YOUNG FOOLS

ALSO BY LIZA PALMER

Family Reservations

The Nobodies

The F Word

Girl Before a Mirror

Nowhere but Home

More Like Her

A Field Guide to Burying Your Parents

Seeing Me Naked

Conversations with the Fat Girl

YOUNG FOOLS

A NOVEL

LIZA PALMER

LAKE UNION
PUBLISHING

Published by Lake Union Publishing, Seattle

www.apub.com

EU product safety contact:
Amazon Media EU S. à r.l.
38, avenue John F. Kennedy, L-1855 Luxembourg
amazonpublishing-gpsr@amazon.com

ISBN-13: 9781662527159 (hardcover)
ISBN-13: 9781662527166 (paperback)
ISBN-13: 9781662527142 (digital)

Cover design and illustration by Philip Pascuzzo

Printed in the United States of America

First edition

Praise for Liza Palmer

"Fresh, exciting, and necessary. A must-read author."

—Taylor Jenkins Reid, author of the *New York Times* bestselling novels *Carrie Soto Is Back*, *Malibu Rising*, and *Daisy Jones & the Six*

"Palmer tells a story like a girlfriend over lunch."

—*People*

"Funny and clever . . . a real crowd-pleaser."

—*Publishers Weekly*

"Palmer is a witty, charming writer."

—Refinery29

"A nice, warm snack."

—*New York Journal of Books*

"Palmer deftly covers the complicated ground of family and hometown loyalty."

—*Booklist*

"Honest, humorous, and whip smart . . . impossible to put down and so much fun to read."

—*USA Today*

"Funny, fresh, and frank . . . Snappy and smart."

—*The Oklahoman*

"Palmer's authentic humor carries the message with a hint of parody."

—*Publishers Weekly*

"Funny, painfully honest, and hard to put down."

—*Kirkus Reviews*

"In a word: genuine."

—*Herald Sun*

For Altadena

I can't forget you. I try all the time.

—Bear's Den, "Berlin"

I could have been someone. Well, so could anyone.

—The Pogues (featuring Kirsty MacColl), "Fairytale of New York"

CHAPTER ONE

Summer 1995

What an extraordinary woman. Too bad she did so very little with her life.

Helen Hicks fears this phrase will one day float through the air at her funeral. Ever the wordsmith, Helen feels ambivalent about assuming the use of "extraordinary." She'd never want to be perceived as a person who thinks too highly of herself. In the end, she decides that—in this particular scenario—she's technically not saying it about herself and bravely perseveres, keeping the word.

She looks out the bus window, writing and rewriting the scene in her mind. Editing her mourners' dialogue, pulling it back when it veers into overt sentimentality, surgically threading in a believable level of awe while trying not to dwell too long on the creeping refrain that she never realized her full potential. At the age of twenty-four, Helen not so secretly thinks contemplating her own death makes her an even more profound and tortured artist.

Caught up for a moment in her reflection in the window, Helen pushes her newly dyed–black hair out of her eyes, careful not to smudge the winged eyeliner she spent far too long perfecting. She likes the way she looks but resents that her rebellious exterior hasn't manifested the requisite fortitude to match it. Moving on quickly from this inconvenient lapse of confidence, Helen muses that the functional decay of the bus, poetically juxtaposed with the lush green hills of the Sonoma County landscape just outside, embodies her own artistic duality.

Inspired by her thought, Helen quickly digs through her backpack for her well-worn notebook and jots it down. Then she rests a pensive hand on her chin, thinking this completes the look of a young writer just before the world discovers her greatness.

"Is that yours?" a youngish man across the aisle asks, pointing at Helen's feet. Jolted out of her reverie, Helen follows his outstretched finger to see her own backpack. Annoyed, she nods a quick yes and pulls the backpack closer to her feet. "Not that." He points again. *"That."*

Helen lets out an exasperated sigh, rolls her eyes, and looks down at her feet. Which is when she sees a bright-pink, plastic-wrapped parcel resting against the back of the bus seats in front of her.

"Is it an inflatable travel pillow?" he asks as Helen plucks her thick sanitary napkin from the bus floor and violently shoves it into the depths of her backpack.

"What? No!" Helen blurts, her pale skin coloring deep red.

"Oh," he says, clearly disappointed.

Helen turns back toward the bus window, resolving that the villain in her as-yet-unwritten but soon-to-be-celebrated debut novel will coincidentally look a whole lot like the man who had the audacity to ruin her perfect literary moment. She looks back over at him, making sure she gets the details right: white-blond hair, flannel shirt, baggy jeans, and a black San Francisco Giants baseball cap turned to the side. Unfortunately for Helen, he mistakes her furtive glances for more than a passing interest in him.

"You wanna make out or something?" he asks.

"It's ten o'clock in the morning," Helen says, barely able to contain her disdain.

"So?"

"Ew."

The youngish man just shrugs.

Hoping to reset the moment, Helen ejects the CD from her Discman and blows on it. She sets it back inside and presses play. Once the first song kicks in, she replaces her hand dramatically on her chin with a sigh as the Napa Valley speeds by her window.

In just a little over an hour, Helen gets off the bus at a pedestrian bus station in the middle of town. She tugs her vintage Samsonite suitcase down the bus's steps, its hard Biscayne Blue shell picking up new dents and dings along the way. She told her parents she simply must take the old suitcase and not the wildly uncool, floral tapestry roller bag gifted to her by her grandmother. Her father scoffed and told her she wasn't going to a costume party; she was attending the iconic Hayward Writing Intensive. The same intensive whose list of attendees reads like a who's who of the literary world. So many great writers, and not one—her father paused for impact—would be bringing an old, dented suitcase. He could barely get the words out, his sneering, tight upper lip curling over the *d* sound with particular disgust. He ended the conversation with an angry shake of his head, cracking his newspaper back in front of his face just to put a fine point on his irritation.

Helen took the Samsonite. Or rather, Helen sneaked out in the early-morning hours with the Samsonite after hiding her grandmother's floral tapestry roller bag in the back of her closet. What she understood, what her father didn't, was that the Hayward Writing Intensive actually *was* a costume party and the character Helen Hicks was dressing up as was An Important Writer. This was her chance, and she wasn't going to blow it by showing up as her actual, real self.

But as she lumbers from the bus and into the station, Helen begins to question bringing the Samsonite on this pilgrimage.

She tries to collect herself in the tiny bus station and watches what is just another quiet Sunday for those hurrying to and from places unknown. She can't believe they have no idea how significant this day is for her. They're just going to get groceries or meeting a friend for lunch, while she's the closest she's ever been to having one of her greatest dreams realized. Helen unwinds the straps on her backpack and settles it comfortably on her back.

Next, she pulls a meticulously folded piece of paper from the inside pocket of her black moto jacket and studies her handwritten directions to the Hayward Writing Intensive shuttle stop, about a half mile away. Helen scans the bus station, trying to find the exit or any signage that matches one of the streets on the paper. As she does so, she sees the man from the bus wandering around the station, clearly looking for someone. He looks different now that he's off the bus. Perhaps it's his growing panicked look, but something about him makes her regret treating him so harshly.

The young man settles in just next to Helen underneath the large platform display, and the clickity-clacking of the ancient departure board echoes throughout the station. He doesn't even notice Helen as he nervously takes off his baseball cap, fidgets with his shaggy hair, and carefully replaces the hat. Seeming to grow more and more agitated, he smooths down his flannel shirt. But, as he does so, Helen notices a large neon-yellow price tag dangling off one of his sleeves. And it's not just any price tag. Helen recognizes that it's from a secondhand store and someone has scrawled the sale price of $1.29 in giant black permanent marker. He is proudly fussing and tidying the new-to-him flannel shirt as a group of teenagers notice the tag, whisper to each other, and then scramble away laughing in the singular piercing tone that only teenagers can access. Watching this hits Helen a little too close to home.

Her gaze flicks from the group of teenagers to an elderly couple just walking into the station. The old woman sees the youngish man and her face lights up. She nudges her husband and excitedly points to where he's standing. Helen looks over at the man as their arrival registers and hears him let out a relieved sigh before exclaiming, "Grammy!" She can see his whole body move toward his grandparents, and in that split second, Helen reaches out and grabs the neon-yellow price tag, spinning the plastic fastener around her finger. Using his velocity as he runs toward his grandmother, Helen lets the price tag pop off in her hand, the plastic fastener leaving a red indentation. He doesn't even notice, lunging into his grandparents for a long-overdue hug.

Helen looks down at the tag in her hand and smiles. By the time she looks back up, the youngish man and his grandparents are long gone. She sees a trash can by the entrance, walks over, drops the price tag in, and sets off for the shuttle stop.

Twenty minutes later, she finally arrives at it dripping sweat. The August heat is a particular circle of hell that seems to drag on for years. It's also not helping that Helen insisted on wearing what she thought was her "coolest writerly outfit," an ensemble boasting the moodiest and blackest finery from her closet, so she could successfully put her most tortured foot forward on this momentous day. Flopping down on the bench, she peels off her backpack, then her black moto jacket, then her thrifted black men's suit vest—careful not to snag her threadbare, oversize black sweater on any of the several button pins fastened to the vest—and finally unravels her thin black scarf from around her sweaty neck. Sadly, because most of her layers are black, Helen fails to notice that with the heat and her copious amounts of sweat, the brand-new black dye job she did on her mop of hair just the night before has begun to run and stain the gray REM concert T-shirt she found at a thrift store.

Completely oblivious, Helen positions herself on the bench as if she's sitting for Hans Holbein the Younger. Her black, shabby Converse All Stars pulled in and pigeon-toed, threads from her ripped black jeans lazing over them like expensive fringe. The choice of reading material cost Helen many a sleepless night, but she finally decided to go with Didion's *Play It as It Lays*, a book she heartily enjoys but also felt sends the right message to the other esteemed writers she'll be meeting throughout this weeklong writing intensive. It's a classic, deep cut, while also being quite thin and convenient to carry everywhere.

Seeing two men approaching the shuttle stop, Helen sighs and dreamily falls into her book as if right on cue.

"My parents used to have one just like it," a lanky man with dark hair, khaki pants, and a short-sleeved madras shirt says to his friend as they walk up to the stop.

"I didn't even know they made them anymore," his friend responds.

"I don't think that one was made recently," the lanky man says with a smirk.

Helen looks up and offers a regal nod—careful not to appear too eager with the official first two people she'll meet at the Hayward Writing Intensive.

"We were admiring your suitcase," the lanky man continues.

"Oh, thank you," Helen says proudly, feeling entirely too smug for someone who has absolutely missed the lanky man's ironic usage of the word "admire."

"We just haven't seen one in a while," the friend adds, flicking a conspiratorial glance toward his friend. Time slows as Helen deflates, watching the two men snicker at her expense.

As Helen's smile fades, the men continue to joyously bond over her earnest misplaced pride. As they do so, she retains her heavily practiced aloof elsewhereness, but internally her mind is a cacophony of all her fears being realized.

Helen had thought that people in her small town of Mill Valley, California, made fun of her because her family was notoriously weird and off-putting. A pack of snobby know-it-alls who stood out in the worst ways possible among aging hippies, commuter families, and people who do macramé for a living. And while Helen understands that she technically didn't do anything to provoke those two men at the shuttle stop, she can't disregard the fact that she is no longer in Mill Valley, California, and that those two men don't know her family. Yet in her first interaction, she was met with the same playful cruelty she's endured her whole life.

When Helen went off to college, she was positive she'd leave behind the **Kick Me** sign that was perpetually taped to her. In fact, the only things that got her through high school were the elaborate stories she made up about how she would roll back into her hometown on Christmas break flanked by her pack of cool college friends, heads back, laughing as they swanned through town. But as her freshman year in college began, she once again found herself on her own, trying not to notice the distant sniggering of her classmates. And when she did go home at Christmas break, she barely left the crumbling pile of an estate her family had lived in for generations.

So Helen did what she did best: She made up more stories. But this time they were about how college was just high school with alcohol and driver's licenses. Of course she didn't fit in there. Her new fictions were about how she'd finally find friends and intellectual peers in an MFA program. People who'd not only recognize their own singular exceptionalism in her but also share war stories about being chronically misunderstood as arrogant snobs simply because they were smarter than everyone else. All she had to do was survive college and get into a top MFA program and she would have the third act of her dreams.

But once again Helen found herself on the outside. And even worse, it was getting harder and harder to blame everyone else when she was the common denominator in all three disparate scenarios. So, on a quiet night, when she was once more on her own—except for a cheap bottle of red wine—Helen finally did the math and concluded that she was the perfect target for ridicule. Not only was she weird and off-putting, but she had, in the words of one of her junior high school teachers, a "breathtakingly bad attitude."

Once she discovered the root of the problem, Helen struggled to find a solution for how to fit in. What could she do—or have done—any differently? Finding herself at an impasse, she broke the problem down as if she were a character in one of her own short stories, asking herself what they would need to change in order to invoke a different reaction in the reader. The answer came roaring back: everything, but ultimately nothing. Helen concluded that what her particular character feared the most wasn't not fitting in, but a life of anonymity and never making it as a real writer. Not fitting in didn't even break the top ten of the worst things that could happen to her.

She then began to piece together a character sketch of a single-minded person driving herself toward greatness and that this path was seldom taken by people who fit in. It was her rebellious quirkiness, breathtakingly bad attitude, and off-putting nature that would actually form the foundation of her inevitable rise to fame. She could concentrate on writing while everyone else got drunk with their friends. She could forge her own path while everyone else followed the status quo. She would be an observer of a life most people left unstudied. In short, she determined that it was her loneliness that would spawn the great work that would make her a literary legend. And as she finished off the bottle of cheap red wine, she reassured herself that it would all be worth it in the end. Because, as she finally stumbled to bed in the wee hours of the morning, Helen triumphantly concluded that hers was not a story of trying to fit in, but one where she yearned to stand out.

Unfortunately, Helen is still waiting for this theory to prove itself out. And it doesn't help that her loneliness—which she doesn't even notice anymore—accelerates with every passing year. It's one thing to be a successful writer while also being an off-putting recluse. There're plenty of examples of famous writers who fit that bill. But if she's not a famous writer . . . Helen can't bring herself to finish the thought as the desperation builds inside her.

The Hayward Writing Intensive is her last hope. Along with forbidding Helen from taking the old Samsonite, her parents made one other stipulation before she left for Hayward: Since she has finished her MFA program, it's time to follow in the quicksand-like footsteps of her failed-artist parents and become an embittered professor, teaching the subject they were unable to succeed in themselves. They have already called in favors and set up interviews. They have already assumed she will fail just like they did. They have already given up on her.

But Helen hasn't given up yet. She still has one more shot. Every year the Hayward Writing Intensive awards the Edith Glending Fellowship to one writer under the age of twenty-five. Glending attended Hayward back in 1929, when she herself was barely twenty-five years old. And it was at Hayward that she wrote the very beginnings of what would become her now legendary debut novel, *Quiet Was the Meadow*. A book Helen hates and will fail to mention, should she win. So precious, so tedious, and so very, very boring. She imagines herself holding court years from now at an exclusive gathering of Glending Fellowship alumni making a joke to those gathered that maybe Glending should have fudged it a little, writing her masterpiece about a louder meadow, thus making the novel far more interesting. She envisions herself throwing her head back in laughter, her expensive champagne sloshing haphazardly out of its coupe glass as everyone joins in.

If Helen can win the Glending Fellowship, not only will she forever (publicly) lie that she is a huge fan of *Quiet Was the Meadow* but, more importantly, she'll secure the one-year, $25,000 living stipend the fellowship provides so the winner can spend that time working on their debut novel. The stipend isn't enough to live on, but Helen believes that, combined with the ongoing one-on-one mentorship also provided, it'll be just enough to convince her parents that she must postpone those interviews and the looming shackles of professorship while she fulfills her duties as a Glending Fellow. What Helen is less comfortable admitting is that she hopes winning the distinguished fellowship will make her parents proud. That they'll see writing is her true calling and she, in fact, is rather good at it. A point of fact they have yet to acknowledge.

Without the Glending Fellowship, there is no Helen Hicks. Without the Glending Fellowship, there is only Professor Hicks.

She has to win it.

She just has to.

The shift in Helen's demeanor would have been imperceptible to the two men. But if they'd been paying close attention, they would have noticed Helen's gaze home in on them, her eyes narrowed and hard.

And as she turned her body to better face them, not unlike a cannon aimed at a far-off dreadnought, her jaw is set and her breathing is steady.

"You haven't seen a suitcase in a while?" Helen asks, dipping into her ample stores of experience, dealing with people who are far less intelligent trying to make fun of her.

"No, we've seen a suitcase. I . . . know what a suitcase is," the lanky man says, stumbling over his words.

"Oh," Helen says, looking back down at her book. And then, with just the right level of shrugging disregard, she adds, "That's weird."

Defenseless against Helen's impeccably utilized adolescent indifference, the two men are left unsatisfied. Helen imagines that they were depending on a little ego boost to really kick off the week with a bang. Instead, she's left them worse off than if they'd just mustered up the courage to be civil.

As the shuttle stop fills with every kind of writer, Helen doesn't even attempt to make a connection. She's also pushed the big blue suitcase as far under the bench as she can, hanging her black moto jacket over it to hide its unsophisticated conspicuousness. When the shuttle finally arrives, Helen makes sure to board at the front of the line so she won't have to drag the suitcase down the main aisle in front of all her esteemed literary peers.

As the shuttle trundles up the mountain, Helen turns away from the other writers while the shuttle erupts with introductions as mutual friends of friends network and greet one another. Little pairs of writers cramped shoulder to shoulder wade into conversations, asking prying questions about where they went to school, who they know, and what they're working on this next week. Each answer is carefully edited with just the right level of fabricated humility, while also making sure to highlight their impressive pedigrees as clearly and unimpeachably as possible. It's a high-wire act that this particular subsection of people has had to master. But through rigorous practice they have heroically endured.

With a sigh, Helen leans her head on her hand, trying to appear as apathetic as possible about their impending arrival at the historic literary campus. But her mind keeps replaying that moment at the shuttle stop. Her face colors as she's reminded time and time again of how stupid she was for being so open. She should have known better. How could she have let her guard down so fully? Unable to focus on the flora and fauna speeding by just outside her window, Helen turns back to the other writers on the shuttle.

As Helen is jostled and rumbled up the windy mountain road, she looks from happily chatting duos to groups of laughing writers who lean across the shuttle's aisles. Which is when she realizes that she's the only person no one chose to sit next to. No. That can't be right. Now consumed with disproving this fact, Helen risks life and limb to crane her neck and looks toward the back of the shuttle. Right in the middle of more groups of delighted, chatting strangers is one other person sitting by herself. Helen exhales a sigh of relief. It's a young woman who has made the rookie mistake of sitting on the aisle, where her aloneness is on full display. She's also trying to lean her way into other people's conversations. And watching her giggle along with a group she's clearly not a part of, her face open and expectant, is hard. So Helen turns back around in her seat and stares out the window, secure in the knowledge that she's at least in better social standing than one other person on their way to Hayward.

When the shuttle finally comes to a stop, everyone begins to stand and gather their belongings. The driver opens the large door, and one by one, the crowd of the literary world's future elite file out onto the iconic redwood-lined pathway that leads up to the main Hayward campus. Helen doesn't move. She needs to get herself together before she steps out onto this hallowed ground.

"You comin'?" the driver says, looking at Helen in his rearview mirror. Helen nods, organizes her many black layers of clothes, and exits the shuttle.

Regardless of whatever existential crisis she had on the long ride up the mountain, the first sight of that oversize wooden sign marking the entrance to the Hayward Writing Intensive takes Helen's breath away. There are no words on the sign, just the iconic logo of a coast redwood branch as a quill burned into the wood and painted in white. When she was in high school, she found a photo of this exact vantage point in an old English textbook and ripped the photo—and the entire page along with it—right out of the book. It's been hanging on the wall over her desk ever since. She can't believe she's standing here. She's dreamed of this moment for years. She sets her suitcase down and lets herself get lost in the moment.

Scanning the full panorama spread out in front of her, she becomes emotional. It's more beautiful than she ever could have imagined from the photo. Redwood trees as tall as skyscrapers dapple the forest floor, dark-brown rustic cabins just visible between the trees' thick, thousand-year-old trunks. And the scent. Nothing could have prepared Helen for the woodsy musk that is somehow both warm and embracing, yet bright and alive all at the same time. She feels as far away from her old life as possible, wondering how this magical place seems to exist in a rip somewhere in the space-time continuum.

The chittering and buzzing of the wildlife who call these woods their home combine with the echoing, far-off voices of excited writers to make the most rhapsodic symphony she's ever heard. Has she experienced real beauty before now?

But, far off in the distance, she hears a voice getting louder and louder. Annoyed that someone has the insolence to corrupt this enchanted place, she narrows her eyes at the person racing toward her yelling, "Hey, man!" at the top of her lungs.

To Helen's horror, it's the other young woman who was sitting by herself on the shuttle. She has one of those childlike, feral runs—limbs going every impossible direction. From afar, the woman looks like a bouncing, beige blob. Her lank, dirty-blond hair is parted straight down the middle and blends tragically and seamlessly into her pasty-white skin. Her backpack and duffel bag bounce and shift around her beanpole of a body as she gets closer and closer. The woman wears a pair of tan corduroy pants with an oversize T-shirt and an olive-green sweatshirt tied around her waist. Everything about her doesn't belong at Hayward. Helen quickly looks behind her, hoping that there is some other reason to explain why this woman keeps barreling toward her. Finally—

"Hey, man," the young woman says again, breathless from the run.

Helen's face is contorted in a contemptuous medley of terror, disgust, and condescension. The young woman doesn't even notice and continues speaking.

"I had to come back. I gotta tell you . . . Look, there's no easy way to say this, man, but uh . . . your hair dye has, like, totally stained the back of your shirt." The young woman has one of those ways of speaking where she runs out of breath midsentence and inhales whole parts of the statement in an excited gasp.

"What?" Helen asks, tugging the back of her shirt around to see it drenched in black splatter worthy of a grisly crime scene. She lets out a frustrated sigh, replaying the moment when she pulled off that young man's price tag and that she felt downright self-righteous at how benevolent and dignified she was. Turned out, they were two of a kind.

"Maybe put one of those on before you head up to the main hall," the young woman says, gesturing to Helen's pile of black clothing, stacked high atop the old suitcase.

"Oh, I—"

"My name's Cherry, by the way! See you later, whatever your name is!" she yells before Helen can finish her sentence.

Helen stands there in a daze, still holding on to the collar of her stained T-shirt as Cherry runs up the path, looking like an old sentient beanbag chair lurching toward freedom.

CHAPTER TWO

As Helen waits in line for her turn to register for the Hayward Writing Intensive, she appears just as indifferent to those around her as she was throughout the entire shuttle drive up the mountain. But this isn't the same performative ennui she prides herself on. No, Helen is overwhelmed. And as she nears the front of the check-in line, she's on the cusp of shutting down completely.

Having a dream come true is new for Helen. She's known only yearning. And as the itchiness of happiness vibrates inside her, she grows fidgety and struggles to process this new slate of emotions. Even worse, she can't stop herself from making little "ha" sounds as she fights to tamp down her growing delight. And every time someone turns around to look for the yawping culprit, she, too, turns around as if to say, "Yeah, ugh! Which weirdo is doing that, right?"

Helen's discomfort with her unabashed joy finally crescendos as she reaches the front of the line. After spending far too much time worrying she'll be unable to say her own name without a rush of giggles cascading out, she steps forward to meet the pointed gaze of the very studious-looking woman checking in those lucky enough to attend the Hayward Writing Intensive. But just as she's about to speak, a tiny slither of a thought whispers in Helen's ear: Maybe this has all been a big mistake and her name is not actually on the list.

"Name?" the woman asks.

"What?" Helen asks in a horrified daze.

"Your name?"

"Oh. Um . . . Helen Hicks?" Helen's voice lilts up as if she's unsure.

Without any fanfare, the woman finds Helen's name and, using a ruler, highlights her information in yellow, confirming that she has been checked in. The entire process will go down as one of the most anticlimactic moments in literary history. The woman then leans over to a large box at her feet and pulls out a thick canvas tote bag with the Hayward Writing Intensive's iconic logo at its center. The woman extends the bag across the table to Helen, who quickly grabs it.

Helen finds a quiet spot out of the way, then sifts through the tote bag in search of the promised map of the campus. After locating where her housing assignment is relative to the check-in desk, she turns the map around to match the real-life geography in front of her and strikes out toward where she'll be sleeping for the next week.

Helen wends her way down a wood chip–covered pathway through the dappled thicket, spying on the other writers as they disappear into the tiny cottages that pepper the Hayward campus. Each little cottage has a corresponding number as its address. As she continues down the pathway, she reads them off in her head as if counting down at a NASA rocket launch.

Then she sees it right at the end of the pathway: cottage number eleven. Its deep wood tones blend in with its surroundings, and the small porch is just big enough to hold a built-in bench and a small writing table for one—a detail Helen is sure confirms her theory that aloneness is a cornerstone in the pursuit of literary greatness. Someone has put a vase with a spray of greens inside on the table. They've really thought of everything. Helen scans her surroundings, noticing that the simple, rustic structure is nestled in between a massive redwood tree and a burbling stream. She looks back down at the paper and confirms she got the number right before getting attached to what is clearly the best little cottage on campus. She heaves the old Samsonite onto the porch with a loud creak. She opens the door and steps inside.

Helen sets her suitcase down and takes in the cottage's interior. On one side she sees a small wooden dresser and a neatly made-up twin bed with a wooden frame; on the other are a small desk and a simple wooden chair. Because there is no electricity in the cottages, she's been provided a lantern for the evenings. There is also a handmade, circular rag rug at the center of the floor. She looks at the map and sees that the communal bathroom and showers are about halfway back up the pathway and decides to take her flashlight on any late-night bathroom adventures.

She unravels herself from her backpack, setting it down on the chair, and sits on the bed. Helen has never felt stillness like this before. Or at least, the stillness she's felt up until this point has felt foreboding. Her brain cycles through trying to figure out what this feeling is that warms every cell of her being. She finally catches it by the tail as her shoulders lower for the first time today.

Helen feels safe.

Sitting in this quiet, tiny cottage that is all hers in the middle of a rustling wood with nothing but writing on the schedule for the next week feels sublime. Helen lets out a soft sigh as she finally understands the scope of that word—"sublime."

But almost as quickly, the spell is broken, as Helen feels her time at Hayward already ticking down. She can't waste one single moment of this week. And tragically for Helen, she quickly categorizes letting herself sink into the feeling of being safe for the first time in her life as a waste of time.

Helen gets up from the little wooden bed, takes off her jacket, and hangs it on the back of the desk chair. She then begins unpacking, carefully putting her all-black wardrobe away in the small wooden dresser, which smells like pine. She putters around the little cottage setting out her things, and with each item she places, she grows more and more comfortable in this daydream come to life. When she finally finishes and pushes the now-empty Samsonite under the bed, she looks around the cottage and lets herself bask in how *her* it is. She lives here.

This is where she is staying while attending the Hayward Writing Intensive. She smiles to herself, loving how cool that sounds.

Finally satisfied, Helen sits down at the desk and begins to go through the tote bag she received at check-in. She examines each handout, the schedule, the map, and the list of writers who will be workshop mentors this summer session with a microscopic level of scrutiny. She then walks through her schedule and gets acquainted with all the places she'll have to go on the first day—Helen is famous for her dry runs. She'll eat her meals in a large tavern-like building called the Public House, which is located right in the center of campus. Her workshop is in one of the classrooms in a cabin called the Retreat, which is located almost directly behind the Public House. Helen is relieved that she won't have to run all over the woods, hurrying from one place to another like others whose workshops are in farther-flung places, down dirt pathways, and up steep hills. She's also happy to find that most of the panels, Q and As, and tonight's welcome mixer will be held in Hayward House, the original building dating back to 1925 that started this entire program seventy years ago.

Reading through the pamphlet, Helen learns that Hayward House was originally one of the small colleges associated with a now-defunct university. Its subject matter spanned a very loose spectrum of art and social sciences, but over the years, it became known more for its writing program. When the university went under, Hayward House remained standing. And as the years went on, Hayward House became the Hayward Writing Intensive.

As the sun sets and dusk falls, Helen sees on the schedule that the welcome mixer is happening in Hayward House right now. In fact, it started thirty minutes ago. Which, for someone from California, is still early—but she'll take her time walking there to balance it out.

She stands, puts back on her black moto jacket, and using the small mirror she brought to do her makeup, checks to see whether the hair dye is sufficiently hidden. Satisfied with her appearance, Helen looks around the cottage as if she's forgetting something. It feels weird to just walk out without keys or a backpack. Helen begins picking at one of her fingernails, already fidgeting without something to busy herself. In a panic, she empties the tote bag and slings it over her shoulder. She nods approvingly and finally steps out of her cottage and onto the wood chip pathway leading back up to the main campus.

Helen hears the festivities before she sees them. Live music barely drowns out the din of excited voices, laughter, and clinking glasses as they echo and waft through the woods. As she nears Hayward House, she sees writers spilling outside, drinks in hand, and from what she can see, the wall of people looks impenetrable. Everyone is either standing in tight, exclusive circles or huddled in cozy pairs or trios, just like on the shuttle. If there are people on their own, she certainly can't see them.

Usually, in situations like this one, Helen seeks out the unofficial designated area where people who find themselves on their own can congregate, thereby making it appear to be a group even though no one is talking to or acknowledging anyone else. Helen thought, of all places, Hayward would be lousy on the ground with areas such as these. After all, these are great writers, and aloneness, as she's just confirmed back at her cottage, is one of the keystones of artistic excellence. Helen then decides that the truly great writers—who have the strength of character to stand alone, as she does—are inside Hayward House. It's what she would do, after all. Steeling herself, she makes her way to the entrance.

Standing in the crush of people at the door, Helen tightens her grip on the tote bag's canvas straps. As she waits, she employs a long-standing tactic for whenever she's been confronted with a gathering or event she must attend: She acts like she's urgently looking for someone in the crowd. Selling the ruse fully, Helen stands on her tiptoes, looks at her watch, and then, using a now-heightened energy, lets out an exasperated sigh.

"Looking for someone?" the man standing next to her asks, as if on cue.

"Oh—" Helen acts surprised, tearing her attention away from the task at hand and refocusing on the man. "All my friends are just inside, so . . ." She trails off, shaking her head impatiently.

"First time at Hayho?" the man asks.

Helen panics. She didn't understand the last word he said but is now positive she should know it. Using her skills at deduction, honed in the trenches of historically never being privy to insider lingo, Helen concludes that the word is another name for the Hayward Writing Intensive.

"Yep. First time at *Hayho*," Helen says, dipping her voice just slightly as she mumbles her way through the unknown word.

"What's a Hayho?" a woman just behind them asks as the crowd of people shuffles closer to the welcome mixer entrance. The man gives Helen the slightest rolled eye at the woman's ignorance. Helen returns it with aplomb.

"'Hayho' is short for 'Hayward House.'" The woman remains confused. Helen lets out the tiniest of scoffs. The man holds up one hand and begins spelling the word out. "H-A-Y for 'Hayward' and"—he holds up his other hand—"H-O for 'House.' When you put them together . . ." The man threads his fingers together. "Hayho. Easy."

"Oooh, that's super cute. Hayho!" the woman squeals, waving to a friend who's farther off in the crowd. Her friend waves back, yelling the word in excited response, clearly not knowing its true meaning. The woman then begins to wrongly explain to her far-off friend that Hayho is the name for the building they're all lined up to enter and not a nickname for the Hayward Writing Intensive as a whole. Helen and the man share a look as they decide not to correct her.

Finally at the front doors, Helen declares to the man that she'd better get to finding "all" her friends, keeps her head down, and pushes through to the main room. Once inside, she takes in the thick timber beams that make up the room's dizzyingly high raftered ceilings. The rustic barn is counterbalanced by the natural light flooding in from the wall of windows that overlook the dusky, lush green just outside and the hills far off in the distance. It's simply breathtaking.

At the front of Hayward House are three large hanging banners. The first looks to be an almost heraldic flag of the original college's sigil, dating back to 1925. The second large standard simply has the Hayward Writing Intensive logo. And the third is this year's summer intensive's oversize pennant, with the year, 1995, stretched across its triangular face. Helen slides her gaze from the front of Hayward House to the east wall and sees that every year has its pennant proudly displayed. The only difference is the ones on the east wall are covered in the signatures of those who attended the intensive that year. Helen's heart soars as she thinks that, no matter what, her signature is going to be in this room forever. *She* is going to be in this room forever. Regardless of whatever happens after this week is over, she will be remembered. And no one can take that away from her.

Helen looks down from the wall just in time to see a trio of writers striding toward her. She deftly squishes herself into a small pocket of open space as they hurry past without a word of apology. And this is precisely when Helen decides she is officially done with the 1995 Hayward Writing Intensive welcome mixer. She makes an empty promise to herself that she'll find the other writers who keep to themselves some other time and starts looking for a way out. Which is when she sees the elaborate food and beverage offerings lining Hayward House's back wall. Her eyes widen as she sees several tables full of food, coolers full of beverages, and barely anyone partaking. She curls her fingers around the empty tote bag on her shoulder and gets an idea.

She meanders over to the food tables and makes an elaborate show of getting herself a plate and filling it high with crackers, sweaty cubed cheeses, and various and sundry tiny bites of every possible kind of hors d'oeuvres. Helen sets the plate down, scans the area, and sees the extra kitchen bags just to the side of the main food table. Not wanting to ruin her Hayho tote, which she plans to carry for the rest of her life—paired with a sigh and "Oh, this? It's just a tote I got from when

I attended Hayho," freely using the insider term with abandon and acting as though she learned it firsthand several years ago—she pulls a bag from the roll and rips it off with stealthy vigor. She lines her tote with the plastic kitchen bag, picks up her full plate of food, and when no one is looking, dumps the entire plate's contents into her safely lined tote. Now eyeballing the cooler filled with bottles of beer, Helen realizes too late that she's done this the wrong way round. If she dumps the bottles of beer in now, they will crush the food at the bottom of the tote bag. But the thought of having her little treats back at her perfect cottage by the burbling stream without an ice-cold beer is too much to bear, so Helen walks over to the cooler and begins loading up her pockets with bottles.

She's in the middle of tucking her third bottle into the inside pocket of her black moto jacket when she feels the dark presence of someone standing next to her. There is no way she can play this off, but that doesn't stop Helen from coming up with a story that just might work. She turns to the person standing next to her, ready to tell whomever it is that she was just about to wipe off the condensation from the bottle, because one time a bottle slipped from her hands and she didn't want to repeat that now, did she, and since her jacket is leather, she needed the inner lining to wipe it off, okay? Which is when she sees it's that Cherry woman who told her that her black hair dye had monstrously stained her gray REM concert T-shirt. Helen is frozen, the bottle half in the inside pocket and half out.

Cherry takes in the entire tableau, leans down, and pulls her own bottle of beer from the cooler. She finds the church key dangling from the table by a red string, pops open her beer, and then looks over at Helen with an arched eyebrow. Helen nods absently, extending her unopened beer to the young woman. She cracks it open and catches the bottle cap in her hand midair. She hands the cap back to Helen and walks away without a word.

Helen watches as Cherry disappears back into the throng of writers and decides that she needs to get out of there before Cherry regales some cool clique of non–socially awkward writers with the sad tale of the loner weirdo hiding bottles of beer in her pockets. Helen fails to notice that Cherry proceeds to sit at a table all by herself, taking a long pull on her beer as she watches the other writers mix and mingle around her. Avoiding making eye contact with anyone, Helen scrambles out of Hayward House, hoping the live music hides the sound of bottles clanging with her every step.

Once clear of the crowd, Helen hitches the full tote bag higher on her shoulder, takes a long swig of her beer, and walks as far away from the welcome mixer as she can. She steps back inside her little cottage, sets the bottles of beer on the desk, takes off her jacket, and hangs it once again on the back of the chair. She grabs the tote bag and two of the beers and steps back out onto the porch. She sits on the bench and puts her feet up on the banister. She plucks a fancy hors d'oeuvre from the tote bag and pops it into her mouth. Which is when she realizes how starving she is. She hasn't eaten since this morning. She takes another long, hard-earned drink of her beer as the birds chirp high in the canopy.

Realizing she's the only person not at the welcome mixer, Helen lets out a loud, echoing yawp, finally releasing all that combustive happiness she's been trying to tamp down since check-in. And as she stretches out on her porch, Helen can't seem to stop smiling. Whatever happens after this week, she thinks, at least she had this perfect night on this tiny porch with a stolen beer and no one around to judge her for giggling like a little kid.

The next morning, Helen wakes up early enough to see the sun rise. Sitting on her porch, still in her pajamas, she peacefully sips the remnants of the water in the old plaid Thermos she brought from home. Helen heads up to the showers and gets herself ready for the day, going early enough to rinse out her REM shirt without any witnesses.

When she gets back to her cottage, Helen packs her tote bag full of treats into the old Samsonite so as not to attract ants or any other curious, hungry animals. She then decides on yet another all-black outfit, topped off, of course, by her signature black moto jacket, which signals to all that Helen is just another cool, rebellious writer attending Hayho, no big deal.

Stepping into the Public House later that morning, Helen peruses the breakfast offerings before serving herself a healthy portion and sitting down at a table next to the front door. She's made eye contact with exactly zero people. And to those sitting down for their own breakfasts, Helen appears to be completely captivated by the carefully curated book she's read no fewer than twenty times. She quickly eats her breakfast, fills her Thermos with water, and snags a to-go cup full of coffee on her way out. She was the first person in the Public House this morning, and she's the first person to leave.

Now sitting on a rock in front of the Retreat, Helen falls into one of her favorite hobbies: eavesdropping and people-watching. She tells herself that studied observation of the human animal is necessary for good writing, but in reality, it's just another excuse to sit by herself and act like it's an artistic choice. Sadly, her plan backfires, as she fails to realize that by sitting right in front of the Retreat, she's now surrounded by nervous and incredibly talkative writers hovering and pacing in the minutes before their workshops begin. And making it all the worse, she's the only one sitting. As a consequence, everyone looms and hovers far above her like she's somebody's elementary school–age child who's come along for the ride. Helen fears there are not enough black moto jackets in the world to compensate for her actual personality.

Positioned just in front of her, a pack of writers begins unspooling one rumor after another about what they can look forward to this week. No stranger to writing workshops, Helen nods along as each person conspiratorially whispers whatever they've heard at their local writing programs. Apparently, one person heard that the Hayho faculty members get to choose the six members who will be in their workshop that week. And that each day, the workshop will have one piece that's good and one that has potential. The writer puts the word "potential" in giant air quotes, making it clear that what they really mean is that one piece will be good, and one will be bad. When another writer asks how you'd know which one is which, the person just says, "Everyone will know."

So, as the door finally creaks open, the words "everyone will know" begin to dismantle what little confidence Helen had coming into today's first workshop. Oblivious to her breakdown, the gaggle of writers streams in, dispersing into their respective workshop classrooms, where they'll stay for the next four hours. Helen threads herself in along with the other writers and finds her classroom as coolly as she can. Walking into the small room, she sees a number of long tables set in a square, all facing each other. She scopes out a seat that can both be not in the way, but also allow for easy access out of the classroom when she has to use the bathroom. She sits down and begins unpacking her notebook and pencil.

After getting situated, she looks up to see the lanky guy with dark hair who made fun of her Samsonite walk into her workshop classroom. She hates that she looked up at exactly the moment he was scanning the room for a place to sit, because now she can't just ignore him completely. Quickly shifting to plan B, Helen holds his gaze in what quickly becomes a game of chicken as to who is going to look away first. This man has no idea who he's dealing with. When not avoiding eye contact altogether, Helen is a master of staring people down.

But this man is a worthy opponent. Wearing another madras shirt that Helen isn't 100 percent sure is the same one as yesterday, he seems to be enjoying Helen's challenge. A slight smirk curls across his face as he finds a seat opposite her, settling in with a sigh and a practiced tousle of his wavy, dark hair. But just as he begins to unpack his notebook, he drops his pencil on the ground and spends the better part of the next several minutes chasing it around the workshop floor, causing him to welcome the next three workshop members with his backside up in the air and staccato, frustrated humphs as the little pencil thwarts him time and time again. Just across from him, Helen can't help but smile.

Helen is feeling pretty good about herself, but as the final member of the workshop bursts through the open door, she sees that this session has turned into some kind of Dickensian alternate universe in which she is to be visited by all her awkward social ghosts from the last twenty-four hours. Because the sixth and final member of Helen's workshop is none other than Cherry, the beige blob who pointed out her stained T-shirt and then caught her stealing bottles of beer from the welcome mixer.

Trapped by her own vast knowledge of various storytelling devices and principles, Helen is preyed upon by the Rule of Three and braces for the inevitable third humiliation this woman will bear witness to.

CHAPTER THREE

Helen looks down at her notebook and begins scribbling furiously. Anything she can think of—quotes from books, random thoughts, and in what can only be described as a fugue state, she just writes the word "hahahahahaha" over and over again. As Cherry crosses the small workshop room toward the only empty seat, next to Helen, Helen finally comes to her senses. Looking down at her notebook, she sees how absolutely deranged it looks, and if this young woman—or any normal human, come to think of it—sees it, they'll quite rightly conclude that these are the scratchings of an insane person. As Cherry sets her backpack down, Helen flips the page of her notebook over with such a jerk that she rips a piece of the paper off in her hand.

"Hey, man," the young woman says, sliding into the seat next to Helen.

"Hey," Helen responds, now wondering what to do with this corner of torn paper. And while Cherry takes off her worn-in sweatshirt, Helen ends up just shoving the paper into her pocket with a small sense of relief that she's taken care of at least one looming humiliation.

"You get that stain out?" Cherry asks, punching Helen's newfound calm in the gut.

"I rinsed it out this morning," Helen says, hating that their conversation is the only sound in this mausoleum of a classroom while everyone anxiously awaits the unknown writer who'll be leading their workshop for the week.

"Cool, cool," the young woman says, unloading a brand-new spiral notebook, three unsharpened Blackwing pencils, two pristine Pink Pearl erasers, and one pink-and-purple pencil sharpener that, according to the elaborate design on its top, was once a souvenir someone bought at the Roman Baths in the city of Bath. Helen watches as Cherry pulls her feet up underneath her and proceeds to sit crisscross applesauce in her chair. Her fingernails are bitten down to the quick and she's written something illegible on the top of her hand in blue pen as some kind of reminder that—from the faded looks of it—has a very low chance of being of any help at all. Just as Cherry is about to say something else, Deborah Torres strides into the room with a mug of steaming tea and an armful of stapled stacks of paper.

"So sorry I'm late, the photocopier was not being cooperative this morning," Torres says.

There is a moment of utter silence as all six of the workshop attendees have the same thought: Deborah Torres looks nothing like her author photo. She looks better. The rarity of this particular phenomenon happening in a world of authors using twenty-five-year-old photos that have been retouched beyond all comprehension is worthy of a moment of silence. And it's not that Torres doesn't look lovely in her author photo. She just looks like she's the newly minted CEO of a Fortune 500 company who's very excited about taking their company public—all crossed arms, shoulder pads, and pageant hair.

But the real Deborah Torres is none of those things. At barely five feet tall, she wears her long brown hair swept up in a messy bun, and a Milky Way of freckles splashes across her cheeks and the bridge of her nose. Torres is wearing a perfectly aged pair of vintage 501s with an oversize white button-down oxford shirt that falls open just enough to show off a stack of layered chain necklaces—the most dominant of which has a little owl charm that's currently tangled among the others. She also sports a worn-in pair of leather sandals and has her toenails painted bright red.

Gobsmacked, the six students try to laugh at her joke but are far too overcome by her mere presence to regulate themselves. Because while everyone knew that Deborah Torres was a genius, what they hadn't known was that she was also a very real human being who was relatively young and undisputedly cool and, most importantly, had chosen each one of them personally to be in her workshop (rumor has it). So the smattering of shocked and hesitant laughter as they process this new piece of very inconvenient information ranges from nervous giggling to barks and snorts, as if she's entered some kind of petting zoo.

But Torres should be used to this reaction by now. After a decades-long esteemed writing career, Deborah Torres's latest masterpiece is the only thing anyone is talking about these days. It's won every award, been celebrated on every stage in every literary salon, and been at the top of every list since it came out—which is now going on twenty-three weeks. It's rare that a book is able to capture a moment like this, and moreover, that the literary world is in complete agreement that they are witnessing history. Seeing the stunned expressions on the faces of her six workshop members, Deborah presses on and goes through the basic schedule for the next week.

Each day they will read and talk about a select number of students' work—some days it'll be two, other days it could be just one. Deborah assures the workshop members that her only goal is to get through all six stories by the end of the conference. The four-hour workshop will be broken down into two sections: The first half will be spent reading the pieces out loud, and they'll spend the second half discussing, interpreting, and offering any pitches or notes they think will deepen or focus each piece. The hitch is that the person whose piece is being discussed is not allowed to respond or speak. This way, the work must stand on its own, as it will if and when it gets published.

Deborah Torres does not add that one piece will be good and the other will have "potential." Helen can't decide whether this makes the rumor true or false. And what if someone's story is the only one they talk about that day? Does that make it really good or really have a lot of potential? Helen hates that she's going to have to confirm this information the hard way—by assessing today's two pieces and deciding whether they fit these broad, oversimplified descriptions. The part of this experiment that makes her sick to her stomach is she doesn't know whether her piece is among the two slated for today's workshop.

Torres goes on to say that she's found that when she shares her critiques in workshops such as these, hers are the only notes that writers prioritize. So, in trying to solve for that problem, Torres announces that she will hold her feedback until the end. There is a roller coaster of reactions throughout the small workshop room: disappointment at not hearing Deborah Torres's feedback first, so that they then could safely tailor their notes to reflect hers, combined with the growing anxiety at having your work possibly panned in front of all your peers, and then finally excitement at knowing that each workshop member will have their work read by the great Deborah Torres.

"I'm not one for those terrible icebreakers, but why don't we go around the room and introduce ourselves," Deborah says, settling into her seat and taking a sip of her tea. From where Helen is sitting, she can smell that it's an Earl Grey blend. She decides, right then and there, that she, too, will become an Earl Grey tea drinker.

Deborah begins with the lanky guy from the shuttle, and Helen learns that his name is Dan Mishler. Helen also learns that he can't wait to tell everyone that he's a native New Yorker. Manhattan, he clarifies, making pointed eye contact with each individual. He lists his impressive educational background with the detached ennui of someone who flirts with the fine line between confidence and arrogance on a minute-by-minute basis. Dan Mishler ends his introduction with well-practiced humility, punctuated by his gesturing to the young woman sitting next to him that it's now her turn.

The young woman seated to Dan's left is perhaps the smallest person Helen has ever seen. Her delicate, gamine features are set off by giant doe eyes and a tangle of long brown hair that traces down her back. She's pulled her knees up to her chest, sitting in her chair like a small woodland creature, and says in the tiniest voice that her name is Ruth Alexander and she's also from Manhattan. She then lists a far more impressive educational background than Dan Mishler's, cataloging the great institutions as if they are the heaviest of burdens. Ruth ends her introduction with a heavy sigh, as she yearningly gazes at the woman seated to her left to save her from this trial.

Picking up on Ruth's doe-eyed plea, the next woman tells the class that her name is Tala Piñeda and that she's from Chicago. Tala is wearing a pink, floral slip dress with butterfly clips neatly arranged throughout her thick black hair. She has a matching pink Chanel Hobo tote, which she's looped over the back of her chair. Tala lists off her own impressive educational background, emphasizing each item by tapping the table in front of her with one of six bright-pink pencils she's prepped and sharpened for this workshop. Tala looks to her left, but Deborah Torres is seated there. The two women go back and forth, laughing about Torres not needing any introduction, and as the awkwardness fills the room, the look of sheer dread on the face of the young man on Deborah's other side grows. Finally, Deborah gives the young man a nod, and he takes a long, ragged breath before telling everyone his name is Karan Sanyal and he's from Washington, DC. He lists his ridiculously impressive educational background as if hearing his own voice for the first time. He slumps back in his chair with a shrug, and Helen takes this to mean that he is finished and it is now her turn.

Helen introduces herself, saying that she's from San Francisco. She tells herself that no one knows where or even what Mill Valley is, so saying San Francisco is just easier. She even almost believes it. Following everyone else's lead, Helen lists her own extraordinary educational history, making sure to downplay it as much as possible. Not because it isn't notable, but because Helen learned long ago that even though you've made your various alma maters your entire identity, you must act as though you are breathtakingly bored by it all. She turns to Cherry, letting her know it's now her turn.

Cherry bolts up in her chair and exuberantly introduces herself as Cherry Stewart and says she's from Los Angeles. There is a slight hesitation before Cherry shrugs and announces that she never went to college and that Hayho—Helen takes note that even Cherry "never went to college" Stewart knew Hayward was called Hayho—is the first writing program she's ever attended.

Cherry's simple statement sets off a seismic reaction. The other workshop members begin to process what Cherry said in waves, as they're only able to take in portions at a time. That she's never gone to college would be enough to set her completely apart from everyone else in the room, but the fact that Hayho is the very first writing program she's ever attended is unthinkable. It's as if someone were to say that they've never really hiked, but they're going to give ole Everest a shot.

Helen scans the faces of the other workshop members and sees the same looks of confusion and fascination that she no doubt has on hers. But there's something else far more threatening floating in the room's ether, utterly invisible to the naked eye. Underneath the questions and the judgments is the fear that Cherry Stewart is the real deal: a downright literary genius. Someone so gifted that they were plucked from obscurity to attend one of the most esteemed writing programs in the world without having to attend multiple Ivy League schools, revered master's programs, and however many residencies and retreats. People like Cherry come along once in a generation, and as Deborah instructs each person to take one of the stapled stacks of paper and pass the rest down, Helen can see that she is not the only one having a full existential meltdown that will be cured only once it's confirmed that their writing is, indeed, superior to Cherry's.

"The first piece we will be reading is Ms. Alexander's," Deborah says, putting on her glasses and turning to a terrified Ruth. "Ms. Alexander, would you begin reading, but as she's doing so, I advise the rest of you to sit back and listen. Sure, you can jot down some thoughts and ideas, but don't lose the experience of hearing something for the first time by spending all your energy trying to generate the perfect fix or critique. Today's workshop is all about Ms. Alexander and not how good and smart of a workshop attendee you are. Remember we are giving feedback on what Ms. Alexander should do to deepen her work, not what you would do if this were your piece. Ms. Alexander, you may begin."

Helen sits back in her chair and puts on her best thinking face as Ms. Alexander begins reading her piece. She wants to make sure Deborah Torres sees that she's taken her advice and while some others may already be writing down their thoughts, she's the one true and best student in this workshop and oh my god, yes, she would love to be best friends—Helen is swept away making up stories about Deborah Torres coming up to her after the workshop and admitting how desperately she wanted her in her group before asking Helen if she'd like to read a draft of a book that she's currently working on . . . and oh, Deborah hears that Helen is the front-runner for the Glending Fellowship, and would she like the number of her agent? Because Deborah's read Helen's short story and she doesn't mean to play favorites, but she's never seen a talent like Helen's as long as she's been coming to Hayho.

The thing is, there is an actual precedent for this particular daydream, Helen reasons to herself. Two years ago, she was eavesdropping on some classmates in her MFA program one afternoon as they talked about the Hayward Writing Intensive. In envious, hushed tones, the two writers talked about a rumor that after a young writer won the Glending Fellowship, Deborah Torres herself read their short story and fell so in love with it that she forwarded it to her agent, and within just a few weeks, Torres's own editor bought the young writer's upcoming debut novel for over six figures. It was hearing this rumor that actually finally made Helen apply to Hayward after dreaming about it for years.

Because while Helen has lived her entire life as a writer, she has very little knowledge of how to actually make this her career. Her MFA program focused primarily on the craft of writing, never deigning to sully its hands with the business side of things. And unlike Mr. Mishler and Ms. Alexander, she's never even been to New York, let alone made any connections with anyone in publishing. So, for Helen, Hayho became her best shot at getting published before her parents made her "grow up" and "get a real job." If she can win the Glending Fellowship, that would immediately give her a leg up in the publishing world, as well as a community of esteemed alumni available to her as mentors and colleagues and references. The fact that Deborah Torres chose her for this week's workshop (rumor has it) makes even Helen encouraged that the stars may have aligned after all. Because, worst-case scenario, if she doesn't win the Glending, she still has the moments after their last workshop to plead her case and save her writing career.

Helen gets momentarily lost in the vision of being asked to come speak to the new students at her old MFA program. Newly anointed as a Glending Fellow and Deborah Torres's greatest prodigy, Helen envisions herself up onstage, speaking to a packed house of dazzled students about her creative process and enviable literary success at such a young age. Like so many of her heroes, Helen wants more than anything to be published while still in her twenties. To be heralded as an intellectual sensation who achieves great things before she's even thirty years old. That's exactly who the Glending is for: someone so preordained for a life in the arts that they should be allowed to go right from school to the most exclusive echelons of literary society.

Because Helen doesn't want to be someone who inspires people with her tale of plucky resilience. She doesn't want to do her time in the salt mines, only to find herself sitting at some infinitesimal table in a local bookstore being ignored by passersby as she peddles her touching little book of the heartfelt lessons she learned along the way. Regardless of what everyone else says, Helen wants to be put on a pedestal. High above everyone else. So high no one can touch her . . . or make fun of her. She wants that sublime feeling she felt in her little cottage to coat her entire life. Now that she's tasted it, she knows she can't go back to a life without it. If Helen doesn't walk away from Hayho with something tangible toward a career in writing, she has failed. Failed. Just like her parents said she would.

Everything is riding on this week.

Everything.

Because Helen's been lost in her own world, she's surprised to hear repeated references to the Donner Party as she tunes back into Ms. Alexander's reading. Helen quickly scans the first pages, trying to find how an ill-fated wagon train and a group of rich pioneers who ultimately turned to cannibalism back in the 1840s are relevant to Ms. Alexander's piece. Is this nonfiction? Is this historical? Is Ms. Alexander using the Donner Party as an allegory for capitalism? As the pages crawl by, Helen is horrified to realize that Ms. Alexander has used the Donner Party as a backdrop for what can only be described as some kind of accursed hybrid between a bad Bukowski poem and an erotic romance. The sheer number of ham-fisted innuendos utilizing the word "eat" causes Helen to wonder how Ruth ever got into this workshop in the first place.

Next to her, Helen hears Cherry let out a long exhale. She looks over to see Cherry's head is pitched down, with her right hand at her forehead shielding everyone from seeing her pained expression as much as possible. In her left hand is a newly sharpened Blackwing pencil, and Helen can see that Cherry has scribbled the words "please help me" and "dear god get me out of here" and "this sux" over and over again in the margins, while also adding giant question marks throughout Ms. Alexander's unhinged prose in some desperate attempt to have something to say when the discussion portion begins. Something besides "this sux."

Cherry catches Helen looking over at her, but before Helen's gut instinct to act like she wasn't looking kicks in, Cherry quickly writes "do not make eye contact with me or I will lose it" on the bottom of the page Ms. Alexander is currently milking for all it's worth. Cherry tries to regulate her breath, but Helen hears the tiniest little squeal escape Cherry's mouth. She covers it up by starting to cough.

"Oof, sorry. I choked on my own spit," Cherry announces. Ms. Alexander looks over at Cherry as if she's just shot her dog. Helen theorizes that if this imaginary dog were made to listen to this story, getting shot would probably be the better option.

Deborah Torres urges Ms. Alexander to begin reading once again. And to everyone's horror, she picks up three full paragraphs back from where she left off. There is a noticeable deflation in the room as everyone realizes they'll have to endure another pass at Ms. Alexander's cringeworthy build to the final scene. The deflation quickly turns to anger as the class looks at Cherry, blaming her for their current predicament. Cherry returns to hiding her face and writing angry missives all over her paper, and as Ms. Alexander continues, her voice takes on this bombastic, almost slam poetry tone that somehow makes this whole experience even worse.

Which leads Helen to conclude that the rumor about workshops being split into one piece that is good and one that has "potential" is 100 percent confirmed. Because Ms. Alexander's piece has . . . *a lot of potential.* However hard Helen is on her own writing, she is confident that what she brought is, at the very least, far better than this. And being assured of this alleviates much of Helen's anxiety as she considers taking on the rest of the week.

Helen sneaks a look over at Cherry, who is now working on a pretty good stick figure drawing of Ms. Alexander holding a paper that has flames erupting from the top. Behind this stick figure drawing is a little audience of cheering spectators, little stick figure arms in the air, huge smiles taking up the bulk of their giant circle heads. Helen can no longer help herself and lets out the tiniest of stifled, breathy giggles. Cherry looks over and then writes "if you laugh, I laugh."

Helen looks around the room, assesses that the coast is clear, and then writes below Cherry's warning: "we can't risk her just starting back at the beginning." Cherry puts her hand over her mouth, letting out several ragged, desperate breaths in an attempt not to laugh, and finally writes "howdareyou" as if it were all one word.

Helen and Cherry are pulled from their little back-and-forth as Ms. Alexander reads what she must believe to be quite the edgy and shocking climax of the piece. Needless to say, it comes as a shock to no one which part of her doomed sweetheart's body the young ingenue eats first. At hearing this particular detail—and the tediously overwritten paragraphs describing the act—Cherry drops her head and lets out a weary "Oh my god." Hearing this, Helen reaches over and writes "Be strong. It's almost over." Quickly, Cherry adds underneath, "if only some rich pioneer would eat my ears off." Cherry pushes the paper toward Helen so she can read what she just wrote, and it takes everything Helen has to stifle yet another giggle. How long has it been since someone made her giggle? Seeing Helen's reaction, Cherry smiles wide, moving the paper back over to her side of the table. Now mirroring Cherry's body language, Helen puts her hand to her forehead as she, too, tries to cover her face so people can't see that she is on the sharp edge of completely succumbing to just throwing her head back and outright laughing.

As Ms. Alexander finally comes to the end of her piece, the other members of the workshop offer a smattering of applause. Deborah Torres thanks her for going first and follows that up with directions for what happens next. Finally catching her breath, Cherry flips her chunk of paper over, hiding the evidence as Helen fights to quell her own smile. Unfortunately for her, Ms. Alexander misconstrues Helen's beaming as proof of her genius and, to her horror, nobly bows her head and doffs an imaginary cap in acknowledgment of her "awe."

Deborah excuses the workshop for a ten-minute bathroom break, and Helen doesn't quite know how to navigate this moment. Does she ask Cherry what she's doing or does she just get up and go to the bathroom on her own? Does she write her a little note or does she just act like nothing happened?

"You gotta pee?" Cherry asks, standing up from her chair and putting on her droopy sweatshirt. Helen looks up at her and is beyond thankful no one else is in the room at the time.

"Yeah," Helen says, standing.

"You should bring your jacket. We may need to steal some tampons from the bathroom," Cherry says with a wink.

As Helen and Cherry navigate the long, crowded hallway from their workshop room to the women's restroom at the far end of the Retreat, Helen quickly realizes that Cherry is one of those people who absentmindedly herds whoever she's walking with so that they are constantly running into the nearest wall. But for some reason it doesn't bother Helen. In fact, she kind of likes it.

Which is not like her.

She doesn't know if it's because, from an outsider's point of view, it's obvious that Helen and Cherry are together—maybe even jumping to the conclusion that they're friends—simply because of how close they're walking. Or maybe there's something about the feeling of Cherry constantly bumping and rebumping into her, the conciliatory hand on Helen's arm along with a muttered or grunted "oof, sorry" each and every time she is once again herded into the wall. In the end she decides that she likes it simply because Cherry's herding is a constant reminder that Helen's not alone.

For once.

Cherry pushes open the door to the women's bathroom and holds it for Helen as she walks through. As she closes the door behind her, Helen is surprised at her reaction to seeing a line of women waiting to use the three stalls. Relief. She's not ready to have a full uninterrupted conversation with Cherry. It's too much pressure. But small talk where you have to watch what you say feels much more her speed. The tragedy of Helen's misjudgment in this moment is that the concept of "watching what you say" has never really been Cherry's forte.

"This is my first time at one of these things, but that sucked, right? I'm not missing something?" Cherry asks, at full volume.

Helen checks to see if either Ruth or Tala is in here right now, going so far as to look under the stalls and check the shoes of the women hidden within. But while Helen has been checking to see if the coast is clear, the other three women in line have turned to see whose voice is now echoing through the small bathroom with perfect clarity. Helen looks past Cherry's face to the other women and offers a small, apologetic nod. The three women turn away from the pair, their faces contorted in that very specific blend of disdain, combined with the pleasure that comes from letting people know that you think them beneath you. Helen would know. She's mastered that look.

"I mean, all art is subjective," Helen responds, her voice hushed. The door to the bathroom opens, and two more women line up behind Helen.

"Come on," Cherry says with a smirk. Someone flushes a toilet and the line shuffles forward. In the momentary flurry of commotion, Helen quickly answers.

"Yeah, okay, fine. It sucked," Helen says.

"Right?" Cherry blurts, her arms held high above her. Another flush. The door creaks open again as another woman pushes her way into the cramped bathroom.

"It makes me wonder how she even got accepted," Helen whispers as they scoot forward in line.

"You heard her—she said she was from Manhattan. Grew up there. My money? She's connected. Her and that other guy," Cherry says.

"Just because someone is from Manhattan doesn't necessarily mean—" Helen says, shocked.

"No, I know. But being from Manhattan and having writing that sucks and you're at a fancy workshop place?" Helen cringes at Cherry glibly calling the Hayward Writing Intensive a "fancy workshop place" and notices the other women in line recoil at the oversimplification. "Connected." Cherry waggles her eyebrows and Helen can't help but let out a sneaky giggle. She quickly stifles her laughter and glances at the woman behind her, who is now clearly eavesdropping. Another flush.

"I don't know," Helen says.

"I bet I can get it out of them," Cherry says.

"What? Wh . . . how . . . how are you going . . . wait," Helen says. Another flush.

"You all try to be chill, but people here really like to brag." Cherry makes pointed eye contact with every single woman in the bathroom line. Helen watches in awe as each one of them looks down at the ground and away from Cherry's barbed gaze. With a sigh, Cherry continues, "I bet they'll tell me within, like, two minutes." She winks before disappearing into the stall.

". . . in, like, two minutes," the woman behind Helen repeats, mocking Cherry's Valley Girl accent and her very LA usage of the word "like." The other women in line giggle as the woman beams.

"I heard that!" Cherry yells from inside her stall.

Helen huffs out a shocked, giggly wheeze and quickly covers her mouth. She watches as the woman's face flushes in embarrassment. Hearing Helen laugh, Cherry proceeds to cackle from inside her stall. Another flush and Helen lunges into an empty stall, finally away from the line of scandalized snobs and her own bursting laughter.

The secret Helen couldn't tell Cherry was that she actually didn't have to go to the bathroom. She just wanted to talk to her and figured the bathroom was as good a place as any. And now Helen finds herself just sitting on the toilet, waiting for an appropriate amount of time before she can flush and get out of there. But as she sits, she finds that she's unable to fully comprehend the last three minutes, let alone how she feels about them. She swings wildly between complete humiliation and an off-the-charts empowerment that she's never felt before. She tries to understand Cherry's response to being bullied as if it were a feat of close-up magic. Replaying each moment as if it were a little red ball swiftly moving from cup to cup. Helen was unaware you could just . . . not care. This whole time she could have just not cared? Another flush.

"Hey, man, I'm going to wait for you out in the hallway, 'kay?" Cherry yells over the stall.

"Yeah, okay," Helen answers, in a voice usually saved for telephone interactions with her parents' friends.

Helen stands up and flushes the toilet. As she unlatches the stall door, she has this moment of realization that she's going to have to walk past the line of women from before. And while Helen hasn't really unraveled exactly how Cherry was able to pull off the magic trick of acting like she didn't care, she still has her own decades of experience in being in rooms with people who've decided that Helen is not only someone who is easy to make fun of, but a way to bond with those around you in the process of doing so. It's really a bullying win-win.

Helen pushes her shoulders back and strides out of the stall, her chin held high. She washes her hands, pulls several paper towels from the wall-mounted metal container, blithely tosses them in the garbage, and without a glance at anyone else in the room, opens the door and walks out into the hallway. It's only then that Helen realizes she didn't take a breath throughout her entire performance. So, as Cherry greets her, Helen gasps in a deep inhale, realizing she's beginning to feel slightly lightheaded.

"God, right? Someone really lit it up in there," Cherry says, noticing Helen's held breath.

"Oh, I . . . never mind," Helen says, not wanting to sully the moment with her own insecurities.

"What were you going to say?" Cherry pushes, barreling down the crowded hallway back toward the workshop room. Cherry's question catches Helen off guard.

"What?"

"You were going to say something. What was it?"

"It was nothing," Helen says, careening into the wall.

"Oof, sorry," Cherry apologizes. She continues, "I don't think it was nothing."

"It was dumb. It's certainly not worth all this—that's for sure," Helen says, her face coloring as she tries to make her voice sound as breezy as possible.

"I like dumb."

Helen lets out an exasperated sigh as she frantically searches for every possible exit to this conversation. Yet with each failure, she grows ever more frustrated as Cherry beats her to each door, quickly flicking the lock as Helen's shaking hand reaches for the doorknob.

Helen is trapped. And a trapped Helen is not a friendly Helen. And she so wants to be a friendly Helen right now.

"Just forget it," Helen says, trying to smile as they idle in front of their open workshop room door.

"Oh my god," Cherry whispers, covering her mouth.

"What?" Helen asks, looking around.

"I'm so sorry. You . . . it was you who lit up the bathroom. Oh god . . . I'm so sorry, I do this all the time. Just shove my foot in my mouth and ruin everything. Ugh, of course it was you . . . We're all nervous, obviously it's—"

"I did not light up the bathroom!" Helen yells, just to get Cherry to stop talking.

Several people turn to stare, including—to Helen's horror—Deborah Torres, who briefly looks up from her stack of papers, assesses the truly humiliating situation, and respectfully looks away. This is Helen's worst nightmare. But in that moment all she can do is laugh. She's so caught off guard by it that the echoing roar bursts from her like an exorcism. Cherry's face transforms, a wide smile blooming where there once was a tense, worried line.

"I stand corrected," Cherry says, laughing.

The two young women stand in the hallway laughing, shifting from side to side as nervous writers hurry back to their own workshops. Helen and Cherry watch as the last of their workshop members walk into their room and sit down. Deborah picks up her pile of papers and taps them into a neat stack. She stands and begins to distribute the next chunk of writing to the other writers. She leaves two little bundles where Helen and Cherry were sitting and looks to the door, where they still stand.

"Ladies?" Deborah says, motioning for them to come in.

Cherry sighs and begins to step inside the workshop room, but right before she does, Helen stops her by putting her hand on Cherry's spindly forearm. Cherry looks down and then looks up at Helen. Immediately, Helen regrets it, but then she sees Cherry's face. She's not annoyed. She's not mad. She's not even concerned that she's currently being pulled back out of her workshop room by a complete stranger. She's just . . . patiently waiting to know why. Helen lets go of Cherry's arm and finally speaks.

"Do you ever just forget to breathe sometimes?" Helen asks, unable to look into Cherry's giant blue eyes.

"Man, all the time," Cherry says with a shrug, before stepping inside the workshop room.

Helen follows Cherry inside with a long exhale in an effort to calm the butterflies in her chest that are still fluttering in the aftermath of actually being honest with another human being about what she's really thinking. Helen slides in next to Cherry and fusses with the chunk of papers Deborah Torres left at her seat. As she does so, she feels herself almost crystallizing in place, as if she is now somehow made of glass after enduring just one authentic moment. Careful not to disturb the butterflies or even her own ragged breath, Helen moves through the next few moments trying not to break into a million pieces. The perilousness of trusting someone new has always been a high-wire act and Helen has yet to survive the fall.

"Welcome back." The class settles as Deborah Torres waits. "I want to thank Ms. Alexander for going first, but now we're going to move on to our next offering, from Mr. Mishler—oh, wait. Tea. I desperately need tea. Why don't you give the pages a quick scan and I'll be right back," Deborah says, grabbing her empty, stained mug and quickly stepping out of the workshop room.

Cherry zeroes in on Ruth and Mr. Mishler.

"Where in Manhattan are you two from?" Cherry asks, making pointed eye contact with the pair. Helen tries to play it cool, but notices that the other workshop members are calling Mr. Mishler simply by his last name. They're already becoming friends. Without her.

"Oh, you know . . ." Mishler shrugs, playing coy.

Cherry plays along. "I bet you don't even live there," she parries.

"My mom's in Congress. So we have to live there, I hope you know," Ruth says, clearly thinking she's absolutely chastened Cherry and her prying questions.

"And DC," Cherry adds.

"What?" Ruth asks.

"She would have to go back and forth between her district and DC, right?" Cherry absently sharpens her pencil as she speaks.

"Well, yeah," Ruth drawls.

"That's a pretty big job," Cherry says, looking back down at her papers and sneaking a sly, smug glance over at Helen. Ruth puffs up, looks over at Mishler, aghast, and points a tiny skeleton finger across the tables at Cherry.

"Yeah, well . . . and his father is the president of one of the biggest publishing houses in New York. Hm? We could tell you which one, but—"

"Then you'd have to kill us all?" Cherry laughs. Her comment garners a few titters from Tala and Karan.

"No, but . . . maybe." Mishler's voice cracks, trying to lighten the moment.

"Okay, Big Shot," Cherry says.

Cherry Stewart would refer to Dan Mishler as Big Shot for the rest of her life.

Mishler is just about to respond when Deborah Torres walks back into the workshop room with a steaming mug of Earl Grey tea. The floral smell of the tea's bergamot wafts through the small room, adding an oddly flowery note to the building tension.

Deborah repeats that the second piece they'll be reading today is Mishler's, and it dawns on Helen that his will be the "good" one of today's workshop. She allows a small scoff to escape, thinking that anything would probably be considered good, given its predecessor. But then she crafts an entire narrative where Mishler's piece is heralded as good simply because of who his father is. But Helen has to believe that Deborah Torres wouldn't be a party to that level of favoritism. But maybe she doesn't have a choice. Or . . . Helen's entire body sinks as another explanation wriggles up from somewhere dark and corrupted: Another possibility could be that Mishler is a rich, good-looking guy who's popular and from a very connected family while also being—Helen gulps—a good writer. With shaking hands, she reaches for Mishler's story in front of her.

Mishler launches into his piece and it becomes clear that he is good. Immediately and inconveniently so. Helen grinds her teeth as she listens, hating how swept away she feels with every wondrous word. Mishler's prose is clean without being sterile, poignant without being cliché, and cutting without being cartoonish. Halfway through, she looks over at Cherry and sees her scribbling all over the story. But this time she's writing words like "wow" and "this is great," and during one particularly moving section, all Cherry seems able to do is draw three little hearts next to Mishler's words. As the story builds to its stunning ending, Helen begins to feel sick to her stomach, trying and failing to quiet the growing tempest brewing inside her. A storm that brings with it a simple truth that could derail everything Helen has planned.

Dan Mishler is a better writer than she is.

And if he's a better writer—and he's way cool and super connected—then in what world could she win the Glending Fellowship over him? What was Helen thinking coming here? How could she have been so wrong in thinking that she had any chance to dig her way out of her sad little life by winning the Glending, when people like Mishler are also vying for the same prize? And there can't be only one Mishler. Hayho is probably teeming with Mishlers.

Overwhelmed, Helen leans back in her chair. After Mishler finishes reading, Helen has no idea where to begin in processing her tangle of feelings, so she sits quietly and awaits Deborah Torres's instructions. The discussion and feedback portion of the workshop is next. Helen knows that any gathering of writers that involves giving one's opinion on another's writing should be approached as if one is entering a gladiator's arena. Armored up and weapon at the ready, one must be prepared for greatness or death. Or both.

Helen learned the rules of this particular literary blood sport as she has everything else in her life—too late and the hard way. It was her first year in college and she'd turned in a piece she was proud of. When she arrived that fateful day, the professor had arranged the desks so all the students faced each other. Helen took this as a sign of community, impartiality, and most of all, mutual respect. She excitedly sat down, ready to experience her very first literary salon. But as the first student began to rip into another student's writing—mocking them for their plebeian overuse of the word "perfect"—Helen started feeling sick to her stomach. She'd been wrong. So wrong. There was no community here. No one was being impartial. And the only respect given was for one's own opinions.

Helen had looked down at her neatly written notes—naively cataloged and organized so she could be the most helpful—and just felt so dumb. Was she so far off that she didn't see how bad this writing was? What did this woman know that she didn't? What had she missed? Helen looked over at the young man whose writing was currently being eviscerated and was stunned to find him just nodding along, jotting down the hurled insults like they were the ingredients in a lovely casserole that he simply must try. How was he not hysterical right now? Or was he just in some kind of dissociative catatonic state where nodding along was all he could muster up the courage to do? And if she were to look at what he was writing, would it simply read "I will never write another word I will never write another word I will never write another word"?

Helen grappled with what she should do. Should she give her notes as planned and forever brand herself as someone without taste? That'd be social and artistic suicide, as far as she was concerned. But she'd liked the piece. She thought there was room for trimming, but overall, she'd enjoyed reading it. But as the woman continued with a truly haunting level of unfettered joy in ripping apart someone's hard work,

Helen began to reframe her feedback so it'd show the rest of the class that she, too, was someone who could recognize the difference between good and bad art—something her parents had drilled into her. They often said no matter how subjective art may be, there must still be a standard set by those in the more elite echelons of artistic circles for those who don't know any better. And that it was her moral obligation to exemplify those standards, so that great art would not be defiled by those unworthy of its grand and beautiful burden.

As Deborah Torres runs through the rules of engagement for this portion of the workshop, Helen thinks back to that day. How terrible she felt giving that man her feedback, piling on with the rest of the class. How she was almost going to approach him after with heartfelt apologies, but then she remembered how gleefully he'd ripped apart her writing. How happy he looked at calling her work "overwrought" and "pretentious." Two comments, she later thought, that were rich coming from someone who probably just didn't get it. No, Helen knows exactly how today is going to go down because her understanding of it was forged in the very worst of crucibles.

But what she also knows is that all this hinges on whoever goes first and how the rest of the workshop feels about that person. If they respect them, then they'll rework their notes just as Helen did all those years ago. But if they don't respect them, those who follow will get as much pleasure in tearing them apart as they do the work that sits in front of them.

Helen is confident that this group clearly knows not only Deborah Torres's rules of engagement, but the unspoken rules of engagement as well. To even get into Hayho, they would've had to have done their time in the literary trenches. The tricky part is that they're starting off with Ruth's piece. A piece that Helen outright hated. She can't imagine anyone starting things off with all-out praise, but Ruth is connected. She's the daughter of a powerful woman who clearly hangs out with Mishler and his publishing titan of a father. A factor that no one in this room can ignore.

Helen doesn't know what she's going to do, but as Deborah Torres finishes her speech, she starts sketching out some thoughts that could, at best, be construed as indifferent. Helen can live with indifferent; what she can't live with is a burned bridge this early in her writing career. So it'll come down to who goes first and not only whether they liked it, but whether they'll take someone down who is clearly connected in the publishing world. Because it will take a certain kind of person to come out swinging with a deck as stacked as that.

"Ms. Stewart, why don't you start us out," Deborah says.

CHAPTER FOUR

Helen looks from Deborah Torres over at Cherry, her mind an echoing cavern of Cherry's own words that this is her first time at "one of these things." There's no way she could know about the unspoken rules of engagement. In fact, Helen couldn't help noticing Cherry scribbling furiously to jot down even Deborah's basic instructions. Why would Deborah choose her to go first? She's like a lamb to the slaughter. Deborah knows that Cherry is inexperienced—even the shuttle driver who brought them all up here yesterday could easily guess that this is the first time Cherry has been in any kind of literary anything. Helen is haunted by the vision of Cherry looking Ruth Alexander right in those giant doe eyes and telling her that her work sucks over and over again as the other writers gasp and avert their gazes. Not that she'd be wrong, but no one is supposed to say it out loud, is all. Helen has learned that disdain is best when implied, rather than stated outright.

As Cherry sits up a little straighter in her chair and pulls Ruth's pages from underneath Mishler's beautiful piece, Helen is conflicted. There's no way for her to subtly communicate to Cherry even a fraction of what she's learned during the years she's spent in higher academia. In a moment of panic, Helen almost writes on Cherry's papers, "DON'T TELL THE TRUTH!" But as Cherry takes a long inhale and nods at Deborah Torres that she's ready, Helen is just glad she's not going first. And in a moment of cold clarity, she concedes that if someone is going to burn a bridge, it may as well be the writer who has the least chance of ever crossing that bridge in the first place. Helen immediately feels bad for thinking such a mean thing about someone who's been nice to her. But think it she did. And as much as she fights against the callousness of the thought, she can't seem to unthink it.

For Helen Hicks, writing will always come first.

"Okay, um . . ." Cherry starts, flipping through her pages. Her eyes scan and rescan "this sux" and "ugh come on." Helen watches as Cherry dog-ears one of the final pages, smooths out another, and starts nervously spinning her gray pencil over and over in her hand, as she skims and reskims Ruth's writing, her finger tracing down across her onerous words as if she's searching for somewhere, anywhere to begin.

"Anytime, Ms. Stewart," Deborah says, urging Cherry along. Cherry lets out a long exhale and nods. She looks over at Ruth and makes direct eye contact with her.

"This is my first time at one of these things, so I'm not sure what you're looking for here. Plus, you've got to get through all five of us giving you feedback, which can be a lot. So I'm just going to give you two big notes . . ." Cherry trails off.

"Uh-huh," Ruth says. Never in the history of communication has a two-syllable grunt implied so much disdain. Even in the throes of panic, Helen has to tip her hat to the woman. Deborah Torres gives Ruth a look and reminds her that no one but the person giving feedback is allowed to speak during this time. Ruth holds up a hand in silent surrender and pulls her knees up to her chest, her heavy burled-wood fountain pen sagging in her hand.

"I want to start with your main couple. Knowing what we now know happens in the final, climactic scene, and because we don't know if this is just a portion of your novel and whether or not you're writing a romance"—Ruth and the rest of the workshop members bristle at the word—"or a thriller." Another bristle. "Or a short story." Everyone is apparently fine with that last one. "Thing is, I have to care about them so that the final scene can have the impact you're looking for." At these words the whole workshop lets out a little "hm." Those who have been listing back in their chairs lean forward. Those busying themselves obsessively studying Ruth's pages in an attempt to find anything to praise look up. Stunned, Helen looks from Cherry's pages—still graffitied with words usually saved for bathroom stall walls—to her thoughtful visage as she carefully chooses her next words.

Finally, Cherry continues, "I don't know them well enough." Almost as if she, too, is surprised at Cherry's useful feedback, Ruth unscrews the top of her fountain pen and begins writing.

"But let me add my other big note in here and then come back around to stitch them both together." There is a stunned silence as Cherry flips back and forth among a few pages of Ruth's piece. Once again, she looks up and makes direct eye contact with her. "I think you have an opportunity here to play with the gaps in readers' knowledge about who did or didn't survive within the Donner Party. Giving us this young couple set among such a historically tragic backdrop—and now that we care about them and have grown invested in them maybe surviving—I think you'll create some really great tension, as readers will want to know what happens and if this lovely couple lives. So making us care about them not only makes us invest in them, but also ups that tension throughout the piece, as we near what most people will now be sad to find out is a tragic ending." Cherry scans Ruth's words once more, gives a little nod, and says, "That's it from me."

The only sound in the small workshop room comes from the furtive scratchings of Ruth's fountain pen as she struggles to write down every last bit of what Cherry said.

"Thank you for your notes, Ms. Stewart," Deborah says. Cherry smiles so wide that she has to look down at her papers in an attempt to hide it.

In the lull that follows, Helen has just enough time to figure out that Deborah is probably going clockwise around the room. Which means she's next. In situations like this, Helen prides herself on two things: being able to efficiently judge how people are feeling based on body language and the overall vibe in the room and the speed with which she's then able to play out every possible scenario within these freshly defined parameters. It's only after she does both of those things that Helen decides her path. Sadly, Helen has yet to realize that, in doing so, her whole life is a reaction. And for someone who's so obsessed with plot and story structure, she is completely ignorant of the fact that if she were the main character of her own story, she'd be completely devoid of action.

Once she's satisfied with her own astute conclusions, Helen decides to build on what Cherry said about Ruth's piece. But she strategically chooses to use more academic language so that it will telegraph to everyone in the room, notably Deborah Torres, that unlike Cherry, this is not Helen's first time "at one of these things." Buzzwords and lingo that she's picked up over the years in the hallowed halls of higher academia that basically say exactly what Cherry said but, in Helen's view, far more intellectually.

Karan echoes much of what Cherry and Helen said, while Tala decides to lean on calling Ruth's work "edgy" before adding her own surgically neutral notes that gently challenge Ruth to ask some bigger questions. As Tala goes through her notes, she comes the closest to actually trying to give real feedback to help Ruth become a better writer. Ruth doesn't see it that way, of course. So, as Deborah continues to remind Ruth that she mustn't speak during these feedback sessions, Ruth continues to argue with Tala about why the creative choices she made are actually great and that perhaps Tala doesn't fully understand what she's trying to do here. Things continue to get a bit heated as Tala, once again, describes Ruth's work as "edgy" and Ruth snarls back that "just because you don't get something doesn't mean that it belongs on the fringes."

"Well, where do you see it on the shelf, then?" Tala asks, looking to Deborah for her permission to ask Ruth a pointed question. Deborah nods.

"With the other bestsellers," Ruth says without a hint of irony.

"Ah, okay," Tala says. Resigned, she nods, looks down at the rest of her notes, and finally says, "Then . . . that's it from me, I guess." Ruth jolts back in her chair and crosses her arms, looking satisfied she's made her point. What Ruth doesn't fully grasp is that what kept Tala from continuing wasn't her realizing Ruth was right; it was that she concluded, quite tragically, that Ruth is unreachable and no longer worth her time and energy.

All eyes turn to Mishler. Helen is actually really interested to hear what he's going to say. Tala has given him just enough of an opening that he could pick up where she left off. He's perhaps the only person in the workshop who could be even a little honest about how terrible Ruth's piece is. But Helen wonders if he, too, will take the path of least resistance.

"Mr. Mishler, you're up," Deborah says, spinning the tea bag around her spoon and setting it delicately on a small sandwich bag Helen realizes Deborah brought for that exact purpose.

Mishler rests his elbow on the table and brings his hand up to the side of his face, absently tracing his fingers along his jawline as he finds his words. Helen notices Tala watching this motion intently and then, in real time, seeing Helen's confused face watching her swoon over *Mishler*, of all people—causing both women to quickly look away from one another. Helen clears her throat and looks over at Cherry, who can't keep herself from cringing at the entire interaction.

"First, I want to agree with all the thoughtful feedback already given. But I actually want to dig into what Tala was talking about a bit more," Mishler says, ripping apart the temporary accord in the workshop. Helen feels Cherry sit up a little straighter in her chair and sneaks a look at Ruth, who is unable to hide her shock.

"Please proceed, Mr. Mishler," Deborah says, quietly urging him to continue.

"I thought Tala's question about where this book would be on the shelf was such a good one because it helped me to home in on the main issue I have with this piece. I think we have this romantic view of breaking all the rules of literature and inventing a new kind of book. And while that is a noble thing to aspire to, one thing my father has drilled into me over the years is that you have to first learn the rules in order to break them. So, while I admire what you're trying to do with this piece, I think what's missing are the basic tenets of craft—Cherry's point about the main couple and the stakes and tension being a prime example. For me, my note is simple: Go back to the basics and strengthen those foundations before you start trying to break all the rules." Mishler holds Ruth's furious gaze before giving a gentle nod and sitting back in his chair.

The entire class is quiet. Helen can't believe Mishler actually did it. She isn't sure if this proves or disproves her theories about how writing workshops are akin to gladiatorial arenas, where there are no alliances and everyone is fair game. Her confusion rests solely on a feeling that it was actually because Ruth and Mishler are friends that he felt morally obligated to tell her the hard truth. That he didn't want to send her to the publishing wolves with a story that would embarrass her. It's difficult to tell the difference, but Helen now thinks that maybe it's not always a bad thing when someone gives you honest but hard feedback. The truth is in the nuances of how that feedback is given, and Mishler wasn't gleeful in ripping Ruth's work apart or in love with his own ideas or how he would have written it. He was kind, to the point, and most of all . . . he was right. So maybe, just maybe, he told Ruth the truth because he actually wants her to improve as a writer.

Then Deborah Torres gives her feedback on Ruth's piece. Not only does she agree with what everyone has already said—saying how excited she is now about the next several days, based on their astute observations—but she adds her own concerns related to Ruth's work lacking the basics of what a good story needs. She finishes by saying that she loves that Ruth took "a big swing" and can't wait to see how the next draft turns out, given the thoughtful notes Ruth's received today.

As Deborah moves the workshop on to Mishler's piece, Helen slides her gaze over to Ruth, whose knees are pulled up to her chest, and that giant burled-wood fountain pen is lazing in her tiny hand. The thought of having to publicly process that the story you thought would be heralded as a bestseller was actually in dire need of a full rewrite is something Helen can't even comprehend. Looking back down at the table in front of her, Helen laughs to herself that at least she's found something positive about thinking that she and her writing could always use work. Because Helen is certain that it would never come as a shock to her if someone told her that she was completely wrong about something.

The feedback portion for Mishler's piece is much different from Ruth's. Helen was not alone in her complete adoration of his work. Most of the notes orbit around very basic nitpicks, excitement at reading the rest of the work, and an overall reverence for Mishler's craft. Ruth does throw in a few low blows during her feedback session, going so far as to point out a typo as proof that Mishler needs to "tighten everything up a little" so he isn't perceived as "sophomoric."

As Karan finishes his glowing feedback, Helen quickly agrees with everything the rest of the workshop members have said, but as she comes to the end of her critique, she pauses for dramatic effect. She looks out the one small window in the workshop room, breathes in a deep, long inhale, and brings her hand up to her chin in exactly the way she's practiced over the years. She pensively exhales, making it a point to change the timbre of her voice as she dramatically continues: "For me, writing has always been about the why. Not *what* are you writing, but *why* are you writing. And while I concede that this piece is well written and beautiful, I think there's room for more of you in there. Underneath all this writerly perfection, I feel like this piece would benefit greatly from a bit more of your messy humanity. You know? Where in this work is the real Mr. Mishler?" Helen asks anyone and everyone, but mostly Deborah Torres.

Sadly, Helen has gotten a bit too in character and stumbles over Mr. Mishler's name. And as she comes to her climactic moment of poignant thoughtfulness, instead of ending on the emotional plea she was hoping for, Helen instead says, "Where in this work is the real *Mitcher Missler*?" And as she tries to rein the group back from their shaky, spasming sniggering, all Helen can hear is Cherry saying "mitchermissler" under her breath several times before Deborah Torres mercifully cuts in.

The rest of the workshop is a blur as Helen plays and replays her mistake over and over again. *Mitchermissler.* She was so close. *Mitchermissler.* She had them. Mitchermissler. Mitchermissler! MITCHERMISSLER! rings inside her head like a death knell. As the first day of their workshop comes to an end, Helen can only feel deflated. How is she supposed to woo Deborah Torres into being her mentor so she can win the Glending Fellowship, get an agent, and sell her first novel before she is forced to follow in her parents' joyless footsteps now that she's the girl who said "Mitcher Missler"?

"Thank you all for such thoughtful feedback. I look forward to meeting with everyone again tomorrow. Also, I hope to see you at my Q and A in Hayward House with Tess Bayard after lunch. I think it would be really good for you to hear her story since she won the Glending Fellowship two years ago, and that very summer she was sitting right where you are. Good job today, everyone," Deborah says, piling up her belongings and striding out of the room. The rest of the workshop members stream out behind her, falling in with the rest of the hungry writers, all on their way to the Public House for lunch and, if Helen's fears are correct, to gossip about the dumb girl who said "Mitcher Missler."

"Let's eat," Cherry says, standing up from her chair and looping her backpack over both shoulders.

"I've lost my appetite," Helen says, slumping in her chair.

"Is this about the Mitcher Missler thing?"

"Oh my god. How does it sound just as bad every time?" Helen thunks her head down on the table.

"I think people just needed the laugh, you know? I don't think they—"

"Think I'm stupid?" Helen finishes, her voice muffled as she speaks into the hard wood.

"I . . ."

"Why are you thinking about it? Oh my god, this is my worst nightmare." Helen looks up at Cherry, her face flushed and desperate.

"I hesitated not because I agree, but because people think other people are stupid for really gross reasons. It's hella subjective." It takes everything Helen has not to make fun of Cherry's usage of the word "hella."

"I just—"

"I know," Cherry finishes. She nods. "I know."

"We don't know each other all that well, so just to confirm you're seconding my absolutely mortifying desperation at wanting to be a real writer more than anything else in the world," Helen says, finally standing up and gathering her things.

"Yeah," Cherry says, laughing.

"Okay, good," Helen says, following Cherry out of the workshop room.

"Mitchermissler," Cherry says once more. This time, Helen smiles.

"Oh, and by the way? It was so subversive how you insinuated that"—Helen takes a steadying breath before saying her name—"Ruth was writing a romance or a thriller."

"What?" Cherry asks, as they get in the buffet line.

"It was elegant," Helen says, grabbing a plate and a set of cutlery wrapped in a paper napkin.

"What are you talking about?" Cherry asks, serving herself some food.

"How you slipped in a little dig. It was elegant."

"I didn't slip in a dig."

"No, you did. You said that she might be writing a romance or a thriller."

"Right," Cherry says, grabbing a brownie and a lemon bar from the dessert tray.

"Right," Helen says, scooping up a serving of fruit salad.

The two women walk over to an empty table next to the Public House's entrance in an uncomfortable silence. They set down their trays piled high with a precariously balanced array of big, medium, and small plates filled with everything from a basic side salad to a stack of dry brownies. Cherry scans the room, taking in the buzzing hive of excited writers as they desperately trot out what they hope will be their cleverest and most writerly performances in front of all their new friends . . . and their newest set of rivals. Later, after they finish the meal, all the writers will go back to their solitary corners and write down their best lines, lying to themselves that these illegible scribbles are the very heart of their next award-winning story.

Just as Helen is about to continue arguing that not only was there a dig, but it was, in fact, elegant, Cherry cuts in.

"So, what's your deal?" Cherry says, stabbing into her salad.

"Excuse me?" Helen asks, midbite.

"Who are you? Tell me about yourself," Cherry says with a sigh.

"I . . . uh . . ." Helen stammers, completely overwhelmed by the sweep and scope of Cherry's question.

"Why don't we start with why this question is so terrifying for you," Cherry says.

"Could you answer it?" Helen shoots back, buying herself some time.

"Hell yeah," Cherry says, puffing up a bit.

"Then go ahead," Helen says, calling her bluff.

"Fine. I'm twenty years old. Born and bred in Pasadena—it's a town, like, thirty minutes outside of LA. Big Dodger fan, and I want to be a writer," Cherry says.

"Oh, okay. I get it."

"Get what?"

"I overthought it. You're just looking for, like, where I'm from and—"

"I'm not looking for anything. I just asked you what your deal was, and because you acted like I was holding you at gunpoint, I thought I would show you that it wasn't as scary as you were making it out to be," Cherry says.

"I didn't act like you were holding me at gunpoint." Helen shoves a dinner roll in her mouth.

"So?"

"So, what?"

"Oh my god. What is so hard about this?"

"Oh . . . *oh*. Okay, so you were saying 'so' to prompt me to answer the original question. I thought you were saying 'so' like . . . 'so what, you were holding me at gunpoint' and—"

"Look, if you're in witness protection, just, like, blink twice or something."

"I'm not in witness protection, I just . . ."

"Make everything a bigger deal than it is. Yeah, I'm getting that."

The part that Helen can't say out loud is that no one has ever asked her about herself before. She's twenty-four years old and this entire interaction is a first. Helen seriously doubts that that's the kind of answer Cherry is looking for here. Helen wonders what it'd be like if she answered Cherry's question honestly. How Cherry would react if she said, "Oh, what's my deal? Well, I've never been asked this question by anyone. No one has ever been the least bit curious to know more about me. And as you can probably deduce, I have no friends and have never had any friends. In my entire life. Well, not real friends, anyway. Made-up ones . . . loads. No, I totally understand that you'll have to be going now, it was nice meeting you!"

"Well, this is fun," Cherry says, shoveling the last of her salad into her mouth as Helen quietly panics. Helen looks on as Cherry scans the Public House, probably looking for another place to sit. Panicking that Cherry is going to leave, Helen begins speaking before she can think better of it.

"I'm twenty-four years old. I'm from Mill Valley—it's a small town by San Francisco—and I want to be a writer," Helen says all in one breath.

"I'm proud of you, man," Cherry says.

Helen lets out an exhale of a laugh. "It's a big question, is all. Especially here." She bites into her sandwich.

"I get that."

"Yeah?" Helen asks, her mouth still a little full.

"Yeah. This place is crawling with people who just want to make connections with fancy people. I get how you thought that me asking you what your deal was, was me being one of those people."

"Fancy people?" Helen asks.

"Well, what would you call them?" Cherry's face flushes red. Helen immediately feels bad.

"Do you mean people like Ruth and Mishler?" Helen asks.

"Yeah, but also, like, people who just get to go to college. You know?"

"Oh."

"Yeah."

They are quiet.

"It's not a big deal that you didn't go to college," Helen says.

"You're lying."

"No, I . . ." Helen trails off. She was, in fact, lying.

"I won this writing award last year. I entered because the prize money was enough to pay for this place. But when I went to the little ceremony where they were going to present me with the prize money, all they talked about was how little education I had, like I was some wild kid they found in the woods. They even changed my biography to include that I never went to college." Cherry looks down, herding a pile of crumbled potato chips around her plate.

"I don't like that," Helen says.

"To this day, I don't know if I won the award because my writing was good or because I was an inspirational story that made them feel better about themselves," Cherry says.

"Take the money and run is what I say," Helen says.

"Yeah, but—"

"No, I know. It's messed up. I think because my parents are both professors, I forget how . . ." Helen searches for the right word. Finally: "Special it is to be able to go to college."

"It's very special. Four years where your entire job is just to be curious and learn? Who gets to do that?" Cherry asks hypothetically, but Helen feels the weight of the answer in the pit of her stomach.

Helen gets to do that. Everyone in their workshop gets to do that. Helen even got to go to a master's program. And she didn't have to win a writing award to come to Hayho; her parents paid for it. She suddenly feels guilty for throwing a tantrum about the interviews her parents have set up for her. What kind of jerk stomps their foot at the very idea of getting a real job?

Helen Hicks does.

"So, why didn't you say all that when you talked about what your deal is?" Helen asks.

"Say all what?"

"That whole thing about the prize money and fancy people. I would argue that that's way more your deal than being a fan of the Dodgers," Helen says, confused as to why she's saying these things.

"I mean, you have to tell a reader the basics of a character before you dive into the messy, gooey stuff, right? It's just good storytelling." Cherry swigs down the rest of her lemonade. Helen is quiet. Cherry looks up from her drink, clearly thinking she's said something wrong. "What?" Helen knows she must look like she's about to cry. "What? Did I . . . oh no, did I say something wrong?"

"No . . . I . . ." Helen stammers. Finally: "I've just never met someone who spoke my language, is all."

"What?" Cherry asks.

"Writing. You speak writing," Helen says. Cherry laughs. Unable to stay in the far too messy and gooey moment, Helen looks down at her plate and scoops up a heaping spoonful of stone-cold rice pilaf. It is one of the worst things she has ever tasted. It takes everything she's got not to spit it out immediately.

"We should get going if we want to get a good seat at the Q and A," Cherry says, stacking her empty plates onto the tray.

"Mm-hmm," Helen says, her mouth full of rice pilaf. When Cherry stands to bus her tray, Helen grabs her napkin and spits the rice pilaf into it as quickly and discreetly as she can. She then hides the napkin among her empty plates and follows Cherry, tray in hand, over to where they've been instructed to throw their trash away and leave their trays.

"You gonna throw that pilaf into your tote for later or . . ."

"I really would love to live that down at some point," Helen says, exiting the Public House just behind Cherry.

"Maybe stop squirreling things away, then," Cherry says, striding across the main campus toward Hayward House.

"I honestly didn't know I was a squirreler," Helen says, as if meeting a part of herself for the first time. She unpacks this new truth about herself as if she's a scientist looking through a microscope. Overwhelmed not by what she sees there, but by how many other examples of this phenomenon she has been ignorant of simply because there has never been anyone close enough to her to point them out.

As the two women close in on Hayward House, they see a crush of people already waiting to get in. Both of their shoulders slump as they shuffle to the back of the line.

"Rumor has it that Edith Glending herself is going to be here this year to present her award," Helen says.

"Isn't she, like, a hundred years old?" Cherry asks.

"Ninety-one . . . so almost."

"I loved *Quiet Was the Meadow*." Cherry sighs, lazing back against the outside wall of Hayward House.

"What?" Helen asks, legitimately shocked.

"Didn't you?"

"Uh . . ." Helen scans the crowd of writers around her.

"Really?" Cherry asks, understanding Helen's answer completely.

"I just . . . it wasn't . . . you know . . . uh . . . that's the beauty of art. It's not for everyone, and you get to, you know, love it or . . . and timing, you know? For instance, you can't like something one year and then come back to it and . . . you know, really . . . um . . . love it," Helen stammers.

"I just really loved that the whole thing was about—"

"How quiet the meadow was?" Helen interrupts. Cherry laughs.

"Yes and no. I loved that she really explored the luxury of quietness. Like, who gets to be soft and have that gentle life of . . . boredom, really." The line to get into the Q and A begins to move. Helen and Cherry fall in, finally finding seats in the way back of Hayward House, right on the aisle.

"Hm." Helen hates that she never saw that deeper meaning in the book. Like some kind of plebeian, she wrote the book off as trite and failed to answer the very question she posed to Mishler: What was the why of *Quiet Was the Meadow*?

"I gotta say I love that you're a back-of-the-class kind of person, too," Cherry says, taking in the room. The three large banners are hung high above a small stage fitted with two tall director's chairs, each with its own microphone. In between the two chairs is a precarious-looking, spindly table with two glasses of water on top, and a box of tissues.

"What do you think the tissues are for?" Cherry asks.

"Historically, tissues have been used when one has a runny nose or to blot tears caused by crying," Helen says, wading a little bit further in with the darker parts of herself.

"So not for making little ghosts, then?" Cherry asks, parrying Helen's lunge of an answer. Helen laughs.

Helen watches as the other four members of their workshop walk in together and find a free row of seats near the front. Helen notices that Ruth has apparently lessened her revenge plot against Tala and Mishler, as they appear to all be happily chatting with one another, laughing and excited about their blossoming bond. Mishler cranes his neck to take in the full scene, content to be seated with three other people and up front, where everyone can see them. Helen watches as he sees her and Cherry in the back of the room. She's genuinely curious about how he'll react, so when he quickly acts like he didn't, in fact, see them, Helen feels a bit better about finally saying something to Cherry.

"Guess our invite got lost in the mail," Helen says, gesturing to the quartet of other workshop members.

"Yeah, but they're front-of-class people. That's not our bag, man," Cherry says, settling comfortably in her chair.

Helen is struck, once again, by the ongoing realization that Cherry's bravado seems to be the real thing. It's apparently not an act she puts on so no one can pick up on a tangle of jealousy, yearning, and frustration boiling just below the surface—a practice Helen knows all too well.

As Helen staves off unwelcome waves of envy at the foursome of fast friends and of her effortless exclusion from it, Cherry appears to be completely unbothered.

Roberta Lartey, the Hayward Writing Intensive's creative director, stands at the side of the stage. She gathers her long, floral dress and steps up the four small stairs. As she makes her way to the center of the stage, the crowd begins to quiet. She walks over to one of the high director's chairs, picks up the microphone, and switches it on. The clu-clunk of the sound system powering on shushes those in the audience who failed to catch the first social cue to stop talking. Roberta steps to the front of the stage and swoops her long box braids over to one side.

"They could have asked us," Helen whispers.

"But then we'd actually have to sit with them," Cherry quickly whispers back, her eyes still glued to the stage. Helen ever so subtly begins to pout. Cherry notices, mostly because Helen's idea of subtlety needs some honing. "Did you want to spend the next hour fielding probing questions about the Donner Party?" Helen shakes her head. "Yeah, I didn't think so." Cherry leans in and whispers, "You gotta think these things through, kid."

"Good afternoon, I'm Roberta Lartey. It's so lovely to see so many familiar faces. To those old friends: Welcome back. And how about we do a show of hands—who is here for their first year at Hayho?"

Helen and Cherry both raise their hands. Everyone looks around the room to see who is or isn't raising their hands. Of the 25 percent of people attending for the first time, Helen notices that everyone in their workshop also has their hands up. For a brief shining moment, Helen thought that those four had attended Hayho for years and known each other before and that was why they'd walked in together. As she looks at all four of their little excited hands high in the air, Helen must now deal with the fallout of realizing that, aside from Mishler and Ruth, they all just met. And yet, in those fleeting moments of the first flush of friendship, they've bonded over being in complete agreement that Helen and Cherry do not belong.

Roberta continues. "It's so lovely to see so many new people—welcome. I'm so excited for our first event this session, so please welcome Deborah Torres and Tess Bayard to the stage."

The crowd breaks out in applause as Deborah steps up onstage and smiles at Roberta. Helen feels a smug sense of familiarity with Deborah, because she's been in the same room with her for the last four hours, but the rest of those gathered in Hayward House are near hysteria at her sheer presence. While Deborah and Roberta say their hellos, Tess Bayard steps onto the stage.

"Ugh, she's so cool," Helen reverently whispers to Cherry. Cherry allows a slight nod.

Tess Bayard is wearing almost exactly what Helen Hicks is wearing, but while Tess's outfit looks straight from the runway, Helen's is the piecemeal version one buys at thrift stores and bargain bins in small towns across the nation. Tess's black designer moto jacket perches atop her slim shoulders, grayed and scuffed to grunge perfection. Her black jeans are frayed just like Helen's, but Tess's also sport a surgically placed rip at the knee that adds a je ne sais quoi to the outfit that Helen's somehow lacks. Tess wears no makeup, yet her pale skin is dewy fresh and her fluttery eyelashes accentuate her large brown eyes with nary a hint of mascara or winged eyeliner. Her bow of a mouth is the perfect shade of powder pink, and her sun-kissed brownish hair is cut in a swoopy pixie cut that somehow looks better every time she effortlessly brushes it out of her eyes. Tess finishes the outfit with a pair of black silk ballet flats stitched with a tangle of hunter-green vines throughout their narrow silhouette. Tess greets Roberta and Deborah warmly, waves to the audience, and makes her way over to the two high director's chairs as Roberta exits the stage and takes her seat in the audience.

Deborah Torres's words echo through Helen's head: *"I think it would be really good for you to hear her story since she won the Glending Fellowship two years ago, and that very summer she was sitting right where you are."*

"If that's how cool winning the Glending Fellowship makes you, count me in," Helen whispers to Cherry as the women get settled in their chairs, laughing and talking with one another as they scooch and shift onto the high director's chairs.

"Oh, are you going for that, too?" Cherry asks, seemingly unmoved by Tess's coolness.

"I mean, yeah," Helen answers, confused as to why there's any question.

"Oh." Cherry doesn't look at her.

"Are you?"

"Yeah."

"Oh."

Helen and Cherry will not mention the Glending Fellowship again for several days.

Deborah begins the Q and A with the basics of Tess's life and early writing inspirations while the entirety of Hayward House nods along, half listening and half crafting what their own answers will be, if and when they get to sit up on the Hayward House stage alongside one of their literary heroes. Deborah then moves into the era of Tess's life just before she attended her first and only Hayho. Like most of the writers present, Tess attended an impressive university, followed by an even more impressive master's program. She speaks warmly of personal mentors who supported her along the way that cause actual gasps from the audience. Tess muses about her "little short stories" and the seminal institutions who have published them, along with the storytelling events, festivals, and literary salons she's been invited to and the icons she now calls friends. Her voice has this dry giggle to it that makes everything she says sound somehow both wry and adorable.

Helen Hicks is positive that she's on the verge of exploding from sheer yearning with every new fantastical scenario Tess unravels.

Before today, Helen was positive that the life Tess Bayard is describing was the stuff of legend. Something so unattainable that the mere thought of being able to actually live that dream of a life would be downright silly. But here's a woman who is the same age as Helen talking about how nervous she was standing on the stage of the

Kaufmann Concert Hall at the 92nd Street Y reading from her debut novel in front of a sold-out crowd. And revealing that after her book launch, she and her agent sneaked into an SNL after-party and from there watched the sunrise at Battery Park with several unnamed rockers, actors, and comedians.

"I was told not to press you on naming names," Deborah jokes.

"Get a couple amaretto sours in me and I'll tell all," Tess says, her perfect skin flushing pink.

The envy in the room is palpable.

"Let's talk about the Glending," Deborah says.

"That really was the turning point for me."

"How so?"

"I'm in a roomful of storytellers, so I think this will resonate—and I know mine sounds like a very impressive life, but it's just a story. Every day I was unsure. Every day I was surrounded by these brilliant writers, and every day I was positive that I wasn't going to catch a break. But then I got into Hayho, and the week I spent here that summer was . . . let me see if I can put this into words . . ." Tess lets her microphone fall to her lap as she tilts her head back just so. The room is so quiet you can hear the slightest creak of a seat. Finally, Tess continues, "It's one thing to call yourself a writer, to tell that story to yourself and others, right? But it's something else entirely to actually feel like one. And that week at Hayho was the first time in my life I actually felt like a writer. Embodied it, you know? It wasn't just me walking around some college campus playacting Virginia Woolf and begging people to recognize my big, dumb dream."

"I think we can all relate to having a big, dumb dream that others don't recognize until the world did," Deborah says, looking out into the crowd. Everyone is nodding along, riveted.

"But I think the danger is that once you feel that? You start to get scared," Tess says.

"How so?"

"Because how do you go back to a life without that feeling? How do you go back to just the story?"

At these words, Helen begins to cry. This was exactly what she felt that first day in cottage number eleven. The moment she finally not only understood the word "sublime" but felt it in her bones. Helen hears herself sniffling and tries to gulp down the humiliatingly raw emotions she can't seem to control. In a panic, she reaches over to her tote bag and pulls out the big plaid Thermos and takes a long drink, hoping it will quell the growing burning in her throat. She takes several long, deep breaths, one last sip, and returns the Thermos to her tote.

"You okay?" Cherry whispers.

"Just got something in my throat," Helen lies.

"You can just say you were crying," Cherry says.

"Fine. I was crying." Helen uses her sleeve to swipe at her eyes, the black, winged eyeliner and cheap, clumpy mascara now trailing down her face.

"You're not alone," Cherry says, gesturing to the crowd around them.

Helen scans the room and sees that Cherry is, in fact, correct—several other writers are swiping away tears. It's not that what Tess said was particularly groundbreaking; on the contrary, it was quite simple—childlike, even. She related every writer in attendance at Hayho to a little kid running around in a Spider-Man Halloween costume, earnestly fwipping webs as if they're finally able to fully embody their whole self. And for a roomful of writers who'd like the story of themselves to be far more erudite and complicated, that one little anecdote enabled Tess Bayard to pierce through all their well-trained haughtiness and unmask them as just little kids with dreams of a life beyond their four walls.

That's what a good writer does: They put the well hidden into words that are universal in all of us. And force us to do the unthinkable in its aftermath—see that we are not alone, even at our most vulnerable.

CHAPTER FIVE

Tess Bayard's words haunt Helen for the next several days. The sheer panic of having to leave this magical place multiplies with every passing hour. But instead of luxuriating in that safety she felt on her first day in cottage number eleven, Helen spends her time frantically trying to attend every panel, every Q and A session, and every nature hike Hayho has on offer. Until she wakes up early one morning, sore and burned out, on what she's horrified to realize is the sixth day of the Hayward Writing Intensive. She has only one more full day here. Tomorrow she has to pack up that blue Samsonite, say her goodbyes, and lock away this newly found feeling of completeness after she inevitably loses the Glending Fellowship to Mishler (obviously). Then it's back on the shuttle, back to that stupid bus stop where two strangers made fun of her for something she was positive made her cool, and then back home to a slate of interviews for a life and a career she doesn't want.

In trying to suck the very marrow out of her time here, Helen has exhausted herself. And in that exhaustion and momentary weakness comes a wave of sadness that washes over her as she lies in the simple wooden bed she has allowed herself to stupidly grow accustomed to. She can't even remember what her own bed feels like anymore, let alone how dismal it's going to be to not wake up to the distant birdsong floating down from the canopy just above. How harsh her cheap, tinny alarm clock will sound on that first morning home.

Helen had such high hopes for the person she was going to be after attending Hayho. She had visions of this steely, self-assured version returning home after having successfully evolved into the next level of herself. But if this transformation has actually happened, she was ignorant of the fact that this next level would involve even higher amounts of yearning than the earlier one. Helen naively thought that once her dreams became more and more tangible, the desperation to attain them would lessen. Sadly, this could not be further from the truth. As she stares at the cottage's ceiling, lovingly tracing the wood grain in an attempt to etch it into her memory forever, the desire to be a successful writer has grown to a near fever pitch inside her. The sensation mirrors the feeling she experienced as a child when she tried to swim the entire length of the family pool underwater but, just as she neared the other end, the burning in her chest grew and grew and grew until she was positive her heart would explode. On this second-to-last morning in this sublime cottage that was all her very own, Helen lies in her bed with both hands resting on her chest, hoping to keep her poor, desperate heart safely in its rib cage.

All she wants to do is linger a bit longer. But today her piece is going to be read in the workshop, along with Cherry's. And the sheer thought of Deborah Torres actually reading something she wrote propels her to sit upright, swinging her feet to the dusty wooden floor. She walks over to the desk and finds the extra copy she made of her short story sitting on top of her tote. Just as she left it. She was going to show it to Cherry last night after dinner but didn't. She told herself it was because Cherry would read it today anyway, so why give it to her before that. But even Helen is self-aware enough to know that's not the real reason. Unfortunately, she isn't quite able to parse out the real reason from the hundreds of kinda-reasons that are also pinballing around in her quickly degenerating psyche. Is it that she thinks Cherry won't get it? Or does she think Cherry won't like it? Or is it that Cherry didn't give Helen her writing? And if Helen presented Cherry with hers, would Cherry then feel obligated to return the favor? Or is it just that Helen couldn't figure out a not-completely-awkward way to hand it to her, haunted by the vision of her shoving her sweat-covered, wrinkled pages across the lunch table with a grunt of "READ THIS PLEASE I'M COMPLETELY NORMAL." In the end, Helen just didn't. It was easier than any of the other truly catastrophic options.

She flicks through the pages, reading over words she's read and reread, tweaked and fussed with, hated and loved. She wanted to bring something new, but every time she tried to write with Hayho in mind, she became paralyzed at the pressure of producing something for, in Cherry's words, the Fancy People. In the end, she submitted a short story she wrote back in college. There, it went through several workshops, critique groups, and passes by her professors. She then used that short story for her application to her master's program, where it cycled through another set of workshops, critique groups, and passes by her professors. When questioning why she would submit a piece of writing that has already gone through so many reviews, Helen tells herself it's because the goal of Hayho is not to hone her craft, per se—it's to impress someone enough that they give her a shot. And her best shot at impressing Deborah Torres is that short story.

Helen brushes her fingers over the words, hoping that greatness lurks somewhere in these pages. That Deborah will see something in her writing and in her and that that recognition will be passed on to the Glending Fellowship panel of literary greats. Helen puts her hand down onto the pages, her palm flat on the paper.

"I choose this one," she says, acting out a moment in the future when Deborah Torres looks upon all the submissions for the Glending Fellowship and allows her hand to fall onto Helen's pages, singling them out from the rest. Singling her out from the rest. Helen recites the words again as if they are a prayer: "Choose this one."

Helen feels a pang of guilt at imagining Deborah's hand skipping over Cherry's work in order to anoint her own. And as the noise in her head gets louder and louder, she assuages her guilt by telling herself that Cherry's only twenty years old. She has five more years to be eligible for the Glending Fellowship, but at twenty-four, this is Helen's last chance. Ergo, she has way more of a right to win the fellowship than Cherry does and she should not feel guilty if or when she wins it.

In the last moments of having this thought, Helen meekly offers that she'd be happy for Cherry if she won it. But even in the privacy of her own mind, Helen knows this is a lie. She shakes her head, wishing she were a better person. Before the guilt can build once again, Helen tells herself that she is a good person, she's just desperate for a break. And as Tess Bayard said, she just needs that turning point that'll also somehow end with her having her very own book launch at the Kaufmann Concert Hall and the 92nd Street Y, sneaking into an SNL after-party, and then watching a sunrise with famous people in Battery Park. Or, at the very least, getting that monthly stipend for a full year so she can finally sit down and write her debut novel, thereby forging her own path into publishing as a Glending alumna. She needs this. And quite frankly, she's worked longer and harder than Cherry has to get here. Four years of college, then two years in her master's program should count for more than just being a hobbyist. Helen deserves this.

Helen admits that it's been nice having a friend here. Her shoulders slump as she corrects that last statement: It's been nice having a friend, period. Helen hasn't eaten a meal alone since that first breakfast. And passing notes during workshops and panels and Q and As has made the last several days downright lovely. Helen smiles as she remembers last night, when she and Cherry stole a bunch of beer from the cooler and went down to Helen's cabin and talked until the wee hours. Mostly gossiping about the other writers they've met at Hayho, but every now and again something a bit more personal wriggled in. Her guilt rages back, but there's nothing she can do. She wants that fellowship. She needs that fellowship. She deserves a turning point. And if Cherry wins the award at just twenty years old—the youngest person ever to win it—it'll kill Helen. Hell, it will kill her if anyone else except her wins it. And sadly, in this particular scenario, Cherry being a friend has to remain irrelevant to Helen's drive to win.

Regardless of being a friend, right now Cherry is just one more person standing in the way of Helen being recognized as a real writer.

Helen lets out a long sigh, grabs her toiletry bag, slides on her shoes, and makes her way up to the showers for her second-to-last shower here at Hayho. Helen will say this throughout the day: This is the second-to-last time she will get ready in the morning here at Hayho. This is the second-to-last time she will greet Cherry out front of the Public House here at Hayho. This is the second-to-last time she will have breakfast here at Hayho. This is the second-to-last time she will fill up her Thermos with Earl Grey tea here at Hayho.

This is the very last time she will sit in this workshop room here at Hayho.

Deborah Torres closes the workshop door with her hip, her arms full of copies of Helen's and Cherry's writing, fingers curling around a steaming mug of Earl Grey tea. The group has its own ebbs and flows now, having spent four hours of each of the last five days with each other. Deborah hands the stacks of papers to Mishler, who keeps one of each and passes the rest over to the person next to him, and so on and so forth.

To Helen's absolute annoyance, the four other workshop members have become quite the little cabal. Ruth and Karan have even started kind of seeing each other, and the little swoony looks and burgeoning pats on the arm and, oh, what a coincidence that the notes and feedback you're giving on his writing are limited to only lengthy accolades and, oh, look, she can't control how much she's "so in love with this"—Helen's positive if she hears this statement one more time, it will be the last thing Ruth hears as Helen screams it over her mangled body.

Helen is fully aware that she is not one to cast aspersions, shall we say, when evolving one's feedback given that person's position in life—not five days ago she revamped her own critique given Ruth's position in the Fancy People world. Helen is also not immune to feelings of guilt when pondering the act of having to give those harder notes to someone whom you see as a friend. As she shifts her own pages to sit on top of Cherry's, she grows nervous. For a lot of reasons.

While Helen is confident that between her work and Cherry's, hers will be the good one in today's workshop, she can't be absolutely sure until she reads Cherry's writing herself. There is still that slithering fear that Cherry just may be that genius-needle in the Hayho stack who comes along once in a generation. And it would be just Helen's luck to be the other poor sucker who happens to be having her work read the very day that the great Cherry Stewart is discovered.

But what if Cherry isn't a good writer? What if, after all this, Cherry begins reading her story and it's terrible? What if, just like the writing contest that won her the money to come here, Hayho let Cherry in not because of her writing but because she was a sob story that everyone could feel good about giving a chance? The only silver lining to learning that Cherry isn't a good writer, of course, would be no longer feeling guilty when and if Helen wins the Glending. The thought that they would award the fellowship to Cherry for the same sob-story reasons traces up the nape of Helen's neck.

Refocusing, Helen struggles with how she is going to not only give Cherry the notes that she needs to be a better writer but also respect her as an artist if their friendship is going to last more than just six days. And Helen never would have imagined herself thinking such a thing, but she is going to take a page out of Mishler's handbook and do the best she can at respecting Cherry enough to give her the hard notes that will, in the end, turn her into a better writer. It is her moral obligation. But she must put all these worries on the back burner for right now. Because Deborah is beginning her opening remarks for the day, and that means Helen is about to find out if she is the final workshop's good writer or the one with potential.

Deborah calls on Helen to go first. This is a mixed signal, as Mishler and Tala both had the "good" stories for their workshop day, but Mishler went second and Tala went first. And in Tala's case, Deborah spent the entire workshop the next day going back over Tala's story alone. She's clearly trying to make this "one good one and one with potential" rule as opaque as possible. How dare she.

The small workshop room quiets, and Helen begins reading her short story. She hates how nervous her voice sounds. She hates how her voice sounds, period, come to think of it. Has she always sounded so shrill? How do people stand it? Trying to calm herself, Helen pitches her voice down an octave for a brief and humiliating few sentences. She sees Cherry sneak her a concerned look and, after taking a deep breath, lets her voice go back to its regular shrill squawk. The workshop members then laugh at something funny Helen wrote. It's not a big laugh, but it's a slight chuckle, and as far as Helen is concerned, it still counts. Her voice grows more confident, but she makes sure not to rush as the excitement floods through her body.

Helen wrote this particular piece after attending a local community theater performance with her parents. The performance was of an original play written by a woman who taught creative writing out of her living room in Mill Valley, weekly classes that were usually eclipsed by wild stories of the woman's time in Hollywood during the 1940s. Helen had taken one of her classes, in what seemed to be almost an act of rebellion aimed at her parents, and hated that the woman was as inept and ridiculous as they had long suggested. The meat of Helen's short story was the conversation they'd had on the drive home from the theater—a conversation laced with haughtiness and snobbery and that particular melancholy you feel when you realize your parents are just regular, flawed people. She has never been able to find a good title for the short story, choosing instead to melodramatically call it "The Untitled Hicks Project."

As Helen continues to read, she can feel the room lean in to her words. It's an intoxicating moment. They like it, and just like with any good art, they're letting themselves be swept away in it despite what they might think of her personally. It's what she's always loved about writing. That, while she may not be well liked or even palatable to most, her writing has always allowed her access to the more elite circles of academia, whether those within those hallowed halls liked it or not. Proving once more that Helen is correct in her assertion that one can be an off-putting loner only when they're also incredibly skilled at what they do. She understands now that while she may have unequivocally been the former, she still might have a shot at the latter.

As Helen finishes reading, Cherry is the first to clap. Helen undergoes an explosion of feelings as the others join in. First, she wishes Deborah Torres were the one who'd led the round of applause, or even Mishler, nodding his head as if to say, *You're all right, kid. Boy, did I get you all wrong.* And second, Helen's not sure if Cherry is clapping because she liked Helen's writing or if she's just being a supportive friend. Helen knows it shouldn't matter, but as the applause dies down, she finds herself twisting the ovation into some kind of mercy-clap where the little cabal is somehow making fun of her. It happens so painlessly that by the time Cherry gives her a little thumbs-up, Helen is downright annoyed. Helen will later tell herself that this misunderstanding is the reason she does what she does to Cherry during her feedback session. That, in a way, she's protecting Cherry from the very torment she herself is experiencing as she tries to differentiate between an honest, authentic reaction and an unearned rave that is given solely to an already established relationship. She will reason that she is just doing what Mishler did, even though in the dark of the night, she will pick and pick at herself for that not being as true as she'd like it to be.

Deborah thanks her for reading, and Helen is horrified to find herself bending forward in her chair, bowing in response. Worse still, she realizes what she's doing and stops midbow, making it look more like a retching motion, eliciting concerned looks from those thinking she's on the verge of being sick. After a quick bathroom break, one that Helen decides to forgo to further prove she was not nauseous, Deborah instructs Cherry to begin reading her work. Helen sits back in her chair and takes a deep breath, hoping that what she hears is good. Or rather, good . . . but just not as good as Helen's. Or rather, that Cherry's "has potential."

The little scene Cherry has written is less a story and more a character sketch that's a first-person account of a woman—a woman Helen notices sounds an awful lot like Cherry herself—and her two old dogs. The backbone of the story orbits around the conflict that arises when the woman realizes the kitchen sponge she was using to wash the dishes is gone and there is a very high probability that one of the old dogs has eaten it. The truly remarkable thing that Cherry has done, however, is treat the ensuing investigation like a gripping psychological thriller, with the ancient dogs playing the role of the hardened criminals who are impossible to crack.

The group laughs and reacts as if they're hearing the juiciest gossip across the lunch table with every word Cherry reads. And with every giggle, Cherry grows more and more confident until it feels like the entire room is being swept up in some kind of hilarious one-woman show. And while Helen feels that there is nowhere near enough structure and plot for her tastes, she has to admit that Cherry's voice is extraordinary and her natural talent with pacing is downright electric. Cherry finishes reading, and the entire room lets out a roar of frustration at her story coming to a cliff-hanger of an ending. When Mishler presses Cherry about which one of the dogs did it, she laughs and says that he's going to have to buy the book to learn that particular top-secret information. And as Helen looks on, horrified, the two of them share a very touching moment in which Mishler gives Cherry an exuberant thumbs-up, as if he's making a promise to do just that.

Deborah cuts in and shushes the workshop, who are all now actively arguing about which dog did it. Once they've all quieted down, Deborah tells everyone that it's time to give feedback on Helen's story. While Helen understands that she didn't actually hear a groan of disappointment at having to return to her piece over continuing to discuss Cherry's, she'll argue that regardless of whether it happened, the sentiment was nonetheless there.

Helen hangs on to every word and critique, furiously scribbling in her notebook as she attempts to document every last thing people say about her story. Mishler says that the piece is "polished," but then insinuates that it is, perhaps, too polished. As he repeats her own words about the why of the writing and adding a bit more of her messy humanity, Helen can feel her face flush. It's as if he somehow knows exactly the feedback she's gotten in the past about her far-too-perfect writing and how she has a tendency to bend reality to support an idealized version of her characters and the world around them. Helen's feedback is mostly positive, but it's also quite sedate. The critiques are about tweaks here and there, a typo Helen missed (pointed out by Ruth, of course), and Cherry's note about creating stakes with the parents by having the main character standing up more for herself on the car ride home. Helen has received this note before but has been unable to execute it, both in the story and in real life.

But then it's time for Deborah to weigh in on Helen's piece. It's a moment she has both been craving and dreading. Deborah starts by saying how impressed she is by this workshop's feedback. She goes on a bit of a tangent about how giving notes on someone's work is actually one of the hardest things to do, but that these six writers have managed to really offer up some great notes to their peers that will, in the end, make their work all the better. Deborah echoes the group's general thoughts, but then drills down on the personal stakes for Helen's main character.

"I don't think it's made clear to the reader why this particular confrontation matters. Because right now, their relationship feels unchanged—and while that's absolutely a choice you can make because it's incredibly relatable, I don't think humans really know how to handle confrontation in general. And what it does for the reader is make it feel like the confrontation ultimately didn't matter. And even if that's true, we need to see how that realization changes our main character moving forward and whether she thought that finally speaking up—however meekly—would bring about a more open relationship with her parents. It's that transition of emotions that I'm looking for, because in those moments there lies the poignancy of the human experience. But, overall, job well done."

Helen nods along as Deborah speaks but finds herself stuck on "why this particular confrontation matters." As Deborah continues talking, Helen imagines herself walking around the workshop, grabbing her little stapled story, which apparently has nothing in it that matters, and setting the pages alight in one momentous pyre. As Deborah finishes giving her feedback, all Helen can do is smile and thank her, while inside her head she's screaming, "I'VE WORKED ON THIS FOR SIX YEARS AND IT'S STILL NOT PERFECT."

As Helen closes in on herself, Deborah guides the workshop to move on to Cherry's writing. And as Mishler launches into his feedback, Helen finds herself now unsure as to whose piece was the good one and whose "has potential." Maybe it will hinge on whether Deborah Torres thinks Cherry's story matters, which is something that apparently Helen's is lacking.

The workshop members praise Cherry for her voice, her natural confidence with writing, and say that the scene was a "fun read." Cherry beams, smiling from ear to ear. But Helen knows that there's a patronizing bite under the words "fun read," as if Cherry's offering, while pleasurable, wouldn't be something any of these people would deign to read in public. Which is why Helen tells herself she'll be the one person who gives Cherry and her writing the respect she believes the others have not shown her, by giving actual, serious notes, not dismissive notes about her work being a "fun read" with "commercial appeal" and calling this scene "a romp."

When Deborah calls on Helen, she can feel Cherry's gaze bore into her, excited and expectant. Helen doesn't look at her. She tells herself later it was because she was focusing on the task at hand, not because she was already feeling guilty for what she felt she was morally obligated to say to someone—the only one—whom Helen has ever called a friend.

"First, I'd like to say that this is a great start for someone who's attending their very first writing workshop. Your obvious natural talent and innate ability to craft a well-written story are irrefutable." Helen looks over at Cherry, who smiles so openly in response it almost makes Helen rethink what she's planned on saying. Helen quickly looks back down at her notes. "Okay, let's get into it. What I really loved most about your piece was how you subverted the reader's expectations of what a psychological thriller could be and, I think I speak for everyone here, that you made us all very invested in which dog was the perpetrator, as if it were some kind of big Jack the Ripper reveal."

Helen hears Cherry's perfectly sharpened Blackwing pencil scratch and scrape across the college-ruled paper in her spiral notebook as she speaks. She sneaks a glance over at Cherry's paper and sees the words "subvert expectations" and "psychological thriller" scrawled and circled on her paper.

"Where I see room for improvement"—Helen's voice catches, and she clears her throat—"is within the realm of what Mishler said earlier this week about going back to the basics." Helen shakes her head at her usage of "within the realm." In what world is that something Helen has ever said? She refocuses. "Because while this piece is undeniably a fun read, as Karan noted, it also lacks any kind of plot, character development, and most importantly, a why."

Which is when Helen hears Cherry's pencil stop.

Helen takes a long, deep breath and continues, "Once again echoing Mishler's words from earlier, when one sets out to subvert an entire literary genre, the only thing you must absolutely do is do it well. And in this case . . . this piece has not yet achieved that." Helen was going to say "and in this case, *you* have not achieved that" but changed it at the last minute to be more specific about the piece itself. (Later that afternoon, this self-edit will soothe Helen and make her feel slightly better about herself.) She presses on: "You obviously have the makings of an incredible writer—your intrinsic grasp of voice and how expertly you build relatable characters with spot-on dialogue, while also building incredible stakes and tension, is a wonderful foundation for a real page-turner that has the potential to enthrall a wide audience. But at its core, what this work really needs is for you to rise above being a hobbyist and concentrate on honing your craft so that you can be more than just a 'fun read.' It's time to start taking this seriously and get to work." Clearing her throat, Helen cuts through the deafening silence in the workshop room with a quick "That's it from me."

As Deborah Torres begins speaking, Helen can't look at Cherry. But even without looking over at her first and only friend, out of her peripheral vision, she can still see the word "hobbyist" written in block lettering across Cherry's paper.

Once again, Deborah thanks everyone for their notes before launching into her own. Deborah then leans forward in her chair, her whole body softening as she makes Cherry look at her.

"It's not often we get someone here at Hayho that is as new to writing as you are, Cherry. And I know firsthand how absolutely terrifying that can be. Like you, I never went to college, and like you, I didn't have the opportunities that others have to hone their craft. I know how daunting it is to listen to all this feedback and walk away thinking . . . well, nothing good. Am I right?"

"Yes . . . yeah," Cherry says, her face flushing bright red as she clearly tries to tamp down a torrent of emotions. Helen watches this exchange with the composure of someone now assured that theirs was emphatically the good one.

"But I'm guessing you will endure like I did. Because writing is not something we can just walk away from." Deborah waits while Cherry tearfully nods. "So, while I agree with the other workshop members that your work jumps off the page, your voice is clear as a bell, and the characters you've created immediately get under readers' skin, I can also see merit in what Helen pointed out around the necessity of honing your craft. You've got too much potential to remain a hobbyist. From someone who has been where you are, it's time to get to work. Because you're too good to give up this early in your career. Okay?"

“Thank you,” Cherry squeaks out. Helen looks over at Cherry and it breaks her heart. But she also can’t help but feel the teeniest bit of vindication now that *the* Deborah Torres has agreed with her about Cherry needing to hone her craft. In a fugue state, Helen tries to catch Deborah’s eye in an effort to secure this accord, but Deborah looks back down at her notes and launches into her final item on today’s agenda.

“As this is our last workshop session, I want to thank each and every one of you for entrusting your work to us. But I also want to use what little time we have left today for some real talk.” With these words, it feels as though the air has been sucked out of the room. No one moves. Deborah continues, “I know you’ve heard everyone talk about how hard this business is—on panels, in Q and As, and even just sitting down at a meal in the Public House. To consider a career in any of the arts, you must go into it eyes wide open to that harsh reality.” The workshop members look at one another in concern, but then Deborah smiles. “If I can impart one thing onto you, in this final moment—please remember that you started doing this because you love writing.” Deborah scans the room, looking at each and every workshop member. Her striking gaze hits hard, evoking meek nods of assent from around the room. “Because only the love of writing will get you through what will be a very hard road ahead.” The workshop members fidget in their chairs, uncomfortable with Deborah’s warnings about a hard road. And unfortunately for them, she is not done. “And before I let you go, I want to end with a cautionary tale. Hopefully at Hayho you have found an artistic community. Please also remember that a rising tide lifting all boats will always be more powerful than a dropped name, a networking opportunity, or giving a disingenuous compliment in hopes of being introduced to someone’s agent or editor. My door is open to you now. I consider myself a mentor to each and every one of you. I am now a part of your artistic community. But”—Deborah Torres scans the room—“do not squander that open door, or my name, thoughtlessly.”

The little cabal of friends surrounds Deborah Torres as she’s just about to leave, pulling books out of backpacks and satchels with shaking hands, asking for a signature amid tearful confessions of how much she and her work have changed them. Helen rolls her eyes, but hates that she didn't think to bring in her own book and definitely doesn't have the money to buy another copy from the Hayho book kiosk.

As they do so, Helen and Cherry sit silent, locked in a moment where neither is sure how to proceed. Helen roller-coasters between wanting to apologize, saying she shouldn't have to apologize because Deborah did, after all, agree with her, and trying to explain but then getting mad that she shouldn't have to explain until, finally, Cherry begins to pack up her things. Knowing that they only have one more day here at Hayho and Helen doesn't even have Cherry's home phone number, she clears her throat, hoping Cherry will look over. When she doesn't, Helen resorts to saying something. Unfortunately for her, outside of deciding to say something, she had no further thought on the matter. Which is why . . .

"You goin'?" Helen asks, inexplicably leaving off the final *g*.

"What?" Cherry asks, looking up from her backpack.

"You headin' out?" Again. No *g*.

"Yeah, man," Cherry says, hoisting her backpack over her shoulder and then looping it over the other.

"Are you mad at me?" Helen whispers so the others won't hear, quickly packing up her tote.

"I mean . . ." Cherry trails off, walking out of the workshop room. Helen follows Cherry into the chaotic, crowded hallway just beyond. She catches up with her once they get outside.

"I would say that you're mad at me, but maybe the reasons why are complicated," Helen says, trying to catch her breath. Cherry stops. Her shoulders fall. She looks over at Helen, holding on so tight to her backpack straps that her knuckles whiten. Helen notices that a large chunk of Cherry's hair is caught under the strap. Without thinking, Helen gently untangles Cherry's long blond tress from the backpack, patting it once she's done. Cherry watches the whole interaction without a word.

"Don't be nice to me," Cherry says, her eyes softening.

"Trust me, it's not my usual."

"Yeah, I think I just found that out."

They are quiet.

"You were a jerk about it, but I think you're right," Cherry says.

"Deborah also—" Helen starts, but Cherry cuts her off.

"Yeah, okay. You were both right," Cherry finishes, dropping her head to her chest. She begins to rub her forehead, a habit Helen has come to recognize as something Cherry does when she's trying not to get emotional.

"We need food. Let's go eat," Helen says, pulling Cherry toward the Public House.

Cherry continues speaking as the pair trudges toward the busy main hall. "It's always come so easy for me," she says.

"What has?" Helen asks airily.

"Writing."

Helen trips over a small trio of rocks along the pathway to the Public House. Cherry catches her by the upper arm, wrenching her back up into a standing position. Once Helen gathers herself, she ekes out a question she almost doesn't want to know the answer to.

"Writing is easy for you?" Helen asks, forcing a breezy tone as they step inside the Public House.

"Yeah," Cherry says, as if Helen has just asked her if she'd like cream in her coffee.

Helen and Cherry are quiet as they shift and inch forward in the buffet line, filling their plates full of sandwiches, chips, and various cut fruits and vegetables. As Cherry waits for the lemon bars to be replenished, Helen finds herself wondering how the tables have turned on her so quickly. Mere minutes ago, she was giving notes and wringing her hands about whether she should apologize or offer further explanations. And now here's Cherry telling her that writing comes easily to her.

Nothing has ever come easily to Helen. So much so that her teacher presented her with the Best Trier Award at the end of first grade. An award, she found out later, the teacher made up because Helen never won anything or stood out anywhere else. What six-year-old wants to be the best at "trying" and not the much cooler offerings like "Fastest Runner" or "Best Reader"?

Helen Hicks: the Best Trier.

"You want some?" Cherry asks Helen, her hand gripping the tongs as they hover over the freshly filled platter of lemon bars.

"Uh . . . sure," Helen says. Cherry stacks three more on her plate. Helen grabs one and shoves it in her mouth.

Helen scans the crowded Public House, looking for two seats, powdered sugar now dappling her threadbare black sweater. Cherry juts out her chin to indicate the far corner of the room, where two empty seats await them. Helen nods and follows Cherry as she winds her way through the loud and packed room.

"What was I just saying?" Cherry asks, taking a big bite of her BLT.

"That writing comes easy to you," Helen says robotically.

"Right. So when it came time to submit my application, I felt like I needed something new. So I wrote that story in, like, thirty minutes." At this, Helen chokes on her lemon bar. Cherry slams Helen's back, quickly pulling Helen's arms above her head.

"I'm good. Please, I'm fine. I really am fine," Helen says, gasping for air and struggling to understand how a person can write anything in thirty minutes. Her short story took more than six years to write, and Cherry killed it in that workshop with something she wrote in half an hour?

"I went to the library, where they have this one computer, wrote it up, printed it out, and sent it with my application. That was the first and only draft."

"You didn't revise?" Helen asks.

"I've never had to."

"You always have to."

"Not when you're a hobbyist," Cherry says, making very pointed eye contact.

"But it's like what Deborah was saying—you could be so much more," Helen says, pushing past the awkward moment.

"No, I know that. I—"

"I can help," Helen cuts in.

"Help?"

"Yeah. I can read your stuff, give notes, and teach you how to revise. I'll make you a better writer."

"A better writer." Cherry's face is unreadable.

"And then we can have debut novels together!" Helen blurts, trying to swing their awkward conversation around to becoming the inspiring pep talk she envisioned.

"Before we're thirty, of course."

"Oh god, yes. Please. Long before. If I win the—" Helen stops herself.

"No, go ahead. We're going to have to talk about it before the ceremony tonight anyways," Cherry says.

"If I win the Glending, I'll be able to spend the entire year writing my novel. Have you ever imagined something so wonderful? I could be the next Tess Bayard."

"And what if someone else wins it?" Cherry asks.

"I would—" Helen says quickly but stops.

"You would be happy for them?" Cherry finishes.

"Uh-huh," Helen says, looking down at the lunch table. Not able to sit in the awkward silence, Helen takes a giant bite of her tuna fish sandwich and offers an overly exuberant thumbs-up as proof of her commitment.

"You're a terrible liar," Cherry says.

As the tuna fish plops out of the back of her sandwich, Helen takes Cherry's words as the highest of compliments, now feeling safe in the knowledge that she's hidden her true self well.

CHAPTER SIX

On the final night of Hayho, the entrance to the Hayward House is beautifully decorated with an allée of luminaria. Their subtle, warm light flickers in contrast to the loud and raucous crowd of writers actively fighting back the looming dread of having to return to real life tomorrow. Cliques of writers glom on to one another, blurting proclamations of hometown meetups, possible writing groups, and a future where they're all big and famous writers. And to ensure they'll all believe these declarations throughout the night, they head straight to the open bar en masse.

Helen and Cherry decided to meet in front of Hayward House prior to the start of the ceremony, but as Helen walks through the flickering luminaria, she grows uneasy. After lunch today—and the "uh-huh" heard round the world—they each went back to their respective corners under the guise of trying to soak up the very last drops of that wonderful solitude they both luxuriated in while in their individual cottages.

As Helen sets herself up at the entrance, she runs through every possible scenario for how she'd like the night to go, landing on the terrible revelation that if she doesn't win the fellowship, she wants someone she doesn't even know to take it home. She hates that she feels this way. But there's just something deeply unfair about someone who spent thirty minutes writing the piece that got them into Hayho winning such a prestigious award. It should be given to someone who's put in the time, someone who's been working toward this for years, someone who . . . someone who is a trier. The best trier, in fact.

As Cherry lopes through the luminaria, squealing "Beeeeyooooooteeefulll" at the top of her lungs, Helen has to admit that this latest revelation may have something to do with her wanting to continue being friends with Cherry. Because the hard truth about herself is that she knows if Cherry wins and not her, the festering envy she'll feel will erode her. She's not proud of this epiphany, so just as Cherry comes to a bounding stop in front of her, Helen decides to add on that Cherry deserves a better friend than that and therefore Helen winning is in both of their best interests.

"Let's go win this thing, babyyyyy," Cherry says, lacing her arm through Helen's and tugging her inside. Helen smiles, letting herself be tugged, but that familiar yearning looms inside her like a vulture. Helen loathes how comfortable she has become with crippling disappointment.

Tonight, the Hayward House is set up for the big awards dinner, and starched white tablecloths puddle on the rustic wood floor as the waitstaff speed around the periphery in preparation. Just next to the main stage, the Hayward String Quartet offers musical accompaniment for the evening. But this is no ordinary string quartet—this particular one is legendary in literary circles, as it is made up of a rotating ensemble of famous writers. It's tradition that each generation boasts to the younger ones that the Hayward String Quartet that played for their Glending ceremony was the pinnacle of literary greatness. This year, however, is going to be tough to beat, as Deborah Torres on viola is the least famous in the quartet, a staggering fact that will be repeated for years to come.

Looking at the large seating chart, Helen and Cherry are devastated to find that Hayho has implemented assigned seating this evening. Worse still, they've made the diabolical decision to seat all workshop members together for this final evening's festivities. Helen and Cherry share a look of dread, before walking over to their assigned table in the very front of the room, where the tiny cabal, led by Mishler, are already on their second round of free apple martinis.

"Welcome, welcome," Mishler slurs, holding up his glass. The other three writers giggle and whisper, their faces blotchy and red from either the alcohol or the hot summer night with no air-conditioning. Probably both.

"Hey," Helen says, sliding in next to Tala, the least offensive of the three. She slides her black moto jacket off and hangs it on the back of her chair.

"You drunk already?" Cherry asks Mishler as she sits down next to Helen.

"No," he blurts, sloshing his drink around in the glass.

"Okay, Big Shot," Cherry says, scanning the room in search of the open bar. Mishler downs the rest of his drink.

"It's over there," Helen says, pointing to the opposite corner.

"Beer?" Cherry asks.

"Yeah, sure," Helen answers.

"And I'll grab three more to hide in your pockets for later," Cherry jokes. Helen offers a nervous laugh as the little cabal tries to figure out what Cherry means by that.

Helen sits quietly, looking around the room. She sets her elbow on the table and rests her face in her hand, hoping that she looks mysterious and confident as she stares poetically at the Hayward House one last time. She breathes, what she hopes, is a very dramatic and melancholy sigh.

Helen thinks back to middle school and remembers this one girl who used to twist her long blond hair between her fingers, knot it, and then let it loosely tumble down to her shoulders. She used to do it over and over again. Helen remembers hearing some of the popular boys in the hallway talk about how they loved watching her fingers looping and playing with her hair. One of the boys had even said that it was "hypnotizing." So, as Helen tries to put off as mysterious an air as possible on this, the night she may win the Glending Fellowship, she decides to try it herself. Helen brings her fingers up to her hair, wrenches the dyed-black straw between her fingers, and yanks it into a knot. But as she tries to let go so it can fall romantically to her shoulders, the hair becomes tangled in one of the several silver rings she decided to wear tonight. Very quickly the situation goes from bad to worse, as the knotted hair tightens around a set of two stacked rings on her pointer finger. The rest of the room muffles around her as she not-so-silently panics.

"So, who do you think is going to win?" Mishler asks her. Helen quickly takes her hand, the knotted hair, and the stacked silver rings right along with it, and places it up against the side of her head, as if falling into a contemplative stillness at Mishler's question.

"I don't know," Helen answers, knowing it would be arrogant to offer up herself.

"I think I am," Mishler says, proving Helen's point.

"Congratulations in advance, then," Helen says.

Ruth laughs. "Anybody but Cherry, right?"

"Oh, god. Yes," Tala says, cheersing her new friend.

"What?" Helen asks, stunned.

Karan sneers. "That piece today? Come on."

"But you . . . I thought you liked it? You said it was a 'fun read,'" Helen says, her hand still glued to the side of her head. Karan just shrugs.

"I mean, it was entertaining. I'll give her that," Mishler says, as if this is the most insulting thing one could say about another's art.

"Yeah, I thought so, too," Helen says, patting herself on the back for standing up for her friend despite her own petty jealousies.

"But it's not, you know . . ." Mishler gestures around the room. "On par with the rest of us." Helen notes that he said "us," including Helen herself.

"I think she's got a lot of potential, like Deborah said," Helen says.

"Potential isn't what wins the Glending," Ruth says.

"That's exactly what wins the Glending," Helen parries.

"What?" Ruth pushes back.

"The Glending Fellowship is awarded to a writer with the most potential. Like, that's actually, I think, verbatim what it says in the pamphlet," Helen argues.

"Like, that's actually, I think . . ." Ruth mimics, teasing Helen.

"You've been hanging around Cherry too much," Mishler says.

"Who's been hanging around with who too much?" Cherry asks, setting a beer in front of Helen before plopping down next to her. Helen looks over at Cherry, hoping she didn't hear what the others were saying.

"We were just talking about who we think is going to win tonight," Helen says, trying to move past the awkward moment.

"I think it's going to be Helen," Cherry says, noticing Helen's hand, the knotted hair, and the stacked silver rings. Helen turns to Cherry, surprised.

"What? You never . . ." Helen trails off as Cherry deftly untangles her knotted hair from the stacked silver rings, ripping only a few hairs from Helen's head in the process.

"Why? Who did you say?" Cherry asks, taking a long drag of her beer.

"Not you," Mishler says.

"I said I didn't know. I didn't say anybody," Helen says, panicking.

"Well, I know it's not going to be me, so I'm just going to enjoy myself tonight," Cherry says, sitting back in her chair.

Helen looks over at Cherry, wanting to tell her that she's wrong, that she has potential and is exactly the kind of writer Edith Glending imagined when she set up this award. But the moment to say something passes, and Helen says nothing. Cherry's proclamation hangs in the air, floating above the five people who laughed and enjoyed her writing just a few hours ago, but whose silence now all but confirms her worst fears: While no one assembled knows who'll win tonight, they're all in agreement about who won't. Helen can't help but feel guilty. Unable to look at Cherry, she takes another long drink of her beer and laments how exhausting it is to constantly hide her terribleness from everyone.

If only she could hide it from herself.

There is a definite shift in the room, as if something—or someone—has entered Hayward House like a sonic boom. Everyone starts turning in their chairs, looking for the root cause of the disruption. Helen follows the jangle of whispers and screeching chairs being moved out of the way to see Roberta Lartey pushing *the* Edith Glending in a wheelchair, wending their way through the mass of tables, gawking writers, and waiters. Edith Glending is a tiny woman. Known for her eclectic style, Edith sits ramrod straight in her utilitarian wheelchair, decked out in a pink and orange silk shirt, bright-orange silk pants, and lime-green velvet loafers. She's accessorized this outfit with what looks to be fifty pounds of outlandish jewelry, ranging from thick gold chains to a beaded necklace that is so large, it resembles a chain of colorful ocean buoys, bobbing up and down with her every breath. On her lap are two tiny white dogs, who seem as comfortable lazing on pure silk as Edith Glending is with wearing it. And as Edith is wheeled through the crowded room, the dogs nonchalantly take the measure of those writers who are fortunate enough to be in close proximity to get a good look, their little black button eyes unimpressed and bored. At ninety-one years old, Edith and her two little, apathetic dogs, are now the sun around which this entire room orbits.

Roberta parks Edith's wheelchair next to a table right at the base of the stage. Edith hands off the two little dogs to Roberta as she deftly maneuvers herself into one of the empty chairs around the table. As everyone watches, transfixed, she settles in comfortably, and Roberta hands the two dogs back to her. They circle around on her lap, before plopping down and falling quickly asleep. Roberta continues to the stage, steps in front of the microphone, and officially kicks off tonight's festivities.

The night is a combination of an end-of-session celebration and a healthy dollop of self-congratulatory back-patting. Every representative from the Hayho faculty spends the first several minutes of their time at the microphone unspooling a mythological level of awe at Hayho's place in the literary landscape and how lucky everyone in the room is to now be a small part of that epic saga. Everyone present laps up the praise, drunk from a full week of living like real writers, with some help from the open bar. The night passes in a triumphal blur.

But the time to announce the winner of the Glending Fellowship finally arrives. Helen has been unable to eat anything all night, and after those first nervous gulps of her free beer, she has spent the better part of two hours nursing that same bottle until its tepid, flat brew became repulsive to her.

Roberta Lartey stands, walks over to Edith Glending, and offers her some help getting into a standing position. Predictably, the two little dogs are beyond inconvenienced at this unwelcome disturbance. Laughing, Edith passes them to Tess Bayard, who's seated just to her left. Tess takes the two little dogs and lets them fuss just long enough until they accept her lap as an alternate napping spot. Then they both circle around until they plop down, tuck their noses underneath their paws, and fall fast asleep once again. Roberta and Edith laugh and talk as they make their way to the four steps that lead up to the main stage. The string quartet plays a jaunty little tune as Roberta and Edith climb the stairs. With each step, everyone who's eligible for the fellowship gets a little more nervous.

Roberta leads Edith over to the podium, gets her set up—making sure the noise from her necklaces doesn't completely drown out the microphone—and then falls in just behind her, making sure she's close by should anything happen. Edith confidently tugs the microphone down and puts her hands, overly adorned with massive rings on every finger, on either side of the podium. The room falls silent.

"Hello. I'm Edith Glending, and I am a writer," she says, scanning the room. Her voice is a raspy drawl, crackly and arch. She waits for the inevitable applause that roars in response. Finally: "It took me way too long to buck up the courage to say that simple phrase out loud. I don't think I'm alone in that. So why don't we do a little experiment here tonight. Why don't we try saying it together." The room fizzes with nervous anticipation. "Ready?"

"Yes!" the entire room excitedly yells back.

But unlike everyone else, Helen is definitely not ready and says nothing in response to Edith's artsy battle cry. In the chaotic flash of time, as everyone chatters and laughs to those around them, Helen closes in on herself.

What Edith is asking feels . . . somehow dangerous. It is so outside of Helen's comfort zone that she finds herself scanning the faces of those seated at her table for a hint as to whether everyone thinks this request is corny or inspirational, and are they going to do it, and if they do decide to partake, is it going to be done ironically or for real? How will she know in time? She looks over at Cherry, but because she's seated slightly in front of her and turned toward the main stage, Helen can see only her profile. Plus, given her new friend's proclivities, Helen is confident that Cherry is completely on board with Edith Glending's cheeseball public declaration of loud artistry.

In a panic, Helen looks over at Mishler as he and Tala share a very stealthy side-eye along with a not-so-stifled giggle. Assured that her instincts are correct, Helen tries to catch their eyes so she can let them know that she, too, thinks this whole thing is stupid. And, to quote Mishler from earlier, "not on par with the rest of us"—obviously folding herself into the aforementioned "us" just as he did before. They avert their eyes quickly and focus back on Edith Glending. But now Helen has the information she so desperately needed and knows that she'll politely participate in this foolishness, out of respect for Edith Glending and the fellowship that is going to allow her a future as a writer. But she's not going to *participate* participate so she can make sure the cool kids know that she is far too erudite for such trifling exercises.

"I want everyone to repeat after me. Ready? 'I'm'—then say your full name—and then say as loud as you can 'and I am a writer.' And don't try to fudge the rules and say 'I'm a writer.' It's not as powerful as really hitting 'I am.' We're all writers here. We know the power of words, and we know that one is far more powerful than the other. I've done studies." The room laughs with contained anxious energy. "Ready?"

The room erupts in applause, and Helen notices that Cherry's claps are far more muted than she thought they'd be.

"Three! Two! One!" Edith counts down.

The room explodes in a cacophony of "I'm" and then hundreds of different names. But then, as if being conducted by a choirmaster, the entirety of Hayho joins together to yell "And I am a writer" at the top of their lungs.

Even though she only barely muttered the five words, they still somehow managed to get stuck in Helen's throat. And in the noisy, celebratory aftermath, she can feel herself flushing from embarrassment, as if she somehow let a truly mortifying secret slip to a roomful of strangers. Just as Edith launches into the main event for the evening, Helen notices Cherry swiping away tears now trailing down her face.

"You okay?" Helen whispers, leaning forward in her chair.

"Yeah. Yeah," Cherry answers, turning away from her. Helen is just about to press the issue but is shushed by a woman at the next table. Helen sits back in her chair, and Cherry offers no further insight into what it was about saying those dangerous five words that made her cry.

"When I was twenty-five years old, I came to this magical place for the first time, and it changed my life forever. It was here that I wrote the first chapter of *Quiet Was the Meadow*, but more importantly, it was here at Hayho that I first saw myself as a writer. I will add, it was the latter that was a far more difficult endeavor. I started the Glending Fellowship because I wanted to provide other young writers with the time, community, and money that would afford them that same discovery process—in hopes of ending with a piece of writing that they not only were proud of but that could give them a toehold into a bright future in publishing. So, without further ado, the 1995 recipient of the Glending Fellowship is Helen Hicks."

Edith Glending says her name so quickly that Helen can't believe it has actually happened. She continues sitting there, looking around at how real this dream seems, how well her brain has populated this reverie, and how sad it's going to be when she wakes up. But then Cherry turns around in her chair and starts speaking to her, although her actual words are muffled and indecipherable. When Cherry's words have no impact on Helen, Cherry begins gently shaking Helen, pulling her up into a standing position and lovingly pushing her toward the stage, holding her hands out as if Helen is a toddler just learning how to walk.

As Helen shambles to the stage, the applause feels like it's happening in another building of the Hayho campus, and it's for someone else who's just won this prestigious award. Because she can't feel her legs, or any part of her body for that matter, Helen slams into the back of someone's chair. She burbles out what she hopes sounds like "Excuse me" to whoever's chair it was and continues to struggle putting one foot in front of the other. In a haze, she lets her eyes fall lazily on Tess Bayard as she quietly claps, careful not to wake the two dogs sleeping on her white satin baby doll dress.

Instinctively, Helen makes her way over to the four stairs that lead up to the main stage. She proceeds to climb them with the hitched and jittery gait of a space alien trying to blend in with humanity as it desperately attempts to grasp the overall concept of a staircase. Seemingly picking up on her quickly deteriorating state of mind, Roberta Lartey meets Helen at the top of the stairs and walks with her over to the podium, where Edith Glending and the Glending Fellowship plaque—which now has a small gold name badge that says "1995: Helen Hicks"—await her.

Helen can feel Roberta's hand tighten around her upper arm. She hadn't noticed that she was swaying, but from the urgency with which Roberta caught her, it must have been quite a spectacle. At this, Helen lets out a little "ha" sound, finally finding her voice. Helen leans into Roberta as she tries to get her sea legs, but then Edith Glending is saying something to her and all the gold and the shiny jewelry and the bright pink and the lime green and the giant pearl earrings that are aggressively pulling down her earlobes and her truly stunning light-green eyes astound Helen, who feels as if she's watching a fireworks show on the Fourth of July. And to her horror, between the escaping "ha" sounds, Helen hears herself ooh and aah at the ninety-one-year-old icon as if she's a Roman candle lighting up the night sky.

"Congratulations," Edith says, leaning into Helen so she can hear her above the din of applause.

"Thank you," Helen says, taking her extended hand and shaking it. Edith's rings dig into her skin. But thankfully Helen is still completely numb and doesn't feel a thing.

"Helen, we're going to take a quick photo," Roberta says and deftly positions the two women so they hold the plaque between them and the photographer can snap a few shots for the archives. Edith wraps her arm around Helen's waist and pulls her close, but not wanting to manhandle the literary legend in her current fugue state, Helen chooses instead to grip the plaque with the rigidity of a corpse in its final stages of rigor mortis and lets the other arm fall limply to her side, drooping and sagging like that of a well-loved rag doll. The flash from the camera sparks and blazes as Helen tries to make her face do something other than resemble a waxen death mask.

Roberta takes the plaque, pulls Helen away from the podium and back down the stairs. Edith finishes with a raucous retelling of how she got published, her first fancy literary party, and the advice she wishes someone would have given her back when she first started. Roberta tells Helen to wait at the bottom of the stairs. And as the string quartet kicks in, Roberta thanks Edith for her generosity, congratulates Helen once again, and sends everyone else off with tidings of fun, camaraderie, and a last night at Hayho to remember.

Still catatonic, Helen is directed to follow Roberta. She obliges. She asks no follow-up questions, and the fact that she's just won the coveted fellowship is all but absent from Helen's entire demeanor. In fact, by the way Helen solemnly nods and shuffles off behind Roberta, you'd think she was being disciplined or asked to vacate the premises. As Helen walks toward the back of Hayward House, she gets a glimpse of Cherry sitting all by herself at the table. The little cabal of workshop members must have dejectedly filed out as soon as their beloved king lost. The thought of Dan Mishler losing is the first thought that cracks through Helen's numbness, producing a wry smile as she steps into a small anteroom just behind the main stage. Roberta gets Helen settled but is then called out by one of the Hayho faculty. This leaves Helen alone for the first time since she won the Glending Fellowship.

The quiet inside the small room quickly becomes unbearable. Helen stands, feeling itchy and aggravated. She begins to pace, trying to rein in just one of the wild and raging thoughts currently barreling through her brain. The deep desire to be able to celebrate this moment along with the shame and confusion when she can't. This should be a simple moment of triumph. She did it. She won. She will have a $25,000 yearly living stipend that will allow her to finally write her debut novel. She will have an appointed Glending mentor, who will be by her side throughout this entire year and provide her with whatever introduction she'll need to thrive inside the exclusive enclave that is the publishing world. She will be invited to every Glending event, where she will rub shoulders with the literary elite as they ask her what they can do for her and her career. She will be able to return home a winner, tell her parents to cancel those interviews, and maybe even move out on her own because she is a real writer now. And she has the small gold name badge on the Glending Fellowship plaque to prove it. She will be able to write her debut novel, and thanks to winning the Glending, she will have access to agents and editors who will want to be a part of her literary journey. These are all wonderful things that she has been dreaming about for years. She'd played and replayed the moment where her name would be called time and time again. Needless to say, that moment did not go down quite like she had imagined. So, what happened? Helen crumples onto an old scratchy sofa in the corner and leans forward, her elbows resting on her knobby knees. She lets her head fall forward, and her dry and damaged black hair scratches and tickles her acne-scarred jawline.

The truth is, when you are a loser, winning is terrifying.

Helen does not insult herself with her usage of the word "loser." It is simply the correct word to describe someone who has never won anything. But not tonight. Tonight, she won. Tonight, all that trying finally paid off.

But whenever she has imagined winning, she's always written the scene in her head with a version of herself who was dressed a whole lot nicer. Someone who's mastered winged eyeliner. Someone who has her act together. In short, someone who deserves to win. A Helen who would be able to stand at that podium and bask in the applause, rather than be haunted by it as if the roar from the crowd were the far-off shrieks of a vengeful ghost.

She has become so compulsive about this dream that she's failed to notice that it has taken on a life of its own, having little resemblance to her day-to-day reality. And this failure has all but guaranteed that her truly extraordinary win feels like someone made a mistake and the Glending clearly should have gone to someone else. Because the version of herself Helen wrote into that winning scene would have no problem hearing her name being called out, or smiling for a photo with Edith Glending, or holding court as she luxuriated in the accolades and congratulations of her fellow writers. Helen's stomach twists in knots. Taking this line of thinking even further, that winning version of Helen would also have no problem standing up to her parents, moving out on her own, confidently writing a debut novel, boldly querying agents, and all but expecting that she and her book would climb to astronomical literary heights. At this realization, Helen begins to slowly unravel. If she can't even navigate these beginning steps in the present, is there any hope that she'll be able to manage the much greater achievements that await her in the future?

Helen sits up and pushes her hair back from her face. She looks down at herself and then does a quick scan around the room, the muffled din of Hayward House safely on the other side of the thick wooden door. Under threat of shutting down completely, Helen tries to find one single concrete thought or idea among the several thousand buzzing and chirping around her brain that might help her begin to pull herself out of this spiral. But the only thought that's strong and whole enough is one that is the antithesis of helpful. So as Roberta reenters the small anteroom, smiling and excited to talk to the brand-new Glending fellow, all Helen can think about is what will happen now that a loser has mistakenly won this award.

CHAPTER SEVEN

"Why me?" Helen blurts as Roberta settles in next to her on the couch.

"I'm sorry?" Roberta asks, clearly positive she's misheard.

Helen is quiet, initially unable to repeat the question, which took everything she had just to say once. Finally, she asks again, "Why me?"

Roberta's entire face softens. "We felt that your short story showed the most promise. And that, combined with your yearslong commitment to learning the craft of writing, made you the obvious choice for this year's award as a writer and as a scholar," she says matter-of-factly.

"Oh. Okay. Well, I'm grateful, really grateful you chose me. Thank you," Helen says, still looking at the floor as she turns Roberta's addition of "scholar" around in her mind.

"You're so welcome," Roberta says, gently patting Helen's knee.

Roberta opens up a file folder and begins sifting through the stack of papers within. Helen nods along as Roberta goes over the fellowship, key dates, and the best way to communicate with her. Roberta has Helen's Hayho application in the stack of papers and confirms her home address and phone number.

Something takes over, and Helen hears herself blurting, "You know what? I'm moving next month, so can I give you my new contact information when I get it?"

"Oh, sure. Where are you moving?" Roberta asks, making small talk. Helen blanks. "You don't have to—"

"The city," Helen interrupts. There is a painful moment as Helen watches Roberta decide not to press the issue. Trying to salvage the moment, Helen continues, "San Francisco, I . . . uh, I know there are a lot of . . . cities. But . . . yeah. Frisco is where this girl is headed. The old, big bay." Why god why.

"That's actually good news, because we've assigned Tess Bayard as your Glending mentor, and she, too, lives in the city," Roberta says.

"Tess is my mentor?" Helen asks, quickly moving past her little white lie.

"Yes, I thought you and she could speak at the after-party." With every new piece of information that Roberta communicates, Helen finds herself having to abandon the nervousness for the last one in favor of being overwhelmed by the new one.

"After-party?" Helen wonders if she will ever speak in full sentences again.

"The Hayho faculty customarily has a little gathering on the last night of the session. 'After-party' is a generous word for it." Roberta laughs.

"Would it be okay if I brought my friend?" Helen asks, already panicking about having to go to this after-party or little gathering or whatever it is all by herself.

"Oh, sure," Roberta says, ripping a piece of paper from her notebook. She sketches out directions to a part of the Hayho campus Helen has never seen. Helen tries to read Roberta's scrawled handwriting, making out words like "faculty housing" and "the common house," stitched together by little arrows and bold circles. Roberta hands the paper to Helen and sees that her hands are shaking, the paper quivering.

"Sorry . . . so sorry," Helen says, folding up the paper and shoving it into the front pocket of her moto jacket. She tucks her shaking hands under her legs. Roberta softens, shifting closer to Helen on the couch.

"I know this is a lot. But the only thing you need to do tonight is just be proud of yourself. Everything else will unfold in time," Roberta says, patting Helen's leg. Helen smiles and nods, hoping she's managed to hide how truly impossible it actually is to follow Roberta's advice.

Roberta gives Helen her business card and tells her to contact her when she has her new address and phone number. Letting herself get a little bit excited about the prospect of moving, Helen smiles and takes the business card. Maybe she can find the version of herself that's a winner in San Francisco.

Helen and Roberta say their goodbyes and Helen immediately sets out to find Cherry. Walking through the emptying Hayward House, Helen fields congratulations from the smattering of people still lingering in the beautiful old barn of a building. Muttering thanks, along with some questionable peace signs, Helen exits the building and is thrust out into the balmy evening.

The Hayho campus has taken on an almost festival-like aura, filled with groups of writers in various stages of drunkenness, celebration, and melancholy. Someone has even dragged the oversize speaker out of Hayward House and rigged it to play from their Discman. Music spills across the bustling campus as people dance and sing along to the songs, holding on to one another for one last night. In darker corners, new couples sit close, nervous for what will happen to their burgeoning love once the spell of Hayho is broken.

Helen picks her way down to Cherry's cottage, scanning the terrain the whole time, unsure as to where she's gone. As she walks, Helen begins to fear that winning the Glending will cause a rift with her new friend. That even though she announced she knew she wasn't going to win, maybe Cherry just said that to deflect the inevitable rejection while also hoping beyond hope that she was wrong. It's a tactic Helen herself has used liberally in the past. As Helen nears Cherry's cottage, she begins to question herself. Is she really about to roll up with her tale of woe about not being able to process winning to someone who has lost? Helen knows that her inability to truly own this win could be read as disingenuous, but she's positive the general population has no idea how little she thinks of herself. Helen steps onto Cherry's porch and the creaky wood announces her arrival.

"Knock, knock," Helen says for the first time in her life. She shakes her head out of pure embarrassment, muttering "knock, knock" under her breath with particular disgust.

She can hear Cherry get up off the bed and walk the three steps to the door. She opens the door, and it's clear that she's been crying.

"Oh, uh . . . I . . ." Helen stammers.

"Come on in," Cherry says, stepping inside and leaving the door open. Helen obliges even though she wants to run as far away from here as possible.

"I'm sorry if . . . I can leave," Helen says.

"No, it's cool," Cherry says, sitting back down on her bed.

"I wanted to know if you wanted to come to a party with me."

"A party?"

"Yeah, you know . . ."

"I know what a party is."

They are quiet.

"It's not my fault that I won," Helen blurts.

"Yikes," Cherry says, leaning back on her hands.

"Wh . . . why yikes?"

"Me crying has nothing to do with you, Helen." It's always bad when someone ends a sentence with your name. Always.

"Oh."

"I'm just going to really miss this place," Cherry says, swiping at her tears.

"Yeah, me too."

"Congratulations on the win. I'm so glad you won. Your story was just amazing." Cherry pulls her socked feet under her and proceeds to sit crisscross applesauce.

"Thanks," Helen says, still awkwardly standing in the middle of the cottage.

"So, this party?"

"It's more of a gathering, but Roberta threw it out there and I asked if you could come and she said yes, so . . ."

"Yeah, sure, why not," Cherry says, unraveling her long legs and standing. She steps into her shoes, pushing and shoving the backs down in the process. Finally, she reaches down and hooks her finger into the shoe and slides her foot in.

"Can I just say something out loud to you first?" Helen asks, looking at the floor.

"Is this gonna get weird or . . ."

"I mean, probably." Cherry laughs and Helen finally drags in a deep, ragged breath.

"Go ahead then," Cherry says, standing next to the door.

"I feel weird about winning. And I know that me saying that to someone who lost could be . . . no, is insensitive, but . . ." Helen trails off, shaking her head at how knee-deep she's gotten herself into this questionable confession. She takes a deep breath and continues, "I'm terrified I won't be able to write this novel because, despite winning this one award, I've never won anything, and if I couldn't even accept the award right then, how will I . . ." Helen again trails off, unable to say the rest out loud.

"Writing can be hard. It's kind of good you're not taking it lightly," Cherry says.

"Writing *is* hard, but I don't know why they chose me, you know?"

"You don't know why they chose you?"

"Yeah, you know . . . like, why me?" Helen asks again.

"What about them choosing you is confusing?"

"Just like . . . why . . . why me," Helen says, coming undone by Cherry's basic follow-up questions.

"Did they talk about why they awarded it to you after the ceremony?" Cherry asks.

"I mean, yeah . . . Roberta said something about my story showing the most promise as a writer and a scholar and some other stuff," Helen mumbles.

"Oh, that's lovely. So you won because you and your writing were—"

"No, I understand the basic criteria for how one wins an award, I just—"

"Oh, okay."

"What?"

"Just say you need some extra validation, man."

"What? No, I am not looking—"

"Well, why do you think you won, then?"

"I don't know. That's what I'm trying to figure out."

"Right, but you said you know the basic criteria for how one wins an award and Roberta told you why you won the award, yet you don't understand why you won the award?"

"No, I know why I won the award!"

"Okay, so why did you win the award?"

"I . . ." Helen can't say it. She physically can't make herself say it. Hell, she can barely believe it.

"You . . ." Cherry leads.

"They must have seen something in my story that they liked," Helen finally says.

"Yeah, since that's exactly what Roberta said, I'm betting that probably had something to do with it."

"Okay, so fine, I'm a validation-seeking asshole who writes stories about things that don't matter, so of course—"

"Don't do that."

"What?"

"You're being overly dramatic, and you know it."

"I can't . . . I don't know why I feel this way, okay? I don't want to be like this, I can promise you that and . . . I think you're right that I just maybe needed someone to tell me the truth, you know? Someone who can't lie."

"Someone to tell the truth about what?" Cherry asks.

It's at this very moment that Helen realizes that not only does Cherry herd Helen with her body, she also does it with her words.

With every question Cherry pushes Helen closer and closer to the wall, backing her into it and downright making her interrogate her own unhinged, malignant thoughts. Except this time, Cherry offers no "oof, sorry" when the herding goes beyond the known path.

"Maybe it's because even I know that Mishler's work was better than mine. So why did I win?"

"Because you did."

"Right, but . . ." Helen trails off, waiting for Cherry to cut in again. But she doesn't. She just lets the moment hang. Finally, Cherry gives a quick nod and steps past Helen.

"You ready?" Cherry asks.

"Huh? Oh . . . yeah. Okay," Helen answers, hesitant and more than a little unsure of how to proceed.

Helen and Cherry walk in silence up the wood chip–covered pathway lined with cottages. Groups of people spill onto packed tiny porches, borrowing little wooden desk chairs from anywhere that will lend them out. Helen and Cherry pass these loud tangles of other Hayho writers, and while there are polite nods and grunted "hey"s offered to them as they pass, it becomes abundantly clear to Helen that, unlike them, everyone seems to have spent the last week forging bonds with the Hayho community as a whole, rather than just one other person. Unsure if Cherry notices this phenomenon as well, Helen decides to keep this observation to herself while Cherry dangerously herds her into the large drainage ditch cut into the far side of the path. Helen uses her latest method in dealing with Cherry's herding, by using the pathway's natural turns to cut in back of Cherry and loop over to her other side. But all this accomplishes is it makes Cherry herd her the other way, which is how Helen now finds herself saying "excuse me" to various and sundry Hayho writers gathering around Mishler's cabin at the very top of the pathway and just next to the main campus. She sees it register on Cherry's face whose cottage it is and then hears the usual "oof, sorry" as she realizes her herding. Then both of them wordlessly speed up, hoping to sneak by the cottage without having to actually interact one last time with the tiny cabal of other workshop members.

"So, where is this party gathering thing?" Cherry asks once they reach the main campus and are safely far enough away from Mishler's cottage. Still reeling from their earlier fight—was it even a fight?—Helen pulls the sheet of paper with Roberta's directions out of her moto jacket pocket.

"Apparently there's a whole other part of this place," she says, showing Cherry the map. Cherry looks at the map, orients herself, and then sets off toward the faculty housing and the common area where this gathering is being held.

"It's over here, past where we had our workshops," Cherry says, pointing to the small canyon just beyond the Retreat. Helen nods as they continue to walk, creating elaborate narratives around the growing silence between the two of them. Cherry now hates her. Cherry thinks that she's a validation-seeking, selfish brat and resents that she won. Cherry somehow found out that Helen didn't want her to win. Cherry can't wait to get to this party, so she can abandon Helen and network with Hayho's buffet of famous writers, editors, and agents.

"I'm moving to San Francisco," Helen says as they navigate the wide redwood stairs down to the faculty housing.

"Don't you already live in San Francisco?"

"Just outside," Helen admits, desperately sidestepping Cherry catching her in another lie.

"When did you decide this?"

"Tonight, but I've been thinking about it for a long time."

"That's cool."

"Yeah." Helen continues to spiral, wondering what Cherry really thinks about her and how this is their last night here at Hayho and the clock is ticking on how much longer Helen has to shift her perception. It is because of this, she will later say, that she blurts the following.

"I mean, you could move there, too," Helen says.

"To what?" Cherry asks, misunderstanding what Helen said.

"To what what?"

"I could move there to . . . to do what," Cherry clarifies.

"No. Oh. Okay. No, I meant you could move there as well . . . you know, with me if you wanted or by me or, you know, whatever," Helen says.

"I don't want to state the obvious, man, but I'm still broke as hell and didn't just win $25,000. So moving to San Francisco isn't a thing I can really do," Cherry says.

"No, I know. I . . . I'm . . . We could share a place. Find somewhere cheap and I would put down first and last or whatever, but there are jobs there and . . . then we could both write our novels and . . . get published before we're thirty and then that apartment would be made into a historical landmark and people would come and take pictures of it and all our dreams would come true!" Helen's voice cracks. Cherry looks over at her. "I mean, you don't have to . . . I was just throwing it out there. I know it's weird."

Helen's rambling monologue ends right as they come to a stop in front of the faculty common house. She is just about to continue telling Cherry that she knows what she asked was weird and that maybe it was even an elaborate joke, but both of them are completely taken aback by what they see unfolding in front of them.

The Hayho faculty housing is a gorgeous lodge of a building, tucked into a lush canyon that's all but hidden from view of the rest of the Hayho campus. Large dark-brown shingles cover the craftsman building, and a sweeping balcony and porch wrap around both the first and second floors. The warm light from within makes the whole building look like it should be part of a miniature Christmas village lovingly set up year after year on some grandmother's prized antique credenza.

Neither Helen nor Cherry makes a move, because standing in the doorway is perhaps the most famous trio of writers they've ever seen in one place. Laughing and talking, these three literary icons fill the front door so completely, it all but ensures Helen and Cherry will remain completely frozen.

"Is there another way in?" Cherry asks, her voice breathy and panicked.

"God, I hope so," Helen answers, still awestruck.

The two women remain frozen.

"Okay," Cherry says. "Here's what we do: We're going to go in and act like we're looking for someone—" Helen looks over at Cherry, choosing not to tell her that's exactly what she does, too.

"Who are we looking for?" Helen asks, interrupting her.

"It doesn't matter, it's a lie. It's not real."

"What if someone asks? We have to agree on—"

"No, you're right. Okay, let's say we're looking for Deborah Torres. We can say we want to thank her for all her help in the workshop and blah blah blah," Cherry says.

"That's good, okay. We're just here looking for Deborah Torres," Helen repeats, practicing what to say as if she has just been given a new set of lines for a community play.

"We're just going to go in and act like we're looking for someone," Cherry says.

The two women remain frozen.

"We're just going to go in and act like we're looking for someone," Helen mumbles.

The two women remain frozen.

"Okay. I'll count to three. Ready?" Cherry asks.

"And then we go in on three or after three?"

"On three."

"So, one, two, walk—"

"One, two . . ."

"Wait, is this practice or is this for reals?" Helen asks.

"It's practice."

"Okay. Okay."

"But this time let's do it for reals."

"Oh god."

"Ready?"

"Yep."

"One, two . . ."

At three, both Helen and Cherry step forward and climb the few stairs up onto the large wraparound porch. The crowd is packed in, and just as they begin to wend their way through some of the most famous writers on the planet, they begin to lose each other. But right when Helen is about to squat down and ball herself up into the fetal position, Cherry reaches back and takes her hand.

It's not often that one can pinpoint the exact moment a friendship is forged, but Helen Hicks and Cherry Stewart will both look back to this precise moment as when they became real friends. They've known each other for just six days, but in those six days, Cherry has herded Helen into walls, ditches, and crowded porches filled with their enemies. And in those six days, Helen has lied, won an award they both wanted, been breathtakingly self-centered, and also made the majority of their interactions awkward and weird. Leaving Helen to conclude that by the time Cherry took her hand at that fancy Hayho after-party, Cherry knew the majority of the real Helen, fought with the real Helen . . . and took her hand anyway. That despite Helen's fears, Cherry doesn't hate her or resent that she won the Glending Fellowship. And as Cherry's fingers curl tightly around hers, Helen almost starts to cry, because Cherry didn't abandon her to network with Hayho's buffet of famous writers, editors, and agents. In fact, Cherry tugs Helen closer, and together they finally officially enter the after-party.

The Hayho after-party is a rager. The music is loud, empty bottles are strewn everywhere, and famous writers are either draped over other famous writers or drunkenly yelling in other writers' faces about "my agent" this or "it's just always about numbers with them" that. Both Helen and Cherry keep their heads down, not wanting to mistakenly offend their literary heroes or, even worse, find themselves swept up in a conversation they both know deep in their bones would be way out of their league.

Helen catches a glimpse of Deborah Torres and Tess Bayard just off the main room among a larger circle of writers. A shiver jolts through her entire body as she averts her eyes and hurries across the cramped space. Helen may not know much about this exclusive literary world, but she is quite positive that if she has any chance of belonging to it, she needs to be someone else and say as little as possible. It's the only hope she has for a bright future.

Helen and Cherry successfully navigate the main room, and Helen feels a very intentional tug as Cherry pulls her farther inside. Helen both recognizes everyone and yet doesn't know anyone personally. Each writer is more famous than the last, and Helen's brain is a riot of *Oh my god, is that . . .* and *I loved your last book*, along with a healthy dollop of *Please I just want to go home*. Finally, Cherry pulls her through the packed kitchen and out the door on the other side.

The fresh air hits Helen immediately. She looks up to see that Cherry has landed them firmly on the deserted back patio. Far from the noise and literary madness happening just a few feet away, the two young women stand hand in hand for several moments, regulating their breathing and collecting themselves. Thankfully, the back patio is completely empty, save for a smallish hot tub on the far side that's tucked underneath a halo of large redwood trees. They look at one another . . .

"When in Rome?" Helen asks, eyeing the hot tub.

"Do as the Romans do," Cherry finishes.

"Thank god no one's around to hear that," Helen says, laughing.

"We really are pretty embarrassing," Cherry says. Helen likes the way Cherry says "we." It has always just been Helen who is embarrassing.

They finally unclasp their hands as they pick their way across the patio and come to a stop in front of the worn and aged hot tub. They tug the large cover off and, using the diffused light coming from the main building, figure out how to turn the ancient relic on. It rumbles alive, and immediately both Helen and Cherry regret making such a commotion. They look inside the main house, hoping not to see all their literary heroes peering out onto the patio with disgust, questioning who exactly is at fault for ruining their wonderful soiree. But with the loud music and the conversations that are being shouted over the din, not one person is aware that a hot tub from the Jazz Age has been turned on for the first time in sixty years.

"I don't think we should actually . . ." Cherry says, investigating the surroundings.

"Go into a hot tub fully clothed with the threat of Deborah Torres seeing us? Yeah, no," Helen says.

"You were going to go in fully clothed?" Cherry asks.

"Yeah, I . . . what . . . how would . . . were you going to"—Helen looks around—"skinny-dip?"

"No, god no. Not here—"

"Oh, thank god, I really thought—"

"I was going to just wear my bra and underwear."

"What?! Here?!" Helen gestures around at the entirety of Hayho.

"I mean, I'm wearing a sports bra, so—" Cherry begins to take off her shirt.

"Why don't we just put our feet in?" Helen blurts, panicking. Cherry stops. "We can just sit on the side and both be fully clothed and maybe not be found a little bit naked by the writer who just won the Nobel Prize a couple years ago," Helen says, pulling off her Converse one by one, then sliding off her socks and tucking them into her shoes, which she neatly lines up just next to the hot tub. Cherry smooths her T-shirt back down over her beanpole of a body.

"Yeah, okay. That sounds nice," Cherry says, pulling her foot up and tugging first one shoe off and then the other. She rips her socks off and throws them over in the general vicinity of where her shoes were last seen.

Cherry investigates the hot tub further and finds the button to turn on the light, and in all its full cheesy glory, the lights begin to cycle through various colors as the two women decide how to proceed. Cherry holds on to the rickety metal railing and steps down into the hot tub, pulling her pant legs up over her knees. Helen watches from the safety of the patio before finally sitting down, rolling up her jeans, and letting her feet dangle into the warm, bubbling water.

Helen and Cherry are quiet for a long time, splashing their feet in the warm water. Every so often, one of them will glance inside, making sure the coast is still clear, and then they'll be back to wriggling their toes and staring far up into the canopy of trees.

"I saw Deborah Torres in there," Cherry says.

"Me too."

"I'm so glad us trying to find her was a lie, because there's no way I could have gone up to her for real," Cherry says, flapping her feet in the water like a little duck.

"I know I'd say something weird," Helen says, re-rolling her jeans higher and higher.

"Knock, knock," Cherry says in a singsongy voice.

"Oh my god, I thought you didn't hear that," Helen says.

"Oh, I heard it."

"Why do I do that stuff? Why can't I just be normal?" Helen asks, only half joking. Cherry laughs, but doesn't say anything in response. This, of course, sends Helen into a tailspin. "This is where you tell me that being normal is overrated and it's actually my weirdness that's going to make me an even better writer and then you'll close out this rousing speech that you like me the way that I am and that those people inside are boring and I'm so special and different and that's why I won the Glending and I should just be proud of myself."

"Yi—"

"Please don't say 'yikes,'" Helen says.

Cherry laughs. "Look, you wouldn't believe me if I said any of that stuff anyways."

"No, I know. But . . ." Cherry waits for Helen to say it. "Fine. Hello, I'm Helen Hicks and I desire a little validation."

"Is it desire or need, I wonder," Cherry blithely asks, as if Helen's need for constant ego stroking is on par with food and water. Helen is quiet. "Okay." Cherry turns to face Helen.

"You don't have to, I just—" Helen looks away.

"I love that you took beers from the welcome mixer and went back to your cottage to be by yourself. I saw you later that night, you know." Helen shakes her head. She didn't know that. "Yeah, you had your feet up on the banister and you were laughing and drinking a beer—you looked like you were having a blast. I wish I would have done that. The coolest part, though, is that I never know what you're going to do or say. You're a wholly new kind of person to me, and when I'm with you, I . . . feel happy."

Cherry goes back to wriggling her toes in the water as if she hasn't just said the nicest things Helen has ever heard about herself. And because they're the nicest things Helen has ever heard, she has no idea what one says in response, besides . . .

"Thank you," Helen says.

"It's all true," Cherry says.

"I think I'm jealous of you," Helen says before she can think better of it.

"What?"

"I think I'm jealous of you."

"Why?"

"Because you're just you." Helen shakes her head. "You're just you."

"And why would that be something to be jealous of?"

"Because I have no idea who I am."

"That's envy."

"What?"

"Jealousy is if you think I'm trying to take something of yours. Envy is when you want what I have."

"Oh."

"You don't think I'm trying to take something of yours, right?"

"No," Helen lies, knowing the more truthful answer would have been "not anymore," now that she has won the Glending and Cherry didn't. Helen keeps this detail to herself.

As the two women sit in silence, Helen wonders why, once again, she purposefully chose to push their conversation off the gushy speeches and onto whatever this is. Should she try to wrench the conversation back that way, or should she just stay quiet, knowing that whatever she tries will probably make things even more awkward?

"I've been thinking," Cherry starts. Helen's stomach drops as she waits for Cherry to continue.

"About what?" she chokes out.

"You moving."

"Yeah?"

"I'm going to come with you."

Helen lunges into Cherry for a hug, but instead slips off the side and lands in the bubbling hot tub with a splash. Without missing a beat, Cherry whips off her shirt and leaps in after her wearing just her sports bra, splashing and dunking Helen underwater until they both dissolve into fits of laughter.

CHAPTER EIGHT

Summer 2005

Helen Hicks stands onstage fumbling with the microphone. Grateful the audience is cloaked in darkness, she tucks the book under her arm and muscles the mic down. Once satisfied, she pulls the book out from under her arm, squints into the expanding darkness in front of her, and takes a deep breath.

"Thank you so much for coming out tonight. My name is Helen Hicks"—the crowd erupts in applause as Helen patiently waits—"and I'm here to read you a little something I wrote."

A hush falls over the venue as Helen folds the book back, lifts her bookmark out, and begins reading. The crowd is immediately pulled in, ebbing and flowing with each of Helen's words. And as she reaches the halfway point, Helen feels the audience now firmly in the palm of her hand. As she builds to the end, her voice becomes louder and louder, finally ending with a rhapsodic flourish that all but demands a standing ovation. In the moments that follow her big finish, Helen looks up from the book and waits.

"Three . . . two . . . one . . ." she whispers to herself.

And like clockwork the entire crowd leaps to their feet, clapping and whistling as Helen bows and offers her humble thanks. Helen is joined onstage by the emcee for this evening's festivities. The tallish woman, who wears a floral slip dress over jeans, beams at Helen before taking the microphone from her. Helen steps a bit to the side, trying to make out the crowd through the bright stage lights.

"Once again, we want to thank you all for coming out tonight. If you want to get a book signed, we'll have Helen set up in the back." The woman gestures over her shoulder. Helen cranes her neck to see where she'll be expected to go next. "But once again, thank you so much for coming out tonight and happy reading!" Helen waves to the crowd as the house lights come up.

Helen's eyes adjust to the light as the unmistakable sound of a milk frother overtakes the space. The emcee guides her down from the small stage that's been set up in the corner of the coffee shop and back to a curtained snug just next to the men's bathroom. Inside this infinitesimal space, Helen sees that the coffee shop staff has set up an old metal TV tray and a plastic folding chair for her signing, along with a stack of the short-story anthology in which Helen was published nine years ago.

"We're so excited that you agreed to this reading. And before I forget, here's your free drink voucher," the emcee says, handing Helen a bright-red drink ticket that doesn't include loose-leaf teas or signature lattes. "It's not much, but we try to do something for those who so generously give us their time." As the emcee says her goodbyes, Helen takes the free drink ticket and pockets it just before squeezing herself behind the rickety TV tray, scraping the folding chair along the rough cement floor just enough to shove herself into it.

"Do you think I could get an Earl Grey, by chance?" Helen asks a passing barista, holding up her ticket.

"That doesn't work for loose-leaf teas," he says without stopping.

"Oh, okay. I—" The barista disappears into the men's bathroom. "Guess I'll just die of thirst then," Helen says to no one.

"Um . . . hi . . . I . . . I'm such a huge fan," a young woman says, appearing as if from nowhere.

"It's so lovely to meet you. I'm Helen," Helen says, extending her hand.

"I definitely know who you are!" The young woman laughs, excitedly shaking Helen's hand.

"Did you want me to sign that?" Helen asks, gesturing to the woman's well-loved copy of the short-story anthology in her hands.

"Yes, please." The young woman hands Helen the book. "I've managed to get signatures from all of the other writers in the anthology. You're the last one." Helen flips open the woman's book and finds the first page overrun with signatures.

"Oh, wow," Helen says, trying to find a place where hers can fit.

"You can just sign on another page," the young woman says, flipping to the very first page, which also houses the book's copyright information and ISBN. "Here! This one is completely blank!"

"I think I'll try to squeeze it in with the rest," Helen says, flipping the page back to the overrun signature page.

"Oh, sure, sure . . . My name's Jennifer, by the way. With a *J*," the young woman says. Helen's eyes dart back to the signature page overrun with *JENNIFER*s and sees that one author has misspelled her name with a *G*.

"Do you want me to fix this one for you?" Helen says, pointing to the outlier.

"Ugh, I tried to get him to change it, but apparently that was . . . not something he felt was important," the young woman says, looking down at the floor.

"Okay, well, how about we do this," Helen says.

She unscrews the top of her fountain pen and, in bright royal-blue ink, goes over the man's signature just enough that the offending *G* blends in with Helen's correct *J*, making them both appear as one elaborate, twisty *J*. The young woman beams and brings her small hands to her chest as if overtaken by Helen's simple, kind gesture.

"You fixed it . . . I can't believe . . . you fixed it," Jennifer with a *J* says.

"Everybody should have their name spelled correctly," Helen says, signing her name with just a little bit more swagger. She hands the book back to the woman with a smile.

"Thank you so much," Jennifer says, holding the book tightly.

"You're welcome," Helen says, feeling pretty good about herself.

"Can I ask . . . uh . . . Is there any news on your novel? I was at a reading you did a few years ago for Edith Glending's memorial and you'd said you were working on it, but couldn't really say more?" Jennifer asks.

"Still chipping away at it. You know how it goes. Slow and steady," Helen says, her smile faltering just a bit.

"Yes, it's hard to find time to write and I'm not . . . I mean, I really loved hearing this short story again, so . . . it's . . . really good."

"Thank you."

"Well . . . good luck with the novel, and thank you again for the *J*," Jennifer says. Helen waves goodbye to the young woman and sits back in the folding chair. But before she can screw the top back on her fountain pen, a man steps in front of the metal TV tray.

"Hi, did you—" Helen starts.

"They said the bathroom was back here?" the man asks, looking behind Helen as if the men's bathroom is somehow also located inside the smallest snug in the world.

"Straight back and to the right," Helen says. The man continues on without another word.

Helen screws the lid of her fountain pen on and sits back in her chair. She will spend the next hour telling fifteen men where the bathroom is, signing one other short-story anthology, and paying full price for an Earl Grey tea.

As dusk settles, Helen weaves through the crowds out for a big Saturday night on the town. The thick wafting smell of nag champa incense blooms out of the various thrift stores and smoke shops that line the historic Upper Haight in San Francisco. Packs of tourists shuffle toward Haight-Ashbury, the intersection famous for the historic houses that made this neighborhood the cultural center of San Francisco's Summer of Love. Following their homemade maps, they hope their pilgrimage will lead them to the Grateful Dead house or where Jefferson Airplane lived, or even take a picture in front of the place Janis Joplin called home. But as Helen trudges past the Hippie House, with its gigantic, fish-netted legs tumbling out of an upper-floor window of a colorful colonial, she tightens her grip on that old Hayward Writing Intensive tote bag filled with copies of the short-story anthology and makes her way to a mini-mart just off Ashbury. Feeling more than a little bit brutalized after tonight's reading, Helen finds herself going over and over her interaction with Jennifer with a *J* and how good it felt to have a fan, and then how immediately that swell of pride dissipated at the young woman's perfectly normal question about where her much-anticipated debut novel is.

Helen sidesteps a group of people just outside a bar and walks through a giant cloud of pot smoke in the process. Waving her hand in front of her face, she shifts the heavy tote bag over to the other shoulder. Finally making the turn onto the small side street, Helen marvels at how efficient she's been over the last ten years at both not thinking about writing her debut novel and only thinking about writing her debut novel. It's a high-wire act she's proudly mastered day in and day out, for every minute of every day, and if that's not commitment, she doesn't know what is.

She'd bet that Jennifer with a *J* would have very little to say about how well meaning Helen has been about trying to write and how she almost does it each and every day. How her desk is overrun with notebooks and outlines and that she is, even as we speak, Jennifer with a *J*, planning a writing retreat with Tess Bayard where she is confident that she'll finally crack this novel and finish it by year's end. It's just been timing. Helen understands the enormity of a debut novel and does not want to take it lightly. You only get one chance to have a brilliant debut. And it's Helen's new theory that it takes a certain level of maturity to create something truly historic. So now, at thirty-four years old, she's conveniently abandoned her old goal to be published by thirty because she's learned that great art takes time.

Simply, Jennifer with a *J*, Helen respects writing too much not to give this debut novel everything she's got. It needs to be her best. And in being *her* best, it can then be *the* best.

Helen opens the door to the mini-mart and makes a beeline for the beer case. As she peruses the offerings, the "great art takes time" speech echoes in her head. Pulling a six-pack of Pabst Blue Ribbon from the case, Helen understands that the uninitiated may think she's just making excuses. But it's not that she hasn't tried. During that first year, all she did was try. After all, she was the first and only recipient of Hamilton Elementary's Best Trier Award. What paralyzed Helen during those first months of her fellowship was that all the trying in the world couldn't produce a single chapter, let alone a chapter worthy of the Glending Fellowship. No matter how many times she sat down at that desk, scribbled down scenes, brainstormed character arcs, outlined plots, and then ran those ideas by Tess and Cherry, none of them yielded an idea that was load bearing enough to build a novel atop. And no matter how many times she showed up, day in and day out, Helen found herself forever wandering in the dark, aimlessly searching for the idea that would change everything. She swore that she'd seen the corners of an idea dancing just out of reach, coming to her in the dead of night like a whispered dream. Jolted awake by the lightning bolt of inspiration, Helen would dutifully scrawl the dreamy whisper in a notebook she kept by her bedside only to see the banal words "love story with a liar?" awaiting her as dawn broke across her twin-size mattress, still on the floor of her bedroom.

Then one day she just didn't sit down at her desk. And then that one day became two and then three and four, and before she knew it, the first year had passed with no debut novel in sight. It had happened so quietly, the busyness of daily life almost inoculating her from the ache of not writing until it became a hitched limp she no longer noticed. And because feeling disappointment in herself is far too familiar to Helen Hicks, she just went about her life. And as that second year began, she looked for a nine-to-five job that she lied to herself was temporary, while she continued to search and excavate the big idea that would be the backbone of her greatest literary achievement.

But how could Helen say all that to a hopeful fan as various gentlemen asked her where the restroom was?

Now covered in the shame of regret of the last ten years, Helen heaves the six-pack of beer onto the counter, digs some cash out of her pocket, and pays with a grunted thank-you. She then curls her fingers around the beer's makeshift handle, deciding to balance out its heaviness by holding it in the opposite hand from her Hayho tote bag. Slightly proud that she's successfully done one thing today, Helen pulls open the door to the mini-mart and exits onto the Upper Haight just beyond.

Helen walks the two or so blocks back to her and Cherry's apartment, switching the beer back and forth between her hands. Finally arriving at the outer security gate to her apartment, Helen shoves the beer under her arm, sifts through her tote for her keys, and finally conceding, sets the beer on the filthy, trash-ridden ground just in front of their apartment's entrance that definitely does not smell of human urine. She unlocks the security gate, shoves her keys into her pocket, and picks back up the beer, careful not to touch the now-sullied bottom. Taking a deep, bracing breath, Helen begins to climb the two flights of stairs to her apartment, setting the beer on the banister halfway up, thinking sliding it up will be easier. It is not.

Just as Helen nears the top of the stairs, someone flings the front door of their apartment open as the blaring music explodes down the staircase. A group of people tumble out of the apartment, laughing and drinking as they pull packs of cigarettes and lighters from pockets and plunge down the stairs, past Helen and out onto Haight Street. Helen pins herself to the wall as they pass, clutching her tote and the beer as if they are her very own children. No one acknowledges her in any way. Once the coast is clear, Helen gathers herself and continues on inside.

The party is in full swing as Helen weaves her way through the crammed apartment, and a makeshift banner over the large bay window reads HAPPY 30TH, CHERRY! There are red balloons on the ceiling and cheap red streamers hung over everything. As Helen makes her way to their small galley kitchen, all she can see is a lot of stuff that has to be cleaned up, hauled down those stairs, and taken out to the trash. But then Helen reminds herself that tonight is her best friend's thirtieth birthday party, and like her, Cherry must also be feeling the disappointment at not making her goal of being published by now. Helen needs to snap out of her bad mood so she can properly cheer Cherry on as the clock strikes midnight and she's still just the manager of the Second Hand, a thrift store in the Upper Haight, and not a published author as they've planned for the last ten years.

While Helen may still be struggling to write her debut novel, she was officially published before thirty years old, thanks to the short-story anthology. It is this technicality that has saved her from truly sinking below the waterline when she wakes up in a flop sweat at 4:00 a.m. fearing her bleak artistic future. Armed with this insight, Helen has prepared sage advice for when, not if, Cherry succumbs to the same existential disappointment that Helen herself has been grappling with over the past few years. And rest assured, Helen is not above throwing her own myriad failures in front of the bus to make Cherry feel not so alone in this Post-Thirty Unpublished World. Confident she will find Cherry messy drunk and lamenting her roundly rejected novel by night's end, Helen will dutifully pep talk her best friend that life is long, great art takes time, and this will be the year that changes everything for both of them. She promises.

"Hicks!" Cherry yawps from across their apartment.

Helen turns to find Cherry Stewart in the middle of the throng, holding a bottle of cheap champagne in one hand and a giant blow-up penis in the other.

"We don't know who gave that to her, but when we find out . . ." Tess Bayard says, menacingly punching one hand into the other.

"Does it have a little bow on it?" Helen asks.

"It's a necktie, Helen. The giant inflatable penis is wearing a necktie," Tess says.

"Well, it is a birthday party," Helen says, sighing deeply.

Tess falls back in with the rest of Helen's friends who have braved this evening's birthday bacchanalia. Huddled over in a corner, the exclusive group cleave to one another as if they're a modern-day contingent of the Hapsburgs tasked with walking among their subjects. Helen continues into the kitchen, drops off the six-pack, and puts her tote bag safely in her bedroom, before checking her face in the mirror. She looks every minute of thirty-four years old. Studying her face, she notices her furrowed brow is becoming more and more defined with each passing year. She does point out to herself that she's yet to form any crow's-feet or smile lines, but quickly realizes this is a pyrrhic victory. It means that her face reflects the worry of the past ten years as well as the absence of anything to smile about. With a dramatic sigh, Helen reenters the party.

"Hicks!" Cherry Stewart calls out again. This time she points the giant inflatable penis at her best friend, shaking it around just enough to clear a broad four-foot swath in front of her.

"Happy birthday!" Helen exclaims, dodging the penis and pulling Cherry into a tight hug.

"How was the reading?" Cherry asks, tucking a rogue tress behind Helen's ear.

"Kind of terrible," Helen says.

"Then you need a drink," Cherry says, shoving a red Solo cup into her hand.

"What's this?"

"Leni made it. It's good. Drink," Cherry says.

Leni is one of Cherry's coworkers at the thrift store who's also trying to make it as a model. Tall and waif thin, she looks like a throwback to the era when consumption raged through the population, all pale skin and romantically elsewhere eyes. Cherry keeps trying to tell Helen that Leni is "so hilarious" and that she's "just got to get to know her." But from the several times they've hung out, all Helen can glean is that someone so beautiful doesn't actually need a personality to be beloved. As Cherry looks on excitedly, Helen takes a sip of the drink and, as if she needed further confirmation, discovers that Leni has just made a batch of regular old vodka cranberry. Two ingredients that have been clumsily mixed and yet the entire party is raving that "oh my god but no really this is brilliant Leni should open a bar or something."

"Mmm, so good," Helen coos.

"Right?"

"Vodka-y!" Helen yelps in desperation, forcing herself to find something nice to say about it.

"Very." Cherry laughs as someone puts a red plastic top hat on her head.

"I have a little something for you," Helen says.

"Oh realllllly?"

"Follow me to my room please, madame," Helen says with the worst French accent ever.

"Oui oui," Cherry says before chugging her vodka cranberry and handing the inflatable penis off to another one of her coworkers.

Helen gestures over at Tess that she'll be right back. Tess gestures back that they're going outside and to meet them there after. Helen nods. Tess and Helen are no more than six feet apart. But the music is so loud and Cherry's friends are somehow even louder, so that were they even standing next to each other, they still would have had to play some elaborate game of Charades simply to communicate one single thought. Cherry drunkenly wraps her arm around Helen as Helen hauls her back to the quiet of her bedroom.

Once inside, Helen closes the door behind them and the noise muffles just enough for her to keep a single thought in her head. As Cherry wanders around the room slurring, "Is the little something over here," Helen is aware that her dark mood is out of place tonight. Helen has long reckoned with her failings when it comes to being the kind of best friend that Cherry deserves. But over the last ten years, it's been hard enough handling one person with Cherry's personality, let alone the giant circle of friends that Cherry's accumulated. Going from a lifetime of having no friends to Cherry was hard enough, so Helen has learned to navigate these moments by checking in with her best friend, spending some one-on-one time with her, and then retreating before her sullen, wet-blanket temperament can spoil everyone's good time. Sometimes supporting your best friend is not about attending their birthday party but leaving it early so it has half a chance of not being contaminated with one's surly attitude.

"Happy birthday," Helen says, presenting Cherry with a small stack of wrapped gifts.

"Ooh, a little pile," Cherry says, taking the presents and plopping down into Helen's desk chair. Helen looks on as Cherry does her usual shaking of each gift, wondering aloud what they are with guesses that are so off the rails it almost makes the actual present pale in comparison. "Is this one an amulet? Maybe a pair of knitting needles? Ooh, a dagger!" Cherry says, shaking a present that is clearly a compact disc.

"You know, one of these days I'm going to actually give you a dagger," Helen says, laughing.

"Maybe today is that day," Cherry says, opening the CD. Helen reaches out and takes the wrapping paper from her, balling it up in her fist. "Oh, one of your mixes!" Cherry clutches the CD to her chest and spins around in Helen's desk chair.

"It's all the music we listened to that first summer at Hayho," Helen says, looming over Cherry. "Remember that last night? This was the track that was playing on the campus after the awards ceremony."

"Wow . . . this . . . I love it," Cherry says, looking up at Helen.

"I haven't made you a mix in a while. It was actually really fun making it. Remembering back."

"I love it and I shall treasure it."

"I don't think it would fit to play for the party, but maybe tomorrow or something."

"I want the first listen to just be me. That's how I always do it."

Helen beams at Cherry. She's always loved how seriously Cherry takes her mixes. "Open the next one!"

"Is it a puppy?" Cherry asks, holding a present that is clearly a book of some kind.

"Yep. You're so good at this."

Cherry rips into the second present and reveals a stunning leather-bound journal. Her face drains of color as she sees the luxurious gift. "Helen, this is way too expensive," she says, carefully opening the journal and running her fingers delicately along the high-quality card stock.

"That grant I've been working on finally went through, so the nonprofit gave me a little raise and a bonus."

"This is . . . you know how weird I get about nice gifts, so I'm sorry if I'm not acting right."

"No, I wanted to. And you need to get unweird about nice gifts. You deserve them! And I . . . I know that we both had goals for being published by thirty and . . . I just wanted to . . . I figured you could use this journal to outline your next novel. Because who cares about turning thirty, you know? I know I had the short-story thing, but I haven't even started my debut novel, so . . . it's not just you. I didn't want you to be . . ."

"Helen . . ."

"Sad. I didn't want you to be sad."

"It's beautiful," Cherry says, slumping in the desk chair.

"No, don't . . . it's supposed to be hopeful. I . . . okay, wait, wait . . . open the last little one. This one will cheer you up for sure," Helen says, taking the journal from Cherry and handing her the tiny third present.

"Okay. The last little one that I definitely won't get weird about," Cherry says, ripping into Helen's third and final gift.

"What do you think it is?" Helen asks, baiting Cherry, hoping it will cheer her up.

"New car?" Cherry responds with a weary smile.

"Right again," Helen says, taking the wrapping paper from Cherry once again and balling it up in her hands along with the rest. Cherry opens the tiny white box and reveals two cheap plastic necklaces in neon pinks, yellows, and greens.

"Oh my god, I've always wanted one of these!" Cherry exclaims, pulling the twin necklaces from the small box.

"I know! They had them at that terrible souvenir shop by Ghirardelli Square. I couldn't resist," Helen says, beaming. Cherry unravels the necklaces and cradles the cheap pink plastic broken heart with the words "BEST FRIENDS" across it.

"It's perfect," Cherry drunkenly whispers before looping one necklace over her head. The necklace digs into her, the plastic beads rolling up and down on her sweaty neck.

"It looks great," Helen says, laughing.

"Now put yours on!" Cherry says, extending the second necklace to Helen. Helen takes it from Cherry and proudly loops the necklace over her head, situating the collar of that same black moto jacket so it shows off the cheap plastic neon beads properly.

"It goes perfectly with the black," Helen says, doing a little spin.

"Thank you so much," Cherry says, lunging into Helen for a big hug.

Helen is used to Cherry's hugs after ten years, but she has yet to master her end of things. No matter how many times Cherry's lunged into her, Helen has never quite let herself sink into it. In fact, it was at Cherry's birthday party last year that Helen got actual evidence of her incompetence when Leni took a photo of them mid-hug. There was Cherry, looking like just another normal person trying to hug her friend, all closed eyes and sweet smiles. And then there was Helen. Eyes wide open, brow furrowed, and a fully arched back as if she were fighting to free herself from what was clearly death's embrace. It was mortifying. But even more than that, Helen had really convinced herself she'd gotten better at it, only to learn that she, quite publicly, had not.

"You're so welcome," Helen says.

The two best friends break apart and Cherry runs over to Helen's mirror to look at herself, posing with her new necklace.

"And if I'm correct—and I always am—you're pretty much done with the party now, right?" Cherry asks, turning back to Helen.

"Have I told you how wonderful it is to have a friend who gets me?"

"Once the inflatable penis came out, I knew your days were numbered."

"That's actually in my contract rider for book signings. No inflatable penises."

"You going to hang with Tess and that whole gang?"

"Yeah, they're out front."

"I thought she gave up smoking?"

"No, I . . . she was, but . . ."

"It's the only thing that keeps her that thin, I guess."

"I mean . . . that's not . . . you know, it's . . ." Helen can't help but defend Tess.

"No judgment, man. It's not her fault she feels like she has to be that thin," Cherry says.

Helen has always marveled at how casually Cherry is able to say the most delicate and sensitive things. She remembers two years ago, when they rented a car to take a trip down to Los Angeles for the movie premiere for Tess's debut novel. Neither of them attended the premiere, of course, but Tess was given a suite at a five-star hotel, and she let Helen and Cherry order a fancy breakfast from room service on her. As they drove down I-5, Cherry hung her arm out the window and blithely talked about Helen's paralyzing bout with writer's block, suggesting they make a rigorous schedule that'd make it impossible to overthink their stories and just write a messy first draft. They would do it together, and within a few months, they'd both no longer have to reckon with that bully of a blank page. Cherry had even said, "And then bim, bam, boop, we'd each have a book."

"Bim. Bam. Boop. We'd each have a book."

With tears pooling in her eyes, Helen stared out the window as Cherry quietly sang along with the song that was currently playing, wistfully pointing out the almond orchards zooming past. As Helen sat there, unobtrusively having a full-on existential crisis, Cherry talked about "perhaps making a little calendar" and taping it to their refrigerator, and every day they wrote, they would "like, be able to awesomely x out the day." Cherry looked over and asked what she thought, not noticing how shocked Helen was that her best friend had broken their covenant of not talking about Helen's writer's block that she thought was understood. Everyone else in her life knew not to mention it, but here was Cherry merrily suggesting that Helen's literary future be chronicled on a makeshift calendar taped to an ancient, avocado-colored refrigerator that shook twelve hours a day because of a faulty compressor the landlord insinuated was somehow their fault.

"I know writing is easy for you, but I can't just . . ." Helen had trailed off, not knowing how vast what she couldn't do was.

"It's just a draft. It doesn't have to be perfect," Cherry said.

"I don't . . . That's not . . ."

"We can just try it. Like, why not try it?"

What Helen couldn't say was that in order to write something actually good—like Glending Fellowship good—it takes more than "bim, bam, boop." And what Cherry was proposing was fine for her, but for writers of Helen's caliber, it just doesn't work like that. She thought back to Hayho all those years ago, when Helen had urged Cherry to go beyond being a hobbyist, and all she could think in this moment was how she'd obviously failed at being a mentor if this was the level of care Cherry still had for the craft of writing.

"You can go ahead, but—"

"It's crazy enough that it just might bust through your block—"

"I'm not blocked!" Helen yelled, finally breaking the easy-breezy tone.

"Yikes."

"Oh, how I've missed your 'yikes.'"

"You're overthinking this, and it's got you all—"

"Cherry, you can't overthink great art."

"I would argue that you can, Helen." Cherry had drawn out Helen's name in the most drawling, sarcastic tone she could muster.

"What do you know about great art?"

"Yi—"

"Don't say 'yikes' again."

"Fine. Don't do it. I'm sure your plan of not writing at all and having a day job you hate writing grants that make other people's dreams come true will work out great for you."

"Just because I'm not physically writing doesn't mean I'm not working on my novel. You know there's a difference between writer's block and excavating an idea, right? I'm not blocked . . . I'm . . . digging, okay? Every day I'm digging. Trying to get past all the shallow, bad ideas to where the deep and profound ones are. And that takes time."

"Okay, man."

"Yeah."

Helen remembered how quiet the rest of that car ride was and how it wasn't until they'd made it to LA that they started talking again. And even then, it was still tense. They'd formed a fragile accord while they ate their fancy in-room breakfast, but it took weeks for them to get back to normal. And even then, Helen couldn't shake the feeling that she hadn't officially won that fight. It was more that Cherry had just given up. This realization, of course, offended Helen greatly. So as the months and years passed—and Helen still had no debut novel and Cherry put no makeshift calendar on the fridge—she began to twist her past conclusions to Cherry simply being unable to fully grasp what Helen was saying about how great art takes time. And that, just like Helen, Cherry had abandoned her little "put a calendar on the fridge" literary plan because she came to realize how truly laughable it was. Because Helen knew that any art that came from such a plan would undoubtedly be trite and unimportant. And that simply was not the kind of art Helen would ever make.

"You'll come get me when it's time for cake?" Helen asks, pulling at the neon plastic necklace that is now silently choking her.

"Yeah, we'll yell down," Cherry says, gathering up the journal and the CD.

"Cool," Helen says.

"Cool?" Cherry asks, opening the door to Helen's bedroom.

"I'm trying it out." Helen and Cherry walk back into the roar of the birthday party still in full swing.

"Yikes."

"Okay, well . . ."

"Maybe not for you, eh?" Cherry laughs, giving her another hug before peeling off to her room, where she'll put Helen's gifts someplace safe and sound.

Helen winds her way through the party, back down the stairs, and out onto the crowded Haight Street, where she finds Tess smoking with the rest of their small pack of friends.

"You made it out alive," Tess says, blowing out a plume of smoke.

"I was in very close proximity to the inflatable penis and lived to tell the tale," Helen says, declining Tess's offer of a cigarette. With Cherry's words still echoing in her head, Helen can't help but notice how much thinner Tess has gotten. How did she not see it before?

"I think you know everyone here, but—oh wait, you don't know Erik and Jabari. They're out from New York. Erik is legal counsel and Jabari is a literary agent over at McCormick. They're in town for the wedding. This is Helen—a brilliant writer, Glending fellow just like me—and she's in the wedding party. So you'll be seeing a lot of her," Tess says, introducing the two men. Hands are shaken and pleasantries are exchanged as everyone gets to know each other.

"The birthday girl is quite something," Erik says, moving out of the way of a pack of teens as they rumble past.

"Helen has known Cherry for . . ." Tess leads.

"Ten years. We met at Hayho," Helen says.

"Cherry Stewart is certainly one of a kind," Tess adds with just enough edge to make Helen feel bad for not saying something.

"Cherry Stewart?" Jabari asks.

"Yeah, she's the one with the inflatable penis," Helen says, laughing with Tess.

"Oh, I need to go congratulate her," Jabari says, looking up into Helen and Cherry's apartment.

"On the inflatable penis?" Tess asks, laughing.

"No, the book," Jabari says.

"What book?" Helen asks.

"It just sold at auction for huge money," Jabari says.

"Cherry has a book?" Tess asks.

"Not just any book. There was a whole bidding war," Jabari adds before disappearing into the apartment.

"Cherry has a book," Helen repeats, the wind knocked out of her.

CHAPTER NINE

Time stops. In a haze, Helen watches as Erik and Jabari open the security gate and climb the stairs to the apartment she and Cherry have shared for ten years. The party rages on as Cherry's friends spill down the stairs, laughing and yelling over the music. Tess stamps out her cigarette as her phone rings. She flips it open and excuses herself to answer a phone call from Tom, her fiancé.

"I have to take this. He's back in London. I'm so sorry, we'll talk about the whole book thing later." Tess walks a few feet away from Helen, her finger in her ear, while she yells into the phone that she can't hear him, and yes, she's still at Cherry's stupid birthday party.

"Cherry has a book," Helen whispers to herself. Another pack of teenagers rumbles past and one of the girls accidentally bumps into Helen.

"Oh, I'm so sorry, ma'am," the girl says before catching up to her friends.

"Perfect," Helen says, shaking her head.

"Hicks!" Cherry yells from the open window just above Helen. Helen looks up, seeing the very first friend she ever had as if for the first time. How did this happen? "It's cake time, m'lady!" As if on autopilot, Helen raises her hand and nods, watching as Cherry's friends pull her back into the thick of the party, much to her giggling protestations. "No! I'm the birthday girl! You mustn't manhandle me!" Cherry's laughter reverberates and wafts across all of Haight Street. The only thing Helen can hear is the sound of her own ragged breath.

Helen opens the security gate and climbs the stairs to her apartment as if facing the gallows. When did she even write this book? And she got an agent at McCormick? Helen didn't even know she knew how to get an agent, let alone one at McCormick. And why didn't Cherry tell her? Was she ever going to tell her?

"There's cake!" a man in a Viking helmet slurs as he stumbles down the stairs past Helen. Helen squishes herself into the wall as he passes, careful not to get nicked by a rogue Viking horn.

She steps across the threshold of their shared apartment just as Leni emerges from their tiny galley kitchen with the cake, the waxen three-zero flickering as she walks slowly toward the birthday girl. Cherry positively beams as Leni approaches.

"Happy birthday to youuuuuuuuuuu—" the group sings.

Thirty.

Cherry Stewart sold a book by the time she was thirty. Bim. Bam. Boop. She did it. She did it and Helen didn't. Cherry did it and Helen couldn't, not even with a full year, a $25,000 life stipend, and Tess Bayard as a mentor.

"Happy birthday, dear Cherrrrrrrrryyyyyyyyyyy—"

As Helen mumbles along to the lyrics, she wonders if Leni knows.

"Happy birthday to youuuuuuuuuuu!"

Does Cherry trust the beautiful, hilarious mixologist over her best friend of ten years?

"Make a wish!" the crowd urges as the flickering candles light up Cherry's face. Helen watches as Cherry closes her eyes and reverently brings her clasped hands up to just below her chin. Even as drunk as she is, Cherry exudes a level of sheer satisfaction that Helen is sure she's never felt. Helen slides her gaze from Cherry's delighted face down to the numbers; the three and zero shimmer in victory, taunting Helen and mocking her myriad failures.

Helen thinks back to her own thirtieth birthday and how Cherry baked her a cake with a two and a nine candle on top. And every year since then, Cherry has trotted out those same two and nine candles, which she saves in the junk drawer just left of the sink. Last year, on her fifth twenty-ninth birthday, Helen began to notice the wear and tear on the candles, seeing that the red piping that outlined the numbers was chipped and nebulous now, as it had been lit and relit year after year. But now here's Cherry proudly looking down at the three and the zero with a sense of accomplishment, a swell of pride, and a sheer and utter joy that is completely foreign to Helen.

Cherry opens her eyes, looks down at the candle, and blows it out with the childlike fervor she has come to be known for. The entire room cheers and claps.

"Happy birthday!" Leni says, moving the cake to one side before giving Cherry a big hug.

"You're the best!" another partygoer yells. The room erupts in "you're the best" chants, adding their own colorful additions as Cherry claps and laughs. And as the din begins to die down, Helen gulps a breath and . . .

"Congratulations on the book!" she shouts.

There is a brief second of silence as everyone looks around to see who said those last words of encouragement, and then the room quickly fills with the sibilant whispers of people asking each other what was actually said. But throughout the confusion, all Helen does is watch as Leni jerks her head over at Cherry with a look of concern.

Leni knew.

Cherry looks from Leni to Helen, and Helen watches as all the accomplishment, pride, and joy drain from Cherry's face. Helen doesn't want to interrogate why this makes her feel better.

"Who wants cake?" Leni calls out before signaling to another friend to turn the music back up. The party rages back to full volume, everyone gathering around Leni for some cake. But as they set up their little cake-serving assembly line, Cherry excuses herself and motions to Helen to follow her. As the two friends curve and loop through the crowded room, one trailing just behind the other, they say nothing. Heads bowed, shoulders high, they curl around the fringes of the celebration like hired cater waiters returning to the kitchen to restock their silver trays.

Cherry opens the door to her bedroom and walks inside without looking behind her or holding the door open for Helen. This infuriates Helen. *It's already started,* Helen thinks. Cherry already thinks she's better than her. Too good to even hold the door open for her best friend, if that's even what she still is. Helen steps inside Cherry's room and makes a big show of closing the door, realizing too late that closing a door behind you doesn't quite have the same etiquette implication as holding one open for someone. Nonetheless, she soldiers on, clicking the door closed with a polite flourish.

Helen turns around and faces her best friend, expecting apologies and explanations. Instead, Cherry stands in front of her stone faced and silent. This also enrages Helen.

"Well?" Helen finally blurts. Cherry crosses her arms and stays quiet. "Are you really not going to talk to me? But why wouldn't you—you wrote a whole entire book without telling me!"

"Jesus, give me a minute. I'm trying to think. Everything is tangled up here," Cherry says, pointing to her head.

"Just tell me what happened."

"I don't know where to start."

"Can you start with the truth?" Helen's voice is laced with sarcasm.

"The truth is . . . complicated, and I'm worried it will hurt your feelings."

"You've already hurt my feelings!" Helen's anger is becoming out of control. With every moment that passes, new and terrible thoughts crowd her mind.

"Do you remember when we drove down to LA for Tess's movie thing?" Helen nods, unable to speak through her blackout fury. "And I suggested that we make a little calendar and stick it to our fridge?"

"Bim. Bam. Boop," Helen snarls.

"Okay—"

"You thought I had writer's block—"

"You do have writer's block."

"I get to say what I have and don't have." Cherry is quiet. "Do you understand? How many times do I need to say it?" Cherry waits. A long time. Helen struggles to calm herself, breathe . . . get in control. It isn't working.

"Well, I did it."

"Did what?"

"I made a little calendar. Taped it up in my room. And before and after work, I used Leni's computer to try and write something. It took me three months and it was terrible."

"You wrote a full draft in three months?" Helen can barely get the words out.

"And it was terrible. But it was a book."

Helen feels this tidal wave of envy and sadness and yearning rush through her. It almost knocks her off her feet.

"Why didn't . . . why didn't you tell me?" she asks, her voice finally softening.

"This is the part that . . ."

"Just say it."

"Do you remember when I started taking those writing classes at the local community college when we first moved here?"

"Yeah, I was super proud of you for working on your craft and not being just a—"

"Hobbyist." Cherry's voice is flat.

"Yeah."

"Do you remember what you said to me when I told you?"

"No, just that—"

"You said that community college was perfect for a person like me."

"It is, though." Cherry locks her gaze onto Helen's.

"And when my short story was chosen by our professor . . ." Helen scoffs at her usage of the word "professor." Cherry's face colors. She continues, "And when my short story was chosen by our professor to be read at that storytelling event they did—"

"I told you I had already told Tess I would come see her read," Helen interrupts.

"You said, 'It's a warm room filled with other beginning writers. It's not like it's a real event.'" Cherry repeats the words Helen said years ago verbatim.

"I was trying to make you feel not so nervous."

"And when I won the storytelling event, what did you say?"

"I congratulated you."

"You said, 'I love that they gave you that experience. That's so cute.'"

"So is this whole conversation just going to be litigating my poor word choices over the years?"

"How about when I was made manager of the thrift store?" Cherry says, dropping her arms for the first time.

"Okay, now you cannot say . . . I took you out for a fancy dinner, bought you a bottle of champagne, and even baked you a cake! You cannot say that I didn't—"

"Why was your reaction to me being made manager so different from the other stuff?"

"What?"

"Why didn't you take me out to dinner when I was accepted into the storytelling event? Where was the champagne when my short story won?"

"Am I being graded here? Like, are you really—"

"Please, I'm genuinely curious. I'm not being an asshole. Can you ask yourself why your reactions were so different?"

"How did this become about me? You wrote an entire book, got an agent, apparently went through an auction, all while keeping it a total secret from your best friend of ten years. Why isn't that the headline of this fight right now?" Helen is barely able to contain herself anymore. If there weren't a raging party going on just beyond Cherry's closed door, the entire neighborhood would be able to hear.

"Please. Stop being mad for one minute and ask yourself why your best friend of ten years felt they couldn't tell you all of that. Why would telling you good news be complicated for someone?"

"Because my guess is that she is, in fact, *not* my best friend."

"Helen. I'm begging you. Please. I need you to get this."

"Oh, I'm getting it. I'm getting that you want to be best friends with someone who has the intellect of a teapot rather than challenge yourself—"

"Helen! Jesus, just stop!" Cherry's roar shuts Helen up immediately, her face coloring bright red. Cherry steps forward and Helen can barely breathe as she feels Cherry's anger radiate from her.

"I . . . you . . ." Helen tries.

"I'm going to say one final thing, and then I'm going to go back to my birthday party and you can go back to hanging out with your little group of fancy friends who would rather smoke outside than deign to sully their hands with my birthday party."

"Tess's fiancé called, so she—"

"Let's stop acting like she doesn't think I'm ridiculous, okay?" Helen is quiet. Tess has actually used that exact word to describe Cherry.

"Fine. What's this one final thing you're going to dramatically say to me, then?"

"I would like you to ask yourself why you were able to celebrate me becoming manager of a thrift store, but not winning a writing award. And before you say that it wasn't a writing award, ask yourself why you think it wasn't a writing award."

"That's two things."

"Well, congratulations on behaving like a tantrum-throwing brat throughout this entire conversation. When you're ready to talk like a grown-up, I'm here. Until then, I'm going to return to my birthday party and celebrate selling a book before I turned thirty," Cherry says, making pointed eye contact.

"You just had to say it, didn't you?" Helen growls as Cherry walks past her and toward the closed bedroom door.

"Aww, but you said you wanted me to tell the truth. Isn't that what you said?" Cherry opens the door, and the din from the party bursts through the small space.

"Now who's being an asshole?"

"Still you, Helen," Cherry says, walking out into the party without looking back.

Helen stands in the blown-out crater she's left in after Cherry's parting shot. She catches a glimpse of herself in the mirror and focuses on the plastic neon Best Friends necklace. She blows out a guttural scoff. But as Helen reaches up to her neck to elaborately rip it off, she stops. Even in this fugue state, she knows that something about this action is a point of no return. That necklace means something. Feeling magnanimous, she gently shimmies the necklace over her head and pockets it. If Cherry notices she's not wearing it, Helen will just say that the plastic was irritating her skin.

Helen stands in the doorway, looking out into the party. The music is loud and people are dancing and laughing and making out. And there's Cherry right in the middle of it all, surrounded by fifty or so of her closest friends. She's jumping up and down, her arms raised high into the air. Everyone is intoxicated by her. Some jump with her, some hype her up, and then there are others who only watch her and smile, delighted to just be in her orbit.

And then there's Helen.

For someone who's technically lived in San Francisco all her life, Helen has exactly two friends to show for it. And one of those friends is Tess Bayard, who Helen is confident does not see the intensity of their friendship in quite the same way as she does. On the other hand, Cherry rolled into the city for the very first time ten years ago and started making herself at home right away. She made fast friends with every neighbor, then made it a point to go around to each and every shop in the Upper Haight, endearing herself far and wide. And when Cherry got the job at the thrift store, she met Leni, and together they made the entire staff there a family. So much so that they've started hosting Thanksgiving each year for those who have no place to go. Helen, on the other hand, has worked at the same tiny nonprofit for going on almost eight years. She has four coworkers with whom she is civil, but they don't even eat lunch together. Well, the four coworkers have lunch together. Just not Helen.

Cherry used to attend a local trivia night at the local bar, and now she's the quizmaster. She became obsessed with mah-jongg and is now in a league. She signed up for writing classes at the local community college, and now she's mentoring younger students. She's dated, gotten serious a few times, and made out with more people than Helen has had unrequited crushes on. Cherry has even instituted something called Touristy Tuesdays, where she gets a group of people together and once a month they do something "as cheesily touristy as is possible" and end the day at a local taqueria, where Cherry's photo now hangs on the wall between the owner's family and Our Lady of Guadalupe.

Helen rests her hand against the doorjamb, suddenly woozy from her yearslong, voluntary confinement. How has the city been so good to Cherry, while leaving Helen ten years older and no better than she was back in Mill Valley? Helen knows the answer, of course.

"You take you with you," her mother had warned when Helen announced she was moving.

Feeling suddenly claustrophobic, Helen quickly wends her way through the party, back down the stairs, out the security gate, and onto the even more crowded Haight Street in search of Tess. She needs to tell her everything that just happened. She needs to hear someone say how right she is and, more importantly, how wrong Cherry is. She needs to feel vindicated as someone else rips Cherry apart for how selfish and sneaky she's been. She needs Tess to say things like, *What kind of best friend does that?* and *No, you didn't do anything wrong, this is for her to fix,* and *Ugh, she said that? You must be so hurt right now.* She needs Tess to be just as mad at Cherry as she is.

She imagines telling her what happened and begging Tess to not storm up there and give Cherry a piece of her mind. *No, don't,* Helen would plead. *It's her birthday . . . She didn't mean it . . . Let's be the bigger people and let her have her little, unseemly outburst.* And as Helen pulls Tess out of that tacky little party, they'll laugh about what kind of book someone like Cherry could even write and how apparently publishers will buy anything these days.

Helen stands in the middle of the sidewalk desperately looking around for Tess. Finally, she sees her standing in a small vestibule, still talking to her fiancé on the phone. Tess holds up a hand and mouths the word "sorry" as she paces. Helen nods and gestures that she'll wait for her to finish. Tess disappears among the crowd, appearing every now and again like an elusive dolphin bursting through the waves.

Trying to calm down, Helen leans against the apartment building's outer wall and tells herself that she just needs a minute. She just needs a minute. But instead of working to calm herself down, Helen chooses to spend the next several minutes writing and rewriting what she's going to say to Tess like it's dialogue in a story. As she tries to craft her monologue, Helen grows more and more angry at how Cherry insinuated that it was Helen's own fault that she hadn't shared the good news with her. That somehow lying to your best friend for more than two years is nothing compared to not properly feting someone for winning a writing award she won over a handful of scribbling octogenarians. Should she have patronized her best friend and behaved as though Cherry had won the Glending? Maybe if Cherry had properly communicated to Helen that this was a big deal, she would have governed herself accordingly.

How was Helen supposed to know?

Just as Helen cranes her neck to check where Tess is, a barefoot woman selling beaded anklets blows a giant puff of weed smoke directly in her face. Coughing and waving her hand around, Helen sinks back against the wall, watching as packs of people enjoy their big night on the town, all busy and going somewhere. Helen balls up her fists, puffing out one angry scoff after another, stopping only to shake her head in indignation.

"Oh. Hey," Leni says, stepping out of the security gate with a giant bag of trash. Helen looks over at Leni and says nothing but gives her an incredibly barbed scoff and a masterful, in Helen's opinion, shake of the head. Leni rolls her eyes and continues, "Guess it's not just your written words that are blocked, huh?" Leni laughs to herself and continues on toward the bins.

Helen is furious.

That was hilarious.

As Helen thinks of twenty comebacks she could have said to Leni, she has this pang that it should be her taking down the trash from Cherry's thirtieth-birthday party. That it should have been her who walked out with Cherry's birthday cake, beaming at her best friend of ten years and singing "Happy Birthday" with discordant vigor. That it should be her up there right now dancing the night away, laughing, and creating new memories. But she's not. She's down here sulking and thinking up mean things to say to her instead. Helen digs in her pocket, pulls out the neon plastic necklace, and laces it back over her head.

Maybe she has been distracted lately and hasn't been as good a best friend as she could have been. Helen feels herself getting more and more desperate for Tess to get off her phone call and save her from actually having to be contemplative about her ongoing inability to know how to be a friend to someone. Because that is what Helen decides is the issue here. Rather than actually thinking about the questions Cherry posed to her, Helen instead decides to lay this entire misunderstanding at the feet of her inexperience in friendships.

Helen gets a lightning bolt of an idea. She will invite Cherry down to Marina del Rey as her guest at Bibliophile, a yearly literary festival that draws thousands of writers and readers. Helen has been asked to be on a panel and will also be signing her short-story anthology along with a few of the other writers. There are always a ton of parties and get-togethers during this time, and even the greenroom will be the perfect networking opportunity for someone new to the field. This way, Helen can show Cherry that she is supportive of her literary success. She will introduce her to everyone, tell them that she's got a book coming out, and show her all that the literary world has on offer. Helen will be her guide, her protector, and her most ardent cheerleader as Cherry embarks on this exciting next chapter.

Helen looks back up into the apartment, wanting to tell Cherry about her idea right now. She knows it will help prove to Cherry that she listened. That she can get out of her own way and celebrate her best friend. This will work. This will put their friendship firmly back on the rails, and next year, it'll be Helen walking out with Cherry's birthday cake.

Leni turns the corner, her hands delicately held out in front of her so as not to get the disgusting trash juice all over her gorgeous sequin party dress. Endlessly used to people staring at her, she doesn't notice Helen lying in wait.

"Thanks for helping Cherry," Helen says, already feeling smug at how well she's handling all this. Leni looks back at the bins, her germy hands still safely far away from her. "Not with the trash. Well, that too. But I meant her book. I wanted to thank you for letting her use your computer." Leni takes a long look at Helen. Helen shifts, confused as to why Leni hasn't accepted her thanks.

"Uh-huh," Leni says finally, using a tissue to delicately pull open the security gate.

Just as Helen is about to unload all twenty of the comebacks she thought of earlier, Tess appears at her side as Leni disappears up the stairs and back into Cherry's birthday party.

"I'm so sorry. Wedding stuff," Tess says, shoving her cell phone into the pocket of her impossibly low-rise jeans. Tess's plain white T-shirt is knotted and cropped under her brown Alexander McQueen cardigan, her hip bones jutting out on either side of her thin frame.

"Is everything okay?" Helen asks, wondering how long she'll have to wait before they talk about Cherry's book and how keeping a secret from your best friend for two years is way worse than not knowing how to properly celebrate someone.

"We want his daughter, Fizzy, to be the flower girl, but his ex is acting crazy as usual," Tess says, lighting a joint.

"Is she acting crazy or . . ." Helen trails off, as she so often does in these fraught conversations with Tess about her future husband. Tess holds the pot smoke for a few moments before finally turning to the side and unleashing the dank plume onto the masses.

"No, I know. I know, okay," Tess says, her voice choked and smoky.

"If all of someone's exes are suddenly 'crazy'"—Helen does giant air quotes when she says the word "crazy"—"I would maybe look at the common denominator."

"But he's not like that with me." Helen watches as Tess looks away from her and takes another long drag off her joint.

"Sure, but just last week you were saying he threw a fit because his ex wanted to take Fizzy on tour for the summer, and he got the lawyers involved because he said her tours were debaucherous or whatever, but it was his band that got written up for trashing a hotel room, not hers."

"Okay, just . . . ugh, I know you're not his biggest fan, but I love Fizzy and not only want her in the wedding but am trying to figure out how we can get custody moving forward," Tess says, growing emotional.

"No, I know. I love that you're in her life, because you're the only adult who seems to understand that she's just a little girl and not some mountainous border region worthy of a thousand-year war."

Tess absently looks at her phone, scrolling through old texts from her fiancé. She looks up when she hears Helen finish. "Once we get married, he'll get better, and together we'll do everything we can to bring that little girl home."

"Are we going to talk about Cherry's book thing, or do I have to keep acting like we haven't had this exact conversation a thousand times and how you never listen to anything I say and it always ends with you telling me that he'll get better after you get married?"

"Oh god, am I that bad?"

"And I'm even less interested in spending the next several hours regurgitating the same advice I've given you over the last six years while you act like this drama is happening to you, rather than something you are actively choosing," Helen says, her tongue loose and dangerous.

"I thought that was why we're friends," Tess says, making pointed eye contact with Helen. "Because we both excel at that little hobby." Tess blows out a shaft of vengeful pot smoke.

"You should know better than anyone that telling someone to just get on with it and write a novel isn't good advice. It's not that easy," Helen bites back.

"Of course I know that, but—"

Helen cuts Tess off by blowing out the longest, most dramatic sigh she can muster. It's childish, but she finally gets her point across.

"Fine. So, did you ask Cherry about it?" Tess asks, her voice clipped and distracted. Helen doesn't allow Tess's obvious displeasure to stop her as she barrels ahead.

"She said it was my fault that she didn't tell me." Saying it out loud feels as good as Helen knew it would. She knows she's oversimplifying. She knows she's taking advantage of Tess's already strained relationship with Cherry to skew her toward villainizing her best friend. She knows this, and yet she continues, "Apparently I just don't know how to properly celebrate people."

"What are you supposed to be celebrating? When the thrift store has a big sale on used Hawaiian shirts? Give me a break," Tess says. Helen laughs. It feels good.

"I guess I was supposed to make a big deal when she won that little writing award."

"Oh my god, are you serious? Didn't she get, like, a little paper certificate for that?"

"Her professor"—Helen pauses when Tess scoffs—"clearly made it on her computer."

"So embarrassing."

"Right? How was I supposed to know?"

"You weren't. She's jealous of your success. Has been ever since Hayho, when you won the Glending and she didn't. Like there was a chance of that, but still."

"I have a lot to learn about friendships. So I know I can do better."

"You're being way too nice about this," Tess says, stomping out her joint.

"I thought I'd invite her to Bibliophile."

"You shouldn't enable her bad behavior. You've done nothing wrong."

"No, I know. But it could be good for her. She's new to publishing and I can introduce her around. She can go to panels and sit in the greenroom with real writers. There are also some really good panels on just the craft of writing that I'm sure she can learn things from. It'll be fun, and it would show that I am taking her seriously and supporting her," Helen says, feeling like herself again.

"I don't know, Helen."

"What?"

"Are you sure you want to . . . Look, I know you like Cherry and all, but Bibliophile? Are you sure you want to vouch for her like that?"

"Vouch for her?"

"Yeah, you know . . . you would basically be saying to every respected writer you know that this person has been vetted by you, and now your credibility is on the line if she gets all Cherry Stewart on them."

"Gets all Cherry Stewart?"

"Yeah, you know," Tess says and waggles her arms around while saying "hey, man" to everyone who passes.

Helen laughs. "I took Cherry to a book event once and she did fine."

"Wasn't that the reading where she asked that writer how she dealt with her second book not doing as well as the first?"

"I think she was trying to ask how someone deals with the painful process of getting better at one's craft and how when you look back—"

"She called her second book a 'flop,' Helen."

"Yeah, okay. I . . ."

"Now imagine that kind of energy but multiply it by a thousand."

"She's my best friend. I want to show her that I listened."

"Like I said, you're being way too nice."

"She deserves nice."

"Well, I hope you know what you're doing," Tess says, her cell phone ringing in her pocket. Just as she's about to tell Helen that it's her fiancé again, Helen cuts her off.

"I hope you know what you're doing, too," Helen says with an arched eyebrow.

Tess walks away without a look back.

CHAPTER TEN

Helen wakes up the next day to the sounds of Cherry banging around in the kitchen. She reaches over to her bedside table, turns her alarm clock so she can see the time, and is horrified to discover that it is already way past noon. She shouldn't feel guilty; Cherry's birthday party raged until well into the wee hours of the morning. But even so, she can hear her father now: *Day's half over,* he'd warn, looking over whatever tome he was reading at the time. Shaking her head, Helen untangles herself from the sheets and swings her feet to the floor. She is wearing her usual nighttime attire, an old pair of sweats and a droopy pink tank top with just enough holes to warrant throwing it away. Helen pushes her perpetually damaged black hair back from her face and stands, both nervous and excited about pitching her idea to Cherry about being her guest at Bibliophile.

"Come here, you little jerk. Just . . . come onnnn." Helen can hear Cherry pleading with something as she turns the corner into the main room.

Even though Helen has known Cherry for going on ten years now, the singularly absurd vignette she sees when she turns the corner is unhinged, even by Cherry's standards. Half of Cherry's body is hanging out of a small kitchen window as her legs and feet kick and lurch, accompanied by every cursed word she grunts.

"What are you doing?" Helen asks, rushing over.

"It's stuck . . . I . . . I can't get it," Cherry whines.

"Get what? This . . . that window . . . this isn't safe," Helen says, placing a gentle hand on her best friend's leg.

"Ugh, wait . . . Hold on," Cherry says, shimmying back inside with the grace of a bulldozer. She narrowly misses several teetering cairns of glasses and dishes stacked up from last night's party on her way down.

What Helen hadn't seen was that Cherry is holding a long-handled broom with a kitchen knife duct-taped to the end of it. And as she stands in front of her, Helen watches Cherry take in the dirt and grime now covering her shirt from having basically lain down in decades of filth. Holding what looks like a homemade harpoon, Cherry wears the same outfit from last night. Helen wonders if she has even been to sleep. But when Cherry looks up, Helen notices that someone has written "mah honey baby" on her cheek in what looks to be red permanent marker.

"You . . . uh," Helen says, gesturing at Cherry's cheek.

"What?" Cherry asks, swiping at the wrong cheek.

"No . . . it's . . . other side," Helen says, pointing.

"There's nothing there," Cherry says, feeling around her own face.

"I assure you there is," Helen says, smiling. Cherry looks in the reflection of the window and can see just enough to panic.

"Oh, wait a minute." Cherry shakes her head, it all clearly coming back to her now.

"Mah honey baby," Helen reads, laughing.

"I remember not a lot from last night, I will confess," Cherry says with a shrug, no longer attempting to rid herself of the temporary birthday tattoo.

"Who wrote it?" Helen asks.

"I have no idea." Cherry shrugs. Helen marvels at Cherry not knowing who among her innumerable friends felt strongly enough in their love of her to permanently affix the sentiment to her face. Whereas if Helen woke up one morning with "mah honey baby" written on her cheek, she would know without a shadow of a doubt that it was Cherry. Stung by this realization, Helen quickly pivots the line of questioning.

"Are we going to move on to you hanging out of the kitchen window in the same clothes you were wearing last night, mah honey baby?" Helen asks, trying to peek out the window.

"It's stuck," Cherry says.

"What's stuck?"

"The penis."

"Well, this just became a conversation I never thought I'd have."

Helen walks over to the kitchen window and heaves herself up to get a good look out into the cramped space between their apartment building and the one just next door. On her first attempt, she sees nothing.

"You have to really get up there," Cherry says, straightening both of her arms as if she's lifting herself out of a swimming pool.

"Do I really *have* to get up there? Is this . . . why do we care if an inflatable penis is stuck?" Helen asks. Cherry hangs her head. "What?"

"I put my necklace on it."

"Which necklace?" Helen asks.

Cherry looks up. Pointedly.

"No."

"Yes."

"Why?" Helen asks.

"I think we were all wondering where you were last night and if you were going to rejoin the party. When you didn't . . ." Cherry trails off, flicking her eyes out the kitchen window.

"You dressed up an inflatable penis to . . ."

"To be your stand-in. Yes."

Helen walks over to the counter, heaves herself up, and leans out the kitchen window to see if she can see her very own phallic effigy. About fifteen feet down, the inflatable penis has wedged itself between their apartment building and the one just next door. What Cherry didn't say was that she'd also drawn a little face onto the penis, so all Helen can see when she looks down is a slightly deflated, smirking penis wearing a Best Friends necklace and the words "HELEN HICKS" scrawled down the main shaft. Something about seeing it—actually seeing it—causes Helen to break out into hysterics. Struggling to get a breath, she clambers down off the kitchen counter to a worried Cherry.

"So the knife was . . ." Helen asks, pointing to the large kitchen knife shimmering in the midday light.

"To poke it. I thought if I could deflate it, then I could wedge myself through the gate and grab it once it fell to the ground."

"That knife can barely cut an apple," Helen says, pulling the knife down and running her finger along the blade with no injury whatsoever.

"Right, which is why I just pushed it down farther and farther."

"Is it low enough that we can get it from the ground?"

"Not really, but—" Cherry's face lights up.

"What?"

"You're littler than me. I could lift you up," Cherry says, cupping her hands and miming pushing someone up as she speaks.

"I don't know," Helen says.

"No, this is the only way. I'll bring the harpoon, you grab the tongs," Cherry says, taking off toward the front door.

"Cherry, wait!" Helen says, looking down at her droopy pink tank top and sweats.

"Grab the tongs!" Cherry yells, stampeding down the stairs.

"Perfect," Helen says. She walks over to the utensil drawer, fights with the potato masher for a good two minutes, and once she's managed to free the drawer from its clutches, tugs the drawer open and begrudgingly grabs the tongs, along with a bright-yellow pair of kitchen gloves.

Before leaving, Helen grabs a sweatshirt from the floor of her bedroom, throws it on over her tank top, and follows Cherry down the stairs with an adolescent harrumph. She opens the security gate and is met with a bright, sunny Sunday morning that feels like a nuclear blast. Squinting in the sunshine, Helen puts a hand over her eyes and scans Haight Street as if she's a captain watching the horizon for land ho. She sees Cherry just outside the janky metal gate that stands between them and Helen's long-lost penis proxy.

"Over here!" Cherry says, pushing her homemade harpoon high into the air. Helen notices that not one pedestrian blinks an eye at her. *Just another Sunday on the Upper Haight, I guess.* Helen deflates just a little and shambles over to Cherry.

"Ugh, come on," Helen says, looking up high between the two buildings to where the inflatable penis has lodged itself. She is thankful, in this moment, that the little face is pointed upward. She lets her gaze fall to the overgrown patch of grass, which is riddled with trash, used condoms, and random piles of abandoned shoes and clothes.

"It'll be an adventure!" Cherry says, examining the gate. Helen steps forward, settling in next to her, their bodies so used to being close to one another that they're like little puzzle-piece friends, easily melting into a space that's big enough for only one person. Helen has always loved the sound of Cherry's thoughtful breathing, and whenever they've shared a hotel room in the past, she's always found the white noise to be comforting.

Helen curls her gloved fingers around the metal gate and cranes her neck to see if there's a way in. She tries pushing the gate, but the loose chain and padlock rattle with every movement. Cherry puts her hand over Helen's and pulls the gate, the chain's slack revealing about a ten-inch-wide opening. Cherry looks over at Helen and waggles her eyebrows. Helen's shoulders sink as she realizes what Cherry is proposing. Shaking her head, Helen ducks underneath Cherry's arm and squeezes through the small opening and into the wild, grassy area between the two buildings, careful not to slip on the innumerable condoms that lie in wait. Cherry follows closely behind, careful to hand Helen her harpoon before ducking beneath the chain.

No one walking Haight Street even glances at the pair.

Helen and Cherry position themselves just below the inflatable penis. Cherry was right—it is perfectly lodged both halfway up and halfway down, making it impossible to reach on your own. You'd need either a ladder or a kneeling best friend, who is, at this very moment, currently cupping her hands at Helen's feet.

"I've always wanted to do this," Cherry says, unable to keep herself from smiling.

"Of course you have," Helen says, putting a kitchen-gloved hand on Cherry's shoulder before stepping into her hands.

Helen has always known that Cherry is strong. But up until this very moment, she could only intuit this information secondhand after watching her carry a pair of old chairs they found on the side of the road up their flight of stairs when they moved into this apartment ten years ago. The way Cherry lifts Helen into the air with ease stuns her. Coming from a kneeling position, Cherry heaves Helen up toward the inflatable penis in one smooth motion as she stands. Leaving it up to Helen to save the day. She winches her tongs around the lowest-hanging deflated ball in one fell swoop, causing the penis to careen down to the grassy strip. Even though Helen is fully aware Cherry would like nothing better than to catch the penis before it hits the ground, she gracefully lowers Helen down to the ground before lunging over to save the penis from its filthy surroundings.

"We're sterilizing that in alcohol before it goes anywhere near you," Helen says, walking back toward the metal gate.

"That's a lot of alcohol," Cherry says, eyeballing the penis.

"The necklace. We're sterilizing the necklace," Helen says, dipping down under the chain and continuing her conversation through the metal gate.

"We can do them both together. Don't want to separate them. They've already been through so much," Cherry says, passing the penis and harpoon through the gate before following behind.

Cherry's penchant for humanizing everyday items is a long-standing one. From thanking a Blackwing pencil on its last sharpening for its service to feeling guilty for finally "giving up" on a coffee table they found on the side of the road after its second leg broke off in as many weeks. Hearing that Cherry plans on treating a neon plastic necklace and an inflatable penis as star-crossed lovers she doesn't have the heart to separate doesn't even faze Helen anymore.

"You want coffee?" she says, holding the security gate open for Cherry as they climb the stairs together.

"Nah, I'll grab one on the way to work."

"You work today?"

"Yeah, I switched with someone because they got a little too drunk last night," Cherry says, opening and closing various cabinets in search of the rubbing alcohol.

"Drunker than you?" Helen yells from the bathroom, pulling the alcohol from beneath the sink.

"Way drunker," Cherry says, taking the bottle from Helen.

"Okay, well, why don't you shower real quick, and I'll do this," Helen says, taking the alcohol back in her still-gloved hands.

"Oh, thank you. That's a great idea," Cherry says, handing her the inflatable penis as well.

"How long's your shift?" Helen asks, not wanting her conversation with Cherry about Bibliophile to be rushed.

"It's a long one, so don't wait up," Cherry says, kicking off her shoes and socks on her way to the bathroom.

"Maybe we can do a celebratory dinner after work tomorrow? For the book?" Helen asks.

Cherry turns around and the very tip of her nose has flushed red. Helen knows this means that she is trying not to cry.

"I would love that," Cherry says, intertwining her hands at her chest.

"Okay, we'll decide on a place, and I can just meet you there after work," Helen says, set on finding the perfect restaurant to talk to Cherry about Bibliophile.

"I can't wait!" Cherry yelps, skipping off toward the shower, shedding items of clothing along the way.

"And I'll clean up around here," Helen yells.

"What?" Cherry yells back.

Helen walks over to the open door of the bathroom, where Cherry is already in the shower. "I'll clean up the apartment."

Cherry pulls back the shower curtain and peeks out to where Helen is standing. "Why would you clean up after a party you didn't go to? Just leave it, I'll clean it up tomorrow." She disappears back behind the shower curtain.

"I feel bad," Helen says, looking at the floor.

"What?" Cherry yells from inside the shower.

"I feel bad!" Helen yells.

"What?" Cherry yells again.

"Never mind!" Helen yells.

As Cherry finishes her shower, Helen returns to the kitchen and makes herself a cup of coffee, giving the filthy penis a wide berth. She hopes that inviting Cherry to Bibliophile will make up for everything and that the dinner tomorrow night will be the one-two punch of true, best friendship that will help them move on from last night's ugliness, as well as whatever caused Cherry to hide that she's been writing a book for the last two years.

Bim. Bam. Boop.

Cherry's words continue to torment Helen. Because while she's been consumed with Cherry's humiliating assessment of her last night, she's also been grateful that it has eclipsed actually having to process Cherry getting a book deal and not her. Because today feels normal and as if nothing has changed. Cherry is heading off to work at the thrift store, and Helen is spending another quiet Sunday getting ready for a workweek of writing grants and sitting in her little cubicle with nothing on its walls except her various passwords and an old card the rest of the staff signed for her birthday five years ago. Because however much she wanted this time in her life to be different, she's tragically gotten used to it this way. Where she and Cherry are both struggling. Where they're both stagnating. Where they're both frustrated in a life that hasn't quite turned out how they'd hoped.

But that's all going to change now. The little, quiet life that they've built over the last ten years is on the cliff's edge now that Cherry has a book deal and an agent and an editor. She'll have rounds of edits and meetings with marketing teams. She'll quit her job at the thrift store and go on a book tour. She'll get to spend her days writing from home or adorable coffee shops around the Upper Haight while Helen continues to wear cheap polyester slacks and comfortable loafers as she takes the BART to her day job. She'll get to have a bright future, instead of a dim but comfortable present like Helen. And then a book cover will be emailed to Cherry that she'll excitedly show to Helen, and Helen will have to push past her envy to say how beautiful it is.

Envy. Jealousy.

Helen remembers back at Hayho, when Cherry corrected her usage of the word "jealousy." Saying that what Helen felt was probably closer to envy. As Helen gently peels the neon plastic necklace off the inflatable penis, she wonders which word she should use when she both wants what Cherry has and feels as though she has taken something of Helen's from her. Or is that just envious jealousy? As Helen lovingly cleans Cherry's necklace with the rubbing alcohol, she feels a twinge of pride at having possibly invented a new word that will be endlessly helpful to fellow losers such as herself. Envious jealousy seems to encompass the full scope and sweep of what it feels like to yearn at an Olympic level.

As Helen sets the sterilized necklace down on a dish towel, she hears the shower turn off and Cherry pull back the shower curtain. She also hears Cherry carrying on a full conversation with her from the other room, something she's famous for and has been talked to about several times. Helen has told Cherry time and time again that she cannot hear her when she's talking to her from a whole other room in the apartment, unsure as to why this continues to be news to her best friend.

"What?" Helen yells from the kitchen. Cherry continues to talk on and on from the bathroom as she's brushing her teeth and applying a thick SPF to her pale skin.

". . . we can have those little green beans that I like and share the full order of dumplings." Cherry walks out into the main room as she finishes her sentence.

"Are you talking about dinner tomorrow?" Helen asks, running a paper towel soaked with rubbing alcohol up and down the inflatable penis.

"What are you doing?" Cherry asks, catching Helen midstroke.

"What does it look like I'm doing?" Helen asks. Cherry arches an eyebrow. "Oh my god, do you want this penis cleaned and reunited with its great love or not?"

"They must not be separated!" Cherry swoons, tightening the towel around her wet, lanky body.

"Were you talking about dinner?" Helen prods.

"Yes! I was saying we could go to that Chinese place over by that one little card store you like," Cherry says, giving no actual concrete details.

"That would be great," Helen says, knowing exactly the place she's talking about.

"Okay, I'll meet you there tomorrow at 6:15? That way if you get caught up with anything at work, you won't be stressed out thinking that . . ." Cherry walks out of the main room and toward her bedroom and continues speaking the entire time she's changing. Helen catches none of it.

In the beginning, Helen would walk to wherever Cherry was, thinking that doing so would somehow remind Cherry that the person she was talking to was not, in fact, in the same room as she was. Sadly, this only enabled the bad behavior and emboldened Cherry to continue twittering on until Helen came close enough to be a part of the conversation she was, up until that point, categorically missing.

Cherry says her goodbyes, thanks Helen for cleaning up the apartment—while also assuring her that she definitely doesn't have to and that Cherry plans to clean it up tomorrow on her day off. Helen feels good about repeating that she wants to, but doesn't go into why. Cherry lunges into her for a big hug, then bolts down the staircase, already late for her shift at the thrift store. Helen is positive she hears Cherry talking all the way down and resigns herself to not knowing. It's best not to think about the details and whole conversations Cherry thinks Helen was privy to.

As Helen begins cleaning the bathroom, she is plagued with a montage of possible vignettes from the future that haunt her with every scrub of the toilet brush. The day Cherry comes home and announces that she's quit her job as the manager of the Second Hand, a thrift store she's worked at for more than nine years. As Helen moves on to the bathtub, she wonders what selling a book at auction really means and whether it's the kind of money that will make Cherry think about moving out on her own. Is it the kind of money that means that Cherry is now an official writer and never has to find a day job ever again? Or is it the kind of money where Cherry still has to work at the thrift store and their lives will look pretty much the same as they do now, except that Cherry has a book out like Helen did with the anthology? Somehow running these different scenarios through her brain is better than just asking Cherry and knowing for sure their lives are about to be upended.

As Helen moves on to the kitchen, she wonders if Cherry is going to buy her own computer and whether she'll be flown to New York and wined and dined by her editorial team. Helen thinks back to the book event they did for the short-story anthology and how all she got was a black tea in a paper cup and the permanent marker she signed books with . . . which she stole for posterity. She's been invited to lavish events put on by the Glending Foundation and remembers that before she read at Edith Glending's memorial, all the Glending Fellows were offered snacks and drinks in the greenroom. Tess has invited Helen to a few of her book readings and even an exclusive literary salon or two, but that was Tess being wined and dined, not Helen.

And as Helen imagines a life where she's in the front row of Cherry's literary success, she grows more and more troubled. By the time she's tidying up the last bits in the main room, Helen has successfully written an entire narrative in which Cherry has moved out and is living in either a cool brownstone in Brooklyn or a beach house in Malibu, leaving Helen to move back home with her tail between her legs, having to admit to her father that he was right and she is, in fact, a total failure.

"She's going to leave me behind," Helen dramatically says to herself. Of course, Helen doesn't admit to herself that when she was told the short-story anthology was going to be published, she started looking for apartments she could move into on her own, thinking it would become the next bestseller and a precursor of the success she would inevitably achieve with her debut novel. Maybe Helen's fear of abandonment is grounded in her own predilection to leave people behind, rather than Cherry's. This unwelcome memory throws her into yet another shame spiral about how Cherry, time and time again, has proven herself to be a better human being than Helen could ever be. Which is why, as Helen hauls two giant garbage bags full of laundry down to the Laundromat on the corner, she finds herself unable to hide from certain darker truths about herself any longer.

There's something particularly meditative about a Laundromat. This fact infuriates Helen, as that's the very last state in which she wants to find herself right now. She would like nothing more than to stay in shallower waters, where she can skew the events of the last twenty-four hours into more comfortable territory where, like Tess said, she's being way too nice about this whole thing and has nothing to question about the way she's behaving or reacting.

Because as she watches the colorful tempest of clothing tumble round and round in the dryer, Helen is forced to untangle the emotional ingredients currently swirling in her head. And the uncomfortable realization she comes to is that envy and jealousy are just a part of the equation. It's not that Helen is unaware that the way she's reacting to Cherry's book news is petty and not aligned with someone calling themselves her best friend. It's that she's unable to act any other way.

Had she really thought her own self-loathing was a victimless crime?

Of course Helen is its first victim—that's a detail she's never found particularly significant. But up until this very moment, she never fully grasped how Cherry was also collateral damage in Helen's own battle with herself. Because in her inability to celebrate her best friend, Helen's own insecurity has made her all but unable to see beyond her own misery and be unequivocally happy for someone she loves.

As Helen folds the warm and tangled clothes, she looks back at all her other failed friendships—or whatever they were called—and now sees the wake of bodies strewn behind her, broken and bruised from having to perform their love and friendship enough so that even Helen could believe in it. A task that could never be attained, so Helen could safely and merrily roll along with convenient narratives about being a literary recluse too great and misunderstood to ever sully her hands with something as pedestrian as making a friend. No, everyone else was the problem, and Helen was just the misunderstood hero who would have to go it alone.

But as with most breakthroughs, after the swell of relief from discovering a long-hidden pattern subsides, the discomfort with this newly excavated knowledge begins to close in around her. And as Helen's shoulders buckle under the heavy weight, she is forced to sit with the seismic ramifications from what she's just learned about her active role in her own unhappiness.

Unable to sit in the truth of her limitations, Helen continues to wildly swing, pendulum-like, between actually holding herself responsible and desperately trying to find any other explanation for who's really at fault for why Cherry chose to hide that she has been writing a book for the last two years. As she loads up their newly folded laundry and stubbornly hauls it back to their apartment, Helen attempts to make an argument for this whole misunderstanding being both of their faults. Sure, she has work to do on herself, but it was Cherry who chose not to tell her that she was writing a book and then proceeded to lie about it for two whole years.

Still monologuing about who has the higher percentage of wrongdoing, Helen pours the boiled water into the Cup Noodles she'll be having for dinner tonight. Slurping up the hot and delicious ramen as she stands over the sink, Helen hates that with every percentage point she moves over into Cherry's friendship column, she feels better and better. And as the night wears on, she's incrementally being absolved of this being nothing more than an accidental slight made by someone whose own self-loathing made them incapable of showing up properly for their best friend. As she brushes her teeth and puts her newly washed pajamas on late that night, Helen has almost convinced herself that she is only partly to blame for last night's blowup.

Helen tosses and turns, awakened by Cherry finally coming home in the wee hours of the morning. As she hears Cherry crawl into bed, she digs a pencil and an old receipt out of her tote bag and dramatically does the math around how many actual days two years is, in an attempt to find an answer to a completely imaginary equation based on loose details and a paper-thin theory.

"That's seven hundred and thirty days," Helen says to herself, marveling at her own scribbled math on the back of a receipt.

As visions of a bleak future in her childhood bedroom begin to dissipate, Helen throws the pencil and receipt back in her tote bag, angrily crosses her arms, and thinks of every little lie Cherry must have told her in order to write a book in secret in just two years. Was she really at work this late, or was she just hanging out over at Leni's, looking at one-bedroom apartments? And what about when she said she was going home to visit her family back in Pasadena? Did she really do that, or was she on a writer's retreat or even meeting prospective agents? How can Helen believe a single word Cherry has said over the last two years, if this is the level of dishonesty that has been afoot?

Helen wakes up the next morning and gets ready for work, last night's usage of the word "afoot" weighing heavy on her soul. She feels exhausted at the new world she finds herself in. If only this were just about Cherry writing a book in secret for two years, Helen could handle that. But it's that her book sold. Cherry's book sold. And Helen can only imagine how good it feels to cross the finish line with a dream you've had for your entire life. To finally be able to exhale. Cherry's made it. All that noise in her head now quieted.

Not like Helen, who watched as her New Year's resolution went from selling a book, to writing a book, to outlining a book, to generating a list of agents and editors she wanted to work with, to attending a writing conference, to writing every day, to finding time to write on mornings and weekends, to committing to a writer's retreat once a year, to journaling and reading more, and finally to just trying to lose fifteen pounds.

Unlike Helen, Cherry is no longer plagued with waking up at 4:00 a.m. with an elaborate plan to create some new system where this time it's "for real" and she's going to write that book and get out there and start going to book events and build her community and take a writing class and start querying agents. Every night for the past ten years, Helen has crawled into bed having done none of that. And every night she felt just a little bit worse. Until one day, she woke up and didn't feel anything at all.

In fact, she welcomed the numbness. She told herself that living every day hobbled by her own creative shame and paralysis was just too hard on her. Day after day, week after week, month after month, year after year, she'd make the same empty promises, and day after day, week after week, month after month, year after year, she'd create more and more elaborate excuses for why those promises had been broken, as if she weren't the one who paid dearly for it.

Helen doesn't know how to be happy for Cherry because Helen doesn't know how to be happy.

Sitting on the BART on her way to work, Helen thinks about how that statement isn't quite true. Heartbreakingly untrue. Because she has experienced happiness. Fleeting moments here and there that felt so weightless and dreamy she almost cried. She felt happiness in her little cottage at Hayho, sitting beneath the redwood canopy, a whole week of being a writer in front of her. She felt that click of happiness when she finally found the perfect word for a sentence that hadn't felt right through multiple drafts. She was overcome with happiness when she got the call that her short story was going to be included in the anthology, and she cried when she held the real-life copy of it in her hands for the first time. Intermixed with her nerves, she felt an uncomfortable amount of happiness when she was chosen to read at Edith Glending's memorial, standing on that stage and reading her words in front of more than a thousand people.

But the other uncomfortable bit of information Helen must sift through as she recounts these instances of happiness is that these moments are all related to writing and—for the majority of them—not the actual process of writing, but the very public and external validation of having successfully written. So is it writing that makes Helen happy, or is it people recognizing that she is a good writer? Feeling slightly nauseous at this realization, she watches as a toddler across from her smiles and coos at a little stuffed cheetah in her dimpled hand. Helen can't believe she's having trouble with an emotion babies can comprehend at its basest level, yet here she is trying to dissect happiness like it's an embalmed frog pinned to a metal tray.

Even with this painful epiphany, Helen also knows that happiness is hard. She's witnessed how dangerous it feels and has always argued that that swell of ebullient joy made her feel out of control. Like she was sitting in the wicker basket of a hot air balloon, unable to control how high or how far she'd be swept away. And even more debilitating, she wonders how anyone can simply tread around on earth when they've soared among the clouds. Proving her point, even the act of excavating these brief moments of happiness has made Helen feel lower than if she'd just stayed numb.

As Helen walks the rest of the way to work, she challenges herself to recount moments of happiness outside of writing. *There must be some,* she thinks, panicking. She thinks back to a moment last year when she bought a basket of fresh strawberries from a farm stand and stood in the sunshine and ate them all, the red juice trailing down her chin with abandon. Or how that first night in her new apartment with Cherry felt, crawling into her very own bed and feeling that she was at the beginning of a great adventure. Or there was even one moment where she took a train up to Seattle to meet up with Tess after one of her book events, and drank a perfect cup of Earl Grey as the summer sun warmed her skin and the beautiful verdant landscape sped past.

Helen feels better about herself for the briefest of moments, until she realizes that all these moments took place by herself. She runs through all the moments when she and Cherry laughed until their stomachs hurt, or even the times when it was just perfectly peaceful, the pair sitting in silence as they drank their morning coffee. Or the innumerable examples where Cherry finished one of Helen's sentences and vice versa. But as Helen sets her bag on her desk and boots up her computer, she knows why none of those moments made it into the world's saddest highlight reel of happy moments. Put simply, it's because people make Helen nervous. And in that nervousness, Helen is unable to just be. And if what she's gleaning from these moments of happiness is true, then a major ingredient of feeling happy is just letting yourself be—no overthinking, no judgments, and no catastrophizing about the moment after the happy moment.

Just being happy.

And Helen is purely unable to accomplish that level of peace around anyone else, even Cherry. She knows she's gotten close. There was one moment right at the beginning of when they first moved to the city, where she and Cherry were in their apartment and Helen made a joke about performing some dance from a music video and stood up right there and actually did three or four of the iconic moves, going all out without a second thought while at the same time cracking a string of off-the-cuff jokes while Cherry fell out of her chair laughing. It was the freest Helen had ever felt . . . with another person. Dancing? Pop culture? Stream-of-consciousness jokes? Never before . . . and sadly, never since.

As her workday wears on, Helen realizes that this phenomenon is probably why she has always found plot to be way easier than character when it comes to writing. Always able to get that spark of an idea and then harness the act structure to create a compelling story, she grew frustrated with the wooden and robotic characters who populated her worlds. Therefore, it isn't much of a shock that art has imitated life and that it's the people—both real and imagined—who remain an enigma to her, causing Helen to overthink, panic, and back away from any real emotions.

The only silver lining to all these disruptive breakthroughs is that at least Helen is confident that when Cherry inevitably leaves her behind, she'll be able to find a moment or two of happiness in the blown-out remains all by herself. Maybe she should plant some strawberries in preparation.

Helen trudges through the workday, thankful for the mindless tasks, and as she packs her bag to leave finds herself feeling nervous about tonight's dinner. She wants it to go well. No, she needs it to go well. Cherry is the most important person to Helen, so . . . Helen stops, her arm in midair as she packs. She thinks the words again: *Cherry is the most important person to Helen.*

Oh.

Cherry is the most important person to Helen.

Somehow that single, simple fact got lost in all Helen's machinations and excuses over the last couple of days. She's taken her friend and their friendship for granted, and moreover, she's let her own bad attitude and overall ennui cloud what a good thing she has. Has she forgotten what the first twenty-four years of her life were like without Cherry? Does she really want to go back to that? There aren't enough strawberries in the world.

Helen quickens her pace, now absolutely panicking about losing Cherry. She zips up her bag, switches off her computer, and says goodbye to no one as she hurries out of her office building and down the street to wait for the BART. Helen practices speech after speech, fiddling with her backpack strap's buckle until it pops off, crumbling into pieces in her sweaty little hands. Helen leaps up at her stop, and almost runs to the little Chinese restaurant just next to that one card store that she likes only to find Cherry sitting at their favorite table in the back, smiling wide and waving her over. Helen wends through the tiny restaurant, nodding and smiling at the older couple who own and run the place.

"Hey, man. You look—"

"You're the most important person to me," Helen says, looming over Cherry.

"You're the most important person to me, too," Cherry says, not missing a beat.

"I'm so sorry. I'm just so sorry," Helen says, wanting to give Cherry a hug, but since she hasn't had a frontal lobotomy, she can only awkwardly pat Cherry's head, her hair tangling around Helen's fingers as they both wish none of this were happening.

"It's okay, man. Come on, sit down," Cherry says, motioning to the small bistro chair just across from her. Helen continues looming over Cherry and is just about to launch into her newly learned epiphanies about happiness when the owner comes over with several plates of food. All their favorites: the green beans, Zhong dumplings, mapo tofu, dan dan noodles, and a steaming bowl of Szechuan hot pot. Helen looks down at the food and Cherry's open face and wishes she didn't feel so badly about how she's behaved, because she definitely would have cataloged this as a happy moment, for sure. But, you know . . . without the Helen Hicks of it all.

Helen finally sits, setting her work bag at her feet. The owner brings over a pot of tea, wishes them well, and leaves Cherry and Helen alone with the delicious feast now steaming between them. Helen pours them each a cup of tea and then lifts her glass.

"To you and your amazing book," Helen says, extending her hand to the center of the table. Cherry beams, lifting her glass to Helen's with a loud, ceramic clink. And then neither woman takes a sip, because the tea is much too hot. Which makes both of them laugh.

"We've got to take a sip. It's bad luck," Cherry says, forcing her lips to the rim of the mug and slurping up a volcanic glug. Helen follows Cherry's lead and burns her entire mouth in the process.

"What do you think of coming with me to Bibliophile next week?" Helen asks, as Cherry piles her plate high with green beans and mapo tofu.

"Really?" Cherry asks, pushing the plates toward Helen so she can serve herself.

"Yeah, absolutely. I can switch my hotel room to two queen beds and I'd introduce you around and you could even reach out to your publisher and see if they're sending anyone and if they want to meet up with you, because I'm assuming you haven't met any of your editorial team in person yet?" Helen asks, moderately shocked at how much she does actually know about the publishing world.

"No, I haven't," Cherry says, shoving a stack of green beans in her mouth.

"I could get you into the greenroom and some panels—you could talk to other writers and tell them all about your book," Helen says, not touching her food.

"That would be really awesome," Cherry says.

"So, tell me about the book. I want to hear all about it," Helen says, her heart breaking just a little.

"It was actually one of the notes you gave me back at Hayho," Cherry says.

"Really?"

"Yeah, you said that my scene subverted expectations of the psychological thriller genre. And I liked that, so when I thought about what I wanted to write, I was like, let's just do that again," Cherry says, taking a delicate sip of her tea.

"Bim, bam, bop," Helen says.

"Boop. It was bim, bam, boop. But, yes."

"Right. Boop," Helen says, furious she got it wrong.

"So, when I learned about the difference between the thriller genre and the mystery genre, I realized I didn't think my scene was a thriller. It was a mystery." Cherry looks down at her plate as she says this.

"Oh, right. You're right," Helen says, dazed. How had she gotten that wrong, too? First "boop" and now this?

"So I just thought about the book I wanted to read and wrote that," Cherry says, with a shrug.

"That's great," Helen says, her voice cheerily forced.

"And I think in the beginning it was just about finishing it. Like, just to see if I could do it or not, you know?"

Oh, Helen knows.

"Yeah," she says, swallowing hard.

"But then, after I'd revised it a few times, I was at this bookstore, and I was just leafing through one of the books that I kinda thought was like mine and I flipped to the acknowledgments, and she had thanked her agent in them. So I thought if that agent liked this book, then maybe she'd like mine, so why not just query her?" Cherry is now using her hands a lot to talk this whole process out. Helen has never seen this particular conversational glitch in Cherry's arsenal and wonders what's causing it. Is it nerves? Guilt? As Cherry continues, Helen begins to understand. It's excitement. It's pride. It's happiness. "I worked on my query letter for a few months, and oh, this is a funny story, you'll like this—I didn't know what a 'sayse' was, so I mailed out the query on its own, but then I learned that a SASE is actually a—"

"Self-addressed stamped envelope," Helen and Cherry say in unison.

"Completely over my head. So I remailed the query and the agent wrote on top of the letter 'I didn't like it the first time,'" Cherry says, laughing.

"That's a weirdly mean thing to say," Helen says, thinking this story was going to go in a very different direction.

"Right? But I'm glad she was such a jerk because then? I got mad." Cherry scoots forward in her chair. "I did so much research and I made a list and I sent my query." Cherry thrusts a finger in the air. "All with sayses! And three out of the five agents I queried got back to me!"

"When was this?" Helen asks, treading carefully.

"It was . . . um, this was in March? April maybe?"

"Few months ago, then."

There is a lull.

"I know I should have told you. You deserved to know and I know you could have helped. I think—"

"You don't have to—"

"No, I know I haven't handled this well, but I think I just . . . I didn't want the bubble to burst, you know? Like, I was in this dreamworld, and it was just me and the book, and if it didn't work out, then . . . only I would know. Telling you would have made it real, and I don't think I could even admit to myself how much I wanted this," Cherry says.

"But Leni knew," Helen says, pushing things.

"Leni knew, but she doesn't know anything about publishing, or writing even . . . so her knowing was perfect because she—"

"Could just cheer you on."

"Yeah."

"Without all the baggage," Helen says, nodding.

"You're not baggage," Cherry says.

"But you were afraid I would—"

"I know you've been struggling with writing, and I don't want to ruin this lovely dinner by—"

"Telling me the truth?"

"But it's complicated." Cherry sets her chopsticks down and Helen's stomach drops. She continues, "I know you look down on me when it comes to writing." Cherry's voice is steady and low. She looks across the table and makes pointed eye contact with Helen. Helen is quiet. "I also know that you don't like it that you do."

With this, Helen sits back in her chair. Stunned.

"I really thought I'd hidden . . . the ugly stuff."

"Nope."

"That's great."

"And because you're feeling . . ." Cherry trails off, searching for the right word. Helen holds her breath. "Bad." Helen exhales. "I just couldn't have you making me feel bad. And I know how that sounds, but . . . it was just too fragile. I couldn't risk it."

"No, I get it. I don't know what I would have said, but"—Helen shakes her head, ashamed of the deluge of options swirling inside her head right now—"none of it would have been helpful. In fact, it probably would have been downright . . ."

"Misery loves company," Cherry says, her voice impossibly soft.

"Yeah."

Helen and Cherry are quiet. The owner of the small restaurant stops by with a new pot of tea. Feeling the tension, she quickly retreats behind the counter and makes a face at her husband as if to say "steer clear."

"I think Bibliophile is the perfect idea. We love a road trip. We love a hotel. And we get to go together. Both as writers," Cherry says, leaning forward.

"Just like at Hayho," Helen says.

"I hope their greenroom is stocked, because they have no idea who's about to come down there and pillage it for all it's worth," Cherry says, throwing her fist in the air.

"I'll make sure to bring my tote," Helen says, looking down at her plate.

"You're going to be okay, Hicks." Cherry looks at her best friend across the table. Her eyes are steely but pleading. She is begging Helen to pull herself out of this spiral.

Helen finally looks up and tries to smile.

"God, I hope you're right," she says honestly.

CHAPTER ELEVEN

Cherry slides into the driver's seat of their rental and excitedly shows off a jewel-toned CD case to Helen as she clicks on her seat belt. For the cover, Cherry has drawn a windy road with a little red car on it. There are two little stick people inside the car—one blond and one with questionable brownish-black hair. In block lettering, Cherry has written "HELEN AND CHERRY GO TO BIBLIOPHILE—2005!" She elaborately creaks open the case and reveals the burned CD that lies within. On the top of the CD, in red permanent marker, Cherry has written "Writerly Mix for a Coupla Writers."

"I know our rental is silver, but I only had black and red pens," Cherry says, sliding the CD into the car's CD player. "Also, I didn't know what color our rental was going to be."

Cherry starts the car up and the first song kicks in. It's the same one that Helen put on Cherry's birthday mix—the song that was playing that last night of Hayho.

"I love this song," Helen says, trying to settle her nerves.

"I thought it only right to kick it off with an old favorite," Cherry says, looking over her shoulder at oncoming traffic.

Cherry finally pulls away from the rental car place and threads her way into San Francisco's rush hour traffic. The weather is cool; summers in San Francisco are always the perfect mix of sunny and slightly cooler temperatures. Helen looked up the weather for Marina del Rey and saw that it was going to be in the mid to high eighties, which is better than some other parts of Los Angeles. In Cherry's hometown of Pasadena, it's going to be pushing a hundred, so Helen is thankful for Bibliophile's proximity to the ocean, with the cool breezes that make the Southern California summer weather bearable.

The conversation on the way down to Marina del Rey is a good one, but there is a carefulness laced through the pauses, along with things lurking in between the lines. Helen notices that Cherry is making sure to balance her excitement about the conference with seeing her family again and just having some time off from the thrift store. She sees her best friend tiptoe around being excited about having sold her book, so Helen bulldozes through by talking about all that Bibliophile has on offer. When did it get so hard to just talk to her best friend?

As the road trip wears on, Helen begins to see these little spikes in Cherry's mood. It's becoming clear that she's looking forward to the large and impressive stage that Bibliophile is offering her to show and prove that she's just as good and important of a writer as everyone else there. Several times Cherry puffs up her chest as she waxes rhapsodic about possibly seeing Mishler again or Tala or Ruth and Karan. A small smirk cracks across her face as she fantasizes about telling Ruth that she's actually just sold a book. At auction. Cherry looks over at Helen and asks if she thinks any of them will be there. Helen just shrugs that she doesn't know. But she hopes not. Because, while Cherry is daydreaming about taking her victory lap, all Helen can think about is facing any of those people again without a book to show for herself after ten years and the Glending Fellowship.

How had she not thought about this before now? What is she going to do if one of them is there? Or, worse yet, anyone from Hayho. She knows Tess is going to be there, something she has yet to tell Cherry. But it never occurred to her that the other members of her workshop might be there as well. And while she tried to keep up with their careers in the beginning, she abandoned that plan after watching Mishler's debut novel become a bestseller just two years after Hayho. That was enough. She didn't want to see a parade of bestsellers while she sat on the sidelines. It pains her to realize that Cherry not having a book either made her feel a little bit better. Misery does love company. But that's not the case anymore.

As Cherry and Helen go over the Grapevine and descend into the thick layer of smog that hangs over Los Angeles County, Cherry's excitement has reached a fever pitch. They switch driving duties at a gas station in Castaic, and Cherry takes to reading the Bibliophile catalog aloud while Helen tries to navigate LA traffic. Using her little red permanent marker, Cherry puts childlike stars next to the panels she's looking forward to seeing, along with the bookstores and other booths she's long wanted to visit.

As they pull into the festival's hotel, Cherry points out the large fountain at the center of the hotel's entrance, marveling as if it's the Trevi Fountain. Hanging out the passenger's side window, Cherry asks and re-asks Helen if she's "ever seen something so beautiful." Helen tries to muster up as much childlike wonder as Cherry but in the end is only able to manage a grunt and a smile in response. Cherry hardly notices. Both young women grab their own bags, declining the hotel staff's request to take them up to their rooms for them, and continue inside to the lobby. They've arrived a day prior to the festival's opening, but the hotel has already placed full advertisements for this year's popular books on standees at the entrance, banners that hang high from the rafters of the lobby, and even posters stuck to the elevator doors.

Writers and attendees buzz around the lobby, all wearing little lanyards around their necks that boast different-colored ribbons stuck to the bottom of their name tags.

"What are the colors for?" Cherry asks, after they've checked in and are waiting for the elevator.

"Um . . . uh, purple means you're a presenter," Helen says, lifting up her name tag, which sports a purple ribbon. Cherry sees a group of women hurry past on their way to the hotel's bar.

"What about green?" Cherry asks, noticing all the women's name tags have a green ribbon.

"That means you're signing at a booth this weekend, so you're a professional writer with published books," Helen says as they step into the elevator and push the number nine for their floor.

"And what does mine stand for?" Cherry asks, holding up her own tag, which has an orange ribbon, the brightest color of all.

"That means you're just attending this year's conference. So you could be a guest like you or an unpublished writer here to learn and come to the panels," Helen says absently.

Cherry drops her name tag, letting it droop around her neck. "I can't wait to come back and have a purple ribbon," she says.

"It's just a dumb ribbon," Helen says, stepping out of the elevator and searching for their room number.

"It's easy to say that when you have the best one," Cherry says. Helen pretends like she didn't hear Cherry, unable to manage whatever ribbon-based existential crisis her best friend is currently having at the moment.

Helen digs her key card out and unlocks the door to their room, pushing it open so Cherry can go in first. Cherry always chooses the bed next to the window, and Helen isn't sure if she does this because that's the bed she prefers or if she's learned over the years that Helen likes to be in the one closest to the room's entrance and bathroom. She likes to think it's the former, but knowing Cherry, it's definitely the latter. Cherry carefully puts her luggage on the hotel's luggage rack and pulls open the curtains, revealing a large balcony with a view of the water just beyond.

Cherry pulls open the large sliding glass doors and steps outside. She throws her arms wide and immediately starts talking to Helen, a conversation that Helen can hear only about every other word of.

"Okey doke, I'm going to go take a look at this greenroom and see what offerings I can pillage for some hotel room snack time," Cherry says, gathering her things to head out.

"Oh, I have to go with you," Helen says, walking out of the bathroom after successfully unpacking her toiletries.

"No, it's okay. You can finish unpacking. I'll grab us—"

"You can't go into the greenroom without me," Helen says, grabbing the room key and her name tag.

"What? Why?" Cherry asks, walking toward the door.

"The greenroom is only for presenters and writers who are signing, so—"

"Not for us orange ribbons, then," Cherry says pointedly.

"It's okay. Let's just both go," Helen says, trying to de-escalate the situation.

"Nah, that's okay," Cherry says, letting the hotel room door slam shut.

"Come on. Are you serious?" Helen asks, weary.

"Ugh, I'm always an orange ribbon," Cherry says.

"You didn't even know what an orange ribbon was until five minutes ago."

"You know what I mean," Cherry says.

"I would much rather have sold a book at auction than have a purple ribbon, I assure you." Helen steps closer to Cherry.

Cherry's shoulders slump. "I don't think I realized how much . . . these places and these people always make me feel like an orange ribbon. I . . . I'm sorry," she says, looking at the floor.

"You know I get it," Helen says.

Cherry's eyes narrow. "Were you ever an orange ribbon?" she asks, purposely.

"No, but—"

"Then—"

"I have to sit around while everyone talks about their book deals and—"

"Feeling like an orange ribbon and being an orange ribbon are two very different things. And I know you think you understand, but because of your education and the Glending? You're a purple ribbon through and through," Cherry says, getting serious.

"Well, I don't feel like a purple ribbon."

"You're welcomed into every exclusive space, free to come and go. They recognize you as one of them." Cherry gestures to the very tangible purple ribbon stuck to the bottom of her name tag.

"Can we just go get snacks now?" Helen asks, eyeing the door.

"Nah, you can go."

"Cherry, please—"

"Let me throw my little tantrum, and I promise I'll try to be better by tonight," Cherry says, whipping off her name tag with the offending orange ribbon and throwing it on her bed.

"Okay," Helen says.

"I promise," Cherry says before walking out onto the balcony and sitting in one of the two deck chairs.

Helen stands in the hotel room, already feeling defeated. She turns to the door but then whips around and strides toward the balcony, swiping Cherry's name tag up as she walks past.

"No," Helen says, standing in front of Cherry and extending her name tag toward her.

"What?"

"We're not starting out like this. You're going to come with me, and that's that," Helen says, dangling the tag closer and closer.

"But—"

"You're not an orange ribbon, Cherry. You just have an orange ribbon on your name tag because no one knows about you and your amazing book yet. That's what this weekend is for. You're here to network, talk up your book, and steal snacks. And that's what we're going to do. Purple ribbons be damned," Helen says, waggling the name tag one inch from Cherry's face.

Cherry grabs it. "Well, well, well," she says, threading the name tag over her head. She looks down in disgust, but then flips the tag around to reveal her name and the bright-orange ribbon.

"Now, come on—these twenty pockets on my cargo pants aren't going to fill themselves up," Helen says, doing a runway-model turn on the balcony.

Helen doesn't mention to Cherry that she may have ulterior motives for this little pep talk, as there is no way she is going to take on that greenroom on her own. And Cherry and her orange ribbon are just the smoke screen Helen needs to take a little bit of the heat off her first steps back into the literary gladiators' arena.

Helen and Cherry walk down the long hotel hallway toward the elevator in silence. Stepping into the already full elevator, Helen uses another key card the presenters got in their welcome folder to access the concierge floor, where the greenroom is located. This garners a side-eye from Cherry. Helen notices the other people in the elevator—all orange ribbons—notice her purple ribbon, and the impressed look on all their faces puffs her up . . . right up until she sees Cherry studying her as the scene unfolds. Cherry flips her own name tag around, her face hardening.

As the elevator climbs to the concierge floor, attendees of the festival get on and off, and every last one of them spies Helen's purple ribbon. But what Cherry doesn't see—and Helen sees with perfect clarity—is that every time someone sees her purple ribbon, they then look at her name and, upon not recognizing it, look away confused and slightly less impressed. That's the thing with purple ribbons: An orange ribbon will just assume the failure to recognize them is their fault, as if it is their lowly station that has kept them out of the know. A philosophy heartily accepted by the purple ribbons of the world.

When they finally reach the concierge floor, Helen and Cherry step out and make their way down the hallway to where they see a pair of double doors. No sign. No nothing. Meaning, for a room that is so widely talked about, you would have to have a purple or green ribbon to even know where it is. Helen and Cherry stop just outside the double doors.

"You ready?" Helen asks.

"No," Cherry says.

Helen and Cherry don't move. Helen's hand is frozen in midair as the key card shakes centimeters from the door lock to the greenroom.

"We can do this," Cherry whispers, not moving.

"Oh, is it not working?" a writer blurts from just behind them. Helen and Cherry jolt out of their stupor.

"It's . . . uh . . ." Helen stutters. Cherry backs away from the door, making room for the writer to step in front of Helen. The writer puts her key card to the door and opens it easily.

"You did it!" Cherry nervously blurts, her fist in the air. Pushing the door open, the writer looks back at Cherry. Her eyes flick down to the orange ribbon, and without another word, she steps into the greenroom.

"It's fine, we're all fine," Helen soothes, following the writer in. Cherry tries to puff herself up, but enters the greenroom more than a little deflated.

They step inside a large suite with a wonderful view of the water. And in between that and where Helen and Cherry are frozen in place, fifteen to twenty writers sit around and talk loudly, a feast of food and drink surrounding them.

"I hate this," Helen whispers to Cherry.

"You were the one who wanted to come," Cherry says.

"Welcome!" A smallish woman in a floral top and sensible pants appears in front of the pair. Her eyes flick to their name tags and Helen watches as she assesses whether Cherry should be allowed in here.

"Helen Hicks," Helen says, extending her hand. "And this is my guest, Cherry Stewart." The woman shakes both women's hands and is just about to say something when Helen cuts her off. "I don't think we've met before?" As Helen distracts the smallish woman with the always tempting offer to talk about herself at length, Cherry continues on into the large suite.

"Cherry Stewart?" a woman's voice calls out. Helen knows that voice. She looks past the smallish woman to see Tala Piñeda standing in all her pink Chanel glory in the middle of the crowded suite.

"Oh my god, Tala!" Cherry says, picking her way through the crowd toward their old Hayho workshop member. The two women hug, and there is squealing and thundering declarations of how they both look just the same and can you believe it's been ten years, no can you believe it's been ten years?! Helen excuses herself from the smallish woman's clutches and the longest non-introduction about how she and Helen actually met before at a small book festival about five years ago, where they'd shared a table. Helen recollected very quickly having spent three hours with not one book purchase and far too long making small talk about the state of the publishing industry and how the woman felt she was cheated out of a bestseller because her publisher made her change her title.

"Oh my god, and Helen Hicks, of course!" Tala says, pulling Helen in for a big hug that she loathes with every fiber of her being.

"Cherry was just telling me about her book deal!" Tala says excitedly. Cherry's face flushes as Helen marvels at how quickly she must have blurted that news; by her accounts, she and Tala had been talking for under a minute before she arrived.

"Isn't it wonderful?" Helen asks.

"So wonderful. And I saw that your short story got into an anthology, Helen. I'm so glad it found a home," Tala says, tiptoeing around both asking and not asking if there's a novel in the works after ten long years.

"It was the same short story I read at Hayho," Helen says, confused as to why she feels the need to specify information everyone in this small trio already knows. She catches Cherry looking over at her.

"Yes, that's . . . why I was so thrilled it found a home. I really liked it," Tala says, treading lightly.

"And what about you? Are you here for . . ." Cherry trails off, trying to change the subject.

"Oh, no, I haven't written in years," Tala says, laughing. Helen and Cherry share a look.

"What?" Helen asks, shocked.

"Then why are you here?" Cherry asks, bluntly. Her eyes flick to Tala's purple ribbon. Helen eyes Cherry, her lips pursing into a straight line as Tess's words ring out in her head, warning her about her best friend going "all Cherry Stewart on them." After this afternoon's ugly business with the ribbons and now this, Helen is seriously questioning whether she made the right decision bringing Cherry.

"I went back to journalism for a time, tried to sell a book or three, but then I got a job at a big tech company that's starting to really invest in various social media platforms. And now I'm the director of artistic partnerships and I love it." Helen and Cherry have no idea what any of these words mean. "I'm going to be presenting this weekend on how to get yourself out there using social media," Tala says, easily switching into pitch mode.

"We don't have social media," Cherry says.

"I don't think I fully know what it is," Helen adds.

"Yet. You don't have social media yet. I'm hoping to change all that," Tala says, resituating the Chanel jacket that's perched on her slim shoulders.

"So you don't write anymore? At all?" Helen asks.

"No, thank god," Tala says, mugging her apologies to the gathered writers. "But I love it for all of you!"

"You don't miss it?" Cherry asks.

"Not at all. In fact, I remember having this breakthrough with my therapist where I finally realized that I actually didn't like writing. And just like Deborah Torres told us, you really have to love it . . . with everything it puts you through." Tala offers a tight-lipped smile as punctuation.

"You were so good, though," Cherry says, still not able to let this go.

"Good, but miserable. And this job fits me so much better. I've never been happier," Tala says, seeming honest. Her perfect facade cracks for the briefest of seconds. Quickly catching herself, Tala looks past Cherry and Helen to where someone has entered the greenroom. "Ooh, before I have to get to work . . ." Tala leans in, and immediately Helen and Cherry know that what they are about to hear is going to be juicy. "Please tell me you heard about Ruth."

"We haven't heard about anyone," Cherry blurts, before Helen can add that she knows just enough about every Hayho alum to keep her awake most nights from seething envy. Tala leans in even farther, and Helen can sense that Cherry is barely able to contain herself at the prospect of being brought in on such an insider secret.

"Her last novel?" Helen and Cherry nod. Tala shifts her tone to a hushed whisper and continues, "Plagiarized."

"What?" Helen yelps, causing several other writers to turn and look at their secretive little trio.

"Shhh," Tala admonishes.

"What?" Cherry repeats, but this time in a whisper.

"Yep. PR nightmare, but in the end her mother pulled some strings and kept it out of the papers and off social media." Tala waves to another person who just walked into the greenroom. "I loved it, of course. And am naturally telling everyone."

"I can't believe it," Cherry says.

"I mean, I can. That Donner Party thing? Come on." Tala laughs.

"It was pretty bad," Helen adds, absently.

"Feel like the only one out of our workshop to get this whole writing thing right is Karan. Wrote that bestseller, and now he's working on the follow-up while teaching at Occidental. Happily married and—"

"How do you know all of this?" Cherry interrupts.

"I'm telling you. Social media, baby. It's the gift that keeps on giving for us big ole snoops." Tala laughs, waving again to another writer who's just entered the greenroom. "Okay, now I really do have to get to work. So good to see you both again." Tala shoots her arm in the air and calls out to the writer that she'll be right over. "Just like old times!" Tala gets about two steps away from Helen and Cherry before turning around. "Oh! Mishler is here, too. He was up here earlier. Looks just the same. Dreamy as ever. Ooh, let's do a Hayho reunion happy hour or something before the weekend is over, 'kay?" She blows them both air kisses before easily falling into conversation with the other writer.

Helen and Cherry stand in the middle of the crowded suite, stunned and quiet.

"Back to the room?" Cherry asks.

"I'll get the snacks and meet you out there," Helen says.

The two women part ways without another word.

The night passes in a haze of sugary treats and gossip. Relieved to have something else to talk about other than purple ribbons and book deals, the best friends laugh and talk into the wee hours, just like old times. It feels good. They haven't been this easy with each other in a while, long before the news of Cherry's book deal, if Helen is being honest. They go to bed late, but as the sun streams in through the curtains the next morning, Helen finds Cherry already up and quietly padding around the hotel room on her way to the bathroom for her shower.

Helen reaches over to their shared nightstand and pulls the clock toward her. It's just barely 7:30, and if she hurries, she can use the coupons the festival gave her to get a free breakfast before the day's events begin. Helen rolls over and sees the Bibliophile catalog open on Cherry's bed, her chosen panels emblazoned with little red stars. Pulling off her covers, Helen sits up in bed and hears Cherry turn on the shower. With the coast clear, Helen takes this opportunity to quickly skim all Cherry's selections. Flicking through the Bibliophile catalog, she notices that Cherry has put little hearts all around Helen's panel.

Smiling to herself, she sits in the early-morning haze for a few quiet moments, unsure of how she feels about the day ahead. As her feet dangle off the side of the bed, she grows more and more excited about her panel. Helen has chosen what she believes is a perfect outfit—she's paired her black moto jacket with a black, vintage, silk chemise she found at Cherry's thrift store. She's got a pair of slightly ripped black jeans and black ballet flats that Tess convinced her were in style. She loves that her panel is on world-building and that the other three writers are either bestsellers, award winners, or legends in the literary world.

Helen stands up, pulls the curtains open the rest of the way, and opens the large sliding glass doors, letting the cool breeze into the stuffy hotel room. She steps out onto the balcony and lets the sun warm her face, trying to soak up every minute of these next few days. Despite what she told Cherry, having that purple ribbon on her name tag means everything to Helen. Knowing that when she sees Mishler again, she'll have the same ribbon as he does makes her feel like she can actually survive the encounter in one piece without retreating back to San Francisco and the secret, dull life that awaits her there. Because for the next few days, Helen actually gets to live the life she's always dreamed of. She's a purple ribbon. She's an expert on world-building. She can go into the greenroom. She's a real writer.

If only for a few days at a hotel in Marina del Rey.

Unlike Cherry, Helen doesn't have a book to tell everyone about. She has an impressive biography populated with notable institutions and distinguished awards that, along with an author photo taken just after Hayho, she has not updated in ten years. But there are a lot of other purple ribbons in the same boat. For people in the higher literary echelons, taking ten years to write a novel is not just accepted, it's celebrated. She's taking her time. She's a Glending Fellow. She's worth the wait. And while Helen may not believe that back in her cubicle in San Francisco, here with this purple ribbon, she feels a swell of possibility that maybe she'll get that spark of an idea that'll become her debut novel. And maybe, just maybe, her story isn't over yet.

Helen hears Cherry come out of the bathroom, her body wrapped tightly in a fluffy white hotel towel. Helen looks over her shoulder and gives Cherry a wave. Cherry waves back, grabs the little pile of folded clothes she set out last night, and retreats into the bathroom. Cherry's never felt comfortable changing in front of Helen. A fact about her best friend Helen has never quite understood, given her freewheeling inclinations. Once Cherry comes out of the bathroom, she joins Helen on the balcony.

"You ready to con some people out of a free breakfast?" Helen jokes, preparing Cherry for the battle to get two free breakfasts for the price of just one purple ribbon. Cherry plops down in the deck chair next to Helen, a towel wrapped around her shoulders to protect her shirt from her long, wet hair.

"Actually, I think I'm going to splurge a bit," Cherry says, not looking at Helen.

"Splurge how?"

"I know I'm not going to see any of this book money for a while."

"Contracts alone take three or four months," Helen warns. Cherry nods.

"But I have a credit card, and now that I know I can pay it off, why not buy us both a fancy hotel breakfast?" Cherry says, unable to keep herself from smiling.

"Uh . . . yeah, that sounds fun," Helen says, realizing that this means she is going to have to eat breakfast alone.

"My treat, if you want to join me," Cherry offers again.

"Oh, no. That's okay. Presenters get a complimentary breakfast, so I can just do that," Helen says. Cherry gives a quick, curt nod and stands. Before Helen can ask—

"Well, the offer is there if you want it. And I think I'm going to head out early, because there's an orientation meeting for first-time attendees. So I thought, why not lean into my orange ribbon–ness a little," Cherry says.

"That's a good idea. Those things are always great for . . ." Helen trails off, knowing that whatever word she chooses might flare Cherry's insecurity about her orange ribbon.

"And then I'll be at your panel, and after that we can figure out what lunch is going to be," Cherry says, now looming over Helen. Helen puts her hand over her eyes so she can look up at Cherry without burning her ocular cavities from the early-morning summer sun. "Unless you want to do the presenter thing again?"

"Right, well . . . we'll see, okay?" Helen says, not knowing quite why she's being weird about it.

"All right, man. Well, I'll see you at your panel. And if I don't see you before then, good luck!" Cherry says, her voice forced and bright.

"Thanks," Helen says, her voice flatter than she means it to be.

Cherry hovers for the briefest of moments and then finally continues on inside the hotel room. Helen can hear the heavy hotel door slam seconds later and immediately feels bad for turning down Cherry's invitation to breakfast. Truth is, Helen's relieved. Not having to sneak Cherry into the complimentary presenter breakfast after seeing how touchy she got about the whole greenroom thing last night eases Helen's mind during the hours before her panel. What Helen can't understand is that Cherry knew she was a guest at this festival. Helen thought it would be self-explanatory that she'd need to rely on Helen's access to get the perks of the festival reserved for those working the festival, not attending it. It really is a simple equation. Or . . . was a simple equation. Helen thinks that were this the Cherry of a year ago, she'd be happy to sneak into these exclusive spaces and be thankful for the opportunity. Hell, the Cherry of a year ago would have thought that it'd be fun. But now it feels as though Cherry is adamant about seeing every situation as an offense of some kind, rather than just using the next few days to learn from the professionals and network with other writers.

Shaking her head in frustration, Helen finally gets up from the balcony deck chair and begins her day, monologuing about Cherry's annoying bullishness throughout. As she steps out of the shower, she's midsentence arguing with an invisible Cherry about how she is ruining this entire festival and how Tess was right and Helen should have just come down here by herself. As she blow-dries her hair, she's moved on to chronicling each thing Cherry has been ungrateful for, and as she gets dressed, she becomes angrier and angrier as she looks at the candy wrappers from last night that are stacked high in the tiny trash can provided by the hotel.

"Oh, did you not like the free candy I got you? Were the free beers not to your liking?" Helen snipes, pulling on her jeans.

As Helen sits down at the desk, her makeup for the day laid out in front of her, she begins to feel this nagging pull to answer why she's being so strident in her takedown of someone who mere days ago she told they were the most important person in the world to her. Steadying her hand to apply today's winged eyeliner, she feels both good and bad about her endless inner dialogue. Good because it's allowed her to not think about her panel. But bad because none of what she's saying is in any way generous toward her best friend. Cleaving her own purple ribbon to her chest, Helen now fully understands Cherry's sour attitude toward her orange ribbon. Helen would die if she had to wear one. Well, she wouldn't wear it. She wouldn't even come to this festival if not for being promised a purple ribbon.

And as Helen finishes off her look with a nice red lip, she hates that the truth is, she turned down Cherry's breakfast invitation because she wants to walk by the queue of people waiting to get into the panels and signings as they watch her and her purple ribbon effortlessly swan into a room in which they're not allowed. Because while Helen knows the disappointing reality of her life right now, none of the orange ribbons do. And for just a few days, Helen wants to feel that glow of being someone worthy of envious jealousy.

Even if it's a lie.

Helen is painfully aware that Cherry knows all this. She hovered and paused and gave Helen every opportunity to snap out of this violent pendulum swing of a personality of hers and just come eat a fancy breakfast with her best friend. But that's the endless tragedy of being Helen Hicks: She's only able to figure herself out in hindsight. When it's happening, no one in the world is more certain that she's right. That's why she couldn't pull up from her current nosedive and instead just flatly said thanks when Cherry wished her good luck.

"I honestly don't know why anyone is friends with me," Helen mutters to herself as she packs away her makeup, putting it neatly back into its bag. As she puts on her black moto jacket, Helen vows to go to lunch with Cherry wherever she wants. It'll be lovely to debrief after the panel anyway. Helen threads her festival lanyard over her head and lets the majestic purple ribbon proudly loll around her neck. She checks herself out in the mirror, fidgeting with her hair and makeup. After finally smoothing down her name tag and pocketing her room key, she heads out of the safety of their hotel room, her Hayho tote firmly on her shoulder.

The stark difference between the festival hotel yesterday and today is immediately apparent. Helen is joined by a pack of attendees also waiting for the elevator. It takes a good five minutes for one to make it all the way to the ninth floor. And when the elevator does arrive, there are so many people already packed into it that Helen must squish herself in right next to the panel of floor numbers, where she's pinned behind a young man with a huge backpack. Once they get to ground level, everyone pours out of the elevator and into the teeming main lobby.

Festival volunteers run and speed around, while packs of attendees gather around their festival catalogs like cavemen warming themselves by a roaring fire. Helen weaves her way through the crowds, not making eye contact with anyone while at the same time noticing everyone noticing her. She hates how high her chin is jutted out and can hear Cherry making fun of her snooty nose in the air. And she'd be right.

But it feels so good.

Helen can't remember the last time she's felt this good. Her stride smooths as she heads toward the room where the complimentary presenter breakfast is being served. She turns the corner down a long hallway and passes a giant queue for the main signing area. She sees people standing in line, carrying overloaded tote bags and rolling grocery carts filled to the brim with well-loved books. Excited and looking forward to meeting their literary heroes. And every one of those people watches as Helen steps past the sign that says Private Event and into a room where she will eat free eggs and bacon with those same literary heroes . . . without having to stand in line.

Helen pulls the door open and is met with a generic gray room. Gray carpet, gray walls, and around twenty gray tables scattered around inside. The lighting is flat and coats the twenty or so writers huddled over their free breakfasts in a sallow fluorescent hue. The fact that Helen said no to a fancy breakfast with her best friend to eat in one of the most depressing rooms in Southern California feels like punishment enough for her early-morning arrogance.

Along the wall are several silver chafing dishes, all with little handwritten signs in front of them telling people what breakfast food awaits them under the roll-top lids. Helen scans the room while trying to look like she isn't scanning the room and is met with every introvert's worst nightmare: a bunch of strangers sitting together and a smattering of empty seats that promise awkward banter and treacherous small talk. With a sigh, Helen makes her way to the buffet and serves herself a plate, stopping to pour an Earl Grey tea into a much-too-small cup. Her hands now full, Helen turns from the buffet and faces the tables. Thankfully, as she was serving herself, Tala sat down at the farthest table on the right-hand wall and is currently holding court. Helen decides she'll start there.

But as Helen is walking over to the table, Tala stands, says her goodbyes, and hurries out of the room, leaving Helen stranded and standing over four writers she's never met before and a plate full of scrambled eggs and bacon.

"Please, have a seat. We were just leaving," a gray-haired man says in a tweed suit in the height of summer. The three other writers clear their plates, gather their things, and all stream out of the room together, leaving Helen absolutely alone. She doesn't want to confirm her suspicions, so she sits down at the table with her back to the rest of the room, ignorant as to whether she is, indeed, the only writer sitting all by herself. That's the thing about purple ribbons—it's every woman for herself. Helen should know.

Helen eats her breakfast in silence, sipping her tea and acting like she couldn't be more contented. But as she clears her plate, she sees that her hands are shaking. And she already feels like she needs to race back up to her hotel room for a nice private cry while also trying not to throw up. But she can't do either of those things because her panel on world-building starts in fifteen minutes.

After busing her dishes, she grabs her Hayho tote and walks out of the complimentary presenter breakfast and back into the bustling hotel, where she is met, once again, by the line of people waiting to get their beloved books signed. And once again, they all notice her. And once again, Helen puffs up and feels a little bit better about herself. Enough so that she is able to walk all the way to the room where her panel is without taking a detour to have a little freak-out beforehand.

The crowds of attendees just outside the string of panel rooms are buzzing even more than those in the lobby. Helen is exhilarated knowing that some of these people have put their own little red stars next to her panel, and for the next fifty minutes, Helen gets to be an expert. She gets to sit in the front of the room with her name proudly in front of her. She gets to be introduced along with the other panelists and humbly nod along as her impressive biography is read as if she didn't write it herself. She gets to speak into a microphone and say smart things about writing that the attendees will jot down as they try to grasp the writerly concepts she's attempting to make accessible for every level of writer. Now very aware of herself, Helen tries to move through the crowd as unpretentiously as possible, imagining conversations between attendees about how down to earth Helen Hicks was when they saw her in real life.

Helen scans the crowd for Cherry but doesn't see her, so she continues on to the predetermined panel room on her own. She turns the corner to see a large crowd waiting just outside and wades in with a slightly more imperious air than she means to. But what she can't explain to those attendees, who are now backing away from her as she questions the volunteer guarding the locked door about whether she can enter, is that coming off as imperious tends to be an inconvenient side effect of her debilitating insecurity. And that it somehow manages to go hand in hand with an arrogance that resides deep in the marrow of her bones and bloodline.

"The room isn't open yet," an orange ribbon says to Helen as she steamrolls to the front of the crowd.

"I'm a presenter. I'm on the panel," Helen says, lifting her purple-ribboned name tag as proof.

"Yeah, the room's not open yet," the volunteer repeats, sharing a look with the attendee who said the same thing to Helen seconds before.

"So sorry, I'm s—" The door to the panel room swings open, giving Helen a blessed reprieve from having to wade back into the crowd now branded the entitled woman who didn't want to wait along with the unwashed orange-ribboned masses.

Sadly, Helen can't argue that they would be completely off in this assessment.

"Now you can go in," the volunteer makes a point to say to Helen as the crowd streams into the room.

"Yes, thank you. I'm so sorry about—" The volunteer walks into the room without letting Helen absolve herself.

Helen tells herself that only a few people heard the interaction at the door and that if she could just explain that she wanted to go in early because she's nervous and awkward and . . . ugh, maybe she also kinda wanted to feel important. Helen lets out a long, annoyed sigh at the steep, public learning curve this festival is fast becoming for her deepest-held inadequacies. Can she really not have one moment at this festival that is for everyone, or must she continue to flaunt her purple ribbon until it's just her and it exchanging vows in the depressing gray room where she insisted on eating this morning's complimentary breakfast all by herself? How much longer is she going to make this entire festival all about trying to show everyone how celebrated and famous she is? Does she plan on cutting the line at the hotel's coffee kiosk, barking at the hapless hotel worker who works there, "Do you even know who I am?"

Even Helen is distinctly aware that she's only acting this way because the answer to that question would be a resounding no. No one knows who she is, except that now, a lucky few know her as the nobody snob who demanded entrance to the panel room before everyone else, including the three other writers on the panel, who just patiently waited with the attendees like normal people.

Helen quickly makes her way to the front of the room and is reminded of a story that Leni told at a party once about when she was a personal shopper for some high-end department store that was regularly frequented by Hollywood's A-list. With a martini sloshing around in one hand, Leni went through every famous person who was either "super nice" or "way cute" or "shorter in person." But when pressed to gossip about those who had behaved badly, Leni simply said that it was consistently the people who had just barely cracked into the very bottom echelon of Hollywood's pecking order.

"Because who else would need to flex in front of a lowly shopgirl," Leni said, with a genteel sip of her cocktail.

Leni's words haunt Helen now as she settles in at the table at the front of the room behind a large, folded card with her name printed on it. She retrieves the notebook she bought for just this occasion out of her Hayho tote bag, along with her fountain pen, and tries to steady herself. The three other writers join Helen and everyone introduces themselves, shaking hands and greeting one another warmly.

After a few minutes, the festival volunteer from the Door Incident comes up to the table and runs through the schedule for today's panel, making sure to check in with the one writer who will be the panel's moderator, settling her in behind the podium just to the left of the main table. As the crowd settles, Helen looks up from her notebook to see if Cherry has arrived. She's usually easy enough to spot, but as the festival volunteer gives the panel the two-minute warning, Cherry is nowhere to be found. Helen would understand if she decided not to come, but still can't believe she would do such a thing. After all, she told her this morning she'd be here. Maybe Helen just doesn't want to face how weird she's been, and that Cherry has every right to hold her accountable for how she's been acting about the damn purple ribbons.

But Helen was hoping those consequences would happen back in San Francisco after the festival is over. Helen can only laugh. Yes, Cherry should schedule her consequences for when they're most convenient for Helen. Come on.

"Everybody ready?" the moderator says, covering up the now-live microphone.

"Yes," the writers on the panel say in unison. The moderator nods and smooths out her pages of notes. She pulls the microphone down to better fit with her height, and Helen can feel her entire body buzzing with excitement.

"Hello and welcome to Bibliophile. We are so grateful that you chose our little panel as your first foray into what is going to be an incredible weekend of reading, writing, and all things literary. So let me get to introducing the esteemed writers who will hopefully give you more than a little something to think about when it comes to world-building," the moderator says, flipping the pages of her notes to where the authors' biographies are.

Helen pushes her shoulders back and tries to arrange her face so that it looks pensive, yet approachable. She nods along as the first writer is introduced, and just as the moderator is going to begin introducing Helen, the door to the room swings open, and Cherry walks in . . . with Dan Mishler.

CHAPTER TWELVE

Cherry gives Helen a truly embarrassingly large wave and then gestures over at Mishler with a broad, cringey smile, as if to say, *Get a load of this!* Helen responds in kind just as the moderator finishes introducing her. But upon seeing Cherry and Mishler, Helen's mind gets very noisy. It's as if someone's just opened a double-paned window, and now all the traffic noise, sirens, and sounds of the city are barreling in. The short-lived relief at Cherry clearly not being mad at her is quickly replaced with the narratives she's building about how chummy they seem and how excited Cherry must have been to tell him about her book deal and how heartbreaking it will be to hear how kind Cherry was in telling Mishler that Helen still has no debut novel. Tightening her grip on her pen, Helen forces herself to jolt back to the panel and the task at hand. But as Cherry and Mishler settle into the room's very back row, Helen can't stop building scene after scene of the possibilities about how the last hour went between the two.

"Once again, I want to thank everyone for choosing our panel this morning. I know how stacked this year's festival schedule is, and we're grateful that you've decided to put your faith in us . . . for at least the next fifty minutes," the moderator says to a smattering of laughter.

The brief moment of levity breaks through Helen's noisy brain and releases just enough nervous energy to allow her to focus while the moderator asks her first question of the panel. And once her brain has something actually tangible to think about, Helen is quickly swept away in the magic of the panel. With every question, she thrives. Her banter with the other writers is easy, while her answers regarding the craft of writing are clear, relatable, and broken down in a way that would help even a brand-new writer understand how best to proceed when attempting to build a vibrant and believable world for their story.

Helen Hicks is good at this. And it's been a long time since she felt that swell of pride at being good at anything. Maybe that's why she clings to writing as desperately as she does. It's the only place where she is actually able to quiet her brain long enough to become the version of herself she's always longed to be. The version of herself she actually likes.

As the panel begins to wind down, it's clear that Helen is not alone in thinking that she's done well. Every question from the audience is either for her or about something she said. As the minutes tick down, it's clear that she's the one everyone felt was the most able to synthesize the black box that is writing into something that felt, even for a little bit, possible.

As the moderator closes out the panel and thanks everyone for coming, Helen is mobbed by panel attendees with compliments, gratitude, and follow-up questions. The other writers have a few people wanting to snag a signature for a book without having to wait in one of the long signing lines, but no one has the pileup that Helen does. But along with the accolades and attention come the questions: Does she have something she's written that they can read? She tells them about the short-story anthology and then can't help but lie about how she's still working on her debut novel, but it's going slowly. Fingers crossed, she says, that it'll be finished in the next year. They nod along and tell her that they'll look out for it. Their earnestness breaks her heart.

As the next panel's writers start to mill around the front table, the festival's volunteer begins to herd Helen and the other writers toward the breezeway just outside the panel room. Helen quickly gathers her things and notices Cherry and Mishler standing in the back of the room, waiting for her. Helen gives them a little wave and tries to gesticulate that they can head out into the breezeway and wait for her there. Of course, they don't understand her wild hand and arm motions. No one would. Which is how Helen Hicks finds herself awkwardly hugging Dan Mishler in the back of a conference room in a random hotel in Marina del Rey in front of fifty or so onlookers.

"It's so good to see you," Helen says, untangling herself from the hug as quickly as she can. She never knows how long or how hard she should hug someone, so she usually defers to not that long and not that hard. Helen avoids dissecting how truly subpar her hugs are because the only way to get better would be to do them badly and learn from those occasions. But the prospect of going on some vision quest to be a better hugger is not something Helen could ever do, so she's come to terms with the idea that, in this life, she will simply be known to all as a bad hugger.

"You have anything going on right now? We can grab a seat in the hotel café and catch up," Mishler says as the trio is shooed out of the panel room. Helen marvels at how he looks even more comfortable in his skin now than he did ten years ago. While she's been slowly unraveling, Mishler has apparently been thriving.

"I just had this panel, so that works with me." The trio winds their way through the crowds buzzing from one panel to the next toward the hotel café just off the main lobby.

"You did so good on the panel," Cherry says, as they wait for the hostess to seat them.

"Oh, thanks, it was really fun," Helen says, trying to downplay how much the panel meant to her. Feeling that peace settle over her as her mind got to focus solely on writing. Fifty whole minutes where there was no other noise, as if a distant car alarm that had been going off for years was finally silenced. She didn't second-guess anything she said and felt as though she belonged up there. She hasn't felt that in years.

Cherry tells the hostess that it will be three, and she motions for them to follow her. They're seated at a small table in the center of the café among packs of other writers decompressing after a panel, agent meetings, and the random tourist who has no idea what Bibliophile is.

"You should be a professor," Mishler says offhandedly, as he picks up his menu and searches for what he's going to order.

"A professor?" Helen asks, unable to hide her disdain. Cherry looks over at her.

"Yeah, you're really good at breaking things down," Mishler says.

"Well, thankfully I'm not on the lookout for a whole new profession, as I'm currently a writer of books, so . . ." Helen says, smiling tightly at the waitress as she sets down three glasses of water. Helen knows it's a compliment. She knows he's just being nice, but something about Dan Mishler makes even his compliments sound condescending.

"I really loved what you said about making sure to understand the cost of an idyllic setting. How not everyone in that world would have the same circumstances, so . . . you know . . . how would that . . . play out . . . story-wise . . ." Cherry trails off, speaking faster than her brain can keep up with in an effort to save Helen's quickly deteriorating mood after Mishler suggested Helen follow in her parents' footsteps and become a professor after having inevitably failed at the whole writing thing.

"Tala said that Karan's a professor over at Occidental and . . . hell, I was even looking into doing it when I wasn't sure my first novel was going to sell," Mishler says.

"Even you, huh?" Helen asks, sitting back in her chair and crossing her arms.

"Yeah, but I don't think I'd be as good at it as you or Karan, so lucky for me the book sold when it did," Mishler says, laughing.

"Lucky for you," Helen repeats, her eyes narrowing.

"What are we thinking? Tea? Fries for the table? Oysters Rockefeller?" Cherry blurts.

"It's not even 11:00 a.m.," Mishler says, checking his watch.

"We could do a Bloody Mary? Mimosa? Hard-boiled—"

"So, how did you two . . ." Helen trails off, waving her finger around.

"Eggs," Cherry finishes.

"There I was having breakfast with my film agent, and in walks Cherry. Turns out he's also Cherry's film agent," Mishler says. Cherry's face turns bright red.

"Wow, small world," Helen says, the distant car alarm sounding once more.

"I'd never met her in person, just email," Cherry adds. Helen musters up a smile for Cherry, but just for Cherry. When she turns to Mishler, her face is a stoic mask.

"So we all had breakfast together, and the best part about it? She paid," Mishler says.

"She paid," Helen says, allowing a brutally small, fake laugh.

"Do we know what we'll be getting yet?" the waitress asks, appearing next to Cherry.

"Not quite yet, if that's okay," Cherry says. From the looks of the overly stressed waitress, it is not okay.

"We'll do our homework, we promise. Give us two minutes," Cherry says. The waitress gives her a curt nod and leaves.

"And what did your film agent want to meet with you about?" Helen asks.

"Oh, I think she was just being polite taking a meeting with me, because I'm not sure how commercial my book is. Cherry's, on the other hand—"

"She invited us to a little dinner they're having for all their clients tomorrow night. I was going to tell you about it," Cherry cuts in.

"A little dinner," Helen repeats.

"Maybe we should think about what we want to order so the waitress doesn't get mad at us," Cherry says.

"I don't think there's ever a bad time for fries," Helen starts, trying to snap herself out of whatever existential spiral she is caught in.

"Ooh, I like that. Okay, I say we do some fries for the table and maybe some drinks. You're right that it's too early for oysters Rockefeller," Cherry says, elaborately putting the menu down and looking around for the waitress.

"It's never too early for oysters Rockefeller," Mishler says, perfectly contented.

Helen hates how easy they are with each other. Now bonded over film agents, little dinners, and free breakfasts in a world where they've both sold a book and are now fielding offers and negotiating contracts. And then there's Helen . . . someone who would make a great professor.

Something particularly animalistic happens to a person who believes they're being left behind. The sensation floods their body, overriding logic, knowledge, and any possible nuance or gray area. It's especially acute for those who've tried everything within their power to remain in the group but fear that their abandonment is all but inevitable. Helen listens to Cherry blurting out an elaborate order that is definitely too much food, and she feels herself becoming more and more desperate as she tries to think of a way to claw her way back onto a train that she fears has all but left the station.

Imagining these scenarios is something Helen likes to do instead of writing. Some days it's a train leaving the station; other days she's stuck on the top of a mountain and can't find a way down. She's also fabricated whole worlds where Mishler or Tess or Cherry is doing a reading and she's at the door and some bouncer won't let her in even though she keeps telling him, "But I'm a friend . . . I'm a friend . . . and I'm a writer, too!" The bouncer always has a comically New York accent, wears a skintight black T-shirt, but also somehow possesses a collegiate level of understanding of the literary hierarchy, immediately wary that she's no writer *he's* ever heard of.

While that scenario is a particular favorite, she does like to mix up the ways she tortures herself. Some days, she imagines she's actually finished writing a book and asks her "friends" for referrals to their agents. Naturally, they roundly reject her in a gallows-type scene reminiscent of the popular public hangings of the Tudor era. Left to fend for herself, she's forced to sign with an agent who she builds as a cartoonishly disheveled character whose office is located in a strip mall just next to a doughnut place that she's told "is really good." Needless to say, this agent is unable to sell her book, and when all hope is lost, she gives Helen an old coupon to the doughnut place and tells her that the next one is "on me." The big act 3 denouement is a very simple vignette of Helen sitting on a curb just outside the strip mall eating a bear claw and wiping the grease off her mouth with a page from her novel.

When not creating scenarios of public ridicule, Helen likes to do elaborate mathematical equations of just how long it will take her to break back into publishing. Even if she started right now, it'd still be years before she caught up with Cherry, Mishler, and Tess. And that's only if the book she wrote was good enough to get her an agent and sell, let alone sell at auction and become a bestseller.

In the dark of the night, she works out just how many words a day she'd need to write in order to finish a book in a year. She then works out how early she'd have to get up in the morning to use the computer at her office so she could write those words, finally allowing herself to fall asleep only after she promises that she'll start on Monday. And when the alarm goes off Monday morning, she presses "Snooze," telling herself that she'll write double the words tomorrow because she was up late—and on and on, until she goes back to the safety of arguing with an imaginary bouncer outside Cherry's exclusive reading about how she's a writer, too.

She's a writer, too.

As the waitress delivers plate after plate of food to the table, Helen looks around at all the attendees excited to be in a place where they, too, can feel like real writers. She sees the furtive glances at Mishler and becomes keenly aware that any number of orange ribbons would kill to be where she is right now: a purple ribbon who's a Glending Fellow with a short story in a prestigious anthology who gets to sit on panels next to literary legends and eat oysters Rockefeller with bestsellers. So maybe it's not that Helen has missed the train altogether, but that she's just stuck back in economy, rather than living it up in first class with the rest of her friends. And economy wouldn't be so painful if she remained ignorant of how fulfilled and happy those in first class are.

In a moment of tragic synchronicity, Helen tunes back in to Cherry and Mishler's conversation just in time to hear them talking about deadlines and future plans. She gets this image in her head of standing up from her cramped economy seat, walking up the wobbly train aisle to grab a single oyster Rockefeller from first class, and dramatically whipping the curtain between first class and economy closed as the other orange ribbons applaud her revolutionary spirit. Unfortunately for Helen, there is no such curtain, and she must continue to have a front-row seat to the blistering successes of her former literary cohort.

But, of course, Helen knows that she has no one to blame for her being where she is but herself. She has no one to blame for her being left behind but herself. In fact, she's the one who keeps setting off the car alarm, no one else. This is the deepest cut of all. She knows exactly who's to blame. And as much as she likes to spend the time she should be writing creating elaborate narratives for all the ways in which she has been wronged, Helen was actually given a first-class ticket ten years ago and she squandered it. And rest assured, when she was up in first class, she didn't feel guilty at all for popping oyster Rockefeller after oyster Rockefeller as the orange ribbons looked on, mouths watering.

"So, what's the rest of your day look like?" Mishler asks, dipping a handful of fries into ketchup. Cherry and Helen look at one another and instantly know their plans for the rest of the day are different. Once that is wordlessly established, they both defer to the other one as to who's going to answer Mishler first. "I didn't know this was going to be such a controversial question." He laughs. This enrages Helen, mostly because she can't cut in with some impressive plan that was worth the wait and would also—fingers crossed—make him feel just a little dumb.

"There are panels all day that I want to go to and then the keynote," Cherry says.

"Oh, so you're actually *going* going to the festival," Mishler says, wiping the salt off his fingers.

"Yeah, I . . . uh . . . yeah," Cherry answers, confused.

"Writers don't tend to actually go to the panels, is all," Mishler says, picking up on Cherry's confusion.

"That doesn't make any sense. Isn't this a festival for writers?" Cherry asks.

"Right. No, sorry . . . published writers don't tend to go to the panels, I mean," Mishler clarifies.

"So, you're all done learning about writing, then?" Cherry asks. Helen can't help but smile as the color drains from Mishler's face.

"You've got me there," he says, his hands up in surrender.

"Like, why else are you here?" Cherry asks, her LA accent adding a truly advanced level of contempt.

Mishler laughs. "No, you're right. You're right."

"Maybe you should take a look at the panel with all the awesome romance writers. I loved your debut, but dear lord, that main relationship," Cherry says, pushing the festival's catalog toward Mishler. Helen barks out a laugh as Mishler sheepishly pulls the catalog in front of him. Every once in a while, Helen absolutely adores when her best friend goes "all Cherry Stewart" on people.

"Thanks for that," Mishler mumbles, clearing his throat. Helen and Cherry share a sneaky smile at his expense.

"Tess is flying in today, so I'm probably going to see what she's up to," Helen says, momentarily forgetting that Tess also being at Bibliophile is something she has yet to tell her best friend. Cherry looks over at Helen and there is a definite moment where even Mishler can sense this is news to her. And not the good kind.

"It seems I'm not the only one who thinks they're done learning about writing," Mishler says, flipping through the festival's catalog.

"Well, according to you I should be a professor, so . . ." Helen says to Mishler, her face coloring as Cherry pushes away her plate of french fries.

"I didn't know . . . you didn't tell me she was going to be here," Cherry says, clearly hurt.

"Yeah, I'm so sorry, I . . . she . . ." Helen wants to lie. She wants to say that Tess just told her she was coming, but how would she do that—telepathy? Gulping down her chronic failures, Helen soldiers on, "I don't get to see her that often and I knew you were going to be at panels all day, so . . ."

"I thought *we* were going to be at panels all day," Cherry pushes back.

"I'd better get going," Mishler says, setting a twenty-dollar bill on the table for his share of the bill.

"Oh, right. Okay," Helen says as he stands, smoothing out his pants and checking his pockets for his cell phone.

"Hey, I guess I'll see you at that romance panel later," Mishler says to Cherry, handing her back the festival catalog.

"Yeah, okay," Cherry says, distractedly taking it from him. He stands over them for a brief moment and then gives the seething pair a little nod before disappearing into the crowded hotel café.

"I'm so sorry, I—" Helen starts, ready to fall on her sword.

"No, it's okay. I get why the panels would be boring for you," Cherry says, looking around for the waitress.

"I should have told you," Helen says, feeling bad.

"Yeah, well, there's a lot of that going around these days," Cherry says, gesturing to the waitress that she'd like the check.

"We can meet up in the greenroom later, if you want? I can introduce you around?" Helen asks, as the waitress drops the check. Cherry hands her a credit card before she hurries away.

"We can play it by ear, okay?" Cherry asks.

"Oh, sure. Sure. And thank you for the . . ." Helen scans the ridiculous spectrum of items Cherry ordered littering the table. She laughs. "Whatever this was," she says, trying to lighten the mood.

Cherry nods and begins gathering her items, tucking away her catalog in her festival tote. "Best meal of your life?" Helen laughs. Cherry continues, "Shall we dance?" Helen has always loved how Cherry says this. It's so positively corny that Cherry is one of the only people who can truly pull it off. Helen hasn't heard it in a long time. It feels nice.

"We shall," Helen says, feeling a bit better.

"Okey doke, I want to get up to my next panel so I can get a good seat."

"In the back row, right?" Helen asks, knowing her best friend well.

"Naaaaaaaturally," Cherry says, herding Helen into a rogue barstool.

"I'll give you a call later and let you know when we're properly ensconced in the greenroom and firmly surrounded by free snacks," Helen says as they wind their way through the packed hotel café.

"Sounds good," Cherry says.

Helen and Cherry stand just outside the hotel café and say their goodbyes. Cherry quickly disappears into the throng of writers on their way to the spate of panels being offered in the next session. And Helen heads back to the hotel room to recharge after the panel, maybe take a little nap, and wait for Tess to arrive.

As the hotel room door shuts behind her, she immediately relaxes. Housekeeping has been here, and the calm of the newly cleaned hotel room allows her to take her first full breath of the day. She's exhausted from constantly trying to drown out the noise of the festival, along with the noise inside her own head. Helen flops down on the newly made queen-size bed, her arms wide open. And it's in that position that Helen Hicks falls fast asleep for the next several hours, awakened only by the ringing of her cell phone well into the late afternoon.

"Hello?" Helen answers, her voice cracking and rough.

"Hey! I'm here and ready to start drinking," Tess says. Helen jolts up and looks at the time.

"Jesus, I must have fallen asleep," she says, running a hand through her tousle of bed head.

"Where you at?" Tess asks.

"Well, I said I fell asleep, so using your great powers of deduction . . ."

Tess laughs.

"Can I blame jet lag?"

"It's a one-hour flight, so . . ."

"You wanna meet in the greenroom?"

"Ooh, yes. Give me thirty minutes to put myself together."

"Done and done," Tess says.

They sign off and Helen looks at her phone. No missed calls from Cherry. She smiles, knowing she must be having fun at the panels, just as Helen hoped she would. Still smiling, Helen sets her cell phone on their shared nightstand and jumps in the shower, trying to wake up and reset for the night ahead with Tess. The shower feels so good that she finds herself lingering under the best water pressure she's felt in ages. The shower in the apartment she shares with Cherry is often no more than a well-meaning dribble. She finds a more casual outfit, but still tries to craft a certain literary persona that feels good to step into once again. She adds a nice pink gloss and a hint of a winged eyeliner; grabs her black moto jacket, her purple-ribboned name tag, and her hotel key; and steps back out into the madness of the hotel.

Pressing the button for the elevator, Helen is joined by a pack of orange ribbons.

"We loved your panel," one of the orange ribbons says, her voice shaking.

"Oh, thank you," Helen says, her voice velvety smooth.

"We talked about it all throughout lunch," another orange ribbon says.

"So far, it's our favorite," another says.

"Oh, wow. In this crowd, that's high praise. I'm so flattered," Helen says, bringing a single hand to her heart in reverence.

The elevator dings open, and once again, it's already packed full of people. The group squeezes in and Helen is shoved into the front right corner next to the panel of elevator buttons. She presses the button for the concierge floor and the greenroom that awaits her.

"Lobby, please," an orange ribbon offhandedly commands Helen. Helen looks over at the orange ribbon as the elevator continues up, not liking her tone one bit.

"It's . . ."

"What did you do?" the orange ribbon blurts. The entire elevator goes quiet, tense, and uncomfortable.

"I'm sorry?" Helen asks, truly shocked.

"I said lobby," the orange ribbon presses.

"The elevator was already going up?" Helen inflects her voice up in a desperate attempt to de-escalate the situation. She becomes more and more aware at how intensely the entire elevator is watching this exchange, while her name tag and purple ribbon give her zero opportunity to remain anonymous.

"Because you pressed the wrong button," the orange ribbon argues. The door dings open on a floor that is not Helen's floor.

"Excuse us," says a tiny voice from the back of the elevator. Everyone turns, shifts, and moves as two red-faced orange ribbons exit on their floor.

The door closes and the elevator continues up. Helen turns and looks at the offending orange ribbon who dared to come at her about willing an elevator to bend to her selfish desires. She is not the only one. The guilty orange ribbon looks down at the floor and offers no apology. It takes everything Helen has not to say something, or even just inquire why no one else said anything as she was being lambasted for something truly ridiculous. The elevator stops on another floor, and even though everyone in the elevator knows she wanted to go to the lobby, the offending orange ribbon bolts out along with the trio of writers whose floor this actually was.

Now that there are only a handful of people left in the elevator, Helen sees another purple ribbon on the other side of the elevator. They make very pointed eye contact as the elevator climbs to the concierge floor, and when the door finally opens, they both step out together.

"You handled that so well," the other purple ribbon says to Helen just as the door closes.

"I couldn't even believe what was happening, you know? Like, how do you think elevators work, ma'am?" Helen asks, her voice loud and angry. It feels good to finally let it out.

"And those two baby writers just let you take the heat," the purple ribbon says as they walk down the hall.

"Right? And I knew I couldn't say anything! God forbid," Helen says, using her key card to gain access to the greenroom.

"No, you couldn't. You handled it perfectly. I can hear the rumors now if you'd said anything, even though you had every right," the purple ribbon says, stepping inside the greenroom.

"Ooh, what rumor?" Tala yells across the crowded room. The entire room turns to hear about this rumor.

"This wannabe lost her mind because she thought she made the elevator go up and not down to the lobby like she commanded," the purple ribbon says.

"It was so weird!" Helen adds, seeing Tess just next to the open bar. They wave to one another as the entire room rallies around Helen. God, it feels good.

"In front of everyone?" another purple ribbon asks.

"Yes!" the purple ribbon answers.

"The audacity!" another purple ribbon says.

"Well, you're safe now," the purple ribbon says as Tess settles in next to Helen.

"And you never have to leave," Tess says, handing Helen a drink.

Helen takes the drink and clinks glasses with Tess. And then there's another drink and another drink and another. By the time Helen drunkenly stumbles back to her hotel room, it's nearly 3:00 a.m. She kicks her shoes off in the darkened room and crawls into bed fully clothed. When she wakes up the next day, the sun is streaming in and Cherry is long gone.

Disastrously hungover, Helen realizes she never charged her phone, so she decides to plug it in while she is taking her shower. Her head pounding, she lets the hot water run over her without fear of running it cold before Cherry can take her shower, like it does back at their apartment. Stepping out into the steamy bathroom, Helen walks back into the room and sees that she's got missed calls from both Cherry and Tess. She looks at the times. Cherry's phone call came in around 6:00 p.m. last night, and Tess's just came in while she was in the shower. She listens to Tess's first.

"I'm so hungover. I need sustenance. There's a diner across the street. Call me, please—it's urgent I need coffee I'm going to die," Tess says. Her voice is a low, ornery growl. Helen smiles, excited about a good diner breakfast. Feeling slightly less excited about what Cherry has to say, the guilt of being in the greenroom all night finally settles in through the haze of an unknown quantity of vodka tonics. Helen plays Cherry's voicemail.

"Hey, it's me. Just seein' where you are, bye bye bye bye." Cherry always signs off her voicemails with this popping, high-pitched firework, with each bye higher and louder than the last. Helen loves it.

Still dripping wet in her towel, Helen deletes both voicemails and leaves a note for Cherry, saying that she's gone to breakfast with Tess and that she'll give her a call before the dinner her film agent invited them to tonight. Just before she heads back into the bathroom, Helen adds that she hopes Cherry has another amazing day full of panels. She signs it with a big *H* and a smiley face and a heart.

Helen excitedly calls Tess and tells her to meet her outside the hotel by the valet in thirty minutes. She makes a joke about not wanting to sully her hands with the busy hotel lobby again, for fear that some orange ribbon might get some big ideas about Helen's ability to control the very fabric of space and time. She signs off and gets ready for the day, the glow from last night somehow overriding her massive headache. Helen throws on some jeans and a vintage concert T-shirt she found thrifting with Tess a few years ago. She laces up her worn-in Doc Martens, puts on a bright-red lip, and actually manages a pretty amazing winged eyeliner, given her state.

Helen tucks her room key into her wallet, grabs her name tag, and hurries down the hallway to the elevator, thankful that she's the only one awaiting its arrival. She presses the button and realizes she hasn't been this happy in years. She knows her time here is ticking down. But instead of this realization making her sad, she feels an incredible swell of hope that the magic of these last couple of days might be able to revive her just long enough to ride the wave back to remembering who she really is and that she is a writer. Despite the last ten years, she still has a story to tell, and it doesn't matter what the elaborate mathematical equations are, because the years will pass anyway and it's about time she started.

God, she hasn't felt this good in years.

She laughs to herself as the elevator door dings open. She steps inside and smiles warmly at the handful of people already inside. She settles into the middle of the crowd, standing right in front. As she watches the lit floors tick down to the lobby level, she realizes that she's said that she hasn't felt this good in years a lot over the last twenty-four hours. It feels so much better than her usual broken record of excuses and disciplining and shameful, melancholy spirals and imaginary stories about being left behind or having to sit in economy with no oysters Rockefeller. She can feel herself thawing, beginning to recognize herself again. And it both makes her heart ache at having become so numb to her own hopelessness over the last ten years and now soar at the prospect of this sad chapter of her life finally coming to an end.

As the elevator opens to the lobby, she feels herself smiling wide as she weaves through the crowd, striding toward the hotel's front door and the diner breakfast with Tess that awaits her just outside.

Tess is standing a few feet away from the valet stand, cigarette in hand, looking every inch the moody French film star. She waves Helen over, wearing a long maxi dress, which she has paired with a pair of sparkly jelly sandals. Her oversize sunglasses dwarf her small, pale face, and her blunt brownish bob is held back with a small plastic barrette. Somehow she looks even more chic in the early-morning light than she did last night. If this is what hungover looks like for Tess Bayard, Helen is now positive that there's not one state of being where she is unable to look absolutely and completely effortlessly gorgeous.

The two friends set out across the street, the hot summer weather in Marina del Rey made slightly less offensive by the ocean breeze coming in from the Pacific to cool down their short walk to the diner. They talk excitedly about last night, gossiping and catching up. It's fun and easy as they're seated at a large red vinyl booth in the corner. They talk about Tess's wedding and all the planning she still has to do even this close to the event, laughing about how she should try to sell the photos to a magazine to pay for their honeymoon.

"It's not a bad idea," Helen says, sipping her coffee and taking another huge bite of her eggs.

"Oh, I keep forgetting to tell you. Jesus, this wedding has made me stupid. I got you into the party my publisher is having tonight. I talked to my editor and she wants to meet you," Tess says.

"What? Oh my god, are you serious?"

"Yes! I gave her your short story to read and she loves it. I think it might be a good opportunity to get on her radar so that when—not if—you write your novel, you can tell your future agent that you already have someone interested."

"Oh my god, Tess. This is . . . wow. I . . ." Helen can't believe that she feels like she's about to cry.

"Oh no . . . oh, honey," Tess soothes, reaching across the table to her.

"I'm just . . . I just really needed these last few days," Helen says, awkwardly taking Tess's hand.

"I'm so glad you're here," Tess says. And then as the awkward, emotional moment expands: "Let's make out."

They both burst out laughing, and Helen feels like she could fly, she feels so good.

If someone had told her teenage self that she would one day be sitting in an old diner in Marina del Rey with someone as famous as Tess Bayard, she wouldn't have believed them. Let alone that Tess is offering to introduce her to her editor and that she's read her short story and loved it? Is she dreaming?

Ten years.

Ten years of a stupid day job writing stupid grants for stupid people and their stupid dreams. Ten years of sitting on the BART going to and from her stupid apartment to the stupid beige box of an office building. Ten years of packing lunches and taking her morning coffee to go. Ten years of reading the same short story in front of the same small crowds for the same drink coupons in the same run-down coffee shops all over San Francisco. Ten years of watching from the sidelines as all her friends sold their books and had their dreams come true. Ten years of being left behind.

Ten years.

"I love that you believe in me," Helen finally says as their laughter dies down.

"Of course I do," Tess says.

"I don't sometimes."

"I know."

"But not anymore."

"I know that, too," Tess says, picking up the diner's heavy coffee mug and taking a genteel sip.

"This is the best breakfast I've ever had," Helen says, laughing.

They finish eating and float back to the festival hotel. Tess peels off for a much-needed nap now that she's eaten, and Helen stands in the lobby unsure of what to do. Buzzing with nervous energy, she goes back to the hotel room and begins thinking up possible ideas. But this time she finds herself focusing more on what she's trying to say rather than how she plans on saying it. She sees beyond the book, what she wants it to do and how she wants to make people feel. She outlines how her story is going to change the world and where it fits into the literary patchwork that already exists. She is going to make this editor see the impact of the book, rather than get caught on the plot.

Hours pass and Helen gets lost in her imagination for the first time. Not for the first time in ten years, but for the first time. Ever. Always so regimented in her approach to art, Helen has never allowed herself to think beyond the rules and craft of writing. Imprisoned by the rules, she never allowed herself the freedom to just daydream. She's impossibly broken down every story to its structural parts until the very marrow was sucked out of it. She finally sees past every note about depth and shading in and lacking nuance. She finally understands every comment about her prose being too sterile, too careful, and that overall, her characters are far too unemotional and unfeeling.

As dusk settles over Marina del Rey, Helen sits back in the hotel's desk chair and marvels at how she feels. Is this what writing feels like for Cherry? Is this why she says writing is easy for her? Because just like in life, Cherry allows herself the freedom to feel her way through a story rather than beat it to death with precision? This is intoxicating. Helen can't wait to tell Cherry. She can't wait to—

She hears Cherry's hotel card click and the door swings open. Helen leaps to her feet, unable to control herself one minute longer. "Hey!" she says, hurrying toward Cherry.

"Jesus Christ!" Cherry yells, her hands up in a defensive position, all her belongings falling to the floor.

"Oh my god, I'm so sorry," Helen says, laughing. She bends down and helps Cherry pick everything up. "I'm so sorry."

"How long have you been waiting to scare me like that," Cherry says, laughing.

"Untold years," Helen says, now both standing.

Cherry continues toward her bed and drops her tote, plopping down next to it. "You're in a good mood," she says.

Helen jumps over and does a very un-Helen dance right in front of Cherry. "I am in a good mood, and do you want to know why?" Helen shakes her tiny body around in front of her best friend.

"You took a dance class for seniors and you were the belle of the ball?" Cherry asks, taking off her shoes.

"I wrote." Helen stops, her mouth wide open.

"What?" Cherry asks, stopping dead in her tracks.

"I, Helen Virginia Hicks—"

"Virginia?"

"Virginia Woolf. My parents are insufferable snobs."

"Just your parents, huh?"

"Nope!" Cherry laughs, and Helen continues, "I, Helen Virginia Hicks, have written. I have written!" Helen pulls Cherry up from the bed and begins spinning her around the room as she continues to elaborate. "I have used my imagination and I have found the joy in writing and I am untethered from the stodgy rules that have kept me imprisoned lo these many years!"

"I'm so happy for you!" Cherry squeals. And because she's always been stronger than Helen, Cherry pulls Helen in for a giant bear hug and squeezes her so tight, her long arms embracing every part of her. But this time Helen holds her best friend back, pressing her entire body into her and letting herself luxuriate in the warmth of her.

"I wrote about how my book would make people feel and what it is that I'm trying to say and how my book is going to make a difference—"

"This is incredible!" Cherry says, starting to spin Helen around and around. Helen can't stop laughing and saying "whee" over and over like she's a little kid again. This is the feeling that Helen fell in love with. This is the way writing made her feel when she was a kid. She found it again. Helen grows emotional. She found it again.

"I can't believe I found it again," Helen says, crumpling into Cherry's arms. Cherry holds her tightly as she repeats that she can't believe she found it again.

"It's going to be okay . . . it's going to be okay . . . you found it . . . you found it again," Cherry soothes, smoothing her hair down and rocking her in her arms.

"I'm going to make that editor buy it, Cherry. I'm going to make her buy it and I'm going to be a writer again," Helen tearily vows.

Cherry pulls back from her. “Oh my god, what editor?” Cherry is beaming at Helen, so excited.

“Tess gave my short story to her editor and she loved it.”

“That’s incredible! Helen, this is—”

“It’s a miracle. It’s seriously nothing short of a miracle. All I have to do is give her enough tonight to bait the hook. So, when I finish the novel, I just have to pull her in.” Helen mimes pulling in a big fish over and over again.

“Tonight?” Cherry asks.

“Tess got me into her publisher’s party, and that’s where that editor isn’t going to know what hit her,” Helen says, flopping down on the bed, exhausted from catching so many big fish.

“But tonight is my film agent’s party,” Cherry says, backing up.

“Yes! That’s going to be so fun!” Helen says, still on cloud nine.

“No, Helen. You said you were going to come with me.”

“Right, but this could . . . the editor . . . this is . . . I’ve been waiting for this kind of break for years,” Helen says, now sitting up on her bed.

“But—”

“I can do both! The night is young and—”

“Just like last night, when you said we were going to hang out? Like that kind of both?”

Helen’s stomach drops. “I know. I’m so sorry, I got so drunk and . . .”

“Forgot.”

“I wouldn’t necessarily say ‘forgot,’ more like . . .”

“Forgot,” Cherry finishes.

“Cherry, this is . . . I . . . What’s happening right now? Are you pissed?”

“You’ve done nothing but flake on me this entire weekend. Why did you invite me at all?”

“Frankly, I’m beginning to ask the same question,” Helen says harshly.

“Yikes,” Cherry says.

"No! No yikes! You have a book deal. You have a film agent. You have everything and I have nothing."

"You have nothing?"

"This is my chance."

"The life we've built over the last ten years is nothing?"

"What? No, I . . . how did we get here? How do you not see how important this is to me?"

"Oh, I'm getting exactly how important this is to you," Cherry says, starting to gather her things and shove her feet into her shoes.

"Cherry, I . . ."

"So important that it's going to cost you—" Cherry swipes away the tears now falling down her cheeks. "Well, nothing apparently."

Cherry walks out of the hotel room without another word.

As Helen stands in the rubble of their friendship, she finds herself thinking about readers who criticize a story simply because the entire plot hinges on two people having one honest conversation. As if that isn't one of the hardest things two people can do. Helen deflates into the desk chair in a daze. She looks over at her cell phone and wishes she hadn't deleted Cherry's last voicemail.

Because this will be the last time Helen hears Cherry Stewart's voice.

CHAPTER THIRTEEN

Summer 2015

Cherry Stewart can read no more.

Seething, she slams Helen Hicks's debut novel closed and sits back in the hotel desk chair. The room is dark. It's gotten late. How long has she been sitting here? She quickly checks the time, suddenly panicking that she's missed the shuttle that'll take her to the restaurant where her literary agency will be celebrating all their clients in town for the awards show. She has an hour.

A single hour to process that her best friend of ten years wrote an entire book about their friendship and lied about it all.

Cherry doesn't know where to look or what to do, and her anger is growing well beyond what she can control. Feeling the pressure building inside her body, she stands and tucks the chair back under the desk, her hand curling around the old black moto jacket that hangs on its back. Pacing now, she scrapes her hands through her dyed-black hair and looks out her hotel window, hoping it will calm her down, the dusky pink-and-blue Manhattan sky spreading out in front of her.

Cherry turns away from the window and walks back over to her desk. She picks up her cell phone, noticing that she's missed several texts and calls from Mishler. She scrolls through her husband's texts as he gets more and more worried about her and where she's been all afternoon. Still a bit stunned and not knowing where to even begin unraveling all this, Cherry decides to call Mishler back, hoping that talking to him will help her begin to figure it out.

"There you are," Mishler says, picking up on the first ring.

"Here I am," Cherry says warmly.

"Did you read it?" he asks, getting straight to the point.

"Where are you?" Cherry asks, evading his question.

"That bad, huh?" Mishler laughs.

Cherry tries to muster up a playful giggle so he won't be so worried, but instead it comes out as a contemptuous scoff.

"It's . . . it's a lot," she says, pacing once again.

"Marlo and I are just finishing up at my parents'. She's going to go see a show with her mom, but what about instead of waiting for the shuttle, we find a bar or something close to where the dinner is. How does that sound?"

Cherry panics, realizing she owes her stepdaughter a text as well.

As Mishler types away on his laptop in search of a place they can meet, Cherry quickly pulls the phone from her cheek, finds Marlo's phone number, and texts her several heart emojis and exclamations to have fun with her mom at the show. Before she presses send, Cherry debates the heart emojis. Marlo isn't a little girl anymore, and Cherry is unsure how the supercool eighteen-year-old will feel about such an embarrassingly cheesy showing. But that's Cherry. She's always been unable to be anything but dopily gooey for the six years she's been lucky enough to call herself Marlo's stepmom. She presses send.

"That sounds perfect," Cherry finally says, taking a full breath for the first time since she saw Helen's book in the window of a bookstore on her walk home from lunch with her editor.

"Okayyyy . . . let's see here . . . bup-buh-duh, bup-buh-duh . . ." Mishler trails off, and Cherry can't help but smile. She's always loved the little thinking sounds he makes when he's trying to find something. Every morning his low, gravelly voice turns downright melodic as he sifts through the drawer for his "favorite socks," something he continually tells her is a thing. "Ooh, got a live one."

"Can you text me the address?" Cherry asks.

"Nope. Gonna keep it to myself," Mishler says.

"You're doing a really good job of cheering me up," Cherry says, smiling for the first time in hours. She hears a text come through on her phone and removes the phone from her face to see the place Mishler has chosen. She also sees a text from Marlo and can't help but smile. She's texted back a string of heart emojis, along with her own appeal for Cherry to have a good time at her "fancy book dinner." Cherry quickly texts back that she will try to have fun and that she can't wait to hear all about the show.

"I'd take the subway to get there or else we won't have any time before the dinner," Mishler advises.

"That's a good idea. And I'll let the agency know we won't be taking the shuttle, so they don't wait," Cherry says. She takes the black moto jacket off the back of the desk chair. Its weight pulls her arm down to her side, the jacket puddling on the hotel room's rug.

"Okay, see you there in twenty," Mishler says.

"Love you," Cherry says.

"Love you, too," he says, signing off.

As Cherry threads her arms through the sleeves of the black moto jacket, her mind is a riot of every last correction, every detail Helen got wrong, and every real person she happily used as cannon fodder for her own personal vanity project. She grabs the hotel's pad of paper and pen, and as she rides the elevator down to the lobby, she starts making a list—just to organize the cacophony currently raging inside her.

Stepping out of the hotel's main entrance, the balmy June evening makes her immediately regret the leather jacket. But she had to wear it. She had to show even herself that she was the one with the black leather moto jacket. She was the one with the badly dyed–black hair. She was the one with the winged eyeliner. She was the one with the stain on her concert T-shirt. And she was the one who was caught trying to stash three bottles of beer in the inner pockets of the jacket that first night at the welcome mixer at Hayho.

"Why lie about that?" Cherry whispers to herself as she stands on the subway platform writing down every last thing that Helen got wrong about their time at Hayho. She has no idea who this list is for besides her and Mishler, but that doesn't keep her from organizing it as if it will someday be admitted into evidence in a court of law.

Standing in the crowded subway moments later among a pack of commuters on their way home from work, Cherry finally slides the pad of paper and pen into her jacket pocket and steadies herself as the subway car shakes and jostles on its way toward her stop. But without the list to keep her mind engaged, she begins to spiral again, finding herself mumbling arguments and admonishments as New Yorkers get on and off around her. No one gives her and her quiet ramblings a second glance, a detail she loves about being in the city. Although there's a part of her that wishes someone would ask her, so she could yell and scream and get this whole subway car on her side.

"And another thing!" she'd yell as she told the rapt pack of commuters about how it was actually *her* cottage that was right next to the burbling stream, not Helen's. Helen's cottage was actually right next to the bathroom and often had the overwhelming stench of raw sewage wafting through it—definitely not the sweet scent of redwoods and general outdoorsy splendor.

Finally getting off at her stop, she climbs the stairs two by two and exits onto the bustling street just a few blocks from where she's meeting Mishler. As she nears the bar, she regrets not bringing Helen's book, but then thinks better of it. No, she can't be seen with that book, especially given the state that her copy is in right now, marked and highlighted with every last discrepancy between what actually happened and how Helen twisted it to serve her own heroic narrative.

Cherry turns onto the small side street and finds the bar two doors down. A perfect hole-in-the-wall with no sign, a dimly lit entrance, and the promise of a much-needed drink lie in wait. Cherry steps inside and it takes a few moments for her eyes to recalibrate from the dusky haze of outside to the bar's moody darkness. The raucous crack of the billiard balls on the pool table and the squealing guitar solo from the song playing on the old-timey jukebox lead her farther in as the din from the crowded bar drowns out the bustling street just outside.

"Hon!" Mishler yells from the back of the bar. Cherry squints and sees him waving from a small red vinyl booth in the very back, just right of the pool table.

Now in his early forties, Dan Mishler looks nothing like the character that's definitely based on him in Helen's novel. On the stockier side, he still has the body of an ex–rugby player—about as far away from lanky as someone can get. He's neither dark haired nor brooding; Mishler's tousled blondish hair is graying slightly, and he's always had one of those big, open smiles that can light up a room. Something Cherry has always loved about him. Cherry hopes that Helen telling the truth about him being a better writer than she was and making him "dreamy" will make up for the fact that she made him the snobby, entitled villain to her plucky literary heroine.

"Hey, man!" Cherry immediately hates that Helen did get some things right, and as she gives Mishler an exuberant wave back, she vows to at least try to stop saying the thing that came to define her character in Helen's novel. Getting mad all over again, she mutters a sweeping cornucopia of curse words to herself as she threads her way through the Greenwich Village denizens three deep in line to get historically strong pours of their favorite drink. Mishler slides out of the booth and greets Cherry with a big hug.

"I got you your favorite," Mishler says as they break apart. Cherry looks at their small table and sees that he's gotten her a Shirley Temple with three cherries and a bag of sour cream and onion potato chips. Cherry lunges into him for a teary hug.

"You're the best," she says, hugging him way too tight.

"He gave me shit about the extra cherries, but I told him in no uncertain terms that it's only the best for my wife," Mishler says, slightly groaning as her embrace tightens. Cherry finally lets him go and they slide into the small booth. Cherry takes a long drink of her Shirley

Temple and Mishler reaches across and opens the bag of potato chips, grabbing one for himself as he takes a swig of his beer.

"I don't even know where to start," Cherry says, setting her drink down.

"Okay, but before we get into all that, Karan texted me that he has a reading tonight. I told him we would try to swing by after dinner," Mishler says, helping himself to another potato chip.

"I wonder if he knows about Helen's book," Cherry says.

"Honey, I think it was just you who didn't know about it," Mishler says, taking Cherry's hand in his.

"I can hear Tala now, admonishing me for not having social media," Cherry says.

"Oh, we should actually see if she's going to be at Karan's reading. I'm sure she's covering the awards show and all the readings that are happening around town because of it," Mishler says, pulling his phone out of his pocket and finding Tala's number, then quickly texting to see if she's going to be at the reading.

Mishler's extroverted nature has always been a double-edged sword for Cherry. Without it, she would have most definitely spent the last ten years holed up in her little house in Pasadena writing book after book, languidly working in her garden, and going on long dog walks by herself. But, with Mishler, she got Marlo. And now they have an active social life filled with season tickets to the Hollywood Bowl, endless soccer games, and standing dinners with old and new friends alike. Truth be told, Cherry is often relieved that her endless book deadlines excuse her from just a small percentage of Mishler's social engagements. But she eases her guilt by telling herself that most people like Mishler better of the two of them anyway.

"Does this book just . . . Am I the only one who's bothered by this?" Cherry asks.

"I think you were the closest to Helen, so it makes sense that you're the most . . . affected," Mishler says, choosing his words carefully.

"She stole my whole identity!" Cherry barks out.

Mishler is quiet and Cherry immediately feels embarrassed. She pulls her hand away from Mishler's and covers her face. In the furious seconds that follow, Cherry remembers a part of Helen's book where the character based on Tess warned Helen about not inviting Cherry to Bibliophile because she might "get all Cherry Stewart on them" and then the Tess character waggled her arms around and said "hey, man" to everyone who passed. And oh, how Helen laughed at that. Cherry knows it's just a book. She also knows that only a handful of people know that these characters are based on real people. What she doesn't know is why this has absolutely gotten under her usually thick skin.

But that's Helen Hicks. Helen has always known exactly how to pierce all Cherry's usual defenses. And when she used those powers for good, nothing felt better in the whole wide world. But when she uses them for bad . . . Cherry has never felt so violated.

"Why don't you tell me about it," Mishler says, reaching back across the table and taking Cherry's hand. She curls her fingers around his and tries to take a deep breath.

"I made a whole list. Of all the things she got wrong. Of all the lies." Cherry listlessly gropes for the pad of hotel paper in her inner jacket pocket with little success. Finally giving up, she drops her free hand to the sticky bar table and her entire body crumples forward. "I've got a list."

Officially worried now, Mishler slides out of his side of the booth, crosses over to Cherry, and lovingly reaches into her inner jacket pocket and fishes out the pad of hotel paper. Just as he frees it from the torn and threadbare inner lining, he kisses her on the top of her head and slides back into the booth across from her. Mishler fishes his reading glasses out of his pocket, puts them on, and focuses on Cherry's list.

"Black moto jacket. Black hair. Wig . . . wiggy—"

"Winged eyeliner," Cherry corrects, cringing at the state of her handwriting.

"Oh, I remember when you used to do that," Mishler says, smiling easily at the memory. Cherry is forced to see herself in this moment—the unhinged list, the barked and blurted offenses . . . What is happening to her?

"Am I being weird? Why am I so . . . upset about this?" Cherry asks, frustrated—and a little concerned—that she's the only one who seems to be infuriated by Helen's novel.

"Writers steal stuff all the time. Some more than others, but . . ." Mishler trails off.

"It still hurts," Cherry finishes, and Mishler nods.

"She was your friend. Your first real friend," Mishler says gently.

"She was my first real friend," Cherry repeats, the emotion quickly building in her throat.

"You trusted her. You trusted her with your story and—"

"She stole it. She stole it and then made . . . and then made fun of me. She made fun of me like everyone else," Cherry says, gulping down the hurt.

"Oh, honey."

"Do you . . . do you think she gets that in order to make herself the hero of our story, she had to make me the villain of it? I'm not . . . I just . . . I just wanted to be a writer . . . a real writer. Why . . . how does that make me a villain?"

"From the reviews I've read, the general consensus is that the Helen character is the antagonist, not yours."

"That total strangers are debating this at all—" Cherry cuts herself off.

"It's a novel, honey. It's fiction. Just because it's in hardcover doesn't make it gospel," Mishler says.

"Do you think she knows it's fiction? Or do you think this is how she really believes it went down?"

"I don't care what she thinks, quite frankly."

Cherry looks up. "She stole my everything," she says, slumping in the little red vinyl booth.

"She stole your everything because she is a complete cipher. I can't even remember what she looks like, but you . . . you're singular."

"You have to say that because I tricked you into marrying me," Cherry says, offering a meek smile as Mishler hands her a cocktail napkin to dry her tears.

"I know she was your best friend, but I've legitimately never met someone so utterly forgettable in my entire life—and that's saying something, because I went to Yale." This gets a laugh out of Cherry, just like Mishler knew it would. He continues, "When I try to remember her, all that comes to mind is a beige blob."

"She made *me* the beige blob!"

This information hits Mishler hard.

"Oh no," he finally says.

"I don't get it. I loved . . ." Cherry shakes her head. "I loved how she looked. I didn't think she was a beige blob. Don't you remember how pigeon toed she was? Walking around and her little knees always used to bump and clang together. God, and she always used to wear . . . she had a thing about her arms, remember? She didn't like the way they looked, so she always wore these old grandpa cardigans over the same white tank tops that she bought in bulk. Even in summer. She would get so hot . . ." Cherry gets lost in remembering her best friend, and a small smile spreads across her face as she gathers each exquisite detail from the depths of her memory.

Mishler is quiet, deciding that letting his wife linger in the good memories from the past means that, for at least the time being, she isn't sad and upset. Finally, Cherry comes out of the fog and checks her watch with a long, weary sigh.

"We should probably get going," she says before finishing the rest of her Shirley Temple.

"Or we can get another round and skip the dinner and Karan's reading. I can send our regrets."

"No, it'll be good to be out. We don't get to the city enough, and you know how I love New York at night. I think it'll be good to remind myself what my real life actually is, if that makes any sense," Cherry says, fighting to put her tangle of feelings into words.

"No, that makes a lot of sense," Mishler says, sliding out of the booth.

Mishler waits as Cherry packages up the half-eaten bag of potato chips and squirrels it away into her pocket, no longer embarrassed about the habits from her poor-kid past that she can't seem to get rid of. Sure, she has nine mystery novels on the bestseller list and one due out in the fall, as well as a television show adaptation that's been running for five seasons with no sign of slowing. Nonetheless, she's still unable to let uneaten food linger despite having more money in the bank than she ever thought possible. But life is long, she argues, and this whole writing thing can be taken away at any time. It's only smart to prepare for that inevitability now, she tells Mishler. That way she won't burden anyone when she disappears into anonymous oblivion.

This is why what Helen did bothers Cherry so much. It's not cute or funny how Cherry squirrels away food and steals bottles of beer. It's fucked up or, as her therapist says, something she does because of the extreme poverty from her childhood. And she wishes she could stop doing it. But now it's in Helen's book as some kind of cute, character-building quirk that makes the most forgettable person in the world slightly more interesting. Thinking back to the first line of Helen's novel, it enrages Cherry that apparently the only extraordinary thing about Helen was her.

As she and Mishler finally exit the bar, Cherry pulls out the pad of hotel paper and writes that line down. It's a good line, and she can't wait to say it right to Helen's thieving, ordinary face.

Cherry uses the short walk to the lit agency dinner to try and switch into work mode. She tries to push Helen and her novel to the back of her mind as she listens to Mishler recount what he did with his afternoon. A lovely catch-up with Marlo and his parents, meetings with the publisher's PR and marketing team about his newest book, and a conversation around social media that will need Tala's expertise in order to decode it. Cherry nods along, feeling guilty for not being able to fully focus on the ebbs and flows of their easy conversation.

"You ready?" Mishler asks, outside the restaurant.

"I think I'm okay," Cherry answers honestly.

"We can leave at any time, so—"

"Thank you," Cherry says, taking his hand in hers. He melts, as he always does.

"It's going to be okay, honey," Mishler says, squeezing Cherry's hand. Cherry nods but can't fully respond, still unsure if what he's saying is true. Mishler knows Cherry well enough to know that's exactly what she's thinking, so he doesn't press the issue as he leads her inside the restaurant.

The agency dinner goes off without a hitch, and as they say their goodbyes, Cherry finds herself feeling better than she has all day. The distraction worked, and as she and Mishler walk down the bustling Greenwich Village street, she agrees to come with him to Karan's reading in hopes that it will keep the upset of Helen's novel at bay. And with every step, Cherry soaks in the reality of the life that she's built over the last ten years. She loves her life. She loves Mishler. She loves Marlo. She loves their dogs. She loves her garden. She loves that she gets to write books for a living. She loves that she and Mishler get to live in a house with actual air-conditioning and a washer and dryer. She loves that she had the money to buy a plane ticket to come to New York and that she gets to stay in a nice hotel and even order room service. She loves her readers, and she absolutely adores Juno Brannan, her nerdy bookworm detective who's been solving twisty mysteries for the last ten years. Cherry threads her arm through Mishler's and pulls him close, quietly herding him into the oncoming pedestrian traffic as she does so.

"Helen talked about the herding thing I do," Cherry says as Mishler fights for his life, bobbing and weaving through a tide of oncoming people.

"What herding thing?" Mishler laughs, stepping off the curb and taking a few steps in the gutter before he's able to careen back through the crowd and settle in next to Cherry.

"I think I'm also a little scared that she got stuff right about me. You know?"

"Yeah, I get that."

"Like I . . . maybe I don't see myself clearly," Cherry says, unable to look at Mishler.

"I doubt any of us see ourselves clearly," he says absently, scanning the horizon for the bookstore where Karan will be reading tonight.

It makes her uncomfortable, but with Mishler's words, Cherry grows quiet as she reflects on how Helen portrayed her in the novel. She painted a person that was so confident and above the fray, the Cherry Stewart of Helen's novel was far more fearless than she could ever dream of being in real life. But Cherry isn't totally sure if it's awe or just an excuse so she could treat her character with reckless abandon. Just like Helen to create a system where she could make fun of Cherry because she'd convinced herself that it was a victimless crime.

Plagued by insecurities and crippling self-doubt, Cherry's time at Hayho was not the fun romp that Helen made it out to be. Obsessed with the fear of being unmasked as the uneducated fraud that she was, Cherry hates to admit that even with all her success over the last ten years, she still kind of feels like an orange ribbon. She's watched as Mishler confidently accesses every exclusive space, so comfortable with belonging anywhere that if someone did have a problem with him, society as a whole would make sure they knew it was a them problem and not about Mishler at all.

As Mishler pulls open the door to the bookstore and motions for Cherry to go in first, she begins to fear that it's her own fault that Helen's novel is affecting her as much as it is. If she were the Cherry Stewart in the book, she probably would have just yelled some perfectly timed insult over a bathroom stall without a second thought and gone about her merry way. But she's not. She's the real Cherry Stewart. And the real Cherry Stewart cried herself to sleep that first night at Hayho, playing and replaying that moment in the bathroom over and over again, haunted that, once again, some fancy person recognized, without even knowing her, that she wasn't one of them. Purple ribbons always seem to inherently know who's the interloper.

"You okay?" Mishler asks.

Cherry pops out of her panicked haze and manages to give him a warm smile. "Yeah. Glad I'm here," she answers.

The shop is one of those wonderful independent bookstores that's stacked to the ceiling with books upon books upon books. This particular bookstore is one of Cherry's favorites, and every time she's in New York, she makes a pilgrimage. For book events, the store has set up as many folding chairs as they can between the stacks and aisles of books. There are no rows or columns, just a chair here, two over here, and then ten over in the corner. Cherry loves it.

A poster for Karan's newest novel hangs high above the podium set out at the front of the bookstore. A bottle of water sits next to stacks and stacks of Karan's book, along with a cup full of permanent markers. Because Karan takes his time with books, the bookstore is overcrowded with excited readers, family, and friends who have long awaited a follow-up to his wonderful debut six years ago. Cherry spies two chairs over in the corner of the bookstore, and she and Mishler thread through the thick assemblage of fans to take their seats before the reading starts.

Cherry loves book events. So intimate and celebratory. She sees Karan's family and his husband, Nish, trying—and failing—to wrangle their two adorable children. She notices a few fans have brought his debut novel for him to sign, as well as a few elegantly dressed New Yorkers who are definitely his team of editors, agents, and publicist. Cherry is in heaven and finds herself calming down every second she's in this magical bookstore. She is finally able to take a long, deep breath and tucks in close to Mishler, laying her hand on his thigh as she always does, and just as he always does, he drops his hand and curls it tightly around hers. She nudges him and they watch Karan's oldest make a break for the full cup of permanent markers.

Which is right when she sees Helen Hicks walk in.

CHAPTER FOURTEEN

By the time Helen Hicks sees Cherry Stewart in the audience of Karan's reading, it's too late to turn around and slink right back out. With plan A sadly, but irrevocably, in the trash, Helen proceeds to plan B and does what she always does—juts her chin out and continues on as if she's completely oblivious to Cherry's presence.

As Cherry glares at her from across the room, Helen languidly finds a seat in a random single chair that's been set out by the self-help section. And upon sitting down pulls out her cell phone and sighs as she airily scrolls. Behind the glow of her screen, Helen prays that the sensation of all the color draining from her face and feeling violently sick to her stomach is just a visceral one and not something anyone else can see. But even she can feel the anxious clamminess begin to sprout little beads of sweat right at her hairline.

However, Helen's show of standoffishness is working, and as the bookstore employee walks Karan out from the back of the bookstore toward the podium in the front, Cherry is growing steadily more and more furious.

"I love that I'm wearing the leather jacket," Cherry whispers to Mishler. He looks over at her and watches as she continues to nod and mutter about the leather jacket. But even he's only able to catch little bits: "Heh, she can't lie about it now" and "I mean, I'm actually wearing the damn jacket" devolve into just mumbles of "I can't believe she showed her face" and "Ugh, look at her."

"Are you going to be okay?" Mishler asks, clearly growing concerned.

"Oh, I'm going to be okay. It's Helen who's not going to be okay," Cherry says, narrowing her eyes at her former best friend.

"See, it's saying things like that that makes me think maybe—"

"It's Karan's night, I won't make a scene," Cherry says, cutting him off.

"Okay, I—"

"But after? Out on the street? That's neutral ground, baby," Cherry says, scanning the general vicinity like a 1920s gangster trying to assess whether this location is an acceptable venue for an all-out melee.

"Honey," Mishler warns.

"Neutral ground, baby," Cherry repeats, slowly crossing her arms across her chest, the leather jacket creaking and twisting with each motion. Mishler takes a deep breath and shifts to the edge of his chair, apparently readying himself to either hold his wife back or break apart the two former best friends should a fight break out. A situation he likely hadn't thought would be a cornerstone of tonight's lovely book event for an old friend.

Thankfully, the sheer goodness of Karan begins defusing some of the tension. And as the man of the hour makes his way to the front of the bookstore, waving and greeting everyone warmly, his infectious smile begins to evaporate some of the tension created by Cherry and Helen's yearslong feud. But just as Karan says an exuberant hello to Cherry and Mishler, he follows Cherry's fuming gaze over to where he sees Helen sitting all by herself in the very back of the bookstore. Without thinking, he gives her an excited wave, but then it hits him. And because Karan has always been someone without guile or pretense, his mouth drops open as he finally pieces together why the bookstore has begun to feel like a boxing ring moments before the berobed fighters emerge from their respective locker rooms. He's clearly read Helen's novel, and just as the bookstore employee steps behind the podium to introduce him, he is now actively sneaking glances back and forth from Cherry to Helen, unsure of what both of them being here separately means not only for his reading, but overall.

". . . so without further ado, I give you Karan Sanyal!" the bookstore employee finishes to a round of applause from the audience.

"Thank you, everyone, for coming out tonight. It's so lovely to see so many familiar faces," Karan says, opening his novel and putting on his glasses to begin reading.

But something about the way Karan says "so many familiar faces" causes both Cherry and Helen to temporarily forget themselves and that old instinctual pull to one another kicks in, overriding the swarms of seething rage and performative indifference.

And in that moment Helen and Cherry lock eyes for the first time in ten years.

For an instant, they just take each other in. The faces they've loved—how they've aged and changed over the last decade. Cherry notices that Helen still parts her hair right down the middle, but unlike before, her dishwater-blond hair is now dyed a beautiful pillowcase blond, all expensive highlights and thick layers. She's also wearing a full face of makeup, something Cherry has never seen her do. Helen would wear foundation to cover up her acne, but beyond that, if she wore a slightly tinted lip balm it was worthy of note. Her pale skin looks dewy and fresh, rather than blotchy and inflamed, as it did for as long as Cherry knew her. Cherry's brow furrows as the reality of ten years tidal waves over her. It's one thing to say that it's been ten years since you've seen someone, but it's an entirely different thing altogether to see the person you knew better than anyone grow up without you.

But all Helen can see is that Cherry Stewart hasn't aged a day. She looks exactly the same. Helen can't believe she still has—let alone wears—that old leather jacket, even during the height of summer. So stubborn. Her black bob looks as though she's now getting it professionally cut and dyed, so it appears the grocery store hair dye and the winged eyeliner have both thankfully been retired. That face. Helen has always loved Cherry's cherubic little face—her dark-brown eyes forever crinkled from endless smiling. She's always been so open, impossibly and dangerously open. Every thought she's ever had like a ticker tape across her face. Like, take right now, for example: Helen knows that Cherry is furious, because she looks absolutely furious. But

Helen . . . while Helen may feel completely sick to her stomach and like she might throw up at any moment, from Cherry's vantage point, it just looks like she's wistfully taking in an old friend.

Helen is thankful once Karan begins reading, because it forces Cherry to tear her gaze away from her and finally focus on the person everyone came to see. And of course, the minute she focuses on Karan, her face transforms from fury to oozing pride. Helen deflates slightly, remembering how Cherry used to look at her like that.

Helen has played and replayed this very moment a thousand times in her head. What she would say to Cherry when and if she saw her again. She's crafted speeches and created whole scenarios where if she could just explain what really happened that weekend at Bibliophile, Cherry would come to understand Helen's side of things, and yes, fine—maybe she would also admit that she was a little bit wrong for overreacting and blaming the entire downfall of their friendship on Helen. They should have talked about it. It was one weekend, and they'd been friends for years—how could Cherry walk away so easily? Especially when things were just starting to look up for Helen.

In fact, Helen usually starts these hypothetical speeches by telling Cherry that it was actually that very editor Tess introduced her to at Bibliophile who bought her debut novel. And if Helen had gone to Cherry's film agent's thing, she'd probably still be working for that same nonprofit, writing grants to make other people's dreams come true. So technically Helen was right to make the choice that she did, and Cherry should know that.

Helen crosses her arms, fueled by her own righteousness, and sneaks a glance back over at Cherry, who is once again, glaring at her from across the bookstore. But this time Helen doesn't look away. Temporarily emboldened by her own self-absolution, Helen arches a defiant eyebrow. Cherry isn't the only one who gets to be mad.

At this, Cherry can't help but laugh. There's the Helen she remembers—so devoid of any level of self-awareness, she allowed Cherry exactly three minutes to be mad before defaulting to casting herself as the real victim in this scenario. Yes, sure, it was Helen who stole Cherry's whole identity for her debut novel, but what if—just hear her out—Helen is the actual wronged party here. As Cherry rolls her head in circles, her neck cracking and clunking from too many hours hunched over a keyboard, it's as if she's getting ready to do battle.

And just as Cherry brings her head back to center, Mishler's entire body tightens. He honestly doesn't know what's about to happen. "Sweetie, I don't want Marlo having to bail us out of jail," he whispers.

"I promise I'm not going to do anything stupid," Cherry answers. Mishler allows a hesitant nod in response, his body still taut with worry.

Across the room, Helen watches Mishler whisper something to Cherry, their bodies melting and folding into one another. So close. So easy. They look happy. Helen looks down at her lap, that jutted chin now tucked and far less defiant than it was ten minutes ago.

Six years ago, when Helen heard through the grapevine* (*Tala) that Cherry and Mishler had gotten married, she couldn't believe it. She thought they hated each other. But then she remembered that they had been thrown together during that fateful weekend at Bibliophile, something else Cherry forgot to thank her for. Helen straightens in her chair, now actively gathering evidence for the knock-down, drag-out fight she fears is coming her way as soon as Karan finishes answering the audience's questions.

And sure enough, as the audience applauds Karan as he finishes his reading, Cherry bolts up from her chair, points at Helen, and then gestures outside. Helen crosses her arms and sits back in her chair in an attempt to not be told what to do so easily. Helen quickly glances over at Mishler, and it's actually his look that sways her. It's soft and worried and she hates that it cuts through all her excuses and litigation and jutted chins. Because he's right. Cherry deserves an explanation, regardless of how cartoonishly Helen thinks she's behaving.

With a heavy sigh, she stands up from her chair, and as Karan's fans, friends, and family line up to get their books signed, Helen Hicks follows Cherry Stewart outside to answer for her sins.

"Look—" Helen starts, the door barely closed behind her.

"No, you look—" Cherry cuts in. Helen stops talking, but Cherry doesn't have the rest of her sentence mapped out, so there is a long—too long—silence as the women play chicken as to whom should be looking and how long one must look before this conversation continues.

"Okay. My vote is that we maybe try to be grown-ups about this," Helen says, stepping to the side of the busy Greenwich Village sidewalk.

"You stole my whole identity!" Cherry yells.

"Your whole identity?" Helen recalibrates herself. She thought this was going to be about that weekend at Bibliophile ten years ago. She wasn't ready to talk about her novel. Especially not with Cherry. She quickly collects herself and continues, "Okay, that's . . . fine, I will admit that I may have borrowed a few details, but a leather jacket does not an identity make." Helen eyes Cherry's jacket.

"Then why did you"—Cherry makes giant air quotes—"borrow it?" The simple question catches Helen off guard. "Hm?"

"I . . . it . . ." Helen stutters, realizing that they're one minute into this fight and Cherry has already cornered her.

"Exactly."

Cherry's voice is cold and brutal. Helen has never seen her like this, or maybe this is what she's become in the ten years since she's seen her. Even that fateful day at Bibliophile when their entire friendship came crumbling down, Cherry still had that dangerous openness to her, all pain and hurt from Helen constantly prioritizing Tess and flaking on her one time too many. Helen's stomach drops as she realizes the difference between then and now.

Cherry Stewart is no longer her friend. And that wonderful openness and gooey emotion is something Cherry only saves for people she actually—Helen gulps—likes. And right now, that is not Helen.

Cherry waits for an explanation. An apology. Anything. But as Helen stands in front of her, her mouth opening and closing like a hungry goldfish's, Cherry finds herself growing angrier and angrier with every blerp of Helen's lips. Cherry cycles through all the possible reasons for Helen's hesitation: Does she really not have a reason for "borrowing some details," or does she just not know why she did it, or does she know that the answer to Cherry's question would incriminate her beyond a reasonable doubt, so instead of coming clean she's choosing instead to just stay quiet? Cherry can wait no longer.

"You're such a coward," she finally bites out.

Helen hates that she can't argue with that either. "I'm sorry," she finally says, more because she can't think of anything else to say than because she's actually feeling apologetic in that moment.

"You're sorry for being a coward or you're sorry for stealing my whole identity?" Cherry presses.

"Why don't you choose," Helen says with a lazy shrug.

"Are you kidding me?" With every moment Helen hedges, Cherry grows more and more irritated.

"Fine, I'm not sorry." As Cherry is taken aback by Helen's complete lack of remorse, Helen shifts her weight and is just about to suggest they leave it at that, when Cherry cuts in again.

"I have a few theories of my own. Would you like to hear them?" Cherry asks, her words a loaded gun.

"Not particularly," Helen answers, honestly.

"What an extraordinary woman. Too bad she did so very little with her life," Cherry says, quoting the first line of Helen's novel from memory. Hearing her own words laced with such repulsion sickens Helen.

"So?" is all Helen can manage.

"So it appears the only thing extraordinary about you . . . is me." Cherry can't hide the pride she feels in really landing that blow. The dramatic pause, the verbatim quote of her own book, and then the final slam dunk. She hates how happy it makes her to see Helen's face drain of color.

"It's a leather jacket. One stupid leather jacket," Helen growls back, feeling the need to defend more than just her novel.

"A leather jacket. Winged eyeliner. Dyed-black hair. A cottage by a burbling stream. Doc Martens. Mishler bullying you at the bus stop. Calling Mishler Big Shot for the rest of my life? Crying at the Q and A with Deborah Torres and Tess. Drinking Earl Grey tea, stealing bottles of beer—"

"Oh, come on. The bottles of beer? You're mad about that?" Helen struggles to find purchase in any corner of this battle.

"Do you even know why I do stuff like that? Why I'm a 'squirreler'?" Cherry says, quoting Helen once again. Helen's breathing quickens as she's yet again smacked in the face by one of her own quotes.

"Jesus, it's not that big of a deal, okay?"

"It's not some funny quirk you can just take because you're the most boring person on the planet, Helen!" Cherry yells, officially losing her cool.

"We were in our twenties. It was free food and that mixer was stupid and you—" Helen stops talking as she sees tears begin pooling in Cherry's big brown eyes.

"You were never poor. Were you?"

"I mean, we weren't rich or anything, but—"

"But *you* never got made fun of because you thought food stamps were just regular money, so you brought one to school to try to buy a book from one of those book fairs and instead got made fun of by everyone when the teacher told you those were for food for people on welfare and not . . ." Cherry is unable to finish her sentence, violently swiping away the tears now falling down her cheeks. "I was the only kid who didn't get a book." Another violent swipe. "I never got to get a book from one of those bookmobiles. Did you?"

"Yeah." Helen's voice is quiet.

Helen had loved when the bookmobile came to her school. It was the one time being a bookish nerd was a good thing, and she had ruled that day with an iron fist. She had never considered it would be anything but a wonderful memory for everyone, just like she'd never considered that stealing bottles of beer would be anything but a cool thing she envied Cherry for being rebellious enough to pull off. She'd been in awe of Cherry that first night at the Hayho welcome mixer. The black leather jacket, the dyed-black hair—she was everything Helen wasn't. And it never occurred to her that stealing the beer was anything other than the defiant act of someone way cooler than she was.

"I don't . . . I don't like that I do it. It's not funny and I wish I didn't—" Cherry whips out the half-eaten bag of potato chips from the leather jacket's pocket. "I wish I didn't do it, but . . . I . . . I . . . You don't get to just take stuff without having to experience the bullshit that caused it."

Cherry takes a giant, full breath and pulls the collar of her shirt to her face, trying to wipe away the wetness from the crying she told herself she definitely wasn't going to do. It feels good to tell the truth, but she hates that these old, tender memories still make her this emotional. Remembering how she used to pore over those book fair catalogs, putting little red stars next to the books she wanted, knowing full well she'd never be able to get them. And when she found the crumpled food stamp on the passenger's-side floor of their car, she thought she finally had a chance. So excited at school the next day, she stepped up into that little bookmobile clutching the catalog in one hand and the crumpled food stamp in the other. She couldn't wait to finally be like the rest of the kids. The teacher had tried to be discreet, but everyone heard. Cherry can still feel the book being tugged from her little fingertips to this day.

"Why didn't you tell me?" Helen asks.

Cherry looks up, caught off guard.

"It's a strange thing, trauma. It's not something you can easily talk about or say, just put blithely in a novel because you think it makes you plucky," Cherry says, her face angry and pained. She remembers the night she told Mishler the bookmobile story. While it was the single hardest thing she'd ever done, it was also the moment their relationship crossed a Rubicon into more serious, uncharted territory. She trusted him with one of her greatest secrets and he'd held it so gently in his hands, like a little origami crane made from tissue paper.

The harsh reality of the moment is beginning to shut Helen down, and in a desperate attempt to find a loophole for her own deception, she throws a Hail Mary rather than an apology. Because even in this heightened state, Helen is sure that wherever the words "I'm sorry" reside within her, so, too, do the pain and the grief she's been trying to outrun for the last three years.

"Don't I get at least some credit for *not* putting certain things in the book?" Helen makes very pointed eye contact with Cherry.

"I . . . if you're . . . that . . ." Cherry stutters, quickly looking inside the bookshop to assess exactly where Mishler is right now.

"Because you also 'borrowed' something, if I'm remembering that time correctly," Helen leads, her voice desperate and clipped.

"Are you . . . wait—" Cherry barks out, her hands out in front of her.

"And having the character in the book steal—"

"It wasn't . . ." Cherry trails off.

"Oh, it was."

"Just—"

"And having the character in the book steal someone else's essay for their application to Hayho," Helen finishes.

"Jesus," Cherry says, feeling sick to her stomach.

Stealing that essay is the single worst thing Cherry has ever done in her life. The shame she's carried all these years has haunted her like some shackle-clanging ghost. Whenever she's feeling a little too comfortable, she reminds herself that she did this terrible thing and that if anyone ever found out, everything she's built over the last twenty years would be quite rightly ripped from her thieving hands.

She has this recurring nightmare that one day she's going to receive a call from Hayho that they've discovered her treasonous breach of trust and they will be calling not only the authorities but also Cherry's agent, publisher, all her friends, family, and literary peers with the breaking news that she is, in fact, a giant fraud.

Not even Mishler knows about the stolen essay.

She didn't set out to do it. She'd been in the library looking up examples of essays and had found a single bound copy of a local essay contest from the early 1960s. She had found an essay that she'd loved, marveling at how much it spoke to her. She'd tried to write one just like it. She'd tried and tried and tried, but nothing was good enough. In that moment she knew two things for sure: (1) She needed something spectacular if she was going to get into Hayho, and (2) she was not spectacular. So, on the day before the deadline for applications, she'd taken some change from her mother's purse, made a copy of the essay at the library, and copied it over in her own handwriting. She told herself that no one but the library staff would know, but then she'd drunkenly confessed her crime to Helen one night in their Haight-Ashbury apartment. It'd felt good to tell someone, and even better, Helen had seemed completely unfazed by the confession.

Looking back, Helen's reaction should have been a red flag of her morally ambiguous code of ethics. Alas . . .

"And what about Juno Brannan?" Helen asks, hitting Cherry while she's down.

"What about her?" Cherry asks, picking up the pieces of herself.

"Brannan is the perfect detective because she's so fundamentally unremarkable no one ever notices her," Helen quotes from Cherry's book word for word.

"So?" Cherry asks, trying to refocus.

"Look, I don't like it, but that's me and you know it."

"It is not."

"The super-straight part right down the middle of her dishwater-blond hair? And you couldn't have just given me blond hair—it had to be dishwater blond?"

"I don't know what you're talking about," Cherry says, looking away from Helen and knowing exactly what she's talking about. Cherry has long argued (to herself) that Juno Brannan was simply inspired by Helen. But given the last few minutes, Cherry is having a hard time defending her own—shall we say—past creative choices.

"Wow," Helen says, stepping out of the way of a trio of Karan's readers exiting the bookstore. There is a moment where one of the women recognizes Cherry, the broad double take hilariously indiscreet. Cherry notices the woman, and all of a sudden, it's as if she zooms back into the here and now, Mishler's words of warning thick in her foggy and tangled brain.

As if coming out of a haze, Cherry scans her surroundings and notices her husband watching her and Helen through the bookstore's large glass door. Did he not trust that she would keep her promise about not making Marlo have to bail them out of jail post–literary brawl? But then Cherry begins to panic. How long has he been there? Did he hear them talking about the stolen essay? Just then, Mishler mouths the words "You okay?" and Cherry nods, causing Helen to turn and see him looming. Something about seeing him so obviously worried about only Cherry makes Helen feel more alone than ever.

"Fine," Cherry finally barks out, stomping her foot.

"Really? That's it?" Helen blurts, marveling at the childish display.

"Ugh, it's . . . ugh, I hate that . . ."

"I'm right?" Helen gloats.

"No. No, you're not right. We're just . . . both wrong," Cherry argues.

"You're such a hypocrite," Helen says, dramatically shaking her head.

"No way. You don't get to be mad. Yours was way worse," Cherry says.

"How do you figure that?"

"Fine, I stole an essay when I was twenty years old so I could get into Hayho. And yes, Juno may have your hair and your—"

"Fundamentally unremarkable personality," Helen finishes.

"Right. But all of my books are actually written by me and . . . they're about murderers and extortionists and art heists. Your book was about us. You wrote about us. You wrote about me," Cherry says, pounding her fist into her chest.

"'Us' is also me," Helen argues.

"It wasn't your story to tell!"

"You're just pissed you didn't think of it first."

"Are you seriously not going to apologize?"

"Are you?" Helen throws back.

"What do I have to apologize for?"

"What do *I* have to apologize for?"

They stand in silence. Angry, frustrated silence.

"We okay out here?" Mishler asks, the door to the bookstore closing behind him.

"Oh, hey. Look who it is," Helen says, turning away from Cherry.

"Helen," Mishler says, his voice laced with forced politeness.

"Mishler," Helen responds.

"So . . ." Mishler leads as Helen turns back to a furious Cherry.

"Are we done here?" Helen asks.

"Are you seriously not going to apologize?" Cherry asks. Mishler watches the two women like a tennis match.

"Are you?" Helen volleys. Cherry's face colors red as she shakes her head in frustration.

"Yeah, we're done," Cherry says through gritted teeth.

"We sure are," Helen says, forcing a sarcastic smile.

"Ooh, what a great line of dialogue. Just like how you wrote that you never heard my voice again after Bibliophile even though we lived together for a whole month after that, and if I remember things correctly, I think—and correct me if I'm wrong—I think I may have spoken, like, maybe once or twice within those thirty-one days," Cherry says.

"I think I may have spoken, like, maybe once or twice within those thirty-one days," Helen repeats, mocking Cherry's LA accent.

Just as Cherry takes a step toward Helen, another pack of Karan's readers streams out, all lovingly cradling their signed copies of his books. This time the entire crowd recognizes at least one of the writers currently brawling on the busy New York street just outside their friend's book launch.

"Oookay, so before we all get written up in some gossip rag—" Mishler begins.

"Don't worry. I'm going," Helen says, pulling her purse tight on her shoulder.

"Bye forever, then," Cherry says defiantly.

Cherry's words hit Helen hard, just as they're meant to. Even Mishler sneaks a glance at his wife. As her childish anger hangs in the thick humidity of summertime in New York, Cherry's face falters just enough to make Helen hesitate for the briefest of seconds. Finally, Helen turns away from Cherry and Mishler without another word.

"You okay?" Mishler asks, stepping in front of Cherry, who's watching Helen disappear among the people on the crowded New York street.

"No," Cherry answers, crumpling in her husband's arms.

"It's going to—"

"I need to tell you something," Cherry blurts before she can change her mind.

"Okay," Mishler says, his voice just a little bit wobbly. But Cherry just stands there, the years-old confession spiny and sharp in her throat.

"What did you need to tell me?" Mishler asks, his voice gentle and soft.

"I can't look at you when I say it," Cherry says, holding on to his arms before closing her eyes.

"You're worrying me," Mishler says, pulling her closer. Cherry stumbles a bit, her entire being a terrorized riot.

"The essay I used to get into Hayho wasn't mine. I found it in the library in this little stapled book someone had made of local writers' essays from 1962." Cherry opens her eyes and finally looks at Mishler. "I stole it."

"Oh, honey," Mishler says, pulling her in for a hug.

"I'm so . . . sorry and ashamed and . . . I should have told you, but I just . . . I didn't . . . I hated that I did it and I know it was wrong and—" Cherry cries, her face buried in the crook of Mishler's neck.

"Honey—"

Cherry pulls away from Mishler, terrified. "I totally understand if . . . if this is a deal-breaker and . . . we . . . I . . ."

"Cherry." Mishler's voice is serious.

"Just . . . if we do . . . if this is where we end things, just . . . please don't tell Marlo. I can't . . ." Cherry crumples into tears.

"When I was fifteen, I copied one of Matisse's cut-out paintings and turned it in as my own," Mishler admits, drying her tears with the pulled-down cuff from his button-down shirt.

"That's . . . that's not the same thing. You were a kid," Cherry says.

"So were you." Mishler tucks a rogue tress of black hair behind her ear.

"I'm just as bad as Helen," Cherry says.

"I don't know about that, but what I do know is that we all make mistakes." Mishler gently nudges her. "Would you make the same choice today?"

She finally meets his gaze. "No. Of course not."

"Then . . . why not use this essay thing to show yourself how far you've come, hm?" Mishler asks.

"I . . ." Cherry trails off, trying to steady her breathing.

"It was twenty years ago, and you've written several books and essays and outlines and treatments and even a few episodes of the show. Do you think maybe you can forgive yourself?"

"I can try," Cherry squeaks out.

"That's a start," Mishler says, smiling.

"But forgiving myself for 'bye forever, then' is going to take a bit longer," Cherry says, trying to lighten the moment. "Why would I say that?"

"Things got heated," Mishler offers, trying not to laugh.

"I'm a writer, for chrissakes, and that was the best I could do? Bye forever, then!" Cherry yelps.

But there's something in the way Cherry says it that causes both of them to start laughing, and as Mishler squeaks out, "Bye forever, then," through wheezes of hysterics, they both dissolve into fits of healing laughter. For years, she's feared this exact moment, and now that it's finally come to pass, she feels lighter, but . . .there's a tail on it.

Up until now, the only person who knew all of her was Helen, and when that friendship fell apart, Cherry convinced herself it was because all her chickens were coming home to roost. She was flawed. She was too intense. She had driven Helen to Tess because she'd wanted to be a purple ribbon so desperately, she'd lost herself. Just as she'd done when she stole that essay. Somewhere so deep and gooey inside her, Cherry feared that Mishler would come to feel the same.

Breaking apart, Cherry just shakes her head, waiting for any of what transpired over the last five minutes to sink in. When it finally becomes clear that processing this is maybe going to take a tad longer than a few seconds on a crowded Greenwich Village street, she agrees to follow Mishler back into the bookstore, where they join the long line waiting to get their books signed. Karan invites them both to his aunt's restaurant just down the block for a postlaunch meal and they happily agree, anxious to reset the evening.

As twenty or so of Karan's family and friends stream into Karan's aunt's small Bengali restaurant later that evening, Cherry finds herself replaying moments over and over from her fight with Helen. At first, she pulls out little conversational snippets as if she's a scientist checking and rechecking the contents of a petri dish, studying it and chronicling how it's changed and transformed over the course of a moment, an hour, and a day. But as Karan's aunt brings out plate after plate of mouthwatering food, she finds herself almost in a trance as she desperately tries to make herself remember each word and every look as best she can.

"Cherry? Hon?" Mishler's voice pierces through the looped highlight reel, and Cherry focuses back on the here and now.

"I'm so sorry. I missed that, sweetie," Cherry says, her brain still being pulled in every direction.

"Karan asked how your conversation went with Helen," Mishler says carefully.

"If you're okay talking about it, of course," Karan adds, leaning in.

"It was weird," Cherry answers honestly.

"And this was the first time you two had spoken . . ."

"In ten years," Cherry finishes.

"Wow," Karan says, sneaking a look over at Mishler.

"Did you . . . Have you talked to her at all?" Cherry asks Karan.

"Yes, when I was in town for the Brooklyn Book Festival." Karan stops to think and looks over at Nish. "It was right around when Arpita was born, so two, two and a half years? Maybe a little more?" Nish nods, his eyes locked on two-year-old Arpita as she shovels a handful of Gobindobhog into her tiny mouth.

"Was she visiting or at the festival or does she live here or . . ." Cherry asks, more curious about Helen's interaction with Karan than telling another talented writer that she said "bye forever, then" to another grown person in a fit of pique.

"She was here to take a bunch of meetings with editors but wanted to pick my brain about agents. I guess she'd spoken to Tess's agent but wasn't sure about her," Karan says.

"Yes, she was always so very impressed with Tess," Cherry says, her voice way more acerbic than she means it to be.

"I didn't really know Tess all that well, so . . ." Karan says, dodging the invitation to pile on. There is a slight lull in the conversation as Karan and Mishler wait for Cherry to return to the question at hand. She finally picks up on it and tries to figure out where to even start.

"I know that we all pull from our lives for the books we write, but . . . I don't know," Cherry says, still piecing things together herself.

"The leather jacket, right?" Karan asks.

"Yes!" Cherry says, wrapping her arms around herself and the leather jacket.

"What I thought was fascinating was how she was just as hard on herself, but it was very strategic," Karan adds.

"Oh, that's . . . What do you mean?" Cherry asks, all of a sudden unsure of what he means.

"Like, why attribute all of the condescending literary criticism to the workshop members, when she was the one who said all of that stuff?" Karan says, nudging Mishler. Both Cherry's and Mishler's faces drain of color.

"What?" they ask in unison. Karan looks instantly mortified.

"I haven't read it yet," Mishler says, his voice getting caught in his throat.

"Oh . . . um, so in the Hayho section at the awards dinner, she has our characters saying all of the things she actually said about Cherry and her writing when . . ." Karan can't bring himself to say it.

"Wa-wait. She wasn't the one who defended me?" Cherry asks, barely able to say the words out loud. Mishler and Karan share a long, pained look.

"No, honey," Mishler finally says, placing a hand on her arm. Cherry is fully shutting down at this point, the loud restaurant muffling around her.

"And don't get us wrong. We were"—Karan looks over at Mishler, who gives him a nod—"insecure dum-dums who didn't fight her or tell her to stop, so . . ."

"But Tala did," Mishler adds, coming clean.

"Tala?" Cherry squeaks out.

"Yeah, she was actually the one who defended you. She would always ask—"

"Oh, I loved how she did this," Karan cuts in.

"She would always ask, 'What do you mean by that?' when Helen would say something mean," Mishler says.

"And Helen would always backpedal, acting like she wasn't saying what she definitely was saying," Karan adds.

"I can't believe it was Helen. What about Ruth?" Cherry asks in a daze.

Karan laughs. "Well, first I'd like to point out that Ruth and I were definitely not dating." He gestures over to Nish and their beautiful family.

"Oh my god, I didn't even . . . Oh, Karan. I'm so sorry," Cherry says, horrified that it's taken this long for it to dawn on her that everyone who attended Hayho in 1995 became fodder for Helen's novel.

Except Tess.

Cherry's anger flares as, once again, Tess is just as immune to the slings and arrows of Helen's poison pen as she was to her sharp tongue in real life. And Cherry bets that it didn't even occur to Tess that her character was a complete fiction—all enviable and cool, instead of the deeply troubled woman with addiction issues that everyone else knew her to be. From what she can remember, smoking cigarettes was the least of her vices. But like Cherry said before, Helen was always so very impressed with her.

"Nish and I got a big laugh out of it," Karan says, putting his hand on Nish's shoulder.

"We now refer to her as Karan's ex," Nish says, laughing.

"As in, 'Your ex's book just got flagged for plagiarism,'" Karan says.

"Or, 'Oh look, your ex continues to fail up and just became an agent at one of the big five agencies,'" Nish says.

"She's an agent now?" Mishler asks, stunned.

"And I'm sure it's a complete coincidence that she landed her mother's tell-all memoir that went for seven figures at auction," Nish says, shaking his head.

"You're kidding me," Mishler says.

"Nope," Nish says, tidying up the mess around Arpita's plate. Mishler can only shake his head in frustrated disbelief.

"But Helen got Ruth right. She was always cartoonishly awful, and from what I remember, she seemed to rather enjoy the gossiping. But it felt like Helen liked . . . not so much the gossiping or even Ruth, but . . ." Karan trails off, thinking about what he wants to say.

"Having a fancy friend," Cherry finishes, putting broken-hearted air quotes around the words "fancy friend."

"Yeah," Karan agrees.

"I honestly don't understand what happened to her," Cherry says, now spiraling.

"I mean, I think cancer changes you," Karan says softly.

"What?" Cherry chokes out. Karan and Mishler share a look. Nish looks away, giving the trio privacy.

"Helen. She mentioned at our lunch that she had been battling cancer"—Cherry bolts up in her chair, so Karan quickly finishes his sentence—"but that she caught it early. Last I heard she's been cancer-free ever since."

"Oh, thank god," Cherry sighs, rattled by how terrified she was about someone she apparently hates.

"Kind of explains . . . things," Mishler says to Cherry.

"Does it?" Cherry asks.

"I mean, if she thought . . . you know, she was . . . not going to be here much longer, it explains why she was desperate to finally write her debut," Mishler says, choosing his words carefully.

"And absolve all of her sins in the process," Cherry adds.

Mishler nods. "That too."

"It almost makes it worse," Cherry says, locked in her own world.

"Does it?" Mishler asks, looking over at Karan.

"Why live your life as a good person, when you can just use your debut novel to rewrite history and make yourself into the hero you never were in real life. Oh, and while you're at it, why not make up a bunch of lies about every single person you've ever met and make them into cowardly jerks who were definitely not as smart and brave as you were. Ugh!" As Cherry gets more and more animated, she accidentally hits the table and sends at least one water glass flying. Cherry is instantly mortified and sops up the spill with a stack of napkins from the middle of the table.

"Honey . . ." Mishler stacks the sodden napkins onto his empty plate.

"I'm sorry. I'm so sorry . . . I don't know . . . I honestly don't know why this is . . . why I'm acting like this," Cherry says, quickly losing control.

"It's okay . . . really, it's okay," Karan soothes.

As Karan's aunt wheels out a giant cake with Karan's book cover on it, the entire group begins to applaud the man of the hour, hooting and hollering his name and then calling for a speech! Speech! Speech! As Nish pushes his beloved husband to stand, beaming with pride, all Cherry can do is get lost in a single question.

Did she even know the real Helen Hicks?

CHAPTER FIFTEEN

Having successfully staked out her favorite table at the coffee shop, Cherry strides over to the long line and falls in just behind a woman with a giant white poodle.

"She's friendly," the woman says as the dog nuzzles Cherry.

"Look who's a good girl, look at this little sweetie, yes you are . . ." Cherry coos, petting the dog.

"Do you have dogs?" the woman asks.

"We have two. My old girl is twelve, and our daughter's ridiculous puppy is four now," Cherry says as the poodle nudges her for more pets.

"And do they get along?" the woman asks, concerned.

"Not in the beginning, but they're like two peas in a pod now. It's actually really sweet," Cherry says, pulling out her phone and showing the woman a photo of her old dachshund curled up next to Marlo's mutt of a puppy, all giant paws and gangly legs.

"Next!" the barista calls.

"Nice meeting you," the woman with the poodle says before stepping forward and ordering.

"You too," Cherry says. She looks down at the poodle and continues, "And you too." Cherry continues to pet the dog as the woman orders, finally saying a dramatic goodbye as the woman's drink is made and she and the poodle head out of the coffee shop and into the bright, sunny July morning. Cherry steps forward.

"Earl Grey tea and a morning bun?" the barista asks.

"Oh, yes please," Cherry answers, always taken aback when any of the standoffish baristas actually remember her.

Cherry collects her beverage and pastry and returns to her favorite table, setting out her laptop, headphones, a worn-in spiral notebook, three unsharpened Blackwing pencils, two pristine Pink Pearl erasers, and one pink-and-purple pencil sharpener as she takes a deep inhale of the tea. Cherry has a perfectly good office at home, but on days when her brain is particularly noisy, she ventures out to her favorite coffee shop to write. She remembers the very first day she got to write in a coffee shop on a weekday. She'd always dreamed of joining the others as they set out their laptops and ordered some fancy coffee and a pastry, settling in for a full day of writing. For years, she'd enviously stare at them as she waited in line for her morning coffee on the way to her shift at the thrift store. Every morning, she would tell herself . . . one day.

And truth be told, the magic of writing in a coffee shop on a weekday has yet to fade for Cherry. She still feels like a little kid playing hooky even now, and that swell of excitement at being able to buy a cup of tea and a pastry still fills her with unmitigated joy. But ever since her run-in with Helen a month ago, Cherry's brain has been noisier than ever, and crossing the finish line on this latest deadline has taken every ounce of focus she's had.

It hasn't helped that she's had to spend the entire month of July with Juno Brannan, a character inconveniently inspired by Helen herself. In fact, she's even felt the character shifting and morphing beneath her feet. Talking back to her. Fighting her . . . mocking her. Asking and re-asking: Are you sure you actually know me? Well, what if I did *this*? How is it that after ten novels in ten years, Juno Brannan has decided to go rogue? Of course, it's not lost on Cherry that this is all happening after her fateful run-in with her ex–best friend where she learned that their entire friendship was built on lies.

But it wasn't all lies.

Cherry has caught herself obsessing over all the factual discrepancies in Helen's novel while, at the same time, elaborately tiptoeing around some of the more nuanced truths that are too tender to even touch. Cherry can't face those strobing neon arrows just above the observations, conclusions, and personality traits that Helen annoyingly got right. And while Cherry has managed to dodge those inconvenient truths in her real life, she is less able to ignore them when it's Juno Brannan doing the prodding.

Cherry has always hated how books seem to know what they're about before the writer does. And even more dangerous, Juno Brannan seems to be hell-bent on pushing Cherry into darker and darker corners of the world she has created. A circumstance that Cherry feels is wildly unfair, because writing these mysteries was supposed to distract her from the darker corners of herself, not illuminate them.

Cherry takes a sip of her tea and opens up the latest book document, setting her fictional detective loose on her noisy mind. Cherry puts on her headphones, sets her timer, and shuffles her latest writing playlist.

And then proceeds to just sit there.

And sit there.

And sit there.

The blinking cursor is both inviting her in and taunting her at the same time. After far too long, Cherry grabs her phone and opens her text messages. Thank god, there's a text from Mishler.

What time are you and Marlo leaving for the concert?

You'd better ask Marlo, because if left to me, I'll get there way too early and then we'll be uncool, Cherry taps out.

As Cherry waits for Mishler to text Marlo at her summer job, she scans the measly 537 words she wrote yesterday and is relieved to find that they're not totally terrible. And even better, she has a good idea of where she has to go next and is confident it's not somewhere Juno will try to hijack with her newfound independence.

Always more comfortable with a printed outline, Cherry pulls the twenty-nine-page monstrosity from her bag, undoes the binder clip, and shifts between pages, reminding herself of the finer details needed for today's writing. But as she flips back and forth between two pages,

Cherry finds a plot point that no longer works now that Juno has had a bit of a makeover and is no longer "fundamentally unremarkable." Cherry sits back on the coffee shop bench and crosses her arms, both annoyed and excited about Juno's inability to just blend in and let people's underestimation of her be their downfall. This new Juno is loud, unapologetic, and—after ten novels—finally comfortable with how good she is at her job. And as this new Juno finally grows up, she's forcing Cherry to admit her true parentage.

Because while the plots of Cherry's books have very little to do with their yearslong friendship, Juno Brannan herself is very obviously the love child of both Helen and Cherry. Skillfully crafted as an absolute blend of both women, Juno holds within her all of Helen's phenomenal intelligence and wry wit, along with Cherry's sincerity and plainspokenness. But the realization that began to dangerously thaw Cherry in the weeks that followed her run-in with Helen in New York is that so much of Juno is based not only on those aspects of Helen and Cherry that they share—the feeling of being an outsider, the yearning to belong, and the constant fear that just maybe they are the singular human being on this planet who is officially unlovable—but that Juno also has those attributes within Cherry that are because of Helen. The curiosity Helen instilled in Cherry, the joy of learning, and the ability to dream beyond her own small vision for herself.

In the dark of the night, as Cherry tossed and turned, she was forced to admit that Helen changed her. Despite how angry she's been with her over the years, when Cherry sees Juno, in all her objective glory, she has to admit that Helen has changed her—and Juno—for the better.

It's hard when a friendship comes to an end. But it's even harder to admit that it wasn't all bad.

Cherry thinks back over the last ten years and how impossible it's been to navigate the aftermath of the breakup of her friendship with Helen. When she tried to talk about it with anyone, there was this shrugging confusion as to why she was so broken up about it. Helen was just a friend, what was the big deal? But Helen was the biggest of deals in Cherry's life. To her, they were like sisters. To everyone else, the demise of their friendship didn't seem to muster the same level of care and concern that would've happily been offered had Helen been a romantic partner. And not even one who lasted ten years. In fact, Cherry got more support after a six-month fling ended than she was ever offered after Helen left.

She remembers how excited Leni was to gossip and bring up all Helen's shortcomings after she moved out. At the time, Cherry was grateful for the outlet. But when gossip became the only thing she was allowed to talk about when it came to Helen, she found herself struggling to perform the level of joyous outrage that everyone seemed to want from her. Yes, she was mad. Yes, Helen had acted poorly, but Cherry was also hurt and sad and, quite to Leni's surprise, still loved Helen. And whenever Cherry wanted to talk about the ache she felt and how much she still missed Helen, she was met with dismissive affirmations about how she'd won the friend breakup. Then Leni would shut the conversation down with some trite cliché that felt more like a perfunctory shove back out into a life that no longer included the single most important person to her.

Leni finally distanced herself from Cherry because she grew weary of her still being upset about Helen mere months after she'd left. Frustrated with her because she still checked Helen's social media or kept that one mix she'd made or refused to throw away that stupid neon plastic half-of-a-heart necklace with the rubbed-off letters *Be Fri* on it. And it wasn't that Cherry was thrilled with herself for not being able to move on, but however much her own reaction confused her, it did confirm that her friendship with Helen had been just as intimate as any fling, affair, or full-blown relationship Cherry had ever had.

Looking back on those lonely months and years now, Cherry can see that she absolutely funneled all the grief she felt over losing Helen straight into Juno Brannan. All the things she missed about her friend were infused into Juno, and time usually spent with Helen became time spent with Juno. And year after year, book after book, Juno Brannan became a proxy for Helen Hicks, right down to the way Cherry talks to Juno when she writes, using the young detective as a sounding board, confidante, and therapist.

Cherry takes a sip of her tea and thinks back to those two years when she wrote her first book. Hindsight continues to be a humbling experience for Cherry because, of course, now she can see all the things she'd do differently. She would have told Helen about the book, the agent hunt, and the auction. She would have confronted her about her snobbery, but . . . Cherry scrapes a hand through her hair and shifts on the coffee shop bench . . . no. Cherry has to admit that the Helen of ten years ago wasn't ready to have those conversations either. In fact, from what Karan and Mishler said about Helen being the one who actually said all that mean stuff about Cherry and attributing it to them in her novel . . . the Helen of right now is not ready to have the conversation either. It's hard for Cherry to face that their friendship was doomed, but that's exactly what it was. Because the only way their friendship would have worked was if Cherry remained small and only Helen got big. That's what Cherry finally realized that fateful day at Bibliophile.

The hard truth that still makes Cherry's entire chest hurt is that if and when Helen had sold a book, she probably would have dumped Cherry for Tess anyway, thus ending their friendship with a fizzle instead of the blaze of glory it went down in.

Because while Cherry considered herself Helen's best friend, she has to face that Helen would never actually choose her over Tess or even defend her among her academic peers. In fact, Cherry was right in keeping her book a secret from Helen, because even though Helen was her best friend, Cherry is positive she would never truly consider Cherry's writing as important as her own. No, Cherry was her friend because, on top of being her constant companion, she was also someone she got to feel better than. And even though it pains her to admit it, the care and feeding of Helen's low self-esteem was actually who Cherry was in a friendship with, not Helen herself.

And what's confused Cherry for years: why she loved Helen so completely, knowing that all that was true. She doesn't yet have an answer, but feels it's somewhere in the realm of . . . well, she wasn't like that all the time, and those glimmers she got of the version of Helen that would choose her over Tess and defend her among her academic peers and celebrate Cherry's writing were heartbreaking and beautiful enough to fuel a ten-year-long relationship that changed both of them forever.

But then the version of Cherry that Helen portrayed in her book whispers in her ear. She, too, has faults; she, too, has things she can work on; and she, too, was part of the downfall of their friendship.

"Those damn orange ribbons," Cherry mumbles to herself. The girl at the next table over gives her a sideways glance. Cherry gathers herself and acts like she was reading something she wrote aloud. As if the girl cares at all.

Cherry had just signed a three-book deal worth hundreds of thousands of dollars. She was about to be wined and dined in some of the most exclusive restaurants around Los Angeles in a race to secure her television and film rights. Within two years, she'd be sitting on set next to the young actress playing Juno Brannan as her story, her world, and her characters were turned into one of the most successful shows on television. And yet she let a stupid orange ribbon corrupt her so fully that she was about to come to blows over access to snack-size pretzels and free subpar wine.

It was the bookmobile all over again.

What Cherry has learned in the years since, is that purple ribbons don't just exist at Bibliophile. A lesson she, naturally, learned the hard way, having naively thought that once she'd sold a book, she, too, would be anointed a purple ribbon. But that simply was not the case. And frustratingly, how good her books were had nothing to do with the classification. She was a welfare kid from Southern California who never went to college and was writing genre fiction—ergo, she was an orange ribbon through and through and would be forever, regardless of how many accolades she racked up.

Cherry learned this lesson when Mishler got invited to a fancy literary party when they first started dating and invited her as his plus-one. Having nightmarish flashbacks from Bibliophile, Cherry agonized over what to wear, what to eat prior to the party so she wouldn't get nauseous, and basically how to change her entire personality so she would better fit in with the purple ribbons. The plan was that she would meet Mishler at the hotel in downtown Los Angeles where the party was being held after he finished his panel at the *LA Times* Festival of Books and they'd go in together. This was a plan that sounded way better in theory than in practice, because it left Cherry sitting by herself at the entrance to a party watching as purple ribbon after purple ribbon swanned past her with nary a passing glance.

By the time Mishler arrived, Cherry was officially closing in on herself. And as he checked them both in, her mind was a riot of pep talks, soothing mantras, and desperate pleas to get herself together. As she stepped inside—all wild eyes, clammy hands, and highly combustible digestion—she finally found herself at a real purple-ribbon party. She vowed to herself that this time would be nothing like Bibliophile. This time, she was no longer the manager at a thrift store in the Haight, but a successful author with five books on the bestseller list and a TV adaptation already in its second season. This time, they would have to accept her. Of course, she'd glossed over the fact that, just as at Bibliophile, she was only able to gain entry because of someone else. She pushed that fact to the darkest recesses of her psyche.

Once inside, Mishler and Cherry found a spot in the corner of the restaurant and Cherry just stood there, taking in the luxurious spread of food and the bustling open bar that served expensive mixed drinks as well as beer and wine. She observed obsequious cater waiters darting between exclusive groups of purple ribbons as they offered tiny appetizer versions of dishes found on menus of the most exclusive Michelin-starred restaurants.

But as she stood there, pulling and tugging at the new clothes she'd bought especially for the party, she was shocked to find how comfortable all the purple ribbons were with being feted. They had not bought new clothes for the party. They were not nervous or sick to their stomachs. Quite the opposite, in fact. They took their time assessing the appetizers, unbothered by the cater waiter having to stand there motionless and holding the tray up so they could better see it. They laughed with friends as they ordered expensive drink after expensive drink, never deigning to tip the bartender, who they'd then call "chief" or "sport."

And as Mishler and Cherry finally made their way to the bar, she overheard a writer she'd seen on a panel at Bibliophile tell an entire group of purple ribbons that he'd just gotten back from "a surfing trip to Mexico." The very same writer, she thought to herself, who she knew had spent the last ten years writing a breathtakingly boring memoir while his wife not only took care of the house and kids but bankrolled him by working tirelessly as an ICU nurse. The writer had an educational pedigree that looked a lot like Helen's, an agent he met while at Harvard, and an editor who had a house next to his parents in the Hamptons. His novel went on to become a bestseller and won several awards. An outcome he was not only comfortable with but expected.

Seeing him at that party broke something in Cherry Stewart. Up until that point she'd assumed that these purple-ribbon writers were just like her—constantly questioning whether they were talented and relentlessly unsure as to the merits of both themselves as writers and the books they wrote. But that simply wasn't true. That night, Cherry came to learn that the entire publishing industry is run by purple ribbons for the benefit of purple ribbons, who are then reviewed and celebrated by purple ribbons. And there she was, with her little crumpled food stamp, joyously left out of something that she had every right to take part in.

And what pained Cherry was Helen turned out to be no different from any of the purple ribbons at that party. Looking back at their time together, Cherry had to admit that Helen got off on seeing people left out. She got off on being in the greenroom and that Cherry needed her to gain access. She got off on others wanting what she had, even when what she had was all an illusion. So much so that she chose it, instead of hanging out with Cherry, every chance she got. Even if it was the difference between an incredible hotel breakfast with her best friend and a sad gray room filled with joyless purple ribbons eating flaccid bacon.

And what killed Cherry was, like the people at that party, Helen was never able to see her as anything but an orange ribbon. Even now, what stings Cherry the most about that dumb book of hers is that it all but cemented Cherry's orange ribbon–ness, not only within Helen's story but to the entire world. Because just like all the purple ribbons who came before her, Helen's debut novel was lavished with praise, while Helen herself was the subject of countless lovingly painted profiles about how a plucky Glending Fellow persevered through thick and thin to create the kind of great art that takes time . . . *unlike those sell-out orange ribbons,* Cherry added, reading between the lines.

What frustrates Cherry is she knows it shouldn't matter. Regardless of purple and orange ribbons, she gets to write for a living. She gets to sit at a coffee shop on a school day and order tea and pastries, writing books she loves for readers she adores. And unlike her entire family before her, Cherry won't have to do backbreaking work for pennies well into her old age just to have society abandon her when her body is no longer strong enough to be useful. She will be safe. She is safe.

But . . .

Cherry also isn't completely sure she wouldn't have a meltdown if there was a mix-up at some conference and she was accidentally given the wrong badge—a badge without the privileges she apparently needs in order to feel like a Real Writer. A badge that makes it possible for her to cosplay a purple ribbon as if each and every book conference is some kind of comic book convention. So maybe it wasn't only the care and feeding of Helen's low self-esteem that was in play during that fateful weekend.

Cherry's phone vibrates on the table, and she dives for it, thankful for the distraction from a few too many uncomfortable epiphanies about herself.

Apparently people have been camping out since last night, so Marlo says you can leave at 4 so she can at least get some merch, Mishler texts.

Cherry's heart soars at the thought of leaving early.

Camping out since last night? she texts back.

I know it's a young person's game my back could never. Mishler adds a laughing-face emoji at the end of his sentence, something Marlo ribs him for with abandon. Of course, it's made him do it more.

I'll try to get home around 2 just in case she wants to leave earlier, Cherry texts back, happy for the excuse to stop writing early.

She opens her laptop back up, scrolls through yesterday's writing, and fiddles with a word here and a word there, trying to trick herself into finding the momentum she most definitely doesn't have. But after another Earl Grey tea and a lusciously moist brownie, Cherry is able to finally shut out all today's noisy breakthroughs about purple and orange ribbons and get to work on Juno Brannan's latest mystery.

Hours later, feeling a calm that can only come from a good day of writing, she sits back on the coffee shop bench and lets out a gloriously long exhale. Her shoulders now lowered below her ears, she saves the book document for a paranoid hundredth time and shuts down her laptop. She packs everything back into her bag, buses her dishes, and walks out of the coffee shop with a contented sigh.

As Cherry drives home, she wonders when it all got so complicated. She remembers how she used to dictate stories to her kindergarten teacher before she could even write. Back then, the sheer joy she felt making up stories had nothing to do with stealing essays or purple and orange ribbons. She was a writer because she wrote. And she did it because it made her happy and that feeling of happiness was all that mattered.

Why did she know she was a real writer at five years old, but at forty she's not so sure?

Still in a haze, Cherry pulls into her driveway and beeps her car locked. She remembers the first time she pulled into this driveway after she and Mishler bought this house after a lifetime of having to park in numbered spots, shared parking lots, or just battling it out with street parking with the rest of the neighborhood. Mishler had been confused about why she was so emotional, and when she told him that this was not only her first home but her first driveway, he'd hugged her for an embarrassingly long time before trying—and failing—to carry her over the threshold. As Cherry unlocks the back door, she smiles to herself that Mishler is pretty okay . . . for a purple ribbon.

"I'm home!" Cherry calls out, closing the back door behind her. She hears Marlo before she sees her, heavy footsteps running down the long hallway and barreling right toward her.

"You're early thank god we should probably go the line is super crazy right now," Marlo says without taking a breath, trying to show Cherry a grainy photo from someone's social media of the scene outside LA Live, where the concert starts in five and a half hours. In Marlo's other hand is a poster board with four giant pictures of her favorite member of the group that she's printed out from the internet, along with their group name made from some shiny gold wrapping paper Cherry found in the back of one of their closets. She's also got a homemade sign that Cherry helped her make out of three glued-together paper plates and a Popsicle stick handle that has just the face of her favorite group member on both sides.

Mishler sidles up behind his daughter, just shaking his head and mouthing that he's sorry. But Cherry waves him off. She couldn't be happier. Marlo asking her to come to this concert with her is the coolest thing that's happened to her all year. Because both she and Mishler are in complete denial that their time with Marlo is ticking down before she starts college in the fall, a night at a concert with her favorite group feels like a gift. And while Marlo is going to be less than thirty miles away at UCLA, she'll be living in the dorms, and the days of it being just the three of them in this house will change.

Watching Marlo buzzing with excitement, Mishler crosses his arms and purses his lips, and Cherry knows that he's, once again, trying not to get teary at the thought of Marlo going off to college. He leans back against the kitchen island and gooily takes her in. Marlo is dressed in a pair of jean shorts and a T-shirt she decorated with the group's name spelled out in rhinestones. Her wavy blond hair is pulled back in a sparkly headband, and she's attempted to put glittery eye shadow on, along with a shimmery lip gloss that smells like strawberries. Her round face looks just like Mishler's and that open smile of hers could make Cherry do anything . . . like drop her workbag on the counter of their kitchen and wear the same clothes she wore to the coffee shop just so she can get her beloved stepdaughter to a "super-crazy line" full of fans four and a half hours before the concert starts.

Standing in the staggering July heat, Cherry is beyond thankful she took the Dodger cap Mishler handed her just before she left the house. She watches as Marlo excitedly shows the pack of girls in front of them the poster board she made and stands in awe as the entire line explodes in fan chants that they all seem to know, excitedly trades photocards and stickers with one another, and performs bits of impossible choreography Cherry is stunned to find out that Marlo knows and, even more miraculously, actually does in front of other people. Of course, she doesn't show that she's surprised or even paying attention, knowing how shy Marlo can be. In fact, she acts like she's just surveying the packed Nokia Plaza and the line of hundreds upon thousands of young fans that snakes back so far she can't even see the end of it. Which is when Cherry notices a trio of friends passing through the plaza area, probably about the same age as Marlo. One of them points to the long line and laughs, while another makes what is clearly a snide comment as they mock some of the choreography the excited fans in the line are doing. Seeing this, two fortysomething couples on a double date laugh along with the trio of friends, and the group of strangers bond and laugh at the silly young fans waiting in line to see a music group they've decided is uncool.

Cherry immediately becomes protective of the joyous young women in line, but then notices they don't need her to be. Because it's not that they don't see them or sense they're being mocked—orange ribbons tend to have a sixth sense about those things. But thanks to the sheer numbers of other superfans that surround them, they feel emboldened to not hide or apologize. They feel safe to just be themselves and love something with their whole heart.

"Okay, how are we going to do this?" Cherry asks Marlo as the time ticks down for them to be allowed inside the venue. Marlo's little face gets serious, her brow furrowing as she considers Cherry's question.

"We have our seats, so we don't need to rush in to get those, but—"

"The merch," Cherry finishes, solemnly.

"Right," Marlo says, nodding.

"Okay. How about I run to the merch line and you grab our seats? That way if it takes forever, you won't miss a minute of the concert," Cherry says. Marlo's entire face flushes, but before Cherry can ask what's wrong, Marlo speaks.

"That . . . that sounds great," Marlo says, scrunching up her mouth just like she did when she was little and trying not to cry. Cherry wraps her arm around her stepdaughter and pulls her close. Marlo melts into her, resting her head on Cherry's shoulder, already overwhelmed. Cherry wonders how this lovely kid is going to handle actually seeing the group perform and worries she may not make it.

Within minutes, Marlo is back to fanchanting, dancing, and singing along with the other fans. Cherry sneaks a few photos of Marlo and sends them to Mishler.

I've never seen her this happy, Cherry writes, sending a photo of Marlo mid-choreography, her arms raised over her head and her face beaming with the biggest smile Cherry has ever seen.

SHE IS THE CUTEST KID IN THE WHOLE WIDE WORLD! Mishler types back immediately, along with a string of crying-face emojis.

Cherry sends back a string of hearts and pockets her phone, settling in and just letting herself bask in the sheer, unabashed joy these young fans are currently getting lost in as they are finally let inside the venue.

After a barely contained thumbs-up, Marlo races to their seats while Cherry gets into the long merch line that trails around the venue's lobby. And then everything slows down and Cherry finds herself standing at the center of it all: the sheen of sweat that feels cool against the blast of air-conditioning, the excited squeals of delight in happy, bright voices, and young people from every walk of life being brave enough to lose themselves in the freedom that comes from truly loving something with your whole heart.

Just like Cherry loves writing.

And then everything that's been troubling her over the last month shifts and converges inside her. The group of people who mocked the young women in line for the show. The greenroom at Bibliophile.

Helen and her metastasized view of art. Purple ribbons, orange ribbons . . . it doesn't have to be so complicated. Looking around at these young women, it's simple. So simple. She used to be like this. Hell, she was just like this today at that coffee shop. She got lost for hours making up stories, just as she's done her whole life. And that contentment had nothing to do with who talked to her at some stuffy party or whether she was allowed access to a free snack-size bag of pretzels. When it's just her and writing . . . Cherry gulps down the building emotion now gathering in her throat and steadies herself to finish that sentence.

When it's just her and writing, Cherry Stewart is free.

She shakes her head. Again and again. So, if she's free when it's just her and writing, why does she keep inventing things to chain herself to? Because while purple ribbons are very real and the entire world is quite unfairly lousy on the ground with them, it's Cherry who's made the choice to prize their opinion over all else. It's Cherry who's made them into some kind of brutish bogeyman that holds her entire future happiness in the palm of its disapproving hands. It's Cherry who's chosen to keep their condescending remarks on a loop inside her own mind as she's burdened herself with a chip on her shoulder that's only gotten heavier and heavier over the years.

Why?

Because freedom is terrifying. Loving something with your whole heart is terrifying. Holding up a homemade poster with gold wrapping paper letters that announces to the world that you love something . . . is terrifying.

In a daze, Cherry looks around at the life she gets to live. A life that twelve-year-old Cherry would weep if she saw. And it's remembering herself as a twelve-year-old that finally breaks Cherry open. The tears fall as she remembers the little crumpled food stamp, the dictated stories, and the impossible dream that one day she could be a real writer. Cherry brings her hand to her chest, hoping it will push her now fully exposed heart back inside. But it doesn't. In fact, the bloody thing grows and thumps with abandon, now free of its solitary confinement.

In a futile attempt to try to distract herself from her own exposed, beating heart, she scans the wall of merch that now rises in front of her. A smile breaks across her face as she realizes she can buy Marlo every single thing that's hanging on that wall. She's not that little kid anymore. She can buy her a sweatshirt, a T-shirt, a poster . . . all of it.

"I'm going to get that kid everything," Cherry quietly mutters to herself as she realizes she's next in line. That kid. The tears burst through her.

That kid who stepped into that bookmobile with a crumpled food stamp. That kid who just wanted to buy a book like the rest of the kids. That kid.

"I'm going to buy that kid everything," Cherry chokes out again through tears.

Cherry steps to the front of the line and orders two of everything. One for Marlo and one for herself.

Arms full of sweatshirts, T-shirts, posters, little red light sticks, and a handful of photocards, Cherry makes her way back to their seats, where she finds Marlo laughing and jumping up and down with the rest of the young fans in their section. She unloads the armful of items she bought, and Marlo fully loses it, lunging into Cherry for a hug. They break apart and Marlo carefully stows their haul in the seats they definitely won't be sitting in for one single second. But just as the lights go to black and the entire theater erupts in screams and cheers, Cherry pulls her T-shirt from the perfectly folded little pile and puts it on over the shirt she's already wearing. In the beautiful twinkly light of thousands of little red light sticks in the pitch black, Cherry looks down at her T-shirt and then over at Marlo.

This is real.

CHAPTER SIXTEEN

Helen opens the door to the café and steps inside. She shifts to the side of the entrance, swapping out her prescription sunglasses for her regular glasses, while deftly scanning the new terrain. There are two refrigerator cases full of grab-and-go sandwiches and salads, eight tables, one long banquette extending along the wall, and a smattering of outlets peppered throughout. She homes in on the lone empty table pushed up against a built-in planter full of plastic plants, a prized socket all but hidden by a rogue artificial fern. Eyeballing the long line full of people with large computer bags, Helen quickly crosses the main room, sets her computer bag territorially atop the empty table, pulls out her wallet, and settles into the back of the long line, now full of people wishing they'd thought of doing that.

Helen got to the café two hours early, planning to get a little work done before her lunch with Tess's stepdaughter, Fizzy. But as she scans the pastries the café has on offer, Helen has pivoted her plan to maybe less working and more scrolling through social media and enjoying a nice coffee and pastry.

"Large iced Americano and a pain au chocolat, please," Helen orders when she finally gets to the front of the line. She pulls a credit card from her wallet and hands it to the café employee. They take the card, run it through the machine, and hand it back wordlessly. Helen awkwardly stands there, unsure as to whether they are going to give her the stuff she ordered now or bring it to her table later. Furious that she spent the last ten minutes waiting in line looking down at her phone so she wouldn't feel bad about stealing the last empty table, but failed to notice what this café's protocol was. This is exactly why she's been going to the same café that's located within walking distance of her house in the center of Mill Valley for years. Helen appreciates the slower pace, locals-only vibe, and the fact that she's pretty sure all the teenage employees are a little bit scared of her.

"Yeah?" the café employee asks in an apathetic growl.

"Do I wait or . . ." Helen trails off, trying to match the employee's apathy pound for pound.

"Huh?" The employee sighs. At this, Helen has to admit she's outgunned. There is no way she can compete. She knows that now.

"Do I wait for my order here, or is someone going to bring it to my table?" Helen asks, her aristocratic diction making her absolutely repellent to the employee.

"Bring it to your table?" The employee scoffs, their pierced eyebrow raised. Sadly, Helen doesn't pick up on the sarcasm—which is shocking, considering it's her native language—and walks back to her table, taking them at their word.

She sets up her computer, pulls her headphones and notebook from the depths of her bag, and waits for her coffee and pastry. After a few minutes, she's forced to open her book document and flips her notebook to where her scribbled notes reside. Her entire body sinks as she's met with the scant few pathetic ideas she's managed to come up with for her second novel—a book that her publisher gets a First Look Option for and that her agent assures her would be better to turn in "sooner rather than later." All she needs is a synopsis and the first three chapters. But she can't even seem to manage that. After spending a few minutes typing the words "chapter one" in a myriad of different ways, she decides on all lowercase letters and confidently minimizes her book document to begin trolling through social media.

Finally, after a full fifteen minutes, she defiantly scooches over on the banquette and strides up to the counter, ready to light up the café employee about what could possibly be taking her order this long. Which is when she sees a pain au chocolat and a large iced Americano—the glass slick with condensation and the ice now slightly melted from sitting out for so long, waiting for her on a little black shelf next to where she'd ordered.

"Thank you so much," Helen coos to the employee, her face a mask of disdain.

"Oh, you're so welcome," the employee coos back, their tattooed hands clutched to their chest in mock gratitude. Helen grabs her drink and pastry and returns to her table, ruing the day she ever decided to agree to come to a brand-new café in Tess's old neighborhood.

Helen takes a sip of her Americano and hates how delicious it is. The perfect blend of bright and bitter, it's annoyingly the best one she's ever had. As she bites into the pain au chocolat, the flaky pastry tumbles down in shards, landing in swaths all down the front of her beige smock dress. She swipes the flakes off and onto the floor, hoping beyond hope that it's that employee's job to sweep under the tables at the end of their shift. She finishes the pastry, furious that it, too, was utterly delicious, and sets her plate on the far side of her table, as if clearing the decks to get to work before Fizzy arrives in a couple of hours.

Instead, she continues to sip her Americano as she jots down a few more phenomenally terrible kernels of ideas for her next book and then finishes seven crosswords from the activity book she bought at the airport when she returned from New York a few weeks ago. After doing this for almost the full two hours, she tells herself that right now is just about showing up and that, each time she does, she's that much closer to closing in on what her next novel will be about. But as she slides her laptop into her workbag, she can feel that reasoning growing thinner and thinner. The days have become weeks and the weeks have become months, and all she's got are pitches that even she knows are derivative and shallow. It took more than forty years to write her first novel—how in the world is she supposed to write the second "sooner rather than later"?

She naively thought the second book would be easier, now that she'd written the first one. But it's been quite the opposite. And it doesn't help that Cherry's words have haunted Helen ever since their fight in New York—that she and their friendship were the only extraordinary things about her, and without them, Helen has nothing of consequence to write about. It'd be one thing if Helen were overflowing with ideas, emphatically proving Cherry wrong. But she's not. She's got nothing. Just as Cherry warned.

And what really bothers her is that there seems to be even more pressure on her to produce a second novel in quick succession with the first, rather than finally getting to rest on her laurels after publishing her long-awaited debut novel. She thought this time would feel wonderful—going on book tour, talking to readers, and finally having that distant car alarm turned off for good. Instead, she's been blindsided by an unholy blend of wild vulnerability, debilitating expectations, and paralyzing performance anxiety. Not quite the victory lap she envisioned.

A small voice breaks Helen's descent into artistic panic. "Aunt Helen?" She looks up and there's Fizzy. Now in her early twenties, she looks just the same as she did when she was little. All giant blue eyes, some unnatural hair color (today's hair is bright pink), and a lovely curvy frame swimming in a pair of vintage overalls.

"Hi, sweetie. Sit . . . sit," Helen says, nervously half standing and gesturing to the chair just across from her.

"I can't believe you got a table. I just assumed we'd be perched on the curb eating our sandwiches," Fizzy says, her little British accent still just as adorable as Helen remembers.

"I have my ways," Helen says, smiling.

"Did you want to—"

"Should we—" Helen and Fizzy say in unison.

Helen's entire demeanor softens. She's been so in her own head, so lost. For so long. But this is Fizzy. Sweet Fizzy. She knows that it's dangerous, but Helen lowers her guard and finally lets herself relax . . . just a little.

"Why don't we go order," Helen says, smiling.

Still uncertain, Fizzy smiles, stands from her chair, and waits for Helen to slide out of the banquette. They walk over to the refrigerator case, and each picks out a sandwich before falling back in line. This time when Helen gets to the cash register, she attempts to be nice to the surly café employee. And when they ask for a couple of lemonades and bags of chips, Helen acts as though she has no idea why the employee is condescending and rude in return.

They sit back down at their table and Fizzy begins unwrapping her sandwich, but Helen can wait no longer. She lifts her workbag onto the banquette and pulls from its depths a large glass obelisk. Trying not to make a big deal about it, she hovers the obelisk just over the table, not wanting to slam it down.

"This . . . here is the . . . uh . . . you know," Helen says, extending the glass obelisk across the table. Fizzy looks up from her half-unwrapped sandwich, sees the obelisk, and deflates. It breaks Helen's heart. Fizzy brushes her fingers on a napkin and takes the obelisk with two hands.

"Thanks," Fizzy says, looking at the award.

Helen sits across from her and doesn't know what to say. She starts and stops a thousand different sentences in her head. "It's heavier than I thought it would be," she finally offers weakly.

Fizzy nods, but doesn't look up from the award. "Tess Bayard," she reads, brushing her fingers over the lettering.

"She would have hated the ceremony," Helen says, desperate to make Fizzy a little less sad.

"She would have hated the ceremony," Fizzy repeats.

They fall silent.

Helen watches as Fizzy continues to stare at the award and feels herself already holding back tears. She knew today would be hard, but she hadn't factored her own weakened state into the already impossible equation. She thought maybe Fizzy wouldn't want to talk about Tess or how hard things have been in the years since she passed away. She thought maybe Fizzy would choose to shut down all emotion and carry on as a husk of herself, as Helen had done—not that she would wish that life on anyone. Being one of the only adults left in Fizzy's life, Helen musters all her usual methods to shut down all emotion enough to push the tears back down her throat.

"I didn't know it would still hurt so much . . ." Helen starts. Fizzy looks up from the award. "This many years later."

Helen is careful not to say any of the words that might upset Fizzy, like "dead" or "died" or "drug overdose" or "possible suicide" or "gone forever" or "sadness" or "grief" or "breakdown."

"Me either," Fizzy says, finally setting down the glass obelisk.

"I miss her," Helen says, her voice impossibly soft.

"Me too," Fizzy says, looking down at the café table. Helen takes a deep breath.

"Do you want to talk about it?" she asks, bracing herself.

"I . . . uh . . . I have a therapist now. She's really helping . . . um, helping me," Fizzy says, still looking down at the table.

"That's great. That's a great idea," Helen says, not knowing how much enthusiasm she should be showing to a twenty-something kid for seeking out a mental health professional for the incapacitating grief that comes from losing a parent. They fall silent again, but this time it's because Fizzy is clearly working up the courage to say something.

"Aunt Helen?" Fizzy says, and her voice is so small it breaks Helen's heart.

"Yes, sweetie?"

"I think you should go to therapy, too," Fizzy blurts, fidgeting with her sandwich.

Helen sits there with her mouth hanging open—like, actually hanging open. A first.

"Oh, I . . . uh . . ." she stammers.

"It's helping . . . is helping me handle . . . you know," Fizzy says, finally looking up and meeting Helen's gaze.

"I . . . I don't know, sweetie. It's a busy time with the book tour and trying to write the second book. I . . . but I . . . I'll think about it, okay?" Helen says, now the one fidgeting with her sandwich. Fizzy nods and Helen begins unwrapping her sandwich, ready to move on to how Fizzy has been doing, how she likes the new internship, and if there's anything that's making her happy these days. She needs Fizzy to be okay, so Helen works hard to make her voice as sunny as possible as she prepares to launch into what she hopes will be a lighter topic. But just as she's about to speak, Fizzy cuts in.

"Can I say something?" Fizzy asks, surprising Helen. She really thought that would be the end of it.

"Sure, honey. Always." But also . . . no. Even in her depleted state, Helen knows she's hanging by a thread.

"I'm worried about you."

Helen stifles a bark of a laugh. It's visceral and comes from someplace so deep it shocks even her. Fizzy looks up, confused and more than a little hurt. Helen quickly recovers. "I think we're in a contest for who can be the most worried for the other one, then," she says, offering a gentle smile.

"Aunt Helen, please," Fizzy says, clearly struggling to find the courage to be heard.

"Sweetie, please don't worry about me. Really. You're too young to be worried about some mean old lady like me," Helen says, trying to make her laugh. It doesn't work.

"You're not a mean old lady." Helen laughs, ready to take the compliment and move on, but Fizzy isn't finished. "But you're becoming one."

Helen's entire body goes numb. "Oh my god, if I've been mean to you, I'm so—"

"No, never to me. But . . ."

"But?"

"To everyone else," Fizzy says, motioning over to the café employee currently terrorizing a middle-aged couple over their question as to which of their iced teas is decaffeinated.

"Oh, come on. They kind of deserve just a little bit, don't you think?" Helen asks, desperately trying to lighten things up again. Fizzy digs in the pocket of her overalls and pulls out a pinkish slip of paper. She slides it across the table. Helen picks it up and unfolds it.

"It's my therapist's phone number. I think you should call her. She . . . helps me make sense of things," Fizzy says. Taken aback by Fizzy standing her ground, Helen looks down at the woman's name and phone number, still unable to process what's going on. Finally, Helen looks up from the paper.

"Is this why you wanted to meet me? It wasn't . . . about the award?" Helen asks, holding the slip of paper in her hand. Fizzy shakes her head and Helen sits back in her chair. This whole time Helen thought she was ambushing Fizzy, but it's been the other way around.

"You don't have to even call her if you don't want to, but just someone you can talk to . . . anyone," Fizzy says, her little brow heartbreakingly furrowed.

"I don't—" Helen purses her lips and stubbornly doesn't finish that sentence. She knows abstractly that she has no friends, but over the years she's worked very hard to conceal that information from herself through keeping busy with book stuff, trying to write the second novel in various coffee shops around the Bay Area, and convincing herself that she needs to focus on her burgeoning writing career.

"After the whole thing happened when we spread her ashes—" Fizzy starts.

"Wait, is that what's made you worried about me? Look, your dad and I have never seen eye to eye and—"

"But do you still think it was your fault she died?" Fizzy blurts.

"Wh-what?" Helen asks, now officially feeling sick to her stomach.

"Do you?" Fizzy waits, those giant blue eyes boring into Helen. She can't lie to this kid. She's never been able to. But she can divert where this conversation is going.

"Sweetie, I really am okay. It's a sad thing I need to deal with, but that's . . . it's life. It's just life," Helen says, stumbling over her words just enough to infuriate her.

"You had cancer," Fizzy says, sounding like she's about to list the aforementioned sad things, and Helen can't have that.

"We caught it early. It was stage 1 and . . ." Helen puts her hand to her throat, where the scar from her thyroid lobectomy has healed nicely, as proof that it's well behind her.

"No, you had cancer and then we lost Tess," Fizzy continues, and Helen's hand falls away from her scar. "That's a lot to happen to a person in a year."

"I . . . I was lucky. They got it all and I didn't even need chemo. We don't have to—"

"My therapist says that even having a doctor tell you that you have a cancer is a traumatic moment regardless of—"

"Fizzy." Helen's voice is harsher than she means it to be and Fizzy recoils. "I'm sorry, I . . . I'm sorry, but I don't want to be the kind of adult that dismisses your concerns or tells you that you'll understand when you get older, but . . ."

"It sounds like that's exactly what you're about to do," Fizzy says, picking at her fingernails.

"What happened with Tess was complicated, and addiction can be hard, but—"

"She didn't want to be here anymore, Aunt Helen," Fizzy says, tears now welling up in her eyes. "Why can't you . . . why won't you see that?"

"No. It . . . it was an accident and—"

"No, it wasn't." Fizzy shakes her head, tears now streaming down her cheeks. "It wasn't an accident."

"That's just what your dad thinks, and of course, he wants you to think that, too, so he doesn't have to admit that he failed her just like I did."

Helen looks down at the table, reminded that Cherry always told her that she never saw Tess clearly. How infatuated she was with her. How desperate she was for Tess to be her friend. Hell, she even built an entirely fabricated version of Tess for her novel. A version that resembled the wild and free woman she met in 1995 at Hayho who partied with rock stars, wore the coolest clothes, and epitomized the absolute height of literary success. In the aftermath of Tess's death, Helen couldn't bring herself to add the dangerous mood swings, the troubling paranoia, and that time she found her standing in the open window of their apartment, her arms reaching out over the bustling crowd below. When she'd asked her what she was doing, Tess had laughed and joked that Helen needed to "mellow out" and that she was "just playing." Helen had thought Cherry was jealous of Helen's friendship with Tess. But now she knows that Cherry was right and it was Helen's own blindness to Tess's addiction and mental health issues that eventually led to her overdose. And that wasn't the only thing Cherry was right about. In fact, ever since their fight in New York, Helen has struggled to think of one thing that Cherry was actually wrong about.

"Dad's come with me to therapy. We've talked about it with—"

"I know we're trying to act like I'm not a mean old lady, but just because someone goes to therapy doesn't mean they're all of a sudden right about everything," Helen growls. Stung, Fizzy sits back in her chair. "I'm sorry. I . . . I'm sorry. That was about your dad, not you."

Fizzy wraps her sandwich back up and puts it, the glass obelisk, and her bag of chips into her backpack. Helen stutters appeals for her to stay, that she's sorry, she didn't mean it, and can't they just talk this out. Fizzy picks up her lemonade, stands, and loops her backpack over her shoulders, swiping her tears away with the denim bib of her overalls.

"You know what really happened, Aunt Helen." Fizzy brings her hand to her chest. "You know it in your heart." Fizzy meets Helen's desperate gaze. "Too bad you no longer seem to have one."

It's the kind of dramatic line that only a twenty-something kid can deliver. But goddamn if it doesn't land.

"Fizzy, please—"

"I love you, but until you get help . . . I need to keep my distance," Fizzy says, clearly repeating something her therapist told her to say should things go pear-shaped.

"I love you, too," Helen manages. Fizzy waits. And waits. Then Fizzy is forced to watch as the hope that her words might make Helen ask for help fades. It's the saddest thing in the fucking world. Completely deflated, Fizzy walks out of the café without looking back.

Helen is quiet. She won't continue to argue with Fizzy about this, but she also cannot in good conscience agree with her either. Fizzy is young. She doesn't see the world as it is or even Helen as she is. Maybe she's already the mean old lady Fizzy warns her she'll become. She's spent the last few years stealing her ex–best friend's entire identity for her own book, attributing all the terrible things she said about Cherry to the perfectly lovely workshop members who were just too scared of her to speak up, and abandoning Tess when she needed her most.

For years, Helen told herself that there were good reasons why she did the things she did. The circumstances at the time, the other person was doing far better than she was, so what would they care, or just that it wasn't that bad. But it was all lies. And every time she lied to herself and chose to do something that some invented excuse absolved, Helen remained ignorant of the kind of person she was becoming.

In her twenties, Helen had a mean streak, but she was also wry and arch and funny. She had big dreams, and the hope, delusion, and ambition to make them come true. She was awkward, too smart for her own good, and had trouble making friends. But she was still trusting enough to let down her guard and let someone in. She was stubborn and strong willed, but also fought to free herself from her parents' frigid, cruel dysfunction. She was chaotic, messy, and held all these disparate traits within her—some good, some bad, and everything human in between.

By the time she'd reached her thirties, Helen's mean streak became protective and brittle, her sense of humor being one of the first casualties. She still had big dreams, but now they were laced with resentment and bitterness. And that hopeful ambition that used to drive her to create and make art was transformed into a razor-sharp machete that chopped through anything and anyone standing between her and the endgame she decided would make her unimpeachable to all who regarded her. Her intelligence calcified as she traded curiosity for certainty, no longer open to anyone's opinions but her own. Friendships became trinkets she put on display for those around her to envy. And she no longer trusted anyone, for fear they'd somehow turn out to be just like her. Her stubbornness built a wall to keep people out, and her strong will fortified it brick by brick, year after year. She was no longer chaotic and messy as the need for control grew inside her. Control felt clean. Control felt safe. Control felt powerful. And as the years passed, she happily signed off on every facet of her own corruption.

Now in her forties, Helen has become so out of touch with being human that she's unable to engage with anyone outside of her own walled existence, choosing to live in the suffocating safety of her own beliefs. Helen's opinions and thoughts have become gospel, while she relegates everyone else's views to the far-off chatter of the ill-informed and foolish.

It all happened so quietly, so painlessly, that Helen still sometimes likes to think of herself as the chaotic and messy twenty-something version of herself, blissfully ignorant of the person she'd become. The husk who now sits utterly alone after hurting the one person she had left in her life.

Before the torment of the last hour can settle into her bones, Helen gathers her things and gestures to a woman pacing the coffee shop that she's leaving. The woman hurries over and thanks her, sliding into the banquette as Helen grabs her uneaten sandwich, bag of chips, and full lemonade.

"Is this yours?" the woman asks, holding up the little pink slip of paper with Fizzy's therapist's phone number on it.

Helen's shoulders slump as she reaches for the paper. "Oh . . . yeah, thanks," she says, taking the slip of paper and quickly pocketing it before it can infect her with actually having to face all that she's experienced over the last several years.

In a daze, Helen walks up to the counter and drops a five-dollar bill into the tip jar. The café employee stands behind the cash register in shock. Neither one of them says a word.

The way Helen is able to shut herself down in order to make it all the way home feels nauseatingly familiar. She felt this numbness after being told she had thyroid cancer. She left the doctor's office and stopped for gas on the way home. She remembers watching the numbers turn over on the gas pump, feeling the slowness of her own breathing and the beat of her own heart as if someone had separated her from her own body.

Ten months later, she felt that numbness again after hearing Tess had passed away. That day she'd been sitting at a coffee house writing what would become her debut novel when Fizzy kept calling and calling and calling. After finally picking up, Helen had listened to the news, nodding along and offering soothing words to the little girl. She'd said everything right. Then she hung up the phone and went back to writing. Helen stayed in that coffee house for nine more hours, right up until it closed. After that, she sat on a bus bench just outside, scrolling through social media as the staff cleaned and closed for the night. When she finally had to go home, the sadness hunted her, hovering and looming like a wild animal circling her in her own bed.

But Helen Hicks is and always was a storyteller. So by the time the sun shone through her bedroom curtains early the next morning, Helen had already begun building the story that Tess hadn't actually taken her own life as Fizzy had said, but instead had accidentally overdosed.

She'd just taken too many pills, and the friend Helen had known and loved in life got to remain the person she needed her to be in death. Tess hadn't left her. She didn't do this. She was beautiful. She had a thriving career as a writer. She had money and fame. She was happily married. She had Fizzy. She had Helen. She had everything. Why would she . . . sure, she may have had problems, but it couldn't have been that bad. Helen would have known. Helen should have known. Helen . . . no, it was just an accident.

It had to have been an accident.

Armed with this complete fiction, Helen began to feel that sweet cleanliness of controlled anger that finally allowed her to breathe and stoke her own rage and run as far away from grief as she could possibly get. The next day, she sat down at that very same table, at that very same coffee house, and began to construct the character of Tess in her novel. A character who was warm and lovely and, most of all, alive and well. And Helen was able to live safely within this fiction for a long time . . . right up until they spread Tess's ashes in Big Sur. The small group of Tess's nearest and dearest had gathered on the one-year anniversary of her death, and everything was going fine—relatively speaking—right up until Fizzy's dad announced that he was donating the proceeds from Tess's last book to the American Foundation for Suicide Prevention. Which is when Helen slapped him across the face. She hadn't meant to do it, but she needed him to be quiet. She needed him to stop talking so she could remain in her little dreamworld, where her conspiracy theories allowed her to stay angry and functioning, rather than grief-stricken and catatonic.

She was so sure other people would join her, but they hadn't. And when she was ostracized from the group, it only fed her conspiracy theories, along with her bloated and overactive ego, and continued to support her belief that she was Tess's one true friend. She knew the truth and she alone would fight to clear Tess's name. The only person who continued to talk to her after that was Fizzy. The same lovely kid she just . . . Helen crumples against the hallway wall, letting her bag fall to the floor just inside the front door. In a fugue state, Helen pulls the little pink slip of paper with Fizzy's therapist's number on it out of her pocket and is just about to ball it up and throw it in the little trash can in the half bath just off the hallway. But it's Fizzy's handwriting. Her little stationery. She . . . just can't throw it away. She folds it up and tucks it safely into the depths of her wallet. She needs it out of sight. She needs it gone.

Once that's properly expelled, Helen digs deep into the sticky depths of her own delusional, made-up world and is able to once again push down the gathering storm of emotions by scrolling through social media, cleaning the house, reading a book, doing some light online shopping, and finally smoking a joint and watching travel vlogs of people exploring quaint British villages.

But the next day she doesn't get up from the couch to go write. She tells herself she just needs a day to rest and that maybe she's coming down with a cold. But another day passes and another and another and she's still wearing the same pair of pajamas she's had on all week. By the third and fourth weeks, Helen's platinum-blond hair, which Tess's stylist told her would look "omg so cute," is now streaked with her own natural dishwater blond, and hangs greasy and knotted against her neck. No one has called, and the only emails she's gotten over the last month have been from her agent pressing her on how the pitch for book two is coming. Helen thinks about just sending a photo of herself at that very moment to really drive home the fact that it's not going well, Beth Anne. It's not going well at all.

Without friends, Helen has no one to check on her. Without a job to go to, she has no one who's aware that she hasn't left the house in weeks. In short, Helen's descent has turned into an absolute free fall, as if she's been pushed out of an airplane without a parachute.

By the second month, Helen is now leaving the house only to get groceries and has taken to wearing the same stained black sweats, a bucket hat pulled low over her face, and an old gray T-shirt with Han Solo on it that she borrowed from Cherry years and years ago. Helen sees her own reflection in the glass door of the ice cream section: Thin as a wraith with pale, crepey skin and dark circles under her eyes, Helen barely recognizes herself. Lost and clearly in the throes of a long-overdue breakdown, she homes in on the T-shirt.

"It's not borrowing if you never give it back," Helen mumbles to herself, running a bony hand down the front of the shirt.

A woman pulling a bag of frozen spinach out of the freezer section gives her a quick glance. Helen notices, but feels as though she's gotten the wrong idea, so she decides to explain to her that it's really not as bad as it looks.

"This isn't my shirt," she says to the woman. She watches as her statement fills the woman with absolute dread, her entire being unsure of how to engage with someone in Helen's state.

"That's nice," the woman offers, dropping the frozen spinach in her grocery cart.

"It was my best friend's shirt, and I stole it," Helen says.

"Oh," the woman says, making eye contact with another woman who's stumbled upon Helen during her weekly shop. Helen follows the first woman's gaze, and thinking they're all now in a conversation, she turns to engage them both.

"I've actually stolen a lot worse than this from her," Helen says to the two strangers.

"Well, if she's your best friend, maybe she . . ." The two women look at one another, and the second woman gives the first a nod that she's handling Helen well. "She doesn't mind that you have it."

The two women wait to see how Helen will process this information, but all Helen feels is completely overwhelmed. In her weakened state, all her guards obliterated, she is forced to see these two women without the usual stories and lies and conspiracy theories and machinations and mental gymnastics she filters every personal interaction through. These two women aren't bonding over her stained sweats. They're not laughing at her dishwater-blond roots. They're not secretly texting each other to meet up later and gossip about the state of her.

They're simply being kind.

And this beautiful lightning bolt is finally what shatters Helen into a million little pieces.

"I think I've done it wrong, you know," Helen finally says, her voice a whisper.

"What's that?" the second woman asks, her voice gentle and easy.

"Life." Helen's voice is hoarse and pained as she gulps down the agony of wasting forty-four years thinking the absolute worst of people. The two women share a look of concern.

"Are you going to be okay?" the first woman asks.

"I don't even like Earl Grey tea," Helen answers.

And as the two women look on helplessly, Helen lets her basket of groceries drop to the ground. Not because she's too weak, but because she simply forgets it's there. And as she stands in the frozen-food aisle of the small local grocery store in the center of Mill Valley, the grief of the last several years finally catches up to Helen Hicks. In the chaos of the moment, she finally sees herself through the newly made cracks of her imaginary world. This is who she really is. This is the truth of the choices she's made. These are all the people she's hurt. These are the lies she's told.

The pain is instantaneous and takes her over so wholly that the vastness of it terrifies her. Waves and waves of it made up of flashing memories, echoes of voices from the past. And for once, Helen has no words to unravel it or bully it back into its box. The numbness already thawing, she understands that this is not the optimal place for her to be at this juncture of her quickly eroding mental state, so she says a polite goodbye to the two women, steps over her grocery basket, and shambles to the exit. The grocery store doors slide open, the gorgeous late-August morning showing the first signs that it'll be fall soon. Helen closes her eyes and lifts her face to the sky. The sun feels good. Feeling a bit lightheaded, she stumbles over to a plastic bench just outside the grocery store and plops down onto it in a heap.

She looks down at herself. The shirt. The sweats. Her little pigeon-toed feet. She can see the bones in her hands and lifts them up as if inspecting them for the first time. She allows for an anemic shake of her head, before riffling through her purse and pulling out her wallet. She finds the folded-up piece of pink paper with Fizzy's loopy handwriting on it and pulls out her cell phone.

With shaking hands, Helen Hicks dials.

CHAPTER SEVENTEEN

Fall 2025

As her plane touches down, Cherry Stewart texts the family thread that she's landed safely in Iowa. Both Mishler and Marlo text back their excited responses, wishing her good luck and saying they can't wait to hear how her talk goes. As the plane taxis to the gate, Cherry nervously tucks her headphones back into their little pouch and then tucks that little pouch into a bigger pouch and on and on with a never-ending Russian nesting doll of travel pouches. Once the plane comes to a stop, she stands along with the rest of the passengers, quickly grabs her carry-on luggage from the overhead bin, and files out of the Jetway and into the busy Eastern Iowa Airport.

She's supposed to meet someone from the university, so as she nears the exit, she scans the people holding signs with various names printed on them until she finds the one that reads STEWART. A kind-looking man wearing a crumpled blazer with a rolling collapsible basket at his feet excitedly waves Cherry over.

"Hello and welcome! You're my first to arrive," the man says, pulling a water bottle from the basket and handing it to her.

"Hello! Oh, thank you," Cherry says, taking the water.

"We're waiting on two more," the man says, craning his neck to see beyond her.

"Cherry Stewart," she says, extending a hand to the man.

"Frank Pawlowski. I'm one of the volunteers," he says proudly.

Cherry and Frank make polite conversation for the next five or so minutes until they're joined by the other two writers who've been flown in to speak to the university's creative writing classes. Frank hands them each a bottle of water, and then all three writers follow him out of the airport like little ducklings to where his silver minivan awaits them in the short-term parking lot.

On the drive to the university, the three writers get acquainted, introducing themselves. One is a poet, and the other is a short-story writer. Cherry has met the short-story writer before, but this is her first time meeting the poet. When Cherry begins to introduce herself, they look to one another and nervously laugh. Cherry, being Cherry, is immediately mortified, fearing she's already made a mistake.

Picking up on this, the poet speaks quickly, clearly hoping to clarify the situation. "Ms. Stewart, everyone knows who you are," she says, her face flushed and nervous.

"Oh, I . . . I'm so sorry, I—" Cherry barks out a laugh and continues. "I think I've been in the writing cave a little too long." The other two writers laugh, likely relieved that Cherry appears to be as down-to-earth as everyone says she is.

And even though the conversation that follows is an easy one, Cherry comes to realize that she's way more nervous about this talk than she previously thought. But it's a new kind of nervous. Because even though this event has all the old hallmarks of everything that would have triggered her in the past—a fancy university filled with fancy professors and fancy students who are enrolled in an even fancier creative writing program—Cherry no longer feels she has anything to prove. She is a proud orange ribbon. And over the last ten years, she's come to realize that being an orange ribbon is actually a feature, not a bug. Having potential is good. Learning is good. Being a work in progress is good.

Her path to success was different; ergo, she is different. And different is good . . . despite what our teenage years try to drill into us.

It always sounds so after-school special when Cherry tries to talk about this with up-and-coming writers. But there, too, she's come to realize that her open and earnest cheesiness is different and something she should be immensely proud to still retain after everything she's been through in the last fifty years.

She's been invited to the land of the purple ribbons, and she's said yes because this is just a bunch of kids who are still trying to figure out who they are. She's proud to represent the orange ribbons. She's proud to represent the different path. She's proud of herself. As they pull into the university campus, Cherry figures that the nerves are there because, without the chip on her shoulder, she's walking into this event as the real Cherry Stewart.

And that is still taking some getting used to.

Frank invites the three writers to leave their luggage in the minivan and follow him to the holding room, where they'll be met by the faculty member whose class they will be speaking to first. They will be speaking to three different classes over the course of the day, as well as a few panels here and there, and finally concluding with a signing in the campus library. The three writers join the other five or so writers who have already congregated and make awkward small talk. They pour coffee and pick over pastries. Cherry pours herself a cup of Earl Grey tea and sits on a sagging green couch. She sets the tea down on the chipped and frayed wooden side table and flips through the pages and pages of notes she printed out that go with her slideshow. She finds a Blackwing pencil in the depths of her bag and jots down a few notes here and there of quick thoughts or examples that might help the students absorb the concepts she's talking about today.

"Cherry Stewart?" Frank calls out.

"Here!" Cherry answers automatically, as if she's back in elementary school and the teacher is taking attendance.

"Your faculty member has come to collect you," Frank says, as Cherry shoves her notes and her Blackwing pencil into her bag. She stands, grabs her Earl Grey tea, and crosses the room to where Frank stands next to Helen Hicks.

"Oh—" Cherry puffs out in disbelief.

"Hi," Helen says.

"If you could follow Professor Hicks, Ms. Stewart," Frank says, picking up on none of the awkwardness.

Helen opens the door to the holding room and gestures for Cherry to go first. Cherry does, but only because it has yet to register that any of this is real. Just as the door closes and they are alone in the echoing hallway beyond it, Helen stops and turns to face Cherry.

"Don't get mad," she says.

"I . . . I'm too shocked to be mad, but give me a minute," Cherry says as they take each other in for the first time in ten years.

There may be more wrinkles and some gray hairs, but both Cherry and Helen let themselves soften just a bit as they take the other one in. These are the faces they've known almost their whole lives. Faces that appear in stacks and stacks of old photos piled high in plastic bins in crowded closets. Faces that defined eras and embodied lessons that hurt to learn. They were friends, best friends, roommates, sisters, writers, enemies, and then long-lost acquaintances. They fall into a heavy silence, weighted down with too many things left unsaid, ten years of hard lessons, and an even harder climb out.

Another professor zooms past and charges into the holding room, leaving the door open as Frank calls another name. The professor and the poet from the drive from the airport appear in the hallway, speaking excitedly as they walk toward their first class. Instinctively, Helen and Cherry begin walking toward Helen's classroom.

"I was the one who put your name in to come speak today," Helen blurts.

"You teach here?" Cherry asks, not knowing how to broach the issue of whether Helen is still writing books. It's kind of a rule among writers: Never ask how the new book is doing. Better to wait for them to bring it up.

"I've been here for two years, but I was with a few other universities before this one," Helen says.

"That's really cool. I'm happy for you," Cherry says, genuinely meaning it.

"Thanks," Helen says, turning the corner to her classroom's hallway.

"I thought I was going to see you at the Hayho's hundredth this past summer," Cherry says. She'd gone into the reunion fully ready to see Helen. She'd prepared what she would say. She practiced it with Mishler. She didn't quite know what she wanted, but the overwhelming sense of disappointment she felt at Helen not being there gave her a good idea.

"I thought about going, but . . . turns out those kinds of places don't bring out the best in me," Helen says, raising an eyebrow.

"That's the understatement of the century," Cherry says, and Helen laughs. It's not a scoff or a sneer; it's an honest-to-goodness belly laugh. And Cherry hasn't heard one of those in years, if ever.

Helen and Cherry stand in front of Helen's classroom. Helen puts her hand on the doorknob, but then stops. Cherry waits, her brow furrowed. The door is cracked open just enough that they can hear the excited voices of the students within.

"I thought maybe we could get a coffee after this," Helen says, her voice strained and nervous. The few seconds of silence that follow Helen's request are interminable, the din from just inside the classroom acting as its very own tense soundtrack. But then . . .

"I'd like that," Cherry says, just as one of Helen's students pushes the door to the classroom open and breaks the spell.

Helen gently admonishes the student as she and Cherry walk into the classroom together. Helen's shoulder scrapes along the narrow doorjamb as Cherry herds her right into a large bookcase just as the door closes behind them.

"Oof, sorry," Cherry says.

"It's okay," Helen says, turning away so Cherry doesn't see the tears welling up in her eyes.

ABOUT THE AUTHOR

Photo © 2006 Edwin Santiago

Liza Palmer is the author of *Family Reservations*, *The Nobodies*, *The F Word*, and *Nowhere but Home*, winner of the Willie Morris Award for Southern Fiction. A two-time Emmy-nominated, internationally bestselling tea enthusiast who gets to write for Marvel sometimes, Liza lives in Los Angeles, where 95.3 percent of people call her Lisa. For more information, visit www.lizapalmer.com.